Forget Me Not

Forget Me Not

Christina D. Kennedy

Order this book online at www.trafford.com
or email orders@trafford.com

Most Trafford titles are also available at major online book retailers.

Printed in the United States of America.

ISBN: 978-1-4269-7341-3 (sc)
ISBN: 978-1-4269-7342-0 (hc)
ISBN: 978-1-4269-7343-7 (e)

Library of Congress Control Number: 2011910672

Trafford rev. 06/26/2012

 www.trafford.com

North America & International
toll-free: 1 888 232 4444 (USA & Canada)
phone: 250 383 6864 ♦ fax: 812 355 4082

Dedication

To my Heavenly Father who provided a way for me in my life at times when there was no way. He led me through the darkest times in my life and provided me with unconditional love. For with Him I will never be alone.

Prologue

Forget Me Not is a story based on true events that are woven together with undertones and overtones of fiction. It is written this way for a reason; to get myself through a very difficult and emotional childhood story.

For years I have been told to write a biography, and for years I worked at one. I believe I got about halfway there at one point or another when those old drudged up feelings took me so deep into the darkest of dark, the only way back to the light was to stop. I couldn't just put it down and start again. I always felt I was stuck in the biography where I left it.

I came to realize that a scar is a scar; a wound can heal but there is always something left behind to remind us, and if you rub it hard enough it becomes inflamed again. Forget Me Not is written in and out of reality, in a way that the scar is looked at deep enough to recall, but not rubbed long enough to ignite the fire to its hottest point. It is disturbing to some to know that many events in Forget Me Not actually happen. We don't want to believe it, but it does happen. It is happening today, it will tomorrow, and it happened yesterday. There are many stories such as this, and these stories are not written about. If they are bad enough, they are brought to the public's attention and then quickly swept under the rug. A short burst of acknowledgment and then so soon forgotten.

The failure/success rate of child services in Canada has likely never been measured. I am here to tell you from firsthand experience that it is highly insufficient. We are asleep in this country when it comes to the children next door. Some of us just don't know, some of us have a feeling, some of us do know but don't want to get involved. Lastly, some of us know and just don't care one way or the other. Time after time, when we review high profile cases, witnesses tell us, "I knew something might have been going on . . . it was obvious . . . I never would have known . . . or, how could anyone not know?"

Child Services' policy and procedure techniques need to change. It isn't for a lack of their presence; it's what is lacking in how their system operates. It seems they have their noses so far into low risk cases while their tails are hardly touching the surface of something high risk. That high-risk case would require much work out of them, work that could make the difference in a child's future. My husband put it to me all too well one day. He explains it like this: "Would a police officer forewarn a suspected grow-op owner that they have an eye on them? Would they say, we have some complaints so we are going to stop by Monday afternoon at around 2:30 PM?" The answer is no of course; they just don't work that way. Innocent until proven guilty or not, those policemen are there pouncing when they least expect it. It is important to them to get the job done. Well, what about children? What about the work that needs to be done for them? I don't know any worse crime than one performed on a child.

I don't think I can count how many of these planned drop-in Child Services meetings occurred in my childhood. I do recall the outcome though. None! My parents would put on their best face and warn us to shut the hell up. They maybe even joke around a little with the worker. Case closed until the next complaint. Great strategy . . . you think? What are we really paying them for? To go out to homes on coffee dates with a note pad?

How about an unannounced drop in? A reality check-in to see what really happens in these children's day-to-day lives. Then maybe they'd have something, like these police officers do when they are storming in to someone's grow-op unannounced. When I was a kid, would I ever have loved it to see help walk in the door when my father was kicking me around the living room like a soccer ball, when one of us was taking a beating by a two-by-four, or being led down the stairs backwards by the hair while being punched in the face. Hmm . . . is child services equipped for that? If not they had better start. These are the complaints; this is what is happening. Yet they come back from their prearranged visit and report that all seemed pretty good at the Smith's home, but their coffee could have been a little stronger. The failure rate for the policies and procedures they practice is guaranteed.

There were many opportunities for me and my siblings to be saved, but it never happened. We got out when we were basically old enough to walk out. When we walked out we had a lot of wounds that needed to be healed, which can take years. I thank God for being with me through it all. I don't feel sorry for myself nor spend my time reminiscing. That had its day and that day is done. That molded me and made me the person I am today, and amongst many other things, I find I have a passion for change and awareness for children, these children whose needs stay hidden in a society that is inactive for them and that enables their victimizers. Don't close your eyes to the children next door and don't think what happens behind closed doors isn't anything beyond your imagination. Here's to eyes wide open and looking out for the children, and here's to Forget Me Not.

Acknowledgment

To my two wonderful foster parents; Anne Mackay and John Bellamy. With their genuinely loving hearts, they took the time to show me the skills to heal and the tools to keep going. Crystal Brouwer, my dear friend, who has motivated and inspired me to write. Crystal was the first person to read my book as it was being created and encouraged me to press on, my sincere thanks Crystal. I would like to express much gratitude to my daughter and re-editor Courtney Brucks. Of course my family; my husband David and children Jesse, Courtney & Jayden who's love follows me everywhere I go.

Contents

Chapter 1

I trembled in absolute fear in the early crisp morning air. Fear of what was, and fear that if I didn't go back, what the other options would be.

Dusk was pushing the night away as I carefully tip-toed through all the boards and various junk my father and his girlfriend left around the yard. Suddenly, I felt myself start to topple over. Protecting my now 6 month pregnant belly, I caught my footing with my knees almost touching the ground. It was late August and the morning was already very chilly.

How was I going to explain this to my father? I had been gone from home for seven months now. Worst of all I had been living with one of his valued customers and hunting buddies. Not to mention family friend, who I might add is more than twice my age. Of course there is the little issue that I have now been carrying his baby for six months. Yep, good old long term friend of the family Frank Shamanskii, or Uncle Frank. He has known me since I was about five or six years old and has now made me five or six months pregnant. I couldn't be sure as we were pretty confident it would not be a good idea for both of us, if I were to see a doctor, considering I was fifteen.

Leah

I left home like my two older sisters as the abuse we had been enduring was getting way out of control, and more impulsive since our father met Leah.

Leah was a strange woman; a junk collector. She was quite attractive with her dark almost black hair and her pale blue eyes. She was slim (at least when she first met my father) and seemed to love her horses. But she was a schemer; if she was bored she would concoct an incident just so she could beat us (which she took sheer pleasure in doing) or at least severely punish us. One of her favourite punishments was to withhold food for three to four days and lock us in the dugout basement where we had the pleasure of sleeping in the dark on one of the old dog blankets. If we were lucky we might get locked in the unfinished attic which had an old creaky bed with a saggy mattress.

Our father would be pretty convinced that she was justified in all she did, even though her own two children were taken away. The courts declared her an unfit mother a few years back. A long time ago she was nurse (so she said) but was caught stealing prescription drugs for some of her friends. Leah says the doctors were just too afraid to diagnose them and that her diagnosis was right. They were mad that someone who didn't have to go to school as long as they did had all the intelligence and ability, so they took her licence away.

It was very obvious to us that the sex was undeniably good for my father (as he always bragged of this to friends) and he wouldn't trade that for anything.

Father/Mother

Anyhow the beatings were getting to be too much after my mother suddenly passed away. My mother was a petite woman with the most beautiful smile and light brown hair. She was very orderly, kept a clean house, and was very mindful of her parenting. She was a religious person and often taught Sunday school and Crusaders. She had the most beautiful singing voice and would often perform on the church stage. As a child she was always an honour roll student and later attended Bible College to become a laboratory assistant.

My mother's identical twin sister Marilyn said she could take in two of the four of us. I know it was very hard for her to come to that conclusion, but she lived by herself and had only one income. My oldest sister Rose and second oldest sister Faith would do well with her and I was happy to hear they had gone. Father would never let my younger brother Derrick leave, no way, no how. You see my dad was somewhat of a chauvinist, and Derrick carried the family jewels that would pass on the family name.

Father was a gunsmith by trade and also worked doing as a hunting guide throughout the seasons. He was rough and abusive, stood about 5'7" or 5'8" with thick, dark brown hair. He was often up and down with his weight. In fact, his weight fluctuated almost to an extreme. He would be heavy and depressive for years and then bounce back to an average weight for his frame (or thinner). His eyes were a sea blue, and he would often change his facial hair. Sometimes a moustache, or a beard, but most often he was clean shaven. He walked around with the most explosive and unpredictable temper which often lead him to beat my mother for no reason. He was as he described himself to be, a natural racist. He believed that deep down most people were.

I remember Grandmother told me how happy she and mother were that Derrick was finally born, because mother was finally allowed to quit producing babies. In my mind, my mother was beautiful inside and out. She knew how to cook better food than any chef. She also kept the house spic and span, as well as herself and all four of us kids. Leah was always extremely jealous of her and begged father to see her faults. All he could say was that she was soft spoken and a push-over.

He thought that when he married her, her virginity would be exciting for him, but apparently she was frigid and he basically had to beat sex out of her on their wedding night. Leah would have her little laugh every time they talked about that.

In my mind, I was thinking great dad, now you have a filthy whore who doesn't clean, cook, and has no idea how to take care of children. But to him it was fine and dandy as long as she put out.

Good Will Hunting

So after the girls left, father had planned on a two week hunting trip. He asked Frank if he would take over the gunsmith shop while he was gone. Frank, who had broken his arm while playing hockey, was happy to do it. Since he lived about two towns away Father even let him spend the night to avoid travel. Of course he got the unfinished attic bedroom with the old bed and saggy mattress. But it did also have a toilet and a sink, where you got to hide yourself with a lovely, old army green shower curtain around you. You're pretty much alone once you are up there anyhow.

Well this is how it all started with Frank and I. Once my sisters left, I was Leah's main target and slave. Derrick, he got a little bit, but Leah knew he was always semi protected by my father. And if you can believe it she kind of appreciated his chauvinism. I think she knew she was kind of exempt from its rules because she provided my father with unlimited and highly valued sex.

So Leah went to stay with Ed's wife Sara while father went on the two week hunting trip. He took my brother and a group of customers who were paying him to go, with hopes of the best and biggest game. Leah loved to stay with Sara because she was rich, and Leah was manipulative and could act practically normal in front of her. Leah provided Sara with some company out on her lonely multiple acres of caribou prime land in their mammoth house. She would be completely treated by Sara. Sara made the most exquisite meals and served them with their complimentary bottles of wine.

So off they all went. I don't think my dad even thought twice about Frank being alone with me. This was strange as he most certainly didn't trust any men around us. He would say "I know-I am one. I know what we are capable of." And of course he would agree with Leah that all us girls are whores and that we will, when old enough, seduce men.

So for now I had stopped going to school as I was a little traumatized from something Leah had pulled at my mother's wake. It was haunting me to the point of being unable to concentrate. Not to mention, Leah said I wouldn't amount to anything, and she needs me at home. Since everyone was gone, I just had to keep up the house chores, feed the cats and dogs, walk all the way across our tiny little town (where we rented acreage with a large barn) to feed the seven horses.

"The Real Frank"

To my surprise, coming home from feeding the horses the first night, I noticed that Frank had closed the shop down a little early. When I entered the house a burst of yummy filled my nostrils. Scents of garlic, tomatoes, oregano, and cheese were in the air. I actually heard my tummy growl. I quickly took my boots off in the large entrance way and stepped into the kitchen.

"Christina, come in my dear. I was just making us some spaghetti just the way my grandma used to make it. I have all the ingredients in but it will take at least a few hours to cook. You see that way all the flavours combine together and become one." He spoke in a very animated fashion, gesturing with his hands the whole time. That was Frank, he could often make the whole family laugh with his Italian accent and hand gestures.

"Wow!" I responded, "I don't think I have had anyone actually cook anything good for me since my mother . . . and that was a long time ago." My eyes stared past Frank and over at what he was cooking on the stove.

"Yes, yes, that Leah, uhm . . . she can't cook, you know. That is why when I come here and I need to spend the night, I offer to buy the take out." Frank smiled as he gently led me to the kitchen table. "You work too hard you know? For someone so young, I don't know why you do all the chores and slave after that . . . that Leah. Don't think I don't see this. I do, I see this with my eyes all the time when I come here. Do I say something to your father? No, no he is a friend of mine. But more importantly, you Christina, are part of that friendship, and I think you need someone to take care of you sometimes." Frank finished dishing me up a pretty large bowl of salad and began to pour me a glass of red wine.

I laughed and said, "Frank, hello Frank, do you realize you just poured me a glass of wine?" I put my hand out to try to stop him from pouring as I saw he had already poured himself one, and I didn't want him to waste it. Frank looked down at the glass of wine with a slightly contorted face.

"You don't drink wine? I've been drinking wine with my parents at every dinner since I was nine; it is the Italian way. Never hurt me." Frank said, with both arms stretched out, one with the cork screw and the cork still attached, the other with his cast on still holding the bottle of wine "Won't hurt you. Besides, your father is not here and Leah is not either, you drink it. It will relax you, you need to relax. You know, I don't think you ever get to relax. When I am here you are going to relax, okay?" Frank crouched down and crossed his arms beside me on the kitchen table and looked me in the eyes with a very warm smile. I picked up the glass of wine and raised it.

"Here is to relaxing!" Frank rose to his feet. "You know that is a very fine Italian wine. I would only give you the best. I brought this. In fact, I brought many more from my own personal collection from home. When your father asked me if I would run the shop, (despite the fact my arm is not completely healed) I was excited to do it, but not to do a favour for your father. I was excited to spend some time with you, treat you and help you relax." Frank continued his hand animation. I felt a bit of a shiver run down my spine, but I wasn't sure if it was because I was eating his delicious salad so fast, that some was caught in my throat, or if something made me feel strange? Maybe it is just like Frank said I haven't been shown any niceness for such a long time.

"Mmm, hmm," I rattled out, as I gulped a few large swigs of wine to clear my throat. "Sorry, I just don't know what to say this is all very nice and sweet and unbelievable. I can only thank you so very much. I'm glad you're here. It would not have been the same if Leah had not have gone to Sara's."

Frank pulled up a chair and proceeded to toss some salad into his bowl. "Yes, well I had a hand in that. Sara can't stand Leah. Ed, he always has to beg Sara to have her. You know, to kind of appease your father. So this time she got it from both Ed and I. I told her I could not bear to bunk down at your house with her for two weeks, and Sara knew that meant the trip could be cancelled. She knows your pappy moved out and there would be no one to tend to business and keep an eye on you. I know how much she loves her Ed, and I'm not going to get in the way of that!" Frank smiled mischievously, and I could see those handsome dimples in his face come out; the dimples I always admired . . . Did I?

"Crazy, Leah always talked like Sara couldn't be without her when Ed was away. She said she would get so lonely out there by herself." I so curiously replied, hoping to hear more truths about Leah.

"Lonely she has six grown children four of which are daughters; one would always be available if she were lonely. I think I recall her saying she would rather be locked in a casket for nine months than have that crazy woman set foot on their land ever again." I grabbed my chest to keep from bursting out laughing, or worse, choking again. Sometimes Frank has the funniest way of throwing you off guard without even knowing it.

I ate the whole salad and had seconds while still waiting for our spaghetti. After the most delicious spaghetti I had ever eaten, we retired to the living room. Frank was so wonderful, he demanded I sit on Father and Leah's forbidden love chair with him, and he put their ottoman under my feet.

"This is how you, a princess, should be treated," he retorted with his many hand movements. I could definitely feel the wine, but the crackling fire and someone who wanted to talk to me, someone who was interested in me, was so unbelievable, incredibly, special. Frank poured more wine and dished me up the most delicious dessert. "I promise you, from scratch, my love, I will make you a real Italian dessert tomorrow night. I will be more prepared and will pick up some supplies from town." Frank looked down at me in the love chair, as if he was inadequate. I was stricken by the wine and in awe by the extreme effort. I wasn't used to anyone caring for such a long time, it felt odd. I had been pretty down on myself, and Leah had been so down on me. I mean, I was never going to make it scholastically. The only thing I felt confident about was my experience in martial arts, but Leah stopped that right away. At this point I haven't felt like I have many successes in life. But Frank, he's been making me feel remarkable, better than I've ever felt.

I couldn't help but notice his striking, hazel eyes with incredibly long lashes. He almost looked like he was wearing eyeliner because his lashes were so thick. He was always a clean-cut guy, with the sexiest chiseled features, topped off with that irresistible rustic look. He is a tall man, I would guess about 6' 2" with broad shoulders. He says he is forty years old but I remember his ID being on my dad's counter indicating he was forty one. I don't know why, but I think at the time I just wanted to know because I thought he was cute. My sisters definitely thought he was cute. After that, I hadn't put too much thought into it.

Tonight I questioned if he was feeling even a little like I was. I didn't know if I should be feeling this way, but no one made me feel this way. I know boys in school liked me and I didn't feel unattractive. In fact that was the problem, they were all just boys. Boys are just interested in looks, but Frank, he was a man. He was genuinely interested in, well he was interested in my best interest. Young boys only tried for one thing. They tried but they never succeeded.

As the night proceeded, so did the laughs. I soon learned that Frank could do imitations of people and could he ever do a good one of Leah. He had her whine, her snarl, and how Leah's voiced changed when my father was around, even when she tried to sound sexy. His imitation of my dad was outstanding. He pretended he was standing at the shop counter with one of my dad's richest customers that he wanted to impress most. He imitated my father showing off how he made a new barrel and stock and even engraved the customer's family crest on the side. Then he did an animated version of father telling the customer of how he knew what his family crest meant.

My tummy started to get so sore from giggling, I mean really sore. I hadn't had a giggle like that in such a long, long time. I couldn't even recall how long. Leah didn't tolerate much laughter to begin with. Then after mom died there wasn't much to be laughing for.

Suddenly, in the middle of laughing while Frank was stoking the fire, he just casually took off his shirt and put on another log. My laugh started to fade as I gazed upon his rock—hard biceps. I noticed what looked to be a tattoo about four inches in diameter. It was actually an attractive Celtic cross. I've known Frank for so long that I knew his mother was Irish/Italian and his father was Italian. He thought highly of his mother, so I could see him getting something Celtic for a tattoo.

Right now all that mattered about Frank was that his pectorals' looked like he had been just been pressing weights two minutes ago, and his abs looked like he just did several sets of sit-ups. His chest had just the right amount of hair, a small amount in the middle, and then just a sparse trail down the middle of his abs, where it disappeared into his jeans.

Now it has just come to my attention that I was no longer laughing and my mouth was open. I needed one part of my brain to tell the other part of my mouth to shut. Oh yeah, and Frank did notice. Thank God, a log had partly rolled out, and Frank had to fight it with the fire poker to get it back into the fireplace, but not without trying to look at me at the same time, and smile. I'm sure he noticed my mouth was open. Well that was obviously because my brain did not send the appropriate and much needed message. I will not be kept off guard like that again.

Once Frank wrestled the log back into the fire he closed the glass doors. "Well with all that's flammable in here, if I'd have gone up with a bang at least it would have been with my favorite person . . . But don't worry, I would never let that happen." Frank laughed as he casually wiped the sweat off his brow with his t-shirt.

He sat himself beside me on the love chair placing his arm around me. "I hope you don't feel uncomfortable around me Christina, you know it is you I have always loved . . . I know it sounds strange for a man my age to say this to you." He paused and searched me with his eyes.

Aside from having to digest all Frank was saying I was realizing I had never been that close to a man, not to mention a man with no shirt, and with that many muscles. His eyes looked so deep piercing, like he was absorbing my reaction to his words. His scent was so raw and arousing. I was completely vulnerable and yet, here he was right up and wrapped around me, looking deep in my eyes, talking to the depths of my soul. It was like he knew exactly what to say.

Frank started again, "Your eyes, they are beautiful green. They are eyes that have seen many years, many things they should not." Magnetically our mouths connected, and we kissed the most beautiful kiss, but I panicked and tried to resist by pushing at his face. He laughed while still kissing me and grabbed the top part of my arm and shoulder. He held it up against the love seat until the kiss was over.

I never had a kiss like that. I felt weak to his animal magnetism. I really didn't want to fight it. I just wasn't sure if we were doing the right thing.

I pulled away to take a breath. We were looking deeply into each other; so deep it was like we could consume each other.

"Don't be afraid Christina. This was meant to be. Why do you think I haven't moved back to Italy to be with my family? I have been waiting for you. I have been waiting for the right time. I have been waiting for you to mature into a young lady. Don't think I haven't been watching you. You are the right woman for me. Any woman in between was just to pass time; not a woman that would enter into my heart. You are the woman who is going to have all my children. You are going to meet my family and move back to Italy with me." Frank seemed very serious.

"Do you think anyone here will miss you? Really, do you? Because if you do, I will make sure we come back to visit whenever you want to visit them. I know you will want to visit your sisters and maybe even that brother of yours who is put on some kind of pedestal. I will still take you back, I promise."

I think he could see I was overwhelmed. "You're tired my love. This is too much for you to take in at one time and too much for me to explain at this time my love. You need to sleep! Let me take you to your room."

With that Frank picked me up into his naked upper body. At that I had nothing to say and nothing I could say. My face was pressed into his chest muscles and I could hear his heart beating as he walked to my room. The smell of his body mixed with some really amazing cologne was intense. "You are tired my love and I have told you too much for one day I apologize, you sleep now."

Before I knew it Frank was starting to lower me onto my bed. I didn't want him to go as much as I afraid of him staying. I slid my hand down his extremely toned stomach as he lowered me down. "I don't want you to go," I whispered to Frank with my eyes half-mast but still aware of his extreme attractiveness. "Okay sweetheart, okay, I will lie here with you until you fall into complete slumber. I will be here for you and I will not leave. I promise you this Christina." Frank walked around to the other side of the bed. With this I slipped away into a very comfortable, secure sleep.

Pappy

"Open up Christina, it will only make you feel better." I heard the words of who I thought was my pappy. My Pappy was the man my father hired to take care of all his children while he ran his gunsmith shop. Also, Pappy, (whose real name was David) had invested seventy percent into Father's shop. Pappy was very dedicated to us and our father. He taught us so much, Leah even appreciated that she didn't have to cook. Sadly, Pappy came down with cancer and Father decided to screw him out of everything, at Leah's suggestion. We all heard it and we all knew it. Pappy was gone so many times for treatment for so long there was no time for warning. He trusted Father, and that's why nothing was made legal. A certain percentage of the company's income was to go to pappy. Leah, again, had ruined everything!

"Christina open up My Love, My love I am so sorry you were not raised with wine. I tell you, our children will know differently, and then they won't have to go through this. Oh, my poor love it will be different when we are together." I looked up at Frank talking to me as I recognized the sound of his comforting accent.

Last night really did happen. I was surprised he didn't do anything to me. Now he was just trying to convince me to take a couple Advil. Then he wanted to cuddle in front of the fire he built this morning. His plan was that when I felt good enough we would travel out to Kamloops for brunch. Kamloops is a few towns away. He didn't want anyone in our tiny town to gossip, which they loved to do. He knew no one would know me in Kamloops.

My eyes came into focus to see a magnificent man holding out a couple pills and a cup of orange juice. Unexpectedly, I felt like the trust was sealed with Frank, and I would doubt him no more. He was right about everything he had been saying, I was sure. He seemed like he had a lot more interested in me than Leah and father did. He looked so fresh and so sexy standing above me in his blue jeans and with no shirt. He had a small towel draped around his neck like he had been shaving. I pulled his hand closer to me so I could reach the Advil, then I took the orange juice he was holding and swallow it. For some reason I felt safe enough to pull Frank in my bed by his casted arm. I recalled the night before and craved more affection.

Frank laughed in surprise as he almost missed placing the orange juice on the nightstand with his other arm. I grabbed the back of his neck and pulled his face towards mine, and before I knew it we where were we left off last night with that kiss. I found myself in another world that seemed to be becoming my reality. Somehow in this state of pure bliss our clothes were totally gone. I was so entranced I couldn't even recall how one piece of clothing came off. His body against mine was so real it almost seemed unreal. Frank kissed me passionately as we made love for the first time. This was the very first time for me.

The Escape

As the days passed by Frank tended the gunsmith shop while we kept busy planning an escape. Not just an escape but also a way that we could be together forever. The way it was meant to be, like Frank said, him and I forever.

There was one day left before my father was going to arrive home from his job as a hunting guide. Frank drove me several miles to his home in which I had never been. He had moved several times, always closer to us.

We came from the coastal region of British Columbia, Canada, and moved to the Caribou. We had been to Frank's homes before, but since Leah, we were not allowed, any of us. Father repeatedly had refused invitations to Frank's house. The problem was that Leah had flirted with Frank a few times and Frank rejected her flirtations abruptly. So Leah hated Frank and forbid Father to go to Frank's home. Father liked Frank as a consistent business partner and hunting partner (not to mention he did a lot of favors for my father. Such as, take over the shop or bring him clients and hunting groups for his tours). Frank introduced him to rich people who did business with him and just happened to have a passion for hunting.

Frank was at one point, heavily invested in the stock market. He sold his stocks at just the right time and became a financial advisor. He introduced several of his stock market buddies into my father's pool clients. Also the people that came to Frank for financial advice, swore by him, and Frank brought a lot of those clients to Father as well. Frank did a lot of his work flying to customer homes or renting a room in a hotel where he would take several appointments per day. Often he'd teach classes giving financial advice.

We entered Franks home at about 3 AM. Tired as I was, I noticed that most of the furniture was leather, including the dining suite. Frank's house was new looking, in fact, he said he had had it made a few years before he moved to the Caribou. He had it built specifically to his instructions. He admitted to me that he probed my father to know that we were going to make a go of it where we had moved to this time. My father thought it was perfect with all the gaming and hunting in this mid-upper part of British Columbia.

Frank's home was amazing. His bedroom had a four-poster bed with red sheer curtains that were pulled off to the sides. The wood was all dark; actually there were no carpets in the house, just dark hard wood flooring and some area rugs. Although there was only one bedroom there was a den, living room, kitchen, dining room and pantry. He also had an office that had a library of two walls ceiling to floor books, three bathrooms, a steam room and a gym with a glass wall and door that lead to a small indoor pool. I may also mention that there was the most curious narrow door with a rounded top.

"Yes, my dear let's go down-this is one of the things I am most proud of. I opened the door and it was pitch black. I felt something graze over the top of my shoulder and I screamed. A light flashed on and a rope hanging from it flung back into my face. "Relax My Love!" Frank laughed. "You are only on the third step." I looked down at many more stairs. As we were about half way down the walls turned to dirt. It kind of reminded me of the dugout basement Leah used to lock us in.

At the bottom I noticed it was pretty cold, and I wrapped my arms across my chest. "Come here my Christina, and I will warm you with my love." Frank smiled. I inched towards him and he threw his arm around me. He ducked under a beam, and we walked around a rough plywood wall into a dirt room with a small wall of shelves-shelves that contained bottles and bottles of wine. "This is my prized collection. I have collected these from many places, but the ones on this side," he pointed his hand from ceiling to floor. "are from my precious Italy. Many of them were had at family reunions or very memorable times with friends and family." Frank looked like he was reminiscing.

"Well that is it for now my love, you look cold, and I need to get going so our plan goes well. That is important." Frank spun me around and ushered me back up the stairs.

Once we made our way up, there were many hallways leading to different rooms. Attached to the house there was a four-car garage, a shop, a front deck and a back deck. The front deck had a really nice hot tub on it. I could imagine Frank and I using that a lot.

"Okay My Dear, we are going to do as we planned, so I am going to have to leave you soon. You know that sometimes they come home early from those hunting trips if they get the game they went out for. Sometimes they will also come home early if they are tired and haven't gotten anything close to the end."

"I just turned up the furnace, so help yourself to whatever you like. I put your bag of personal belongings on the end of our bed. I also cleared out the top drawer of the long dresser with the mirror. When I get back we will drive to Vancouver and go on a shopping spree to get you some new clothes." Frank smiled holding his arms out.

I was still stuck on the fact he said our bed. How did I deserve such a man? I wrapped myself into his iron chest and waist as tight as I could and he hugged me back so firm and protective.

"So remember tomorrow night (well more like late or the wee hours of the morning the next day). It all depends on what day they get back in." Frank crouched over and pulled my chin up so that we were looking directly in each other's eyes.

"Christina, remember I love you, you have no idea, and I'm going to love you forever." He then placed his lips on mine and what I believe we both expected would be a nice meaningful kiss goodbye, turned into a whirlwind of passion. He pulled our waists close and I started to rip at his shirt before we knew we had flipped over the leather couch and smacked down on it. This shook us back to reality enough to know we had to get back on track if this was ever going to work.

"Okay, you better go," I said sadly as I pulled his hands away. "Remember to tell my dad that I never came back after the second day and you just had no way of getting a hold of him," I said, as Frank started to rise off the couch and compose himself. "No one in the town has even seen me about as you have been feeding the horse across town and doing all the shopping. You should keep the money my father gave you for groceries, or he might suspect something," I exclaimed, frustrated with my hands in the air.

"No, no, listen, if you were gone the next day and he left the grocery money for me to feed you, he knows I would just get my own or eat out. Don't worry, I have this. You just relax, maybe draw yourself a bath. I have some Dead Sea salts in the bathroom cupboard under the shelf with the towels. They will relax you. I will be back." This time he kissed my forehead with sadness in his beautiful eyes. I think we both knew that if our lips touched it would just draw our goodbye out longer, and we needed things to go as planned.

Frank slipped out the door with his head down, paying close attention not to look up at me. As the door started to close I caught a drift of his yummy cologne and the sight of his lowered, handsome rugged looking face. I then saw his waist-length, black leather dress jacket sway with a blast of wind as the door sounded a soft bang. Then I heard the sound of his car start up. It sounded like he let it warm up for a few minutes. It was pretty much close to the second week in February and that was a cold month in the Caribou. A few minutes later I heard the sound of his new car start to drive away. I could attest that his car was definitely as sexy as he was. It rumbled away until I could hear it no more.

Chapter 2

My father knew Frank to be someone who would not leave the shop unattended for any length of time. Frank normally wouldn't, but these past two weeks his head was in another place. Frank kept the door open that lead from the living room to the shop. He did this not to keep Father's business in service but to keep it looking relatively attended to.

Frank loved to hunt. Growing up I remember hearing him talk about it with great enthusiasm. With all the paperwork and people he had to deal with, hunting was a activity he could actually play at. My dad used to give him the old manly whack on the arm and show him some knew stocks he engraved or tell him some wild hunting stories. Now it seemed to make sense; Frank always seemed to have his eye on me now that I think about it. He would tell my dad, "No, let's not go to the pub. You don't know how lucky you got it; my family is back in Italy. It is rare that I get to eat with them. Let's eat together with your family."

Father would yell, "Leah! Lets roast up some chickens and get the children pealing those potatoes and carrots!"

Frank interrupted, "No, no there is the Chinese restaurant right next door! Let me treat you! Then there is no mess, no work, and we can all just enjoy ourselves."

"Are you sure Frank? We can do up some chickens just as easy." My father would say.

I plopped myself onto the leather couch as I tried to recall the last few years with our family and with Frank. How did this come about? I abruptly had to stop thinking about it. I hated to think about my life with father and Leah. I just wanted to think about right now, and right now I missed Frank. He was a hero; he really saved me from a very bleak situation and a potentially pitiful future. I knew I could feel myself falling in love with him. I felt like I should do what I was told and go upstairs and put my personal things that were on "our bed" into the top drawer of the long dresser. Then I would take a bath with some Dead Sea salts.

I slowly pulled myself up and in a daze, I made my way up the dark, wood stair case (admiring the detailed carvings in the dim light) until I reached the bedroom. The bedroom was very large. The four-poster bed was king size and the sheer red curtains and velvet coverings. When I pulled the sheets back they were satin. I had never slept in satin sheets, or velvet coverings before.

I walked over to the bathroom, which was large also, but what caught my eye the most was the bathtub it looked like it could fit four people in it quite comfortably. It had what looked like jets you see in hot tubs at the swimming pool. I immediately pulled up a lever that plugged the tub and started to undress. Where would the salts be? There are an awful lot of cupboards in this bathroom. I found myself comparing the size of this bathroom to my bedroom at home.

Ah, here they are. I should have known the cupboards closest to the bathtub and below the towels, just like Franks said. I pulled them out and placed them by the tub. Now that I was standing stark naked and the huge bath tub looked like it had a long time to fill up I thought, I might go check out that bed. I reached for a towel, in which there were piles of and they were all deep red. Wow, were they ever big. I jumped up and grabbed one. There was a fancy little tag on it that said "made in Italy". I had to laugh at that. Now I wonder if these were a gift from his mother or if he actually bought and brought these back with him. I wrapped it around myself (almost twice) and walked back into the bedroom.

I flicked on an extra light but I could still only see half way across the bedroom. The dark hardwood floor had a massive, red area rug with some possible catholic looking theme on it. The carpet started about three feet after the far side of the bed.

After dropping my red towel on the ground, I pulled back the coverings and sheets and slipped into the bed. If you have ever felt satin sheets against your naked body you will know what I'm talking about. This was amazing! I never felt anything like it. I rolled over onto my back and pulled just the sheet over myself.

Before I closed my eyes I could see halfway down the dimly lit room that there was a natural wood fireplace. Nothing was more relaxing to me than fireplaces, and now Frank of course. I closed my eyes and almost started to drift away when something in my head yelled, "the bath!" I sat straight up and then jumped off the bed, springing into the bathroom naked. To my surprise the water was at least past the jets and bathtub was almost full. I was so tired, I just wanted tomorrow to come so I could see Frank.

The Intruders

I turned the water off and went back to the bedroom to retrieve my towel. As I entered the bedroom again something frightening captured my eye, and I heard myself let out an odd scream. I bent down and grabbed my towel to cover myself while still trying my hardest to maintain eye contact with this huge man that I could barely make out. He was at the far left corner of the back of the bedroom. My heart was pounding so hard I could feel it in my throat and my ears.

"What do you want jerk? I know martial arts and I will kick your ass!" I draped the towel over my shoulder and put myself in a stance. This man didn't talk, and with my heart still pounding I yelled again and insisted he give up his intentions. I squinted to adjusted my eyes, and to my surprise, I realized there were two of them. The other one looked big. God please help me now! What am I going to do with two full grown men, especially when I haven't been in martial arts for almost two years.

"Someone will be here any minute, and I will shout out to them to bring up a gun! We have lots of them. Is that how you want to end up? Answer me! Answer me! Answer me!" Neither of them budged. I thought maybe if I moved a little towards them it would be intimidating. I always found that to work in life, and if I was going to get a beating better to just step up and get it over with. With one hand in front of the other I moved slowly to the other side of the bed with my pulse racing.

I yelled, "What is it that you want?" I noticed a Tiffany pole lamp about another two feet away. "Why don't you answer me?" I said, clicking on the pole lamp as my towel hit the floor. I found myself standing naked, yelling at two life sized statues in the shadows at the end of our bedroom. One was of a Roman soldier and the other of a Japanese samurai. Between them stood a bookshelf with more books, and to the right of the samurai stood another Tiffany pole lamp and a leather Lazy Boy chair.

I grabbed up my towel and wrapped myself before sitting on the floor to do some deep breathing to slowing heart-rate down. I then walked over and turned on the Tiffany pole lamp behind the Lazy Boy and the Tiffany tabletop lamp on the lamp table. I gave the statues a snarl and proceeded to the bathroom.

I placed a scoop of the Dead Sea salts in the water poured some essential lavender oil into the tub then I turning the timer on for the bath jets. As I melted into the tub, its jets massaged my sore and tired body. The smell of the lavender was starting to put me to sleep. As much as I wanted to sleep, I keep one eye open and one eye shut due to my encounter with Mr. Roman soldier and Mr. Samurai I drifted into sleep.

The sudden snap of the jets shutting off jolted me into an upright sitting position. I quickly realized where I was. Yawning I stood up reaching for my towel. I felt so thirsty, but I was too tired to go downstairs. I went over to the bathroom sink and stuck my mouth under the tap and drank from it for a while.

Making my way into the bedroom I could see clear across the room to where my two guests were standing in their battle-like positions. I gave them a glare and decided I was going to look in the second drawer of the long dresser to find something of Frank's to wear to bed. Then maybe I would feel closer to him. I opened the drawer and noticed how everything was folded in perfect little squares. I could see that I had hit the t-shirt drawer, so I picked a white one and pulled it over my head. I walked my towel back to the bathroom and hung it on the towel rack, and then clicked off a couple lights by the bed (not by the soldier or the samurai). Finally I crawled into our bed with the most comfortable mattress and satin sheets.

Homecoming

I bobbed my head up as I heard the latch on the front door creak open. I looked over to the right lamp table where the alarm clock read just after 2 AM. I couldn't believe I slept that long, but then I remembered I didn't get to sleep until after 6 AM, thanks to the statues with the dark sense of humour. Frank said he wasn't going to be home until late in the evening or even the wee hours of the morning. Well I know how those hunting trips can go, home a day or even a week early and sometimes they are back as much as a couple days late. Leah would get so mad if Father was late, that was until she met Sara. Then she didn't care at all, it was as if she hoped he'd be late.

"Christina My Love, where are you?" It was Frank. Oh what was I going to do? I felt so embarrassed that I slept in so late. I was still so sleepy, and there was no way I could fake it.

"I'm up here Frank," I replied, rubbing my eyes and trying to adjust my hair. I could hear him coming up the stairs very swiftly, and before I knew it he was already in the bedroom.

He had an arm full of red roses. There must have been two dozen. The smile on his face showed each of his dimples in their best form. "Everything worked out better than planned," he said as pulled me up and threw his arms around me. He didn't seem to notice my messy hair or bad breath; he seemed as high as a kite. "In fact, your father was apologizing to me that you took off and thanked me that I didn't call Child Services. He was worried about that little prince brother of yours. He was afraid that they would come sniffing around and questioning. As usual, he tried to pay me and as usual, I refused and said that he is like family and that he knows I don't need the money.

I am so happy My Love, I went digging around your father's room and I came upon this old wooden box and look what I found." Frank shoved his hand in his pocket and started waving a small piece of paper back and forth in front of me. "This is your birth certificate and we will need it. You are going to need a shower and to get dressed. We my love, are heading to Vancouver."

I interrupted Frank, "But the roses!"

"There will be many more roses, My Love I will cut these and put them in a vase while you get ready. We need to visit a friend of mine. He knows how to alter your ID. I am hoping he can make you older. If not, he knows someone who can get ID from someone with your same first name who has passed away. From there you can secure all other pieces of ID, the ID we will need to get married My Love."

Frank looked deep in my eyes while holding on to each of my upper arms. I wasn't sure what to say because I was still so sleepy.

"Good because I like Christina," I muttered.

"We will not change that, I have always loved Christina. You are exhausted. Did you have the lights on at the other side of the room all night?" Frank stood and walked across the room."

I stretched as I replied, "Well I was going to spar with your friends there until I realize I would have had all the advantages, since they were stiff and all. However I did keep the light on since they didn't take me very seriously about the not staring thing."

Frank laughed while rubbing his chin and turned off the tiffany lamps. "Well you won't have to be afraid of anything anymore. I will protect you, even from statues. Now go get in that shower. We need to get you a whole new wardrobe. A more grown up looking wardrobe." He walked back over and picked me up. "As sexy as you look in my t-shirts, this means so much to me, I am going to marry you Christina! Mrs. Christina Shimanskii! I love the way that sounds." He placed me on the ground, still looking like he was thinking about the name combination while he patted me on the bottom. "Now go get in that shower, so we can go and start our new life together."

Vancouver

I only had a couple pairs of jeans, a black knit sweater grandma sent me once, a blue winter jacket and a pair of running shoes. I did not look like the girl who belongs to the car I was just going to get into. Frank seemed to disagree. He looked at me and told me how beautiful I was before he opened the door of his shiny 1983 red Ferrari, only a year old.

The smell of the black, wide, leather seats reminded me of the sexy scent I would get when I hugged and caressed Frank in his leather jacket. Even the floor mats were too cool. They were black with red bucking horses. The steering wheel had a yellow round button in the middle with a black bucking horse, same as a square one on the very front bottom hood and a silver metal one on the front grill. I dare not ask how much it cost but I'm sure it was more than my father's green LTD or even his yellow Scout.

Frank grabbed my hand proudly and I noticed that he kept looking over at me in admiration. He did this every once in a while over the whole way to Vancouver. Finally we arrived in Vancouver, but Frank wanted to stop in this huge mall to grab at least a few things. I was pretty tired around eight o'clock, but he assured me there were places still open and that Vancouver is the city that never sleeps.

He was right-he took me to a huge mall and said he knew all the right stores. He took me into a store that looked like it was the focus of a business woman's attire, and it was enormous. "Oh, that is not me," I blurted.

"Christina." Frank raised his voice.

"Sorry I don't mean to get upset with you, but you want to make this work don't you?"

"Yes." I said with my head down. I slowly looked back up a Frank.

"I am a business man and you are going to be my wife. Right now you look very young, and we need you to look older. I promise as I will when we take our vows that I will be with you until you grow old. Then in a few years when you look more like you are in your twenties you can wear whatever you like, ok?" He held up my chin and insisted with his eyes that I look into his and agreed.

"Okay." I replied. We walked around the store until we found a lady who asked if she could help us. Frank responded, "Yes can you find her some classy out fits, shoes, a few jackets, and maybe a couple pairs of PJ's?"

The sales clerk lit up. "Okay, yes we can do that. Would dad like to stay and watch, or is there something you would like to shop for? Then you can come back and retrieve her when you have gotten your stuff done." She had me by my hand and I could see Frank looked irate and was trying very hard not to be. I could see he was always going to cringe if anyone referred to him as my dad.

"You know," he said I do have something I wanted to look for. I will be back in about an hour if you can figure something out by then?" he said rubbing the back of his neck, turning to go.

The lady flicked her hand at him with a fake little smile, "Of course, go on. Done! Don't worry about a thing."

Grabbing my hand, she walked me over to some knee length grey, black, brown, and navy skirts. I couldn't believe it; they got all the bland colors in the same style skirt. "You are so tiny so I am guessing a double zero, she laughed. This is a classic skirt, your dad will love it." She grabbed a few in different colors and pulled them up by my face saying. "umm, mmm, hum. These cashmere sweaters come in all colors and long and short sleeved. They go well with this skirt. Here is your classic white, beige, pink, and baby blue."

Well maybe she had a point there I thought, but the price tag just didn't seem right. These shirts were *$70* each. Still she grabbed them up and moved on to blouses and satin shirts, she also had me try on a really nice black leather dress jacket that I thought would match Frank's nicely. She then convinced me into a very pretty satiny white winter jacket and a red one she insisted on, (I think because it was *$250*). Then we decided on some dress pants and jeans, short boots, tall boots, designer runners, leather slippers, and several different sets of heels to go with the five dresses and two gowns she had picked out.

"Well look, here comes your dad." I didn't even bother correcting her. I didn't think Frank did because he didn't want to draw any attention to us (as much as he didn't like it). "I have the bill and have put everything in bags. It's a little trick I do so hopefully your dad won't refuse you. If he does . . . no big deal. We can put some back and delete some of the items from the receipt." She whispered to me while looking straight ahead at Frank. I think I was looking at her a little stunned.

Frank walked in. I tell you, if he left angry I'd like to know what brought him back looking so slap happy. "How'd we do girls?" Frank said chewing some gum.

"Umm, well exceptionally well. I have the bill here for you. She handed it to Frank and it unfolded. I could see the bottom line. It said total *$4572.72.*

Frank didn't flinch. He just smiled and said, "I see you did."

He proceeded to take out his wallet and hand the stuffy lady his credit card. She grabbed it quickly with bulging eyes before replying, "The shoes are all Italian leather, you know?"

Frank put his arm around me looking deep into my eyes and said to the store clerk, with a smile, "And I am an all Italian man!" I smiled and Frank chuckled a bit.

"If you like, she can try on few things for you, you know just to be sure?" Frank grabbed about seven of the fancy bags off the counter while I grabbed the other three.

"No, no that just won't do. I think I'll have to get her to try it all on back at the hotel when we are alone." He then pulled me over to him with his empty arm and gave me the longest and most passionate kiss. I almost forgot that we were in a mall at this time.

When he finished we looked deeply, entranced into each other's eyes until I head the frustrated sounds of the store clerk. "Um, ahem." she said loudly, with her now beefy, red face, and veins that were popping out of her neck.

Frank somehow still with his gum in his mouth, bowed his head and said, "Good evening Madam." I couldn't help but giggle and neither could Frank as we walked away back to the Ferrari and to the nicest hotel where we ordered room service.

Frank told me that he had to meet with some clients during the day but he had arranged for me to get my hair done and have some pampering here at the hotel spa. He had picked out a gown in a boutique in the hotel that he specifically wanted me to wear to dinner at this very fancy restaurant. He was going to introduce me to some of his very important clients.

He would meet me in our hotel room where I would find the dress and should be wearing it with the blue Italian leather pumps we bought at the fancy place in the mall. "Your hair will be freshly cut and styled, and you will be relaxed and massaged, everywhere. I will make sure you have a female masseuse." Frank laughed. "You will be manicured and pedicured, and your makeup will be done like a lady. That is how I treat my Christina. You will never want to leave me I will be the one to love and protect you forever. When I meet my beautiful Christina in the hotel room I will have the biggest surprise for you that you could ever imagine." Frank ran his fingers through my hair.

"But Frank you have already given me so much. I don't need any more surprises. You are the best surprise; the evening will be a gift in itself. Please don't you have been spending too much money? I won't let you!" I said looking scornfully at Frank.

"Christina, do not tell me how to spend my money. If there is one thing I have plenty of, it is money. I only tell that to you, as you are making me quite upset. I tell you, money doesn't bring you happiness, but love does." Frank's hand was over his heart and his yelling started to quiet down to more of a stern strain. He got down on both his knees and grabbed both my hands. "You are that love for me, and love has no limits. I ask you try to understand this Christina, please. I am sorry for yelling at you, my love I didn't mean for this to happen on our first night away. Please forgive me my love?" He looked up at me with tears in his eyes and kissed my hands softly.

"I'm sorry Frank. I'm young; I just don't understand these things. I promise I will never ever, I mean ever ruin any surprises again." Anger and sadness turned into passion, and we made the best love and then quickly drifted off to sleep.

The Surprise

I awoke to a tender kiss on the forehead and the essence of Franks lingering cologne. "Sleep my love. I have ordered you breakfast to be here at 8 AM then someone will come to take you to the spa. I must go now so I can get my work done. Then I can give you the most beautiful surprise for my beautiful lady. Sleep . . ." Frank kissed my forehead one last time before he switched off the light near the doorway. I peaked up at the clock which showed it was 5:30 AM. As soon as I put my head down, I drifted off to sleep again.

I woke again to a knocking on the door. I looked at the clock which read five minutes until 8 AM. Frank said he was sending breakfast at 8 AM. I jumped up out of bed yelling, "I'll be right there." I noticed I wasn't wearing any clothes . . ."I'll be there in a minute." I opened the washroom door and noticed a couple robes hanging on a rack behind the door that had the hotel insignia on them. I grabbed one quickly, wrapped it around myself and tied it as I walked to the door.

To my amazement three people dressed in white rolled in a whole table.

"Excuse me Madam, where would you like to eat this?" A man asked. I thought for a minute.

"Over by the window I think, thank you." A lady walked ahead and opened the curtains. "Oh my!" I gasped.

"Is something wrong dear?" the man asked.

"I didn't notice we were up so high," I replied nervously.

"Oh yes, the seventeenth floor is where Mr. Shamanskii always stays. It is a wonderful view of the city don't you think? Would you like a newspaper?" He added, as the brunette lady led me to my chair near the window that practically was a wall. I thought for a minute.

"Yes, I'd like that newspaper please Sir." I thought it would keep my mind off the height out the window. I started to take notice of my breakfast spread; one red rose in a crystal vase in the middle of the table. The brunette woman then opened a silver lid and underneath was a small omelette with some red potato hash browns and sliced tomatoes. The man took off another lid and there were mini waffles with whipped cream and strawberries and sliced oranges, melons, kiwis, and pitted fresh cherries on the side. There was a tall silver carafe filled with seeped tea and another with coffee. In front of these was a crystal cream dispenser with a very tall swan like spout. The cream dispenser had plastic wrap around the spout that the woman removed. They also removed the plastic wrap off of a crystal wine glass that was full of orange juice, and off a saucer with a couple croissants. The man picked up a white napkin that had a silver ring around it, slid it out of the ring he placed it across my lap. I thanked him and tried my hardest to look at what was on the table and not out the window.

"Coffee Madam or tea?" a blond lady asked.

"Tea please, I think I'll have tea today." "So does Frank . . . I mean Mr. Shamanskii always stay on the seventeenth floor? I mean how many times has he stayed on the seventeenth floor?" I asked.

"Well, I suppose as long as I have worked here and that has been a good . . . well seventeen years if you can believe that. Ha-ha. He comes here and rents two rooms one he stays in for a week or two while the other he uses to do his business in the other. But my guess is you know that part. Well, there was that time he came to stay and there was a flood on the eighteenth floor and he had to stay on the sixteenth floor. This was a couple years ago, and he was none too happy about that, let me tell you." The brunette lady rambled.

She must have been about fifty five and her accent was definitely English, (that kind of squawky English) and I was pretty sure she was wearing a wig. She finished pouring the tea. "Cream my dear?" she squawked.

"Yes." I started to wonder if these people would ever go away.

"You mean you didn't notice while you were going up the elevator, that you landed on the seventeenth floor? Don't supposed you walked up here and didn't notice seventeen stories?" She had a little squawky laugh to herself. The other two never said much at all.

"I guess I didn't notice, I mean Mr. Shamanskii . . . Frank and I were kissing the whole way up. It just seemed like no time at all." I replied, not even thinking about whom I was talking to; it was like I was still back in that elevator with Frank.

"Oh, my dear, you had me fooled, I mistook you for his daughter or maybe his niece. I thought you were eighteen or nineteen. Well I've never been good with age. You must forgive me. I bet you can't guess my age can you? Well I won't keep you guessing. I'm forty seven and when you're that old you lose your sense of age. Oh well then, will that be all, my dear?" she cackled.

"Yes, thank you, that was more than enough and I appreciate it." The three of them sort of did a slight bow and started to walk away backwards.

"Oh, Madam," The man called. "I have for you from the spa: Crystal will be here for you at 10 AM for a wonderful day of relaxation. Enjoy." He did a final bow and caught up with the other two outside in the hall.

I picked up my orange juice in its fancy crystal glass. Yum! It tasted so freshly squeezed you would have thought they executed the orange in the hallway to get it in here so fresh. Freshest orange juice I have ever tasted in my life. I ate a little of this and a little of that, just so I could sample everything. I wasn't that hungry this morning just excited about the day and what it would bring.

It was 9 AM now, the clock in this room seemed far too slow. I decided that since I had an hour I would try to face my fear of heights I got up walked and directly towards the window without looking at it. I just looked at the carpet until I saw the base of the window at the ground. I opened my eyes and started to topple forward. Clunk! I banged my forehead on the window and in a panic, pushed myself off the glass landing onto my butt. "Oh, that is it; this is so stupid. Of course I would spill my tea. I need to just go take a shower." I was talking to myself now. I picked up my teacup and grabbed my napkin off the table, thinking to myself lucky these carpets are beige. Maybe I can call a flood on floor seventeen and we can go stay on the fifth floor. I think I'd really like the fifth floor or what about the second floor? Who doesn't like the second floor?

I turned the shower on a fairly hot setting and adjusted the showerhead so it would run hard all over. I took one of their mini shampoos that smelled exceptionally nice, lathered myself up with the mini soap, and finished with the conditioner that made my hair slippery soft. Wow, I hope the spa doesn't ruin this. I don't think I have felt my hair so soft.

Finally a knock at the door and I was dressed and ready to go. I opened the door and there stood a rather pretty, tall, blonde woman. She appeared to be about thirty and had the most amazing, pale blue eyes. Her hair was very short and she must have been about six feet tall, (I was pretty sure as she stood almost like Frank to me). She had amazing legs I think they were most of her height.

"Christina?" she asked.

"Yes." I replied

"Can I get you to go back inside and change into this? I'll just wait out here," she said as she pulled a soft blue robe the same color as her knee length lab-looking dress.

"Sure." I said.

"Oh if you look on the shelf behind the bathroom door you will see some slippers." She handed me some oversized plastic slippers in a sealed clear bag.

"Okay." I let the door close and I changed as quickly as I could folding my clothes neatly on the counter. "Darn," I thought these slippers are hilariously huge. My feet are a size four although sometimes a five fit. The lady at the store yesterday pretty much sold me all her size fours.

I opened the door and there was Crystal with a very pretty smile. "Oh, you have such tiny feet. When we get down to the spa we will look for some smaller slippers. Don't worry, once we hit the elevator it does most the work. I wouldn't want to see you trip in those slippers." Crystal looked down briefly and then continued. "I am sorry, I don't think I introduced myself. My name is Crystal. You must be Mr. Shamanskii's daughter . . . or maybe a niece?" She led me towards the elevator.

"Girlfriend!" I responded. Inside really I was getting a little annoyed by the age thing, but I was going to try my hardest not to let it get to me for Frank. He wanted today to be special.

"Wow, well how old are you?" she smiled.

"Twenty-one." I said almost before she could complete her smile. "Well you're one of those lucky people then that will probably look younger for a long time." She replied kindly.

"Yeah, I am getting that. I just wish that I could look my age, you know twenty-one or even a little older as you know Frank is in his forties," I huffed.

"I know," She said, "His age . . . because he has been coming here for so long. I can see how that can be hard." Crystal continued we stepped into the elevator.

"I also date an older man and it is hard when people think you are the daughter all the time. I'll talk to your make-up artist and see what they can do for tonight. I'll also see if they can't give you some tips for later. This is where we get off," Crystal pointed as the elevator dinged.

We turned away from the front counters where everything was white marble. We went under an arch down a hall with more white marble walls and floor until we came to the end where there were two huge double glass doors with handles shaped like a gold sun. Crystal opened the door and ushered me in before the front desk.

"Can I have the program for Christina Shamanskii?" Right then my mouth kind of dropped; no wonder she thought I was his daughter. Frank hadn't informed me that he registered me at the spa under Shamanskii. They handed her a clipboard and she gave a huge smile. Again I could see she was beautiful and seemed to have a really beautiful personality as well—as far as I could tell.

"Well somebody loves you. This isn't just for hair and a make-over Dear this is the works." She leaned over the counter and whispered, "Heather, put me down for Christina here, where my no show is, here, here and here, and here too." Crystal grabbed me by hand "Well it looks like we are going to get to know each other for the day because I have you for your full body, your facial, manicure, pedicure, and he even has you in for a scalp massage before you go off to the hair stylist—now that's a thoughtful man." She almost skipped while she pulled me into a room containing a bed with a doughnut hole for a pillow.

"Oh, and Heather I think this lady needs a fruit and Champaign basket." She pulled her head back in and looked at me. "Don't worry it's free for every customer who has four or more procedures in one day." She looked back at Heather for an answer.

"Done!" Heather laughed, as she picked up the phone.

I had never had a massage before, but from what I could tell, Crystal was really good at it. She started with a pedicure and gave me this really relaxing foot and leg message, then did the body, and facial, and ended with a scalp massage that was exquisite.

We had to break for lunch as Frank had ordered me lunch from one of the restaurants and had it sent over to the spa. Crystal wanted to add acrylic nails to my manicure. She had seen that it said I was allowed to add anything else I wished to have done. I was thinking about the nails and thought maybe I might. I would still have a little time after all was done and before Frank would meet me in the hotel room. Crystal led me into the private lounge room where my lunch was sitting beside a table on another table with wheels. This time there were different, younger staff who placed everything from one table to the other. Again, a young man placed a napkin on my lap and a woman took plastic wrap off everything that didn't have a lid. Then they removed the large silver domed lid off my lunch plate.

"Will that be all?" asked the young lady with the amazingly narrow, pointy nose.

"Yes, thank you," I replied, forcing my eyes from her nose.

Lunch consisted of tea sandwiches, a personal sized veggie platter with about four different cheeses, and fruit tarts for dessert. I didn't eat too much of my lunch and passed on the dessert. I sat for a while sipping my tea waiting for Crystal to come back. She was taking the opportunity to eat her lunch also.

I looked over at the gas fireplace that was roaring from across the room and then walked over to where some empty lounge chairs sat side-by-side in front of them. I sunk down into one feeling relaxed and safe, but at the same time I was panicking inside. I started to think about my mother (usually that would calm me down) but suddenly I just realized how much I missed her. Leah would never let us cry about her or talk about her. I could hear Leah's voice in my head as if she were here right now. She was yelling towards our bedroom from the bottom of stairs, "Toughen up and stop your damn crying you little babies. At least we are going to her bloody wake tomorrow. If it were up to me I wouldn't let you go. You're all too damn soft. But your father he wants to go. I guess he must have some kind of love for her still. Like I'm going to have sex with him again if that's how it is," Leah ranted and raved as she walked back and forth yelling at us to shut up—that was the night we found out our mother had died.

Holding my cup of tea in both hands, I forced my way out of that memory just to find myself in the next one; I was at the funeral parlour in Vancouver, and while I was in this memory I realized this was the first time I had been back to Vancouver since her death. I was twelve years old when she died. I stood looking across a room, down at a white casket with my three other siblings beside me. "Get them ready to go Raymond. Enough is enough, good-bye is good-bye," Leah snapped at my father. I remember feeling scared and numb at the same time.

"Leah, just give them a moment," my father answered.

"Is that tear in your eye? Are you actually crying? Like I am going to play seconds to some dead bitch, Raymond!" Leah slapped my father while she yelled. I was thinking to myself, "Where is my grandmother? Where is my auntie?" They were only traveling from Hope, British Columbia. My father shoved Leah away and insisted that he wasn't crying and that she was crazy.

Suddenly I felt myself being picked up by my jean coveralls and floating over towards my mother's casket. Clearly now she was coming into view. The lower part of the casket was closed and the upper part was open. There was mommy. She had a familiar dress on a white one with different coloured flowers on it. I remembered her going to church in it and I remembered her teaching Sunday school wearing that dress.

Now I was on top of her. My feet and legs were high on the bottom closed part of the casket, so all my weight was on her upper body. She didn't feel like my mommy anymore; she was so cold and when I tried to push myself off she was stiff and hard feeling. I was panicking. Her hair had been freshly permed, and when I tried to pull my head up I could see that her lips were threaded. I didn't want to but I had to push on her cold hard chest to get myself off and slide down the side of the casket hitting the handles attached to the sides.

I heard the other kids crying and Leah and my father arguing. But it sounded like static on a television when a channel keeps coming in and out. I got my feet on the ground, my head was spinning and I saw the door and ran. I ran down the hall while tears ran diagonally through my hair and my face. I was running down a wide hallway until I had run into something—or rather someone, right in the middle of the hallway

"Christina, oh Baby you look like you've seen a ghost." My Auntie Marilyn bent down, picked me up, and pulled me over to the side of the hallway where there was a chair. She pulled out a hanky and handed it to me and began to rock me gently, just like my mother used to. I looked up at her and then the comfort turned to horror again as I was looking at my mother alive. Auntie Marilyn was my mother's identical twin sister. "Hey, hey calm down." Marilyn wrapped her arms around mine so that mine were down by my side and I wouldn't escape. She put her chin on my shoulder and continued to rock me until I started to calm down. "It's going to be alright, Baby, it's going to be alright. You're going to make it through this. I promise you, it's going to be alright."

I jumped back into myself in the spa lounge, looking at the reflection of myself in the fireplace glass plates.

I had tears all down my face and was gripping my teacup like football. "You alright Dear?" A voice to the left of me asked a tissue bobbed in front of my face. I took the tissue and started to wipe my face.

"Oh yeah, I think I am just a little emotional today or something," I replied.

"Well something tells me you're going to be alright Christina . . . Oh, I am going to be late for my facial. I gotta run. You have a nice day ahead of you. Enjoy it." I felt a gust of wind as I blew my nose and looked around. I didn't see anyone, and I was sure I was the only one in the woman's side of the spa lounge when I sat down here.

Wait I thought, does everyone here know my name? I can't see Frank putting this entire hotel up to something like that. I know he thinks I am special, but that is impossible and she was a customer I thought. She said she was getting a facial. I walked over to an area where they had coffee urns, cupboards with snacks, and all kinds of fruit. I turned on the sink and started dousing my face with cold water, when Crystal walked in.

"Hi Christina, Sorry I took so long. I had to take the front desk to cover Heather so she could take her lunch." Her smile twinkled as she stood with her hands folded.

"Did you have a lady that just went in for a facial?" I asked rather over excitedly and fast.

"Well normally we don't give out that information, but because I am the only one who does that this afternoon, I can safely say no, without getting into any trouble." she laughed. "Why? Did you want another?" She smiled and laughed again and then her face got serious. "Are you okay?" she asked placing her arm on my shoulder.

"Oh, yeah I am just so excited about that manicure and decided to definitely go for the French-tip, since I don't know exactly what the dress is going to look like that Frank has got for me. I am only hoping it fits," I laughed, composing myself quite well I thought.

"Okay then My Sweet, let's go down to this other room and, we will get this party going!" Crystal smiled and off we went.

"Okay now I am going to pass you off to the hair professionals. They are very good. They've done hair for many famous people who have stayed here. Oh and the makeup artists, there are two; Marcello and Anthony. They are equally as good and have a lot of experience. I am here for another . . . well wouldn't you know it—five hours. So I want to see you when they are done," Crystal said, flailing her hands and jumping up and down like we were old buddies. It did feel like I had known her for some time. She was like one of those people you meet and you just don't remember, not remembering them.

"You are going to look so good! Also I looked in the computer, and it look like you are here for one week and allowed unlimited services at the spa. So I'm thinking I can probably see you again." She said waving her hands again and then giving me a big hug. I hugged her back as I thought to myself, "I wonder if it would harm our friendship if she knew that I was fifteen. That would make me half her age, technically speaking. Not that someone would, but they could have a child that age and be thirty. But I said I'm twenty-one and I'm going to be twenty-one.

"Okay, I'm going to come by the front desk when they are done with me, and you can believe me when I say 'I want more spa treatments'. Oh yeah and I will be requesting you," I laughed.

"Oh this is Mark and he is your hairstylist for the day. Mark this is my friend Christina; she is looking for an older look. As you know tonight is a very special night. Well I guess it is a pretty special night for everyone really. Not for me if I don't get out of here, but I won't leave until I see your final result and of course until my last customer is cared for." laughed Crystal.

"Oh, you girls are so giggly tonight. Don't worry Crystal, I will take care of your friend and make sure she keeps that smile just the way it is," Mark lisped.

Off my hair went, well not a lot. My hair was long to begin with. Mark said that older woman cut their hair short to look young and because I didn't want to look young, he didn't want to do this to me. He was really funny and kept me laughing just like she said. Next he shampooed and conditioned. I must admit that this conditioner was way better than the hotel's. He put in what he called highlights and lowlights. Then he shampooed and conditioned again and cut it again to texturize it. He straightened it and put these huge rollers in it to give it some volume, but assured me it would still be straight. Then he put in what he called 'hair silk' and sprayed it with four different things that smelled good. When he finished I looked in the mirror and I didn't look like me. I did look about four or five years older. "Wow . . . oh my." I covered my mouth. "I love it, it's beautiful, still down my back, not too short, it's so soft and shiny. I love it!" I almost cried.

"You're welcome My Dear. We must get you off to Anthony, he is waiting for you down the hall. Come with me," Mark escorted me quickly.

I walked along taking as many glances as I could at my new self. I never had that many dark streaks in my hair and streaks that were that blond, but they blended together so well. Still, I thought about how this night was, a special night for everyone, like Crystal had mentioned. Was there something I didn't know? How stupid was I? Obviously there was something I didn't know.

"I leave you with my friend Anthony. I have full confidence that he will give you that look you're wanting. Anthony, this is Christina and I assure you, she is very much a sweetheart. I hate to be rude but I must leave you, for I would not want to be late for a date on such a special occasion," Mark said as he began to walk out of the room.

"I love my new hair Mark, thank you," I waved.

"You're welcome My Dear." He replied and darted out the door.

"Well, Crystal has told me all about you on her lunch break and at the front desk. Needless to say, I understand you are going for an older sort of look. I guess it can sometimes be annoying to be graced with that eternal youthful thing. Well I think it is a little overrated myself. I remember getting ID'd until I was twenty-seven. Not a popular thing with the chicks," Anthony explained. He sat me down on a chair that moved every way. I was in front of a huge mirror, with lights shining in my face.

Anthony had a kind voice; it was low and sounded like a cowboy (of all things). Never thought a makeup artist would sound like a cowboy. I really wanted to, but I didn't think it was my place to ask what his story was, and I could tell Anthony was the type that would in time.

"Well you do have some young skin here. Almost like that of a twelve year old." He smiled at me, "now that's a compliment." He continued, "We can give you an older look without making you look haggard is the good news. The bad news is . . . Well do you want to hear the bad news."He looked over at me with his head tilted and his face solemn.

"Yes, I do want to know the bad news," I answered pulling my head and shoulders back from him. He started laughing. "I'm just kidding, there is no bad news. I'm just trying to get you to loosen up. So relax Kiddo. Sorry. I mean Madam." He smiled.

"Oh, you really scared me there; I thought you were going to have to mould me a mask or something," I said, as I began to laugh a bit.

"Well let's begin now, that we have loosened up your facial muscles. Shall we?" asked Anthony.

"We shall." I answered.

Anthony shaped my brows and then put some awesome cream on my face that he calls his magic base cream. Then he turned me away from the mirror towards some bright lights and went to work on my face as if he was an artist with a fresh canvas. Before I knew he flipped me around and there I wasn't,—well it was me, but a much older version of me. I thought I looked twenty-five or at least pushing twenty-five. This was great just being in this place had made me age a whole ten years. "Now don't cry and ruin it all," Anthony warned as he passed me a Kleenex. "So what do you think? Your husband gave me a sample of the color of your dress as well. Not only do you look older, you match your dress." Anthony exclaimed with his arms swung out like he was waiting for applause on a stage.

"Husband?" I thought that to be odd. "I love it! I love it beyond belief!" I felt my heart beat a little faster in happiness.

"Here, now flail your hands in front of your eyes. I don't want to put you in front of the fan because it will ruin your hair. You know that's the thing about working with women, they're so darn emotional." Anthony stood hands on his hips, looking at me while I waved my hands in front of my eyes in the mirror." You need to get upstairs and get that dress on, but wait one minute. Are you done crying now?" He asked sarcastically. I nodded, break into action on my next task at hand. "Can I just get you to slip into that white tub dress and quickly go up against that backdrop over there so I can get a few pictures for my portfolio?" He asked, squinting his eyes. I didn't even think.

"Yes, yes," I replied grabbing the dress as I walked behind the folding wall.

Chapter 3

I entered the hotel room a different woman. There was a very big vase with about two dozen red roses and a card beside them. Frank didn't lie when he said there would be more roses. As I walked over I saw a beautiful cobalt blue gown hanging from the armoire. I pulled it down and laid it across the bed. I was beautiful. It tied behind my neck and had a plunging neckline that came down to the middle of my breast. Under the breast-line there was a three-inch-thick row of tiny Austrian crystals. It was long and tapered but not snug and had a huge slit up the left leg.

I leapt off the bed feeling my hair bounce and grabbed the card. It read:

> My love,
>   I will be back at the hotel room at 7.
>   I hope you like the dress. Please put it on, we don't want to be late. Dinner is at 8 in town.
>   I love you with all my heart.
>   See you soon.

My eyes caught the wall clock it said 6:30 a.m. He was going to be here in a half an hour. "I really have to hurry." awkwardly, as my acrylic nails felt strange and heavy I unzipped the bag that held my dress very. I unzipped the back of the dress and slipped in, zipped the back up just to mid section and tied the top. I looked at the clock again; it had taken me twelve minutes because of my nails. I looked at them wondering if they were worth it. I thought to myself that they are very pretty, and will make me look older.

I went to the closet by the front door, but something made me stop; the full-length mirror. I hadn't seen my whole self yet. I covered my mouth in disbelief; I couldn't believe that was me. Don't think I ever saw a picture of a girl in a magazine that looked so pretty. I shook my head as I opened the mirrored drawer, telling myself that I don't want to be getting all conceited.

The shoes were right out front. Perfect. Wow and the color was a dead-on match. I sat on the edge of the bed and struggled to do the strap up. The first strap took me five minutes and it had been two minutes getting them from the closet. Frank was going to be here any minute. I wanted to be ready and perfect for him. Just as I thought that, I heard the door rattling around and in walked Frank in a tuxedo. He looked magnificent, better than any Ken Barbie I ever owned. Oh I really had to stop thinking in children's terms.

The Question, the Answer

I stood completely up and straightened out my dress. "Oh my Lord, you're the most beautiful woman I have ever seen in my life! You're absolutely perfect. I really wanted this moment to be special and now it is so much more special. I can't even feel my heart beating." Frank's eyes looked a bit watery. He placed some long boxes and some other things up on top of the armoire.

"Are you okay Frank? Is everything alright?" I was looking at him very concerned.

"Alright, it is perfect, please My Love, you are stunning absolutely, stunning, and you have taken my breath away. Just give me a moment to get it back. Can you stand over there by the roses?" He asked. I moved over as quickly as I could. He was reaching up on the armoire for something.

"Do you like the dress?" I brushed my hands down my waist. "I think it looks simply perfect on you. You know, I was going to get you red but that is so cliché. You know how many women are going to be wearing red tonight?" He asked while he turned around towards me with whatever it was he was looking for.

"I love the dress! And yes, I could tell that red is your favorite color and blue is mine. So that works out perfectly." I said with a big smile, and Frank sank to his knees in front of me. "Frank!" I couldn't believe what was happening.

Frank looked up at me with a smile and watery eyes. "Christina, you are my dream woman, my soul mate, the woman I want to be with for the rest of my days. I want you for the rest of life, My Love." Frank then opened a black velvet box. The diamond was so big and sparkly that I had to pull my head away. "Will you marry me Christina?" Frank asked with the most intense eyes.

I looked down into his eyes."YES!" Frank smiled and picked me up and gave me a big hug.

"Let us put this baby on you. You are now my fiancé and that is who I will introduce you as tonight. Now, this ring is a two-carat, princess cut, in case any of the other ladies ask you. It is a little big, but the jeweller shop gave me one of these transparent little clips that pops on right here, behind your finger. Now look at that, it fits pretty snug. Oh yeah, and if this isn't ironic, my friend Ray came up with some fake ID's for you today—your last name is Valentino. Italian like mine and like Valentine's Day, the day we are engaged. This makes you twenty-one years old. Still makes me a cradle robber, but not a criminal," Frank smiled with his eyes still watering.

That is so strange, I was wondering why people kept saying this was a special day for everyone. That was so perfect, as I had told Crystal today that I was twenty-one. She is so nice and I really want to stay friends with her.

Someone started knocking at the door. Frank burst by with a smile on his face and opened the door. "Your champagne, Sir?" A man wearing some strange get-up with a hat and shoulder pads announced.

"Why thank you, and we have just enough time." Frank pulled the champagne bucket on wheels into the hotel room. I found myself mesmerised as I stared at my ring.

"Congratulations from the management and staff Sir," the funny little man said.

"Thank you kindly." Frank slid some unidentified amount of money into the man's hand. The man smiled and then he slouched and walked back down the hall as our door slowly closed.

"Quick grab the glasses." Frank was excited as he popped the cork. "Here is to a long and happy life together. And let there be children," Frank said looking elated. We raised our glasses and drank.

"Okay, sorry to rush you but I have a few accessories for you. Open this box. See here is an Australian crystal handbag, and in here, a shawl that matches your dress. In this one, are two things to put in that handbag—the lipstick Anthony informed me he used on you and Chanel perfume. Now you can stand up to those rich women in the powder room." Then he looked me in the eyes and said, "But they will never stand up to you in personality or beauty." His eyes absorbed me. I kissed him softly on the lips and told him thank you for everything and started to tell him of what an adventurous day I had as we head out the door. Suddenly I froze as the door opened.

"Oh my goodness, I'm late for Crystal! I told her I would show her my end result. I promised her. Please let me call down to the spa to see if she is still here!" I looked at Frank with pleading eyes.

"Okay, but be quick, they are pulling the car around." Frank hurried me. I picked up the phone and dialled 'Zero' and asked for the spa. It rang twice and a man answered. I asked if Crystal was still working. He told me he thought she had stayed a bit longer, but she may have left. Suddenly I heard, "Is this Christina?" and then the phone was all muffled. "Christina, its Crystal, is this you?" Crystal asked. Frank was holding the door open now, waving me to come out. "We're coming downstairs, meet us by the entrance." Then I hung up.

"I'm coming," I said, running over to Frank and out the hotel door.

We reached the entrance level of the elevator. I was wearing my shawl and carrying my Australian crystal handbag. Frank was carrying the white, satin winter coat as I refused to wear it. I didn't think it went with a gown, and he refused for me to leave it because he knew I would be begging for it later.

I was looking all over for Crystal when I spotted her by the entranced doors. I could see she was looking all over for me. "Crystal!" I waved. Franked looked at me funny. Crystal came running over to me.

"You look unbelievable, totally unbelievable! Didn't I tell you they were professionals?" She exclaimed as she gave me a huge hug. I hugged her back. "Well aren't we the handsome couple. You look like Barbie and Ken." I laughed out loud. I was glad I wasn't the only one who thought on children's terms, Crystal did too. "No, really you do, you guys could be on the front cover of a magazine. If you guys don't do something amazing tonight, that's it, you've wasted the moment," Crystal asserted, looking at both of us.

"We already did." I let her know pointing at my ring. Frank smiled.

"Oh my God, you're kidding me. I take that back you didn't waste a thing. I think I helped though? You have to relax the lady to have her say yes. Or you have to get one of these two or three carats."

I interrupted, "Two carats princess cut." Frank laughed.

"Congratulations!" Crystal uttered as we hugged again.

"Oh this is us," announced Frank, as he grabbed my arm and we waved to Crystal.

We entered the vintage restaurant and yes, I did give in and put on the satin, white, winter jacket. It was as cold outside as Frank thought. It was that humid kind of cold. Frank had explained to me that the coastal region's air was much more moist than the interior. It made the cold creep right into your bones.

After we got past the valet and the front door, I wondered if we had enough money for the meal. The hallway was most spectacular. I was in slow motion. I was thinking to myself that there were way too many hallways in our lives. A hallway seems harder to get from A to B. I almost always liked doorways. They were much more direct and leave out a lot of missed interpretation. We have all heard the saying, "When one door closes another one opens." Where in hallways we lose ourselves and often take the wrong turns.

This hallway was on the other hand, spectacular. The hanging chandeliers were timed and expected, but the doorways and side running hallways were very random and unpredictable. The art along the long path was exquisite, large paintings with posed dancers, a matador with a bull, and famous buildings from all over the world. Before we reached the ballroom, the last painting was an abstract one of a man and woman embracing each other naked.

My eyes lit up when I entered the ballroom. Long tables with white table clothes were all along the sides of the room. Along the tables there were tall crystal vases filled with deep, red orchids. All the china was white and lined with gold. The utensils were gold, and there were many at each placement. The napkins of deep red were neatly folded in a triangle that stood up. Each setting had a half fold card with individual names on it. They matched and were white-lined with gold and deep red. Mine, however, was different than all the rest. It said "fiancé of Frank Shamanskii; Christina Valentino." Frank squeezed my hand with a look of pride and told me he phoned in ahead to see if it wasn't too late to have it made up special. I could see that he was more than pleased that they were able to do it. Through the middle of the table were bottles of Dom Pérignon champagne in silver coolers. Beside each bottle of Dom Pérignon champagne stood two vintage bottles of red wine, one in front of the other.

I was so excited about the whole day and the whole evening event that I had forgotten how nervous I was. I asked Frank what I was supposed to do with all those utensils and dishes. Was I to start with the outside pieces or the inside pieces? Frank didn't look nervous one bit about me or about him. Well I suppose he had no need to worry about him; he has gone to these kinds of affairs numerous times. I remembered he had told me if I forget and I get lost, to just follow what he is doing.

Frank's Fiancée

Frank pulled chair a out for me when an older gentleman said, "Frank talk about luck we are right beside you. And who is this ravishing young lady?" Almost before he could finish, Frank piped back with the proudest look, grasping my hand and lifting me out of the chair.

"This is my fiancée, Christina Valentino. My Christina, this is Joe Burton and his wife Lily. He is one of my VIP customers." I placed my hand out to Joe who had well-groomed salt and pepper hair. He looked to be about in his mid-sixties. He had the thickest, dark eyebrows that made his salt and pepper hair stand out. Joe grabbed the tips of my fingers and kissed my hand. Next his wife shook my hand with a huge smile.

"Will you look at that lovely dress! The days when I could wear something like that? I tell you, gravity has its way with you eventually," She laughed.

I thought her to be quite a pretty woman myself. She looked to be about ten years younger than her husband. Her hair was a medium-brown and about the length of her jaw. Lily's hair had a single streak of grey near the front. Her dress was white velvet with a red sash across the waste. She had a large white fur shawl and was holding a red sheer one to replace it for indoors. She also had a handbag made of red sequins.

It was so nice to feel like I fit in. Frank really thought of everything. I could just see him being so loving, and I was thinking that there was no need for me to ever doubt him. For the first time since my mother's death, there was someone in my life who truly had my best interest and truly wanted to make me happy. I knew I just had to trust.

"Congratulations Frank and Christina. When is the big day?" Joe enquired.

"We just got engaged this evening. I plan on getting a hold of my mother when we get back home so we can start planning immediately. I am hoping in the next month or two. The sooner the better is the way I am feeling!" Frank smiled. I found myself to be a little shocked. Frank and I had not really talked about dates. But as I had told myself,

Frank has my best interest in mind and I will not doubt him. He is like my saving angel.

"Well I don't recall ever seeing you this happy Frank. I will be looking for our wedding invitations in the mail," Joe smiled.

"Well isn't this marvellous? How very spectacular! Imagine the story you will be telling your children; engaged on Valentine's Day. Are you planning on having any children?" Lily asked. Frank pulled me close.

"Plenty, I am from a big family and I think big families are the best." I didn't know what I thought. I nodded my head with my eyes wide at the thought. Mostly the thought of how those babies make their way out into the world. I knew that Frank knew best since he always had a plan that worked. It caught my attention that a crowd of people that knew Frank were lingering around listening. There were a lot of open mouths and a lot of congratulations. Some younger man even picked up my name card and passed it to a crowd of people as if to convince the crowd furthest away that weren't in earshot.

Abruptly, Frank yelled out as he was still standing, "Okay, Okay!" He reached out for my name card and it got passed down a train of people back to him. He raised the name card in the air above himself as he looked up at it. I felt weak at the knees and sat myself down. Most of the other people in the room sat at their designated spots. Frank then picked up a champagne flute and a gold knife. Clinking one against the other, he said, "I don't even know if this is allowed, but I wasn't expecting my engagement to be the icebreaker of the evening. So I would like to make a toast." At that, about twelve fancy dressed waiters came forward and took the Dom Pérignon champagne out of their silver chillers.

"Anything goes for you, Frank!" yelled a man about Frank's age that was almost directly across the table. I could only remember men by their faces and suspected ages as they all had tuxedos on. Frank began to speak again.

"I know that it has come as a surprise to some of you that I am engaged. And yes, the date of the wedding will be ASAP, but still TBA." He then grabbed my hand and pulled me up. Oh, I was so hoping this wouldn't take long. I heard a fairly loud "ohhhhh" across the crowd and thought maybe my dress had come undone from around my neck. But by following everyone's eyes, I could see the way that Frank had my hand and my finger bent back, so that you could really see my ring.

Frank went on. "That may be a lot for some of you to take in. Those who know me know that I have never been married before. For me though, it is not enough I could never get enough of my Christina, and this day will never be forgotten. All of you have become a part of it. This is to spending the rest of my life with my soul mate." One of the waiters that had been going around the tables pouring everyone champagne nudged Frank so Frank lowered his glass for a moment to get a fill. "I could not imagine my life without my Christina, my love." Frank raised his glass in the air and so did everyone else, Frank then clinked glasses with me and the people closest to us. It would have been impossible to clink with everyone as there were at least a few hundred people there. One thing I did know for sure was that this day and this evening was the happiest I had ever seen Frank.

The dinner went smoothly, Frank unfolded my napkin and placed it on my lap. When the soup came I used the same spoon Frank used and remembered to spoon away from myself and to sip from the side of the spoon. I followed Frank with all the utensils as each course was served and placed the fork at the right end of my plate, slightly diagonal when I finished. Before I knew it, the entire meal was over and I wished to go back to the hotel. The waiters had cleared the table and the lights dimmed as some slow music started playing.

Frank was talking quietly to his friend Joe beside him while I tried to eye all the other woman's dresses. I noticed my Frank was right again, most of the woman had red dresses. There were a few pink dresses, Lily's dress was white with red, I saw others that were red with white, and one pale blue with pale pink. I was the only one with a cobalt blue gown.

Frank pulled my arm up until I was standing and lead me onto the dance floor. No music was playing, but I could see his friend Joe up on the stage talking to the band. White light like crystals twinkled all over the floor and the walls. A man on the microphone announced, "To the newly engaged couple, Frank and Christina. We're going to let the DJ take this one." The crowd started to clap, and a few of Frank's friends howled some. Then the DJ started to play a popular eighties love song.

"Frank, I don't dance! I don't know how to slow dance!" I loudly whispered in his ear.

"Don't worry My Love, just let me lead you around slowly. These people are far too drunk to see anything past three feet," Frank laughed in happiness.

It actually went quite smooth. I even felt like I knew what I was doing. Frank just gave me that kind of confidence.

As we left the dance floor there was clapping again. I asked Frank quietly,

"When can we leave? I want to be alone with you."

Frank replied, "You are already reading my mind like we have been married for many years. I don't think it would be rude if we did right now. Everyone knows that we just got engaged tonight. But when we go back and get our things, lets grab our name cards for memory's sake." Frank whispered as we slipped through tables and almost into the hallway.

Close Call

"Frank, how are you? Come over here for a moment. I want to take a look at that young, soon to be wife of yours," a man in a white tuxedo pressed us before the hall. He looked to be around the age of sixty-eight and was puffing on a big brown pipe, a man I recognized very well. He was a customer of my Father's and Frank's. His name was Stan Goldstein and was a German man my father really liked. They had a lot in common. Frank introduced him to my father. I don't think I had ever formally met him, just seen him while I was doing inventory for my father on some new hunting knives. I remembered I had brought him and Father coffee once. This Stan had been on a couple guided hunting trips; Father does a lot of work for him.

I could see Frank's nervousness and his skin turn a shade paler. "Yes, in this light you do look so familiar, but I just can't place it. Gloria come here now, do you recognize this Christina? Now what did you say your last name is?" He asked very inquisitively.

"Valentino," I answered in a quiet voice.

"Oh, Italian as well you are? Well, I think it is good to stick to your same race. We shouldn't go around messing up God's business I always say. You don't look pure Italian to me though. You're white skinned, not olive like Frank here, and your eyes are mighty green," he muttered with his head tilted and one eyebrow cocked.

"Oh enough already Stan, we don't know people her age. She looks all of twenty-four." That felt real good to me. "Let's just congratulate our friends and let them be for once Stan." Gloria snapped.

Frank cut in, "She, like me, has a mother of a different race. My mother is Italian/Irish and my father, Italian. Her mother was German and father Italian." Frank looked down at me while Stan pulled his pipe out of his mouth leaving it in the shape of a little circle.

'Yes. Hmm." I said. Frank took my hand and said good-night to Stan and Gloria. While leaving we could hear the sound of Gloria reprimanding Stan for drinking too much. We scurried through all the people, noticing there were a lot of people on the dance floor now. We picked up our things and made sure we didn't forget our name cards. Then we slipped off unnoticed.

The valet brought the car around and we made our way back to our hotel room without regret. Frank must have quickly slipped off his tuxedo while I was in the washroom. I wanted this night to still be even more perfect I touched up my makeup, brushed my teeth, and tousled my hair. By the time I stepped back into the bedroom Frank was under the covers naked and propped up on a pillow with his hands behind his back. I still had my dress and shoes on.

"Hello," Frank's voice sounded low.

I smiled, "Hi." I walked in front of the bed towards his side, and undid the upper part of my dress while standing sideways so he could see the side of my breast. I tried to pretend I wasn't trying to tease. But I saw through my peripheral vision that he was in a strong gaze. I unzipped the back of my dress."That sure was close with Stan and Gloria hey Frank?" I looked behind myself, letting my hair fall down the side of my face. I made the zipper slowly slide down even lower to the small of my back.

"Yeah," Frank agreed. My dress dropped to the ground. "Close!" Frank repeated as he sat up in the bed now watching more intensely. I bent down and put one foot up on a chair to undo the strap on my shoe. My backside was facing Frank as I looked over my shoulder, letting my hair cascade over to one side as I spoke.

"I knew Stan was racist like Father, but that was pretty bad. I admit it was really nice to hear his wife guess that I was twenty-four." I looked back at him to see if he could respond. He didn't, but he wasn't ignoring me. I looked forward with the biggest smile, trying not to laugh, and managing to get one strap undone with my annoying acrylic nails. I switched my other foot up on the chair to undo it.

"I really enjoyed that butternut squash soup. Too bad they took it away so fast I could have just eaten that all night. What was your favorite dish Frank?" I asked, slipping off my the second shoe and looking over my shoulder.

"Frank, are you listening to me at all?" I jokingly snapped, putting my hands on my hips.

"Oh, yeah I am My Love. I really liked the . . . the champagne. It was so good." He replied starry eyed. I walked closer to him and he looked up at me. I love that puppy-eyed look he sometimes gets. I brushed my hand through his thick hair.

"Could you please?" I pointed down to my leg.

"Oh, yeah I can do that." Frank responded and started to roll my legging down gently until he pulled it off the end of my toe and repeated the same thing on the other side. He then pulled my wrist lightly, just enough to lead me onto the bed beside him as he dimmed the light.

The remaining days at the hotel were excellent. I felt like I had a whole new life, and a whole new set of friends that respected me. But the one friend who was very dear to me and that I was going to miss the most was Crystal. I could talk to Crystal about anything and Frank let me go down every day to the spa. By the end of the week she had come up to our hotel room at least twice for room service dinner with Frank and I. She tried to pay or leave a tip but Frank insisted she didn't. He was happy that I had made a good friend out here because he would be taking me to work with him in Vancouver. He wouldn't dream about leaving me behind.

Crystal and I were excited that we would be seeing a lot of each other. That made leaving not so unbearable when the time came. We left with a huge hug and a kiss on the cheek and now she also gave a hug to Frank too. I assured Crystal we would see her in two weeks and stay for that long. For now it was time to travel back to the Caribou to make wedding plans.

The Frank I Never Knew

The drive home was turning out to be extraordinary. We were going over all the wonderful times we had in Vancouver. We were constantly holding hands, stopping off at all the beautiful sights and taking pictures. I just really had the urge to thank Frank for all the wonderful things he had done for me, and he assured me it was not going to stop. I didn't want to question it, as I knew how mad it made him. I felt I already owned more clothes than I had ever owned in my life at one time. I really didn't see how I needed more.

We both went on about the transformation the spa, the hairdressers, the makeup artists and how they really all came together. Frank told me that he got a hold of Anthony and Mark before we left. He put in an order for all of the hair, makeup and skin products they used on me.

He seemed to feel like he had to assure me he would have married me still even if I had of been the same girl from my father's gunsmith-shop which was just weeks ago. Then he wanted to make it clear that we had to change my looks so that we could be safe and so no one would recognize me. I told him that I understand and that I was so happy and glad for the change. I then asked him if he could get a copy of some of the pictures that Anthony took of me in that white tube dress.

All of a sudden, the cab of the car became completely quiet . . ."Ok, let me just get this straight," Frank raised his voice. The car started to accelerate. "Anthony took pictures of you, my wife, or my future wife for his portfolio? Am I right? Am I right? Am I right?" Frank was furious.

"I'm sorry, I thought that was normal. I thought you knew that happened?" I was getting fearful as the car continued to accelerate.

"It is not normal for someone to molest my wife, you are mine. Do you understand that? You are not a Barbie doll!" Frank screamed at me.

"Frank, please slow down, you are scaring me!" I yelled back. I guess the Barbie doll thing was out the door. How could I be thinking that right now?

"I hope you are afraid right now. I hope you know that I won't share you." Frank's yelling was the last thing I remembered until I woke up to Frank outside the car. The Ferrari was taking up two lanes and we were in a bend on the Hope-Princeton Highway. He got a truck to pull over and I could hear him talking to a man. "Can you please flag this corner? My wife is unconscious in the car and I need to see how she is doing. If she dies, I will die," Frank raged dramatically to the man. The man agreed to watch and flag the corner. Frank came over to my door, but it wouldn't open. I even tried from my side, but soon passed out again.

I woke to Frank beside me crying, "My God, My Love, I am so sorry, I will never forgive myself. The camera and the travel cups were flying through the air and hit your head, and I think your head hit the side window. Oh my God, please be okay!" Frank begged, as I felt myself fade out again.

I awoke again at Franks home or "our home." Frank was right by my side, half asleep as I woke. I stirred a little and realized how mad I had made him feel. I remembered when I made my father mad; I was the only one to blame. Making a profession of blame-taking seemed to be my life. I was the one to blame, and if I didn't like the title I just needed to learn to shake it by doing better.

Frank started talking to me, "My love, Christina, I am so sorry, do you hear me? My life will end if you don't hear me!" He cried. I didn't hear this from my father, so Frank has got to be good. He has got to be so much better, I convinced myself.

"I am sorry," I wailed. "I am sorry, I belong to you, I am not a Barbie. Frank I only want to be yours. Please forgive me. Sorry!" I begged.

Frank rose up above my head. "Don't, stop, I was wrong Christina, Anthony was wrong. I should not expect you to know beyond your years. Just to make people make you look beyond your years. Now I see what I have done to you. What I have done to your face, but please don't worry. It is only swelling and bruising and it will subside. I will give you the best care. You have a concussion and that is my fault. I will not let you see a mirror until you look better. They say about a week and a half. I will be with you night and day until we return to Vancouver. When we go back, My Love, we will fly with your new ID. Sleep now. I will make it up to you.

The next few months went well. We didn't talk about the incident in the Ferrari, except that we had the right side replaced. Frank said he wanted to get a new car. He knew I liked the Ferrari so much that he wanted me to have it while he got something else.

I visited the most I could with Crystal—she was my saving grace. I felt like I could trust her and I made her my maid of honor for the following week. I really felt a love for Crystal, but I still had a fear for Frank. I didn't tell her my real age, the accident, the fake ID or anything.

I never felt quite right since the accident. I was nauseated and tired. We had a visit from Frank's mother Maria and she thought I was pregnant. Frank jumped up elated, and his mother Maria was batting him with a broom. She moved the wedding up to the following week and made Frank pay for all the plane tickets from Italy. He didn't seem to mind.

Maria was a heavy-set woman who had ten children and many grandchildren. Her cooking was delicious, but I could only eat a few times a day. That is what made her think I was pregnant. She was constantly trying to feed me. Frank thought she might be getting offended that I wasn't eating her food, until she came to the pregnancy conclusion, then she knew why.

She got Frank to go into town and purchase a home pregnancy test, and to our surprise, it indicated that we were indeed having a baby. She insisted that Frank's sister, who was a nurse, check me over. Frank's sister Alyssa checked me over carefully and suggested Frank and I get some books on pregnancy. Frank seemed more than thrilled to buy them and start reading them with me.

The Wedding

Our wedding took place in the Banff Springs Hotel in Alberta, Canada on May 27th, 1984. I could not keep up with all of the family and friends, but I was just happy that Crystal was there and she was my maid of honour. But because she was my maid of honor I really felt like I had lied to her. I felt like she didn't fully know me by not knowing my age.

I felt more emotional being pregnant and now married. Still, I walked down the aisle in my long, elegant dress with a four-foot train. My bouquet was simple but elegant; long cut, red roses (of course). The stems where wrapped with white satin ribbon and ringlets of white satin ribbon hung down.

Home again

Here we were, home again, and things started to go as usual. I started to trust Frank again like I promised myself. Frank's sister Alyssa had determined that I was three months pregnant in the beginning of May, but I still wasn't showing. Frank seemed really frustrated, he wanted me to show but I still had a really flat stomach. What I did have was morning sickness and a lack of appetite. Frank's sister had dated my pregnancy from my last period, which was February 1st. This meant I would have conceived on that Valentines' Day night.

There was no way I was going to be able to see a doctor until we could get the marriage certificate and my medical card in the mail. We were both really nervous about being discovered and our dreams being taken away from us forever. As the months passed by we figured that I was finally about five to six months pregnant. Still, I have just a small lump but Frank is elated. He often woke up to me wrapped around him with my stomach pressed against his body and the baby kicking. At this point Frank refused to go to Vancouver to work unless I went with him. He wouldn't leave his family.

Still no medical card—however, our marriage certificate came in the mail. Frank was so proud that he bought a beautiful frame and placed it above our bed. He decided that if the medical card did not come in another two weeks, he would call their office. Frank said there was no way his baby wouldn't be born in a hospital as there was just too much that could go wrong. From all the books we had been reading together it seemed quite possible, which scared both of us.

Carlos

Frank doesn't have to go back to Vancouver for two more weeks so he told his brother Carlos that he could stay until we leave. Frank would love more of his family to move to Canada and he would love to teach Carlos a little about the business. Carlos is twenty-six and very flirtatious. I am very nervous about him, but Frank seems to trust his brother, (he always brags about what a beautiful young wife he has). I have noticed Carlos' eyes on me and I have not reported it to Frank. He had walked in on me naked two times in the past two weeks. I did make it very clear to Carlos that I was upset with him for this.

This time Frank was outside in the garage buffing the Ferrari for me. I was in the kitchen when this overwhelming nauseous feeling came over me. Carlos came up behind me while I was in my satin robe just after I had splashed water on my face. Carlos pinned me up against the counter and started kissing my neck and pushing his hand under my robe and up my leg. I screamed, "No, stop please. Let me go! Right now! I knew that Frank heard something from the garage. I head the door to the living room, and then the kitchen door opened. Carlos continued as he didn't know the layout of the house that well and I don't think he thought Frank was listening.

"Oh, you want it," he uttered as I saw Frank walk in soundlessly. "You're a Shamanskii now; next you're going to have my baby." Carlos pushed my upper back so I was over the counter and pushed his fingers up my leg until my robe was up to my waste. He then started to slide his hands down my legs.

Frank went flying up towards him and punched him in the face, and he didn't stop. He beat him and he beat him. Blood was pouring down his face and Frank looked happy to see the blood—still he kept punching. I was so afraid that I ran into a kitchen closet, feeling our child flop about inside of me in stress. Peeking back in I saw Frank tie Carlos to a chair and drag him down to the wine cellar. I heard each thump. "I don't care if you are my brother; you are going to die now. There are some lines you just don't cross!" Frank yelled.

I knew I had but a little time, so I ran upstairs and grabbed about three outfits and put them in the old backpack I came with. I ran to the fridge, stuffing food into sandwich bags for the drive. All the while I could hear Frank beating and yelling at Carlos, while Carlos pleaded for him to stop. I grabbed the keys to the Ferrari as I headed to the garage. All I could think about was whether or not Frank thought Carlos was taking advantage of me just as he thought Anthony did. I wouldn't let him take anything out on me now that I have this baby in me. I needed to protect more than anything, and out of everything in this world it had to come first. It seemed odd me that I had to be thinking this about Frank. I couldn't believe I was feeling like I had to protect our unborn baby from him.

In my panic I didn't know where I would go. I couldn't place this much of a burden on Crystal and her fifty-five year old boyfriend. I needed to forget. The only road ahead seemed to be the road back home. Father had talked about grandchildren before, so maybe he would be happy. This was all I had and all I had to go on and I had to think positively. I couldn't think of anything else. I was afraid that this time Frank would kill me.

While driving the two hours back to my father's little town I thought of calling Frank's mother. But I didn't want Frank to know where I was if this was my final decision, and I don't think that Frank would think I would choose this path.

Prisoner

I ditched the Ferrari about a mile from town and started walking. It was when I got into the junk-covered yard that I tripped on the two boards with barbed wire between, and suddenly my knee hit a can. Abruptly Leah was flying at me! The sun had risen just enough for her to recognize me.

"Raymond, Raymond, you're going to shit!" she yelled. Out comes my father with a loaded shotgun as if I was a wild rabid moose. Leah pulled me up by my hair and then looked down over my shoulder. "Raymond, I think the damn whore has gotten herself pregnant. I am saying that is a baby bump. You know this girl has two empty legs and the metabolism of a race horse?" Leah exclaimed.

"Christina, is this true, are you pregnant?" Father came closer. "You little whore, you are. I can't have you gallivanting around town ruining our business and our family name." my father yelled, looking at me up and down until his eyes came to focus on my belly.

"You know that," Leah agreed with Father.

"I'll stay indoors and I'll help Leah with the cooking and cleaning," I begged, with my hair still pulled back—which made it hard to look straight ahead at anyone.

"Raymond . . . you know what? I was trained to do abortions, and they can be done at any stage. You know that is what needs to be done here," Leah looked seriously at my father. I thought to do the same.

"Father, this is your grandson or daughter—you don't want to do this! I am five to six months already. Daddy I love you, don't do this I feel it moving all the time! Don't listen to her!" I screamed. My father was silent for a minute.

"Oh Raymond, don't be a baby. She's a damn slut doing this behind your back. And who do you think the Father is?" Leah went on.

"Yeah who is the father?" Leah grabbed the back of my hair and punched the side of my cheek as she yelled. "Tell us or we will kill it."

"Ok, don't kill my baby then. It is Frank, like Uncle Frank, Frank Shamanskii!" I cried.

"That son of a bitch! Take her to the attic, we are getting rid of it! You know how to do it Leah?" Father yelled. Leah grabbed me by the hair and led me backwards into the house. I felt the warmth that brought no reassurance as we went in. We entered through the boot room, then to the kitchen and finally the hall. Leah continued to drag me by the hair backwards up the narrow staircase until she threw me on the old saggy bed. "Don't worry my dear, I am locking the bottom door and there is no way out. You will have two days maximum with your little bastard until I get the right materials to retrieve and dispose of your little problem. If I don't get it in time I will just talk your father into burying you and your bastard in the dugout basement. This place is supposed to be condemned because of some asbestos problem. That problem is in the ceiling, and they won't even look in the basement. I got your dad wrapped right around this baby finger. You rest now little whore, cause I'll be coming for you and your bastard later." Leah never looked happier when she had a project in the making.

I am not sure if it was a coincidence, but my baby was kicking the heck out of me just then. Feeling that life inside me panicked me as the doom and darkness of the one bedroom attic closed in on me.

Chapter 4

I heard Leah double latch and lock the door at the bottom of the narrow staircase and I knew there was no way out—especially in my condition. There was the one double-locked little door and a small window at the top of the bed that was hard plastic and opened upwards. It took a lot of muscle just to open it. If you did get down you were two stories up, and below were a bunch of thick, prickly stick things that were darting straight up and growing out of the ground. Then there were a couple huge piles of old broken boards.

I knew that it was essential for the survival of my baby to know exactly Leah was planning. I knew that there was only one way I could find out; that was through two vents at either end of the attic in the floor.

In the daytime I could hear Father and Leah below the unfinished end of the attic, which was closest to the kitchen/living room area. At night the best way to hear was through a vent at the end of my bed near the makeshift bathroom. It led strait down to Father and Leah's room.

I knew Leah would be scheming with Father about her new project at bedtime. Living with her as long as we did, I could hear her unload to Father in the evenings. During the day you could hear her nagging voice through the attic vents if she locked us up there as a punishment. I hoped she would be doing just that, but in the kitchen or living room—not the shop. The vent didn't lead that far (or at least give good enough sound quality to the shop).

The Battle

I tiptoed across the squeaky floorboards until I got to where they were really loud. Then I actually got on my hands and knees and tried to glide across the floor. I went as slow as I could until I reached the vent. Thank God I could already hear Leah's nagging voice. "Raymond, killing Frank should not be your objective here. Really think about it, that little slut seduced him. Forget about blaming Frank." Leah tried to convince my father.

"She was my little girl once," my father barked back at her.

"Oh, really, Raymond how many times do I have to tell you we all turn into whores as soon as we hit puberty. Then later we get it out of our systems and turn into women. They have a lot of making up to do for their mother; you remember her being so frigid. Ha-ha, they don't even have a hope," she laughed.

I heard my father slap her. "Oh yeah, what happened to you then, your mother wasn't frigid, she was a damn prostitute before your father saved her." Father was getting angry with Leah.

"Raymond! Enough! Business is business and Frank brings you a good portion of your business. We can't lose that, just act normal around him. You would do that if you were smart, but do what you want," Leah cried.

"Well since you have all the answers, what will we do about this situation with this baby?" Father asked.

"I already know. I will get my friend Ellen who works in a doctor's office in 100-Mile House to bring me a speculum, or pop one in the mail. We won't feed Christina for a few days; since she is pregnant she will be pretty weak by then," Leah schemed. I looked over at the backpack with a sigh of relief. I knew I had some carrot sticks in a sandwich bag, a chocolate bar, some digestive cookies, as well as one juice box. I knew I would have to take them out and hide them to start rationing them right away.

"I will use leather straps to hold her arms down and tie her legs to the outside metal rails of the bed. Open her with the speculum and insert a long straw deep into her cervix. Once that is done I just need to blow air up into her uterus. You won't have to worry about that little

Shamanskii; she will be giving birth within hours, maybe days. It is one of the oldest methods out there. I am so excited to finally show you some of my skills on humans rather than just animals," Leah boasted.

"I suppose if that works," Father replied.

"Hell, its Frank!" Leah said rather shocked."Raymond, now stay very calm, remember who puts food on our plate, and just imagine this didn't even happen." Leah reminded Father.

"Ok, I got it. Just go put a pot of coffee on," Father replied. My heart sank, I knew I couldn't be with Frank, but there was so much about him I loved. Couldn't Frank could just be my hero one more time? I didn't want him not to be involved in the raising of our child. But I also didn't know what he did with Carlos in the wine cellar. Did he kill him?

Frank Searching

I could hear Leah clinking around. She was probably trying to remember how to make coffee. Then I heard Father. "Well just come on in here Frank. Leah was just putting on a pot of fresh coffee. You were saying your Ferrari was stolen and someone in your family was possibly in danger ?" Father asked. I thought about Carlos and really wanted to know if he was still around after what Frank did to him. He just went crazy with jealousy. More crazy than he did on the highway when he heard Anthony merely took some clothed pictures of me. Frank began to cry.

"Yes, I just want her back so bad," Frank cried.

"You mean your Ferrari?" Father asked.

"No, I don't care about the Ferrari. I mean my um . . . you know who I mean. This is making me crazy. I mean my youngest sister. She was down here, she has a disease that kills, and she took my car. My brother Carlos is out looking for her also. Did he stop by?" If Frank was asking this, I thought Carlos has got to still be alive.

"What disease does your sister have?" asked my father.

"I don't know, I mean does it matter? Well it is a cancerous one." Frank began sobbing quite loud. "Oh dear God forgive me. I am so sorry to have bothered you folks. They found my car near your home and I know you haven't met Alyssa, but Alyssa doesn't know anyone out here. I thought maybe she found an address or your business card. I will come by to check to see if you have seen her over the next while unless I have found her. Then I will be at peace again." I knew Alyssa had gone back to Italy sometime ago. I knew Frank was desperate to tell such a story.

"Do you have a description?" Father cleared his throat.

"She will look Italian, olive skin like mine, long brown hair and brown eyes. She is beautiful. Like all my sisters. I must go now. I need to see if Carlos has found her." Frank sobbed until I couldn't hear him anymore. Obviously he was talking about me, and making things up just so he could get a look around Father's house. It sounded like Carlos was alive—which made me feel relived.

I wanted to yell out that I still loved Frank, but inside I knew he was incapable of trusting me around anyone who was male. I know what Carlos had done was wrong, but so was the incredible beating he took for it. I just wanted the good Frank back, and I really longed for him now, but I wasn't sure I even knew who he really was. I wanted the Frank from Vancouver.

"Maybe we should give her to him. He would be so grateful he would give me even more customers." Father suggested.

"Raymond get your head screwed on right, she ran must have ran away from her for some reason. If we give her back she will eventually talk. The whole thing will cause us to lose customers. Have you thought of that? When he learns we told her we were aborting his bastard baby he is going to hate us even more. Raymond, they can never see each other again." Leah sounded convincing.

"You are right. We can't take that chance," Father agreed. Damn I thought. I knew I could get away from Frank in Vancouver. Crystal would help, and at least my baby would live and be born in a hospital. Although, I wasn't sure about her boyfriend—he seems to have become friends with Frank. I worried he would tell Frank where I was.

The bell went off again and this time Leah and Father's voices both faded into the shop to greet a customer. I got up quickly, not caring about the squeaky floor. I opened my backpack, ate one digestive cookie and drank my whole juice box. Soon I felt my baby kick and turn around inside me with gratefulness. I then placed the last four digestive cookies under the top head of the bed with the six small carrot stick and the Mars bar. I used my teeth to make a hole big enough to fill the juice box with water for night-time.

Kill Her

I didn't want Leah to think of dehydrating me; I knew that would affect the baby right away. The nurse that visited me at Frank's and what used to be my home, said dehydration could cause early labour fairly easily. I would drink as much as I could during the day from the little sink in the makeshift bathroom, but I dare not run water at night. If I could hear them and the taps and pipes downstairs, I am sure they could hear mine.

I lay in bed for hours until the sun went down. I could feel the baby inside me begging for food and water. I thought I would then get one last binge of water before Father and Leah went to bed and then have a little more to eat. I grabbed the juice box from under the bed and drank it as I walked to the sink. I filled and drank from it five more times 175 ml, per portion I then refilled it for my final night's hydration and slipped it under the bed. I decided from now on that I would always drink from the box rather than run my head under the sink—then I could keep track. I grabbed one more digestive cookie and two small carrot sticks. I laid in bed with the baby kicking as the darkness settled in. A couple hours later, I woke to Derrick yelling good night to Father.

It only took minutes and I could hear voices come up the vent close to the end of the bed near my bathroom. This was the vent that led to father and Leah's bedroom, where all of Leah's daily final conclusions were revealed. It was essential for my survival that I hear Leah's schemes and what she was going to convince my father of next. "Raymond, you remember how peaceful it was when all the girls were gone and it was just you me and Derrick?" Leah asked father.

"Yeah," Father replied.

"I was thinking we already have Christina down as a missing child. Why don't we just stop feeding her after the abortion," I could feel my chest go numb and my brain spin. "She will lose a lot of blood after the abortion. She is small but her stomach measures further along than it looks. If we just don't feed her, between that and the bleeding, it would only be a matter of days and she would die. We could bury her in the dugout basement, or we could even take her way out to that hunting area that you only know how to get to and let the wild animals have her. There would be nothing left to find," Leah suggested.

A long time went by and father never answered. I could feel myself gagging; I covered my mouth with both hands firmly, so I wouldn't make a sound. I was on the floor on my side, leaning on one elbow. Still, Father said nothing.

"Well if my speculum doesn't arrive tomorrow it should be here the next day in the mail. That should give you a little time to think about it . . . Good-night." I could hear the bed creak as Leah rolled over.

"Hmm, good-night," my father said.

"Oh my mother in heaven, how would my father allow this to happen? He obviously wasn't ruling it out," I thought as I slowly got up. I slid into a sitting position and shuffled my bottom across the floor until I was at the head of my bed. I stood upright like a robot, so as to not make a sound. When I heard an old, familiar rumble.

As I was facing the head of the bed I was looking right out the window, and there pulling over to the side of the road next to our backyard was Frank in the Ferrari. He turned it off and got out, but didn't close the door. The passenger's side door opened, and out walked Carlos with bandages across his nose. Frank leaned forward and Carlos looked at him. Frank had his finger in front of his lips. Frank leaned over the hood of the car, scanning the yard and the house, as did Carlos.

I felt so desperate after what I had just heard. I tried to wave my hand in front of the window, without touching the creaky bed. Leah had taken the lamp and there was no way he could see me. I just watched as he looked intensely around the property for about half an hour. They then both got back into the Ferrari started it up and pulled away. I sunk, and sat back into the creaky saggy bed, feeling broken. I cried silent tears until my PJ's were wet around the neckline. Eventually I was so tired from crying that I drifted off.

I awoke at about 10 AM to the smell of burnt coffee and bacon. I immediately ran to the toilet and threw up stomach acid. I quickly drank some water and accepted the fact that I had no toothbrush. I tried to brush my teeth with some water and tissue paper. I grabbed a digestive cookie and ate it with five juice containers of water.

I slowly crept to the edge of the room to the far vent. I got down to the floor to listen for any morning news. There was a lot going on in the house this morning. Oh, I recognized that voice—it was Mr.

Alec Maguire. "No coffee Leah," he said in his Scottish accent I had always loved. "I just thought I would ask Raymond here when he is planning his next guided hunting trip come this fall. Also, I would like to know how those children are? Well most of them are hardly children anymore. I can see why the two older ones would want to go and live with their aunt. I mean, since she is their mothers identical twin, can you blame them? I am truly sorry to hear that Christina has been missing for so long I have always been so fond of her. She . . . she truly reminds me of someone I used to know. Well I have told you that before and I am sure you already know how special she is. I am sure your hearts are just filled of fright, just not knowing how she is. Well, please feel free to contact me once you hear of anything. I would be happy to take her for a summer as I had mentioned before I would provide her with some riding lessons, English style. You know that is always safer. Well, I should be off. I have a long drive ahead of me. God bless you and may he care for you in your time of need." I could hear Alec's feet as he walked through the kitchen.

"I wouldn't worry about Christina. She is alright as long as she doesn't fall into the wrong crowd. Don't you waste your time Alec! Have a good one," Leah sounded put off.

"Hello Frank, I've been meaning to get a hold of you about some recent investments. I do have to go now, but perhaps I will give you a call in the next day or two." I heard Alec say.

"Good-bye Alec!" my father yelled out. Alec must have waved or something because I never heard his comforting accent again that day.

Frank was there now. My heart started to pound. He wasn't giving up. I hope that if Leah tries to take our baby Frank will be there, he will subdue my father without getting shot and get us out on time. "Coffee Frank?" my father asked.

"No thank you," Frank replied.

"I don't want to upset you, but any word on that sister?" my father asked.

"No, none," Frank answered.

"Honey, isn't that funny how Alec always asks about Christina. I know he has always been fond of her. You know, maybe if we had let Christina stay a summer or two at his place and take the riding lessons, she may have never run away. You think?" Leah's voice gloated purposely looking for a response from Frank.

"Hmm, well." My father tried to talk when Frank interrupted; "Well what do you mean? Alec has had a thing for Christina? No one ever told me about this. I've always been part of the family, haven't I? Hey, and who do you think brought you Alec as a client? He is like sixty-three and one of the richest men I known. He was the first client I got you. He still owns half a pharmaceutical industry in the US and inherited millions from relatives in Scotland and millions from relatives in Canada. I put him right in your pocket, buddy!" Frank snapped. I thought to myself yeah, Frank put a scare in them.

"Sorry Frank it just never came up. I didn't know you were so interested in what was going on with the kids. I wouldn't hold anything back from you on purpose." Leah sounded a little worried.

"Of course we wouldn't Frank. Now just calm down here a minute. You're just upset about your sister. Can I get you something? Maybe you need me to come out to you home for a while and be with you until you find out some more information?" my father offered Frank knowing Frank would say no.

There would be too much evidence of me being there. I quickly went over that in my mind—the pictures that Frank had blown up and supersized in every room. The wooden plaque he had made that said "Christina's kitchen." Frank also made a sign at the beginning of the driveway that said Frank and Christina Shamanskii. He made our bench swing where he carved "Frank and Christina" on it as well. Later he carved in "baby" below our names in small letters.

Frank responded, "No, I think I'm just a little out of sorts like you said. Maybe I will go down to Mr. Maguire's house and go over those investments he was talking about. Some work might get my mind off Christina . . . or Alyssa, rather." He said in a trance-like voice.

"Ok, well that will be good for you Frank. I think that will help you a lot," Leah replied happily.

Oh, now I knew what was happening Leah was not a stupid woman, I'll give her that. She just convinced Frank not to look here for me and that maybe I had some sort of bond with Mr. Maguire. I knew Leah planned it so that this way Frank wouldn't be in the way and I would possibly even be dead in the next couple days. Leah's problems would be over.

Scheming

I could tell that Frank left without saying another word when I heard father say to Leah, "You stupid, dumb bitch. Now you've just made me lose two of my best clients." I heard him slap Leah.

"Will you quit hitting me? No such thing will happen. Frank is not going to admit to Alec what Alec won't admit to Frank. At least not past what Alec won't even admit to himself. Frank is going to go up there to look around Alec's place to see if Christina is there. This will keep him away so I can get my job done without interruption. Did you ever think of that?" Leah yelled at father.

"You're right. Okay, I admit, you are right." My father agreed with himself.

"You're damn right I am right! You just got to get used to thinking I am always one step ahead. This clock is always ticking and it doesn't need anyone to wind it. As a matter of fact, I am going to take my notebook and spend the afternoon taking some notes. Notes are good—if there is anything else that we can benefit from this situation, we will take the opportunity. It seems to me, My Dear, that there are a lot of players right now—a lot of rich players and I am in the mood for a game. So take your sorry ass out to the shop while I try to make us some real money," Leah cackled at father.

"You do what you do best, Dear. I won't bother you." My father replied with his tail between his legs.

"Don't worry, I intend to," snapped Leah.

It got quiet for about twenty minutes. I felt my stomach start to roll and grumble. This baby was starving and I needed to eat, but I couldn't stop thinking. What was Leah thinking she had the power to do? What scared me more was that she did have the power to do a lot. She could go from one man's bed to the other and wreak havoc on their lives, and this is what she was doing to Father. The rumours around town about Leah were abundant.

I scooted across the floor and ate the two remaining digestive cookies and one carrot. I was still so hungry so I drank four juice boxes of water. The baby seemed to kick with happiness.

I was starting to worry now. I still had to have dinner tonight and I only had three more carrot sticks and a mars bar. I knew the speculum was going to come tomorrow, but I longed for tonight, for the night when Leah and Father lay in bed where Leah would relay her schemes to Father. I needed a nap. I felt like the baby was having some sort of growth spurt and it was making me really tired. I laid down on the uncomfortable, creaky bed and fell deep into sleep.

The Dream

I saw my mother; she was wearing the dress at the funeral parlour, the one she wore to church on occasion. We were in Sunday school and she was telling the story of Daniel in the lion's den with all the little felt figurines on a board in front of the class. Her hair was straight and brown and her nails and lipstick were mauve. I felt a sense of pride as she told the story.

Suddenly, I was lifted out of the room, towards outer space. My mother didn't notice, she just kept teaching the class. I was lifted up higher and higher. Then I pulled away from the class. They were so tiny and far away until they disappeared. Abruptly, I started to fall. The wind was at my face and I couldn't breathe. I just kept falling and falling and falling. I could see the earth and I was coming towards it fast. It was getting bigger, and now I could see roads and buildings. I shot through a roof without getting hurt and I started to slow down as I went through the first floor, then the second floor, then the last floor. I hovered above for a second, looking at my Father and Leah argue and my siblings. Then I just dropped on my mother's casket. I felt the coldness and the hardness of her body again, and the smell of formaldehyde and perm solution.

I gasped and shot up into a sitting position in the attic. I slowly calmed myself down knowing it was just the dream again. Realizing the true predicament I was in, it was apparent I didn't drink anything since lunch and I never refilled the water. I was so thirsty I just couldn't stand it. I could still hear some clinking around in the kitchen so I decided to see if I could drink and fill up quick. I managed to drink six juice boxes and to fill one. I ate the last three carrots and ate a quarter of the mars bar. I could feel that baby was still alive and appreciated the sweet treat as it danced around.

The house started to get quiet and I heard mumbling near my father and Leah's vent that led to their room. I got myself up and to the ground, slowly pulling myself along until I reached the vent. "Raymond, prepare yourself for an ingenious plan," Leah stated with glee in her voice. "Great", I thought.

"I have been writing out all of our little circles of friends and customers. I then decided to connect facts and information to all of them. I tinkered with it all day when I thought 'screw the abortion idea'," She said. (I felt a huge great relief). "We can make some big bucks here, you know that? Remember that customer of yours that lives in Holland—the one that has the wife that can't conceive. They had the two adoptions fall through, one after they took the baby home for one month. Then about a year ago you had him on a guided hunting trip where he got really drunk and told you of an illegal adoption they paid for, but the baby was stillborn. Remember that? How much did he tell you he paid for that?" Leah asked interestedly.

"He didn't tell me. At least I don't remember. I wouldn't have been interested at the time. I do see your point. The problem with it is that they just broke up last month because of it and she moved back to Spain. She lives with her sister because she was so upset by what had happened. He's been trying to get her back ever since," Father responded.

"Raymond don't you think this would be a damn good reason for them to get back together? I would make sure this was a viable delivery and a healthy pregnancy. You just leave that to me. You call him up and tell him it is about your daughter and that there are no doctors involved. Make sure they know I am a nurse and we have proper equipment to ˙deliver. Tell him that it is not like the other illegal adoption they were trying to do, it that and that this is an embarrassment to our family, and tell them how young she is. I am going to start fattening Christina up tomorrow. I'm thinking that with that couple, we could get around thirty-five to fifty thousand. Let's just play with it for a while and not say a price. We'll see how bad he wants to get that wife of his back," Leah laughed.

"You are a smart woman Leah, good-night," My father responded. I slid my way back and into bed. I thought this would buy me some time and either Frank would come get me, or I would get out somehow.

I awoke to Leah yelling at Derrick, "Hey numb nuts unlatch the door for me there, come on . . . come on. Great, now take your little family jewels and walk away. You heard me, walk away," Leah demanded. I heard Leah slowly walk up the stairs. No one had been up here since they put me here. I knew she was up to something. I just wondered if this time it was going to be pleasant or not.

"Well there you are, Dear," Leah announced, sticky sweet, as she appeared at the top of the last stair about six feet from the end of my bed with a tray in her hand. I was now sitting strait up in the saggy old bed with nervous curiosity. There was food on that tray. Food that looked quite good—not like Leah's cooking.

Leah placed the tray on a lamp table that was beside me and pulled up an old vinyl chair that was dusty with peeling vinyl. She wiped it with her hands a couple times and moved it right up close to me.

"I just want you to know that I completely had your best interest in mind when your father and I were set on us giving you an abortion." Leah tilted her head. Funny I thought. As I remember it, she concocted the plan about giving me an abortion. I am not saying my father didn't put his foot down at any given time, but I am pretty sure she was the conductor.

"I couldn't see you at fifteen, (well you are turning sixteen in a few days) but I couldn't see you wanting to raise a bastard child so young. I know you wouldn't want to shame your father and me.

Well, anyhow, I started thinking, and clearly you are farther along than you look. You have always been the thinnest one in the family, tiny in every way," she laughed. "I think you are all of about five feet tall and last you were weighed you were about ninety pounds dripping wet. So my mothering instincts kicked in. As you know, I have two boys of my own, and practically being a doctor, I think it is better that we bring your baby to term, and have a healthy delivery here at home.

I don't want you to worry. My friend Ellen will be assisting and she delivers babies all the time. She will bring all the equipment we need. Anyhow, I really had to beg your Father about this so you should be really grateful, and realize what a wonderful thing I have done for you.

Anyway, here is some breakfast; you are going to need to keep that baby healthy so nothing goes wrong during the delivery." Leah smiled as she retrieved the tray of food off the lamp table and put it across my lap. "I know what you are thinking, it's not my cooking. Your father is shutting down the shop in the morning for a couple of days. He is cooking up some meals that we can freeze for lunches and dinners. He says he will make breakfast every morning. Don't think I am not aware that I am not a good cook. You can only be blessed with so many things. So you eat up, the side dish of fruit you can keep up here to munch on. Oh, I almost forgot; I am sure you need some laundry done, so go through that pack of yours and I will run it through."

"I suggested to your Father that that bed couldn't be comfortable for a pregnant gal, so he is going to move your bed up later this afternoon. Oh my!" Leah exclaimed, while she opened a small drawer in the lamp table and pulled out an old hard covered Bible. I'm sure it was one that was left over from before we moved here because the place we called our house used to be a hotel.

Leah pulled the window up and on about the sixth try she managed to get it about half way. She shoved the Bible in it right side up and lowered the stiff window back down on it, just so it would keep it open. "You and that baby will need adequate fresh air. It is a long way down from here. Yep, and there would be nothing but large thorny sticks and old broken boards to break your fall," Leah said looking back down from the window and setting her glare on me.

I thought to myself "does she not think I would have thought of every possible way out of here in the past several days?" I glared back at here with my plate of food on my lap, not even caring, as hungry as I was and knowing she could just take it from the baby and I.

There was an important thing she left out and I needed to ask. "Leah after the baby is born, what will happen?" I inquired. Leah snapped from her threatening facial expression and smiled most marvellously.

"Well then you will raise it here until you become of age. When you do become of age your father and I have agreed we will find you a small cheap place and we will pay rent there for you and it for three months. After that you will need to do things for yourself. I think that is more than nice of us. Don't you, Dear?" Leah smiled bright as a saint. I thought it to be mighty nice of her to call me dear, but I knew the plan and knew she had no intentions of letting me keep my baby, or my "it" be with me.

"Yes," I replied and picked up a piece of toast and took a bite. I could tell it was killing her to act so nice.

"I'll be up in a couple hours to do your laundry, Dear." she smiled and bounced down the stairs.

I knew that if she wasn't coming up for my tray, Father would be in earshot if the shop were closed. As hungry as I was, I wanted to hear what she and father were saying more than I wanted to eat. I very quietly put the tin tray back on the lamp table. I got down on the floor and slid across it to the vent until voices came into focus.

"Hey numb nuts get out of here for a while, your Father and I are having a talk, about something that doesn't involve you." Leah snapped.

"Hey how many times have I told you not to say that to Derrick and I?' My father groaned at Leah.

"Well go outside and play. Find something to do. Take some of those trucks of yours out there." Leah suggested a little nicer.

"I am bored of that, I want to walk down to the park," Derrick exclaimed.

"Well go, have fun, make sure you shut the second door in the mudroom this time kiddo," Leah reminded. I could hear Derrick run out and all the doors slam behind him.

"So tell me how did your conversation go with Dirk? Well I can see you are smiling, that must mean it went well. Oh my, are you trying to say he made you an offer? You didn't make him an offer did you? You can only make a counter-offer, Raymond. Remember I have to pay my friend Ellen $2,000 for helping with the delivery and borrowing and stealing supplies from her part-time hospital job on the maternity ward. Why do you keep smiling?" Leah asked.

"Well if you would be quiet for a moment I would tell you. I did talk to Dirk and he has been trying to get Adana back. He is excited of the prospect of offering her another baby, but he is concerned for good reason. He is afraid something might go wrong. I have assured him that he has my word that we for no reason would we want that baby back, and would not let our daughter take it back. I told Dirk that the young man that got her in this state doesn't even know she is pregnant, so his parents are not involved in the least.

He knows you are a nurse with proper delivery equipment and your friend works regularly on the maternity ward delivering babies. Dirk seemed to suddenly perk up and he offered me $50,000. So I said $55,000. He then said, "Tell you what—I'll take your $55,000 and raise you to $75,000 if the baby is a boy." But this of course depends on a long conversation he will need to have with Adana. He said he was going to call her this afternoon to tell her that he needs to talk to about some important information. He is going to explain it as one last try to mend their marriage, and if it doesn't work out she can divorce him.

He will try to call me back this evening so we will know," My father finished.

"You're kidding! Oh she better be having a boy. Honey, do you know how much money this is? Am I genius or what?" Leah asked.

"Mhm, you are. I guess we'll know for sure tonight after Dirk calls, and when he and Adana have discussed it. You know she might have all but given up by now," Father said.

"No way, a woman never gives up. I don't care that she is forty, some woman have babies older than that, and some adopt older than that." Leah laughed.

"Okay, you're messing up my lasagna, now I have two layers of noodles with just cottage cheese in between," Father laughed.

"Oh, cottage cheese is good for babies," Leah said.

I had heard enough. I thought to myself, "this is just going to buy me and the baby enough time to get our way out of here." I got back up on the old saggy bed with my breakfast tray and ate what Father had made. I drank the orange juice, feeling the baby dance about, happy to have been fed. I took the bowl of grapes and fruit off the tray as well as the second cup of orange juice. I put them on the lamp table and placed the tray on the chair. It was nice to smell the fresh air, but it also made me quite tired—pregnancy was so tiring. I imagine the past days of being in the attic and not eating right had taken their toll on me to. I read somewhere that the baby will actually feed off of the mother if they are lacking something.

I started to think about Frank; I think he had given up by now. He would have been to Alec's house and he would know I had not been there. Am I trapped here? What will happen? Will I have to give birth to my baby in this dingy attic? Then have he or she ripped away from me just to be given to some spoiled rich folk because a baby is the one thing they can't have?

I remember Dirk; he would always bring things back from some foreign country. Things that were rare and hard to get, his wife too. They would go on about how there are only one hundred in the whole world or we had to hike on foot for four days in the middle of nowhere . . . or the man who made this is one hundred and four years old . . . the Dali Lama gave this to me, on and on they would brag.

The Ring

I had all of these question but no answers. But I did remember something in my bag of clothes and I wanted to go through it. There were a couple shirts Leah might like for herself. If these were the only nice clothes I have, why let her have them?

I sat up and stretched and across the bed to pull my backpack up to me. I was grabbing it by the strap when I felt a hard lump in one of the outside pockets. What in the world could that be? I slipped my hand into the pocket, and to my surprise out came my engagement ring with the wedding band welded on it. I instantly started sobbing, almost inconsolably.

I went through the laundry and hid the shirts behind a couple of old trunks that were against a sidewall. Getting back up on the bed, I continued to wail and put my chin down on the window frame. I tried to breath in the cold, fresh air to calm myself down. I cried for about five more minutes and decided I needed to hide the diamond ring I was still clutching. I walked back over to the trunks but couldn't see a good place to hide it where it wouldn't be found. The trunks were near the vent where I could hear down to the kitchen/living room area. I heard Leah ask Derrick to undo the latches on the door for her.

Quickly, a picture of the vent flashed in my head. The vent's mouth was completely flat like a table before it dropped down. I had no time. I needed to get back into the bed; I could hear Derrick opening the latches. I ran over to the vent and pulled it up. Ever so slowly, I placed the ring at the far end of the vent furthest from where it drops off and pushed the top back on. I quickly looked back at it and noticed a stream of sunlight shining into the vent, right on the diamond, reflecting color that sparkled all over.

I dashed back to the bed and flopped into it. I heard Leah climbing the stairs when she arrived, I couldn't help look behind her at the light beaming off the diamond in the vent.

"Hello there. Got you a nice wedge of that lasagna your Father has been making in the kitchen downstairs. There's a little salad here on the side that he whipped up, a banana for desert and a glass of milk.

You've been crying haven't you? You know, I have always been trying to get you kids to toughen up. But now you have a baby to think of. Any stress you put on the baby will affect that baby's well being, and delivery. You need to be tough now. I am not going to be hard on you because you are pregnant and I know that is hard enough. I've been there. I think after you have lunch, we will take you downstairs for a nice relaxing bath and your father will bring your bed up here and all you bedding including some of your things. You'll feel so much better," Leah went on.

I was already feeling better because as she was speaking the beam of sunlight started to slowly move down below the vent, across the floor. Also, I did love the thought of a bath, but it did bring another tear to my eye as I thought of my bathroom with Frank. Then it made me have a little giggle inside when I thought of the first night I had a bath in our bathroom and when I thought the statues were intruders.

"You didn't eat your fruit from breakfast?" Leah scrunched up her forehead.

"I was feeling a little sick to my stomach," I replied. "Well you will need to eat all your lunch and have your bath, and then you will need to eat your fruit before dinner. It is essential for your child's development." Leah looked at me seriously, then picked up my laundry and huffed down stairs.

I thought to myself that a few days ago she was going to blow air up into my uterus until my child fell out dead and perhaps I would die from bleeding. But now she says I must nourish the baby. I really wish my sisters were here right now so we could agree on how crazy she was. I wish Frank was here so he could do an impression of her right now. I think being alone up in this attic is getting to me.

After lunch, Leah came upstairs very happy again. "Well let's go get you nice and clean." She smiled and pulled on my wrist. I don't think she knew how to be gentle. This really made me fear what it would be like for Leah and her crazy friend Ellen delivering my baby.

"Ok, I'm coming," I said, pulling my wrist away so I could get the yucky blanket off me and stand on my own.

"Ok, I want you to be ever so careful on those stairs Christina; don't even scare me on them," Leah snapped. I thought to myself I'd like to see how she would feel about this when Dirk gets back after talking to Adana and she says that she is definitely not interested. She'll be throwing me down the stairs.

As I got to the bottom of the stairs and we crossed to the kitchen, it looked like my father had about nine lasagnes done and was now working on about five Sheppard pies at one time.

Leah led me into the bathroom where she filled our old bathtub, the old fashioned one with the feet. She pulled the door with the diamond shaped doorknob shut, (almost all the doorknobs in this old hotel were like this). Leah watched as I slipped off my clothes and stepped into the shallow water. As I did this, she explained that because of my state of mind she will have to watch me close and that I will not be allowed to do anything on my own. She said it will be like this until a few months after the baby is born and my hormones level out.

I just sat there blankly. She grabbed a bar of soap and a cloth and told me to lean forward so she could wash my back. She then told me to wash my hair with our crappy shampoo and conditioner and then she watched me wash myself closely with a weird smirk on her face. I imagined she was seeing dollar signs. When I was done she told me to stand up and she had an open towel. She started to towel me off and specifically dry my belly. "I got it," I said.

"Well let's not be so slow. I have a nightgown here of your older sisters that should fit you. I washed it as well as this nice, purple towel robe. Here are your old blue slippers." I dried and slipped into everything.

Leah led me upstairs where my father had my bed, dresser, and a collection of scary dolls in hoop dresses his mother bought me. She slipped the blankets back, and I got into a much firmer and more comfortable bed. She left without talking, like she was eager to speak to my father. I was too tired now, to even care. I quickly made myself eat all the fruit and drink the juice. I got up and took my hairbrush off my dresser and ran it through my wet hair a few times. I was so tired now, and drifted off to sleep.

I woke up again to the unlatching of the door. I was hungry, but still very tired. Up came Leah with a smile that I was now starting to grow accustomed to seeing on her face. "Wake up Mom, time to feed your little one. You want to be a mother and there are lots of feedings," she glimmered. We got some Shepherd's pie, some salad, and if you eat it quickly enough three scoops of chocolate ice cream and a cupcake.

Your birthday was a few days back so think of it as a birthday cake. Oh yeah and don't forget this big glass of milk. There is some orange juice here for later. I'll just put that on the table here by your bed." She laid the tray on my lap, smiled, and went downstairs. I ate quickly and tiredly. I got the ice cream down, drank half the milk, I put the glass down beside the orange juice, and fell back to sleep.

I awoke a few hours later to Leah retrieving the tray. I purposely reached up for my milk while she was still there and gulped the last bit down. She held out the tray and smiled as I placed the glass on it. Again I drifted off.

Suddenly, I jolted up in my bed to Derrick yelling good-night to Father at the bottom of my door. I let myself slowly stretch out on my more comfortable bed as I pulled myself onto the floor and made my way over to the vent. I could hear the springs rattle around in his and Leah's mattress as they got settled in.

"So Dirk convinced Adana by a hair at first, but now she is extremely excited. He said he is flying her home tonight," my father yawned.

"Can you tell me again, did he say extremely exited?" Leah laughed.

"Yeah, something along those lines would be about right, but they would both still like to see a picture of her—to know she is healthy and see how far along she looks. You know she is tiny and you know you're not going to make her look happy," Father said to Leah.

"Don't even worry. I can add a little cushioning and it doesn't matter if she smiles or not, she is a girl who has shamed her family and is in a condition she would rather not be in. I did talk to Ellen today, and she is going to come down and draw some of Christina's blood. You know, just to see why she seems so extra tired. A lot of it I attribute to being pregnant, but she is just wiped and we don't want to have any problems during this delivery. I mean, if Christina can't perform, it is going to be messy. That means the whole c-section deal and without sedation. We don't want to risk that kind of noise.

I mean, you said they want to be here directly after the delivery, what if they came early? Besides Ellen is going to slowly walk things over here so that the hospital doesn't miss things all at once. She only does so many shifts on the maternity ward and then it is all in a boring GP's office and I know what that can be like. Ellen can do an internal on Christina and measure her uterus to try and get a more accurate date. She will just take the blood back to the lab under another pregnant women's name and lose the results after she prints them off . . . You know I excelled in the ER until some gooney doctors couldn't accept a female being smarter than them and had me thrown out. I'll take the pictures tomorrow Honey, and I make her look plumper and healthy. Smiles? We won't care about smiles," Leah laughed as I almost gagged. It sounded like Leah and Father were beginning a make out session.

I sank back to sleep, thinking to myself about how much I wanted my mother and my sister to be here with me right now. How much I needed a genuine hug. How much I needed a true cuddle from Frank. For soon, if I were to lose his child regardless, of his behaviour, this would be something we would not be able to work through. I sobbed, feeling like I lost my breath, and I drifted off with my face wet with tears. What have I done?

Chapter 5

I awoke to the nasally sounds of Ellen making her way up the stairs with Leah, talk about ruining a good dream. I had just been dreaming about meeting Frank's mother. She was a woman of medium to large build. She bragged that this was good after having ten children. She was a very affectionate lady who continually welcomed me to her family. She was ecstatic to have come to the conclusion that I was pregnant. I dreamed about meeting all of Frank's family members and it made me a bit jealous that there was so much love in their family. The only family member that seemed strange was Carlos. Apparently he was severely bullied in school and had once been molested by a Catholic priest. Frank told me that he had really felt protective of Carlos over the years. I wonder if Frank and Carlos would be able to fully repair their relationship. I really hoped so.

Violated

"Good morning Christina," Ellen said as she came up the stairs with her hands full. She was carrying what looked like a baby scale. On top off that were some blue sterile pads. I could see the dimensions were written on the side of the bag that the pads were in. Ellen's boyfriend Roy followed her with some sort of plastic hospital bassinet. It was filled full of various hospital supplies.

Leah appeared up the stairs with a box of plastic gloves and her arms full of other packaged medical supplies. Father followed behind her with what looked like packaged blankets and some huge sanitary napkins. The napkins were almost as big as adult diapers.

Father and Roy quickly went downstairs and brought up a folding table and opened it where they put the baby scale and all the supplies on it. The table was so long that they put my dresser on the opposite side of the room so the table was right alongside my bed. This table was much longer than my bed. My father darted down stairs quickly. "Roy, you pervert!" Ellen snapped. Roy bounced in the air and started down the stairs abruptly. I knew something seemed strange as I pushed myself up with my feet to the top of the bed.

Ellen came at me with Leah by her side. Both of them smirking as they approached the bed with some articles packaged in plastic. "Well little girl, we are going to take a little look down below and see exactly what you've gotten yourself into. Then we're going to draw some blood and see why you are so over tired. Now I'm going to need you to relax." Ellen started to pull on my sheets.

"No frikin way!" I yelled. I could hear Roy's retarded laugh at the bottom of the stairs.

Then I heard my father say to Roy loudly, but rather calmly at first, "I know this might be rather amusing to you, but if you don't get your ass out of my home. I am going to amputate it. Understand?" Then I heard some really quick footsteps.

Leah ripped all the sheets off of me and made her way around the bed holding my arms and pushing my legs open with her feet. Ellen pulled my underwear down and told me to stay still or I would injure or even kill my baby. I felt myself go limp at those words and Leah whispered in my ear. "Good girl, just relax. This is for your own good. We care about you and we care about that baby."

Ellen squished some clear gel on the spectrum thing that Leah had been keeping in my room for some time. With her plastic gloved hands she roughly pushed the speculum up inside me. She told Leah she needed her down there now to hold the flashlight. She pulled out the speculum and slipped her fingers inside and said, "her cervix feels firm and normal, nothing out of the ordinary, nothing dilated. Now go grab me that tin basin, Leah." Ellen's voice was one of authority. Leah huffed and jumped to grab it.

"There was a time that I was a higher rank than you Ellen," Leah barked.

"Okay, an RN is an RN and this is not about you getting decertified. I would get decertified for this. Either you want me to do this and you are going to pay me for it, or you are not. If you are I am going to need an assistant like we talked about." Ellen looked at Leah with daggers.

"Yes, I'm sorry. I guess I just miss being in charge." Leah handed the tin basin to Ellen. Ellen chucked the speculum into it with a smile on her face.

"Awe, you are my very best friend, remember that. Can you pass me those underwear dear?" She pulled my feet through and told me to lift my bum up as she pulled my panties up and over my bottom. "There now, that wasn't so bad was it?"

I almost forgot that I was in the room. I felt like I had slipped out of my body and was looking down at these two psycho women having a conversation over my half nakedness. They seemed to act like it was quite normal.

"Now put your arm out and relax." Ellen awkwardly held a needle that she pointed towards me. "Leah, I'm going to need a tourniquet." Leah ran over with a rubber band and tied it up high on my upper arm. Soon I could see the blood start to come as Ellen switched the cylinder. She took two cylinders of blood and shook them a bit. She then asked Leah to get her a thermal lunch kit. She placed the cylinders of blood and some swabs she had took from my internal exam into the thermal kit.

Ellen and Leah both started to walk off, chatting to each other when Leah turned around and looked at me. "Your father is making breakfast, so you will be eating in a short while. Get yourself together as later this afternoon I thought it would be nice to take some pictures of you in this state. When you are a little older you will either cherish them, or you will look back at how you screwed up your life. Either way, I just thought you might like them. Freshen up," Leah ordered.

"Now tell me, so what are we looking at for a due date?" Leah asked Ellen excitedly. Ellen answered in her nasally voice, that only she had."You know she measures a little under what she says, but she still looks so small so I am going to say second to third week of November. Still not that far away, no matter how you shake a stick at it," Ellen assured Leah.

"I am so excited, I mean very excited," Leah said as she made her way down the narrow stairs behind Ellen. How could they think I don't hear that? And maybe wonder what they are excited for? For being smart they sure aren't too bright.

I really didn't feel like breakfast after this. I felt like two giant women molested me. I heard the door slam shut and the latches lock behind two nasty sounding giggles.

A few days later, Leah came upstairs. She was extremely happy to tell me that Ellen got the results to my blood test. I had a very low iron level. She told me that Ellen was coming tomorrow and was bringing some special liquid iron that I will have to take every day. "Now it is time to take you down for your bath. Unfortunately we have that little trust issue at hand so I am going to have to come with. I can help you wash those places you can't reach now," Leah smiled.

"I can reach everything fine still," I snapped.

"Yes, I do wish you would put a little meat on. I know you have been eating everything we feed you. So let's just think it's all going to the baby." Leah lit up clasping her hands.

While heading upstairs I couldn't help but recall the way Leah looked at my belly. Her eyes just seemed to bulge into an almost hypnotic gaze. She watched me in the tub and as I dried off and dressed, she made me extremely uncomfortable.

Then she was ever so worried that I might slip on a stair going up to the attic. She reminded me how very steep and narrow they were. She insisted that she follow below in case I lost my footing. I felt like she didn't want to take a chance losing her investment. I am sure if something happened with the baby at this point she would be pretty angry that she worked so long at being nice.

She pretty much tucked me back into my bed, and then told me a really delicious lunch was coming up for me. I just wonder how stupid she thinks I am?

After Leah left the attic, I slipped out of my bed and went to the far vent. It has been weeks since I had gone to it. I had been depresses and tired from iron deficiency. Frank still played back and forth in my mind daily—as much as I tried to block it.

I pulled open the vent and the ring was still resting stably where I put it. I walked over to one of the trunks I had opened before and took out a pair of scissors. I planned to keep these scissors if I needed them for some kind of self-defense, but for now I needed them to hide my ring. I took my backpack and cut a strait slash in the under part of the strap. Then I squished the ring inside and worked it to the bottom of the strap, right up next to the bag. You would have to really examine it to find it, and you still might miss it.

I sat at the bottom of the bed looking out the window as birds chirped. The baby within me kicked and moved like he/she was dancing for some reason at that moment.

It was now early November and I was getting anxious to make some kind of escape. I only had Ellen's calculations to go by, and I was clueless on my own as far as how to calculate a due date. Frank and I tried from our many pregnancy books we had read, and we always came up with the first or second week in November.

I was also encouraged to hear that Frank was coming by the house and shop again. This meant to me that he didn't give up on me. I knew for sure that I would never be able to face him again if I were to have our baby taken away. I could hear the raspy talking at the vent that lead down to Father and Leah's bedroom.

"Raymond I don't think it is a big deal if we induce her now. She mentioned the date of her last period. She is thin because all the weight is just going to the baby. You know we will be careful. We need money now. You have not had as much business and as many clients on you recent hunting tours. Damn that Frank, I think he is on to us. Have you been nice to him like I told you to Raymond?" Leah voice started to elevate.

"Yeah, yeah I have, as nice as a person can be nice, to a man who knocked up my daughter. You know he's more than twice her age." Father banged something loudly.

"RAYMOND, she seduced him. How many times must I tell you? Anyhow I have this herbal stuff that will induce her slowly. Then we will call Ellen. If she is at work she will say she has a family emergency and head here right away. Next we will call Dirk and Adana and they will fly immediately from Holland. You know they want to hold the baby soon after birth. Then if it is a girl they will give us a bank draft for *$55,000* and *$75,000* if it is a boy. Can we please Raymond? It is a difference of a week or so. I have studied and worked in the medical field for many years. You know that I know what I am taking about. She has already had five false calls and uncountable Braxton-Hicks contractions. Last week when Ellen checked her cervix it was softening. Raymond?" Leah barked.

"If you think it will go smooth. You know this is a big investment. And for Dirk and Adana to fly out here to be introduced to their second stillborn child would be traumatic. Whatever you want, as long as you think it is safe," my father agreed.

"Great, we'll start tomorrow." I heard Leah roll over as the springs creaked.

Our investment, their baby, bank drafts, why are they like this? Who am I to them? How can they do this to a human being? I got back to my bed and pushed my scissors right up close between my mattresses near the top of my bed.

Gone Psychotic

I awoke to Leah at the head of my bed, sitting on a chair beside me. "I found these sticking out of your mattress," Leah spoke in my face, leaning her elbow on her knees, her chin on her wrist with the scissors dangling out of her hand. I could barely get them into focus, when she flung them down the stairs. "I don't think you need them. I did bring you a nice cup of relaxing tea though. It is a mixture of blue and black cohosh tea with a little honey." She smiled like the Cheshire cat on heroin.

"No thanks." I replied, rubbing my eyes.

"Sit up and start sipping," demanded Leah. She sounded threatening, which was helping me wake up. It then dawned on me that those were my scissors she threw down the stairs. I started to recall that last night was true. However tea didn't sound like a medicine I thought, so I'll amuse her by taking some sips of the tea.

"Okay," I said reaching for the tea. Leah smiled and passed me the tea. I could see behind her as she leaned back. She had a whole pot of tea sitting on the lamp table.

Three hours later Leah was still making me drink the tea. She ordered my father to leave a new pot at the bottom of the stairs. Leah wouldn't leave the attic farther than the bottom of the stairs, and that was just to get the next pot of tea. By now it was obvious the tea was the labor inducer. Before the end of the first pot I was starting to get bad cramps.

Now after several pots I had a few bouts of diarrhea and Leah was timing me. Soon she called my father to the bottom of the stairs and told him to call Ellen and tell her the contractions were consistently ten minutes apart and to get here quick. I was in pain and I had no idea what these two people were going to do to me. I was completely petrified that they might have trouble getting the baby out. I prayed to God that they would not try to perform a caesarean on me without an anaesthetic.

By the time Ellen arrived, Leah and Father had cleaned up the evidence. They rushed off with the teapot and bag of loose blue and black cohosh. My contractions were now five minutes apart.

"Okay, Leah, let's scrub up, hair nets, gloves, here is a pair of scrubs for you to change into and a mask. We need a clean environment here," Ellen ordered. I started to feel a little more comforted as I yelled out at the start of a huge contraction. "Don't worry dear; I will make sure it all goes smoothly with as little damage as possible," Ellen winked. At this point anything remotely comforting seemed to help.

She place about five blue pads underneath me and started a saline IV. "Okay Christina, I am going to have to go down and check to see how dilated you are. Please try to relax," Ellen looked calm.

Leah came out of the bathroom looking like a nurse; an image I often pondered of her. Now here it was right in front of me. Looking at Leah took my mind off of what Ellen was doing.

"Oh crap, she is nine centimetres, Leah, hand me that amniotome. I'm going to just break this bag of water. She is just going so quickly." Ellen looked over to Leah with her hands open. Leah passed Ellen a long, plastic instrument after taking it out of a plastic wrapper. Ellen put the instrument inside me when she said she was going to tear the bag of water my baby was in. As soon as she did this I could feel a large gush of warm water wash down my thigh. Then came the most excruciating pain I ever felt. I never felt so horrified, I was sure I would not make it another few moments.

"Okay, Christina, look into my eyes I need you to take some deep breaths now. Did you read about how to breathe during labour? Your breathing is way too fast and irregular. That can affect the baby. Inhale through your nose slowly and exhale through your mouth and I want you to keep repeating this pattern, Okay?" Ellen nodded at me. I tried so hard to do what she was telling me but things were ripping, burning, tearing, and stabbing. I could hardly breathe in.

"Christina, you know I love you, you're going to be okay." My mother said. Suddenly I felt as if I was adjacent from my body looking over at myself. I was taking the deep breaths and hearing everyone talk, but my eyes looked blank. I could not feel the contractions anymore; I could not hurt from the things that were being said. I was like a baby that was warm, fresh, fed, and cradled. I knew at that moment it could only be God sheltering me.

"Okay good, we are making progress. Leah you want to get behind her back for this next push and help push with her? This baby is practically pushing itself out. She is looking kind of glassy-eyed so

I'm going to take a blood pressure after this contraction. Raymond, Raymond! Can you get up here for a minute? I need a pair of spare hands," Ellen ordered. I heard the door open and my father stomp up the stairs with a downward looking face."Raymond, pass me that sterile bag on the edge of the table there. It's an episiotomy kit. Don't want your daughter ripping there," Ellen said as if to impress him. My dad tossed it to her without making eye contact.

"Raymond, when do you think Dirk will get here? We're pretty close right now. Just a bit before we will know if it will be the fifty-five or the seventy-five we talked about," Leah sounded excited.

Father, with his back turned to the stairs, answered, "You got me to call at 2 p.m and they were running to get a plane. I think once they get on a plane it takes nine maybe twelve hours. You guys sound like you're going to produce any minute. So figure it out," Father proceeded down the stairs and left me to these two women who were seemingly enjoying playing hospital.

"I don't think I even have to give her anything to numb the perineum—she looks kind of out of it, but her blood pressure is excellent, considering. This baby is coming quickly though and if I don't do it, she will rip like you wouldn't believe," Ellen said a she went down and pulled the area forward with two fingers. She was aiming to cut it with some special scissors in the other hand.

"Wait," Leah said with a big smile on her face. I could see her mischievous smirk as I felt myself in what seemed like a floating state next to my physical body. She was sitting behind my body in order to reclined it. "What if we let her rip? It would teach her a lesson. Ha-ha-ha. Then she would be all loose and no man would have her, ever," Leah laughed so hard I could see my body bounce.

"Or she could bleed to death and I could lose my job like you lost yours, and then go to prison. Sorry, but I don't have the time for this," Ellen said and went in and cut very quickly. "Perfect, here comes the head and here comes another contraction. Time to wipe that look off your face Leah! You promised we are working as a team. The head is going to be born. Look at all that dark hair. Don't push now Christina, I'm just going to do a little pre-suctioning. I'm going to put a little pressure on the baby's head with this next contraction just so that the shoulder can slip out. Okay, there we go, perfect, that's good. Now Christina and Leah, I want you to push with the very next contraction." Ellen got a handle on the baby's shoulders.

I started to inhale now and my belly tightened. I could feel myself come upward as I started to push; I felt the baby slide out of my body as my spirit slipped back into it.

Ellen had the baby in her arms and in a chair at the bottom of the bed; she was suctioning its mouth and nose. "Okay, that's 7 PM, remember that time Leah," Ellen yelled, as if they were going to write it on some birth certificate. I was shaking uncontrollably all over. Leah almost tossed me off the bed as she got up so abruptly and came to a skid. She then started yelling, "It's a boy, it's a boy, it's a boy!" I tried really hard to get a look but Leah had her head right in front of my crotch.

"Leah, you are contaminating a sterile area. Your hair just touched the umbilical cord. Why did you take your hair net off?" Ellen got up with the baby in one hand and guided Leah's head out of the way with the other. I saw her tie my end of the umbilical cord off and then cut it in the middle. I could hear my baby crying loudly.

"Well it's just her right now! The baby was on the other side, and now you've separated them," Leah pointed out. Ellen shook her head. "We still have to make sure the mother is healthy, and right now it looks like she is losing a lot of blood. So turn up the warming light on the basinet. If you could please move back and put the baby in the basinet so he can get warm. I need to deliver the placenta and find out where all this extra blood is coming from." Ellen handed Leah my baby boy.

My shaking had almost turned into convulsing now. I could feel all the blood and amniotic fluid on the pad under me. "Christina I am going to push down on your tummy right now and I want you to push at the same time," Ellen started to push down on me. I was shaking and so cold. I wished I had the comfort of floating back up beside myself, to the place I felt full peace and comfort. But for this moment I had to bare what was in front of me. I took about ten minutes that seemed more like an hour, but the placenta finally came out. Ellen said it looked like it was all in one piece. I still kept bleeding and bleeding. Ellen sewed up the part she had to cut while ignoring rude comments Leah was making. She was basically she was telling Ellen not to bother.

I had a huge bundle of blankets on the top half of me and nothing on the bottom. Leah was trying to keep all the blood from staining. Ellen was babbling to herself that something about my blood not clotting properly and something about the possibility of me being a RH negative and the baby being RH positive—something I didn't understand.

Finally, after about another hour, the blood slowed down enough that Ellen put some elastic mesh underpants with a diaper sized pad on me. Leah couldn't believe she got her to help change the bedding with me on the bed. I was too weak to get up. They made sure to put fresh large, blue pads underneath me to protect the new bedding.

"Don't you have a heating pad or something she can use? I only have three more saline IV bags and she has lost so much blood. I can see why she is shaking so much," Ellen looked to Leah.

"Why the hell do you baby her so much? Why would I want to get my husband's heating pad for his sore back and give it to this little whore?" Leah replied, half between me and the baby.

"For one, Leah, people are people. For another, I agreed to help you deliver a baby not murder. Another he is not your husband. Another I am not babying her. This girl is too weak to even talk, and could die, and if that happens I will sing like a canary. So get your wide ass up and go down and grab that heating pad of your "husband's" so this poor girl can have a little comfort. Close your mouth and go." Ellen ushered her towards the stairs with her hands.

I was so weak I couldn't talk. My body felt numb and cold. I wanted to look over at my baby, but I didn't have the energy. I could hear Ellen bathing him now and she was talking to him at the same time. He was crying different sounding cries. When she first put him in the water his cry sounded startled then after a while he sounded like he was talking back to Ellen in cries. In a matter of hours, people were coming to take him and I couldn't even get a good look at him.

"Got your darn heating pad, where should I put it? Do you want to sterilize it first?" Leah laughed.

"Just one minute. I'm going to dry him and get his weight for the parents. Then, yes, I am going to sterilize it somewhat, Ellen replied, "Seven pounds and seven ounces, that's a big baby. I think you came just in time. Not one problem with you," Ellen said as if she were having a conversation with the baby.

"So you think he is in good condition?" Leah happily snapped.

"Yes but he needs to be fed. Why don't you go mix some of the formula you got, and I'll tend to this girl here," Ellen suggested. I felt Ellen slip something across my chest.

"Oh, no, I forgot to get formula," Leah moaned.

"You forgot what? I brought a birthing station and you forgot baby formula?" Ellen slightly yelled.

"I am sure we can get some first thing in the morning," Leah replied.

"No wonder they won't let you have your kids back. Leah, you should know as a nurse that a healthy newborn needs to eat if it is hungry and shortly after birth," Ellen whisper yelled.

"Well she's got milk!" Leah pointed at me.

"What do you think she is a cow? She hasn't got enough blood in her body. There is no way. The milk comes directly from the blood . . . Okay . . . If it is our only way until morning we need to feed her something that digests easily . . . Soup . . . Wait a couple hours and then try to feed the baby, and then feed her again. We are only doing this until morning, until someone can take the trip out to get some formula. In the meantime I am going to warm some of the bottles of sterile water I brought for him to try," Ellen calculated.

"I'll go get Raymond to start some soup right away. Dirk won't be here until sometime in the morning." Leah reported.

"Wow, will you look at him? His little head isn't so pointy anymore. I remember when that happened with my boys. He looks like a Shamanskii with the dark hair and those long eyelashes. They will be so pleased they might even offer more," Leah squawked and went downstairs.

Even the slight description coming from Leah made my heart flutter. I wanted to hold him so bad. I started to feel the warmth from the heating pad, but energy, I still had none. I was more tired than ever in my life.

Leah, was shaking me vigorously as I woke. I felt as if I had disappeared for a period. I couldn't remember when I slipped off into sleep.

"Leah let me take care of her; you feed the baby this water I warmed," Ellen ordered. It must not have been long that I had been sleeping because I was remembering them talking about soup. I could smell chicken soup, but I had no appetite. Ellen told me that she was going to first change my pad and check down below real quick and then I had to try to wake up enough to eat some of the soup.

When she looked, she said that I was still bleeding, but not half as much as I was—just way more than I should be. "Okay I'm just going to put these pillows behind you and pull you in a semi-sitting position." Ellen started to fluff and prop pillows behind me. After that she spoon-fed me a whole bowel of chicken and vegetable soup. She then gave me a tablespoon of liquid iron. Ellen was pretty nice considering most of the time I had known her she usually went along with Leah. I guess maybe she thought us kids were awful to Leah or something. I didn't really know, I was just glad for the kindness now. She lowered the pillows and adjusted my heating pad while I fell asleep again.

I woke up again to see the blurry image of Ellen rocking my baby boy in her arms. She tapped me lightly "Christina, I hate to wake you but we have a hungry baby here. I want to try and let him nurse just for a few minutes on each side. Leah, can you please take him for a minute? She is going to need some help," Ellen passed the baby to Leah and moved me over to the side a bit. She propped me up with some pillows then sat beside me and unbuttoned the front of my PJ's. She told Leah to hand her the baby. She turned the baby (who was all bundled in a thick white and blue blanket) and put him up to my breast. She put my arms around him but I think she knew I was too weak to take his full weight as she firmly held him in place.

I looked down at the most beautiful baby. When I said a few words to Ellen, he stopped what he was doing and looked deep in my face. His eyes were a mixture of mine and Frank's, and he did have a whole lot of dark hair. His features were so tiny and his lips were like little, tiny rose petals. He seemed so smart and attentive and he really seemed to know me.

Ellen remarked how he looked so deeply at me. Leah got a little mad at this. Ellen explained to her that it is just natural they can smell their real mother. After about five minutes she switched to the other side and let him nurse for about eight more minutes. Then she burped him on the bedside. He made a few little cooing noises.

I loved him before he was born now it was just so much more real. I so wished I had even the energy to reach out and rub his little back. He was so much more than I expected. He had tiny everything.

Ellen passed the baby to Leah to put him back in the heated bassinet. She fed me another bowl of hot soup and gave me another tablespoon of liquid iron. I fell asleep to Ellen adjusting me and Leah shrieking that the baby had pooped and she wasn't touching it.

I woke up again and got to feed my baby with the help of Ellen. For some reason Leah felt she had to stand directly over top and glare down. I felt safe enough with Ellen there as I could see who could put Leah in line for the first time.

I even had a bit energy to touch his little arm that was sticking out of the blanket. When I ran my hand down his arm to his fingers he grasped one of my fingers really hard. I felt a tear fall down my cheek. Leah announced that time was up and I needed more soup. The baby should be full now. Raymond would be taking off in an hour or so to get formula. I was just too weak to say anything as I felt my baby being pulled away from my body. I don't think I could even cry another tear.

Clean up

I awoke to hustle and bustle about the house. The sun was shining through the window, and Leah was saying that we need to clean the attic. Make it look more like a happy place. With that huge pile of blood-drenched pads and rags in the corner it looks like a slaughterhouse.

"Well I'm not getting paid for that Leah, you have already gotten me into more than was agreed. You won't do a feeding or even change a diaper," Ellen pointed out.

"Ellen, please could you just stay until they get here and help? Help by cleaning up and changing and feeding the baby, caring for the girl? We will give you another *$200*?" Leah pleaded with Ellen.

"Well I am going to stay here until I get paid regardless. I think that for all the extras I have done already and the extras you want me to still do *$800* is about right. Maybe you can do some feedings and diapers? Possibly change the girl to?" Ellen teased.

"Okay fine then in total you will get *$2,800*. I can see you have gone beyond your duty. You're one of those annoying, to the book kind of nurses. When I was a nurse in the ER, if someone made a mess and was unconscious I would let them wait for hours. What's the point they don't know it, their unconscious and I'd only be making more work for myself. I think you take too much on your shoulders for no reason Ellen. My advice to you is to take it easy so you don't age yourself." Leah babbled in frustration.

"I am not even going to respond to that Leah." Ellen laughed sarcastically.

I Know His Name

Frank and I cuddled up on the couch in the living room with a crackling fire, Frank, with a glass of red wine, I with a mug of warm milk. We both held a baby name book and one of us would say a name we liked and the other would say no, kind of, or yes. We were laughing and it felt so cozy like we hadn't a care in the world. The crackles and pops of the fire echoed through our laughter. "Luke, I love Luke!" Frank said.

"I just love Luke. I think Luke is a great name." I said in agreement.

"Well then if it is a boy his name will be Luke." Frank gave me the biggest kiss. We pulled each other so tight as our books fell to our laps.

"Now careful going up those stairs, they are very narrow. I will be right behind you here."

"Christina, wake up! My Dear, Dirk and Adana are here," Leah said, as her words pushed my dream far away. I opened my eyes and Adana had her hand out to shake mine. I lifted it as far as I could which was about four inches from my side. Again, my hand was filled, this time with Dirks hand.

"You don't look so well my dear." I couldn't even attempt to respond to him.

"Well I truly hope you will be doing a lot better soon. I want you to know that you have made a wise choice, and we are going to honor you in that. Thank you for the wonderful gift. Dear, you really don't look so good. I hope you get well soon," Dirk said in a Dutch accent. "Is she going to be alright? She isn't looking so good. I know you don't want doctors involved but Dirks brother is a doctor. If we could get her in a plane he could check her out. We would send her right back after." Adana suggested.

"No, no she is fine; she will be better before you know it. She is just a little high on painkillers still. Now, the baby you have all been waiting for is behind this divider we made. We didn't want the sunshine glaring in through the window at him. He's just waking up I see. Now who would like to be the first to hold him?" Leah asked.

"You go Adana, the moment you have been waiting for." Dirk sounded elated.

"Oh My Dear Lord, will you look at this most beautiful baby? He has my dark hair, Dirk! Oh Dirk look! Will you look at those beautiful eyes? Those lashes are so long, I think we better check and make sure it is a boy," Adana laughed with tears streaming down her face.

They came back to my side of the room. Adana sat down on a chair by my bed. It took all my energy to raise my head a little to get a small glance. My head fell and pounded down into my pillow again.

"You should know he was born at 7 PM November 8th and weighed in at seven pounds and seven ounces." Leah announced proudly. I knew Frank's birthday was November 8th. I never realized the date until Leah had said it to Adana. I could only keep it in my heart to myself. I knew no one in the room would be interested nor did I have the energy to think much more about it.

"Well looks like you are going to get a chance to check if it is a boy because I think I smell a poop?" Leah smiled.

"Yes, I would love to change my baby. Dirk, you need to go to the bank—it is an hour away. Raymond, maybe you can just do a transfer rather than a draft. I would like to fly home today. I don't want this to be too good to be true," Adana cried. I could see Leah show Adana where the changing table was.

"Good idea. I will go get Raymond. Dirk, please follow me to the shop. Adana, don't you worry this is not too good to be true, and if all goes well you will be taking your baby home today," Leah smiled again.

"Dirk, you know I want this, make it happen!" Adana said tearfully.

Good bye Baby

I could hear Adana talk to my baby as she changed him. She finished and came back into my side of the room where she sat beside again. "Thank you Christina, I know this must have been so hard for you. You have made all my dreams come true," Adana cried to me. I saw my baby's foot and my hand reached out and grabbed it kind of sluggishly. I had almost no energy to talk, but I at least needed to say something until I could see him again. "His name is Luke," I said in a rather rough voice.

"Luke . . . well I have always liked Luke myself. I promise if I can do anything for you in return I will call him Luke," Adana responded.

"Please tell him about me," I asked.

"One day he will know about where he came from, Christina. I promise you that also . . . I am going to take the baby downstairs to wait so you can sleep. I don't want to make this any harder for you. I will send Leah up to get his things. Thank you again for this priceless gift," smiled Adana. She looked suddenly hardened as she stood up with my baby in one arm and her purse in the other. I used all the energy I had to push myself up on the pillow and lift my head to see her as she disappeared slowly down the stairs with my baby, Luke.

Chapter 6

Over the next month I was still very weak and I found myself in a deep depression over the loss of Baby Luke. I dreamed, lived and breathed Luke. For the first week or so, just thinking about him would cause my milk to appear. I was glad Ellen stayed a couple extra days to care for me. She had stated to Leah that she was going to whether she paid her more or not. She didn't want anything to go wrong that would end her up in jail.

Ellen and Leah

Ellen gave me some medication to dry up my milk. She took all my vital signs and left me with a couple bottles of the liquid iron to take on my own. She also told me a few things about Leah I never knew. Leah and Ellen had been friends since high school, Ellen explained. She told me that Leah's mother was very overbearing and controlling. As a nurse, Ellen says she could see a doctor diagnosing Leah's mother with sever, Bi Polar Disorder. Apparently, she was very abusive to Leah and knew that Leah's father was molesting her. Her mother had even walked in on it and called Leah a whore, then walked out, shutting the door behind them.

Leah's mother died when Leah was fifteen. Pretty much after that, Leah's father molested her more frequently. Leah ended up moving in with an aunt that was diagnosed Bi Polar. The aunt lived just across town from her father. It was because that, that Leah became really rebellious and promiscuous in her late teens and through to her thirties. Ellen really felt sorry for her and always remembered the Leah she met when she was thirteen, the Leah who was shy, caring and very loyal to what few friends she was allowed to have. Ellen said that on the rare occasion she still sometimes sees that Leah.

She thought that once she and Leah completed nursing school that Leah would get some self-esteem and maybe grow and realize that she could be better. But she just became really narcissistic and somewhat like a bully to juniors in college and new employees at the hospital. When she married a foreman for a construction outfit, the bliss was very short-lived. She got pregnant right away and again right after. It became hard for Ellen to even come over and visit, as Leah was so moody.

Ellen said she was mortified at her mothering skills, but she felt bad when she thought about how Leah's mother never mothered her when she was a small child. Eventually, when her husband left her, he got full custody of her two boys. Leah was titled an unfit mother before the judge. It was never really a big deal to Leah to lose her boys. Ellen noted she never really bonded with them. In fact she told Ellen that she was leaving that part of her life behind and was looking forward to a new life. She wanted to put her efforts into her work rather than a couple whining babies. That's when Leah seemed even stranger to Ellen. Leah thought she was even above the doctors. She would have friends come to her home where she would try to diagnose them—even give them medication she stole from the pharmacy in the hospital. Leah would purposely administer to patients in the ER a different prescription than what the doctor had ordered. She thought the doctor was wrong. Apparently, on three different occasions patients had severe reactions to her prescription errors and almost died.

Once, a pregnant woman came in with a chest infection and Leah gave her some medication against the doctor's orders. By the morning they discovered the her seven month gestation baby was dead. That was when Leah had to go to court and doctors witnessed that she had gotten medication wrong on many occasions, often causing harm to patients. Leah lost her ability to ever practice nursing in Canada again, and was charged.

Ellen told me that she knew that when my father and Leah got together and there were four children involved, there was going to be trouble. Ellen explained that when Leah is with a man, she wants all of his attention. Even to the point of it coming down to their own children. The only reason Ellen feels Leah hasn't left my father is because she is unable to sustain a comfortable income on her own. Now that our mother passed and the two older girls have left she feels like she is getting closer to being number one. I am not sure if that conversation with Ellen about Leah helped me understand her more than it scared me.

I was down to one bowl of soup per day now. Leah would unlatch the door and drop the bowl at the bottom of the stairs. It was hard enough getting down the stairs and back up so I would just eat it sitting on the stair and leave the bowl where it was placed. That way wouldn't have to make two trips up and down. I had been wondering what was going to become of me now that Father and Leah had gotten the money they wanted. I only heard the conversations from the vent near to my bed as I did not have the energy to move all the way to the far vent. I had been struggling with slight fevers for about two and half weeks after Luke was born.

Get Rid of Her

The conversations coming from the vent nearest my bed were key, I thought, as that was where Leah would brainstorm and do her decision-making. Lately I had been hearing Leah discuss starving me and burying me somewhere. The other idea she had was to take me up to the deep woods in the cold winter where I would freeze to death. I rather liked that one myself as I had been locked in the attic bedroom for so long. If they set me free I felt that surely I would find my way back to a town. I could get my baby Luke back. However, my fever reminded me that I would have more odds against me.

It was around ten in the evening now as I heard Derrick yell good-night to Father. I quickly got myself situated by the vent, bringing a pillow with me to rest my arm on while I placed my ear over the vent to get the best sound. I could hear them fidgeting about and talking about investments and some holiday they wanted to go on.

"Raymond, I've been thinking again about what to do with Christina and I came up with a plan. I am sure you will find it remarkable. I think I have finally out done myself. I've been kicking around ideas, and thinking about people we know, and it came to me the other day when Alec came into the shop. He had asked about Christina again. You know he seems to be really fond of her and he still keeps offering to take her for a summer so she can spend some time around the horses. He still thinks she might come home. I can only think of one reason why . . . Do you recall that his wife died when he was in his late twenties or thirties and he never remarried. He never had any children of his own. I am betting he would adopt Christina if we were comfortable with that," Leah announced, full of excitement.

"No way in hell am I going to let someone adopt a child of mine. I would rather see them from the cradle to the grave than let someone else be the father of what I created. How the hell do you think that would affect Derrick? Family services would be barking up my back. They are already coming by since the girls moved in with their aunt. The girls have started expressing to child services that they are concerned about Derrick and Christina's safety around you. They told Child Services how you were with them. If you haven't put it together, let me tell you that you don't have the best track record Leah. You were proven an unfit mother before the court, and you have a criminal record. I don't intend on having children with you for more than that reason. But I tell you; this I will not lose my son—he is the only boy I have and he will carry on my family name. That is what I am telling you is going to happen." my father half yelled at Leah.

"Raymond, listen. You are missing out on the opportunity it presents. Alec is rich and I bet due to Christina's age we can get *$25.000* or more for her. He is a lonely guy and he has no family here," Leah begged.

"No way Leah, that is not enough to make me lose my son. I am not going to risk it. How would I explain that to Child Services? My sixteen-year-old daughter comes back home and now I am giving her up for adoption to some man, illegally? Don't you realize there is a process for that and they do checks on people! The fact alone that Alec has no wife, is not in his favor? Not a smart plan Leah." Father snapped.

"Ok then think about this. Sell Christina to Alec in marriage. We can eventually tell Child Services that Christina came back. Christina would tell them that she was fine at home if we promised her that she would be able to leave forever. Once child services processes that we wait a couple of months and then we sign her away in marriage to Alec. By law you can marry under the age of nineteen if you parents sign their approval to it." Leah begged Father again from a different angle.

"Ok Leah even if you could get Christina to say that she liked being home to Child Services, how would you explain this to Alec? Do you remember just over a month ago we plotted against her and sold her son? I don't think she is going to be over that anytime soon. This is as bad as your plan about breeding her again to produce another child for Dirk and Adana. I just don't see Alec going for something like that. Sure he is fond of Christina, but he is law abiding and he has morals," Father explained to Leah. I don't think I ever heard my father say so much at one time.

As far as I felt, this plan was the one I like most whatever way it went—as long as Alec didn't really want me for marriage. This would enable me to get Luke back and I would be away from Father and Leah forever.

"Raymond, I am sure we could sell her to Frank for marriage, but I don't think it would be long before Christina would tell him how we sold his son to an infertile couple. Just go with me on this and we can talk with Alec, see how he feels. We can tell him she went to her aunts', but her aunt can't afford to keep another child and we can say that she obviously doesn't stay around here. Then we can tell him what our plans are. I mean it is not a secret that the whole town doesn't think we are the best of parents. I am sure that is no secret to Alec. He has always checked in on the kids. He's never missed a Christmas giving the kids gifts and taking them to the McCain farm for their annual sleigh ride. That was how he found that Christina liked the horses.

Think about it, we can tell him we are afraid she will keep running away and end up on the streets doing drugs, and God knows what else. Can we just give it a try? We could use any extra money and the kid has been more than a burden to you. She owes you," Leah was trying hard to convince my father.

"Listen Leah, we can start by talking to Alec. I don't want to get Child Services involved in any of this unless Alec even sounds a little bit interested. It would be a long shot if you ask me, but I'll play along, until Alec thinks we're crazy. Then we will have to tell him something like she is going to stay with the aunt, and I am going to send her money just so he doesn't get Child Services involved. That is as far as I go on that one, Leah, and I am dead serious. I think you are rather pushing it myself," Father added.

"Raymond, I promise. It will be fine if he says absolutely not, or if he gets reeled in. I think he would believe the 'going to stay with the aunt' thing and just let it rest. He does live at least five hours away so he won't be snooping around every day. Next Monday you said you will have that gunstock finished for Alec. I think you should phone him before he comes out and you should make him aware you have something to talk with him about. Just so he plans to spend the extra time." Leah's gears were rolling.

"Fine, whatever Leah, but just know I will kill you if you get my son taken away," Father threatened.

I started to get up from the floor slowly as I was quite stiff lying in the same position for so long. As I moved away from the vent I could her Leah babbling something about not forgetting her being the mastermind in selling that bastard child. My father responded to her with something about them not being able to do it if they weren't products of his genes.

By this time I had really given up on thinking my father had any real love for me. I used to ponder it once in a while when I was eleven and twelve. It just got harder and harder over the years when he would let any of his girlfriends treat us however they pleased. Not to mention, he never seemed to really worry or care about what we were doing, how long we were out, and for the most part, who we hang around with. He was, however, dead against us hanging around anyone of African origin. That was about his only rule.

Straight Up Leah

Three days later Leah came upstairs with a tray of food for me. "You look like you are wasting away to nothing. I think we should try to start making you look healthy again. I brought you up some dinner your father made. You know it has taken me a long time to forgive you for getting yourself knocked up like you did, but I think I can finally do it. It had to go the way it did with the boy. He will have a nice home. Much more than you will ever be able to give him. One day you will be thanking me. You don't feel that way now I can tell, but soon enough you will come around. You will know we did you a favor.

"I know you don't like it here and honestly, your father and I are very eager for the days when all you kids up and move out. We have been waiting to start our lives together for years now. That is why it doesn't bother me that you want to leave. The only problem I have with it is the fact that you might affect you father's prize son from staying. Your father won't have that, so I am actively looking for a parent or parents for you, just to get you over these last few years without us. At some point, Child Services will be involved, and at that time I am going to need your word that if they question you, you tell them everything is fine here and maybe something like you 'just don't like the rules'. Or you don't like curfews and getting your homework done, that kind of stuff. If I can't get your word that you will hold your tongue then I promise, you won't leave here alive. Mark my words, I have my ways.

That is all there is, so tell me do I have your word? Because if you even make a signal to Child Services or even a mild suggestion about anything being wrong I can promise you, you won't make it to nineteen! What is it going to be Christina?" Leah looked at me with wild bulging eyes and a beat red face.

I was trying to digest everything she said while trying not to worry that she would attack me just to show me how serious she was. This was common for Leah and Father to do. I knew I had to answer and honestly. I knew getting out of here was good enough. I needed to find Luke somehow, someway. If it wasn't going to be Alec, I just hope someone would take me as a child and Leah and Father wouldn't marry me off. At this point I couldn't tell if Leah was lying about getting parents because my father said absolutely no to that.

"I promise, I would never say anything to Child Services and I would really like it if you could find me a new place to live. If you can, when would I be able to move out? Would it be right away?" I asked. I could see Leah's eyes become less bulgy and her face start to turn a normal color.

"I would get you out of here ASAP. It is no secret, I'm sure. I don't like you and you don't like me. So let's work together on making it possible for us to part ways. One other thing I would like you to promise; once you are gone you are gone. That means I don't care how old you are or how you are feeling, you don't think your coming back to visit your father. There is only room enough for one woman in our household and that woman is me. I am the only female your father needs in his life and I won't ever be second in line," Leah firmly stated with her nostrils flaring. She was breathing really hard; it was strange to discover the things that Leah felt passion for. She was a very strange and hurt person just as Ellen had said.

"I don't like my father. He doesn't care about me and that is clear. I don't care to ever see him again in my life. I would never think of visiting him. I wouldn't even come to his funeral," I emphasized. If I ever spoke that way about a year ago I would expect to be beaten very badly and starved for about four days. But this just made Leah smile and start to light up like Christmas.

"That's right, your Father doesn't care about you at all, and you know I have full control over him and this household. If I wanted to stab you bone through and bury you in the basement I would have your Father's blessing. It makes me happy to see you finally seem to acknowledge this. So to make us both happy we need to work together to get you out of here. I will tell you when we have any further plans. I have to get back to my husband and you should eat your dinner." With that, Leah left seeming like she was more confident of herself and her place in the house.

Sick

I didn't feel too hungry even though it had been a month or more since I had had a good meal. My fever seemed to get worse in the evening and I had some cramping. I never quite stopped bleeding since I had Luke; it was mostly spotting but painful from time to time.

A few weeks had passed since my conversation with Leah. I had gone over everything this woman had done to me and worst of all, to Luke. I didn't care that these people had lots of money and could provide for Luke. I know that no one could love Luke like I could, and I would have found a way to provide for him. I should have had a choice; if I did, adoption wouldn't have even been an option. I knew and could feel how strong my heart was about getting Luke back. I was going to die trying and once I did, I would expose Leah and Father for who they really were.

"Yeah, she is still up in the attic. She has some kind of fever from something and she doesn't eat much at all. I can't get her to beef up. She seems thinner than I have ever seen he," I heard Leah's voice getting louder as she appeared at the top of the stairs to the attic with Ellen. Ellen was carrying a large clothes bag with long handles.

"Hello Christina, you look better than when I saw you last, but you still don't look like you should. Here is a paper gown. You can go around to the bathroom there and slip into it and pop back out here. Everything off underneath please," Ellen said, as I got up from the edge of the bed taking the gown back to the washroom with me to change into.

When I got back to the bed Ellen already had a couple large, blue pads placed on my bed. I laid down and did as she instructed. After a thorough five minute exam, Ellen got me onto roll on my side where she gave me a shot of antibiotics. "Yeah, I think you have a bit of an infection since the delivery. I'm going to leave you with these antibiotic pills that are used to kill certain bacterium we call PID. It develops if a tiny bit of the placenta is left over. I don't know what you are going to do, Leah. I sure hope these antibiotics work, or this poor girl may be sterile for the rest of her life. You should have gotten a hold of me sooner. Unfortunately I can't perform a D&C, which is probably what she does need if these antibiotics don't work. I will be checking on her as you have asked over the next couple months, and I expect a fair amount of cash for all you have asked me to do this time," Ellen glared at Leah.

"Alec will take care of her sterile problems when he gets her. He has confirmed with Raymond today that he wants to take her. He couldn't bear to see the streets get to her. I'm sure he wants more than that, hum," Leah smirked.

"Well I'll be back in a few days. The swabs I took should tell me more about what is going on. Make sure you take those multi-vitamins, Christina and drink lots of water. Your appetite should be back in a few days. Leah, let her bath whenever she wants and keep Tylenol up here for her to use as she needs it," I could hear Ellen's voice start to fade as they disappeared down the stairs, latching the attic doors behind them. I really wanted to be free so bad. Just to be able to sit in the kitchen or living room, but I knew that wouldn't be enough I would like just to run wherever I desired. I missed being with Frank and living as an adult.

The Agreement

The doors unlatched again and in minutes Leah appeared at the top of the stairs. She came to me and sat at the end of the bed. "Alec has agreed to take you. He actually begged your father to take you as his adopted daughter. You know your father when it comes to that. Alec eventually agreed to the marriage, but he won't even do it until you turn seventeen. He offered us way more than we imagined to ensure that we don't go selling you to just anyone. It is unbelievable, for being such a worthless burden, you sure are making us some money. And don't worry, I think I'll just be "frank" about things from now on," Leah laughed shaking her head with her arms crossed.

I actually found myself stunned and with my mouth part open. What did she mean? Why did Alec just want to have me as an adopted child? Why does he care? Then it dawned on me that he probably wanted to look good to my father, but he probably is some kind of pervert. Why else would he want to make sure they didn't just give me to anyone else? I don't know, maybe I was starting to think like Leah.

"Speaking of Frank, he still comes here looking for you. Yep, he has never stopped. Of course he doesn't say it outright; he's too much of a coward. He just looks for excuses to come by and help out around the shop with your father. He's gotten himself a counsellor and he is taking some anger management course. What he needs is to go to AA. He drinks like a fish now. You sure know how to destroy a man. The other day I caught him at the bottom of these attic doors touching the latches. When I asked him what he was doing he said he thought he forgot something in the attic last he stayed. Lucky thing I'm good on my feet. I had to tell him Raymond had a bunch of junk up there that was going to be thrown out soon, and later he could take a look. He couldn't even tell me what he thought he left up there so I could look for it for him. Little does he know, he lost everything in this attic," Leah laughed loud.

"Enough Leah, he is hurting. I don't want to know about Frank. I don't want to hear when he comes by or what he said. He is never going to be a part of my life now. You made sure of that when you sold my baby," I yelled kneeling forward towards Leah on the bed.

Leah pushed me back with her arm and swung back her other arm. "You better think twice before you do that! Child Services could come by any day now and if they see a mark on me, your plan won't work. That would be your doing, not mine." I yelled as Leah pulled her arm back.

"I said I would do my part. We established we don't like each other, but don't come up here and tell me things you think will hurt me in this process. Please just let me be. I already promised you that you will never see me again," I cried.

"Alright then quit you're damn bawling. You kids will never toughen up. You're so soft. I will tell you though that we got a *$25,000* retainer to hold you until you are seventeen. After we sign you over to him in marriage we will receive the additional *$75,000*. I plan to have you healthy and irresistible by then. Ellen will help me with that; she has a few friends that work in the beauty industry. I want you to look as good as you did when you last came home, but even better. You know Christina, you really should be thinking to yourself that I did you a great favor. I not only set your kid up with the best future he could ask for, but I will have set you up for the rest of your life. Alec McGuire is big money; I mean he makes Frank Shamanskii look like a piggy bank. I know we agreed to not visit, but when you grow up there in your head, you'll be thanking me and when you do, remember to throw some appreciation my way." Leah looked at me most seriously. I sank down in my bed, frustrated.

A little More Freedom

Months had passed and it was nearing September; my birthday was just around the corner. I had regularly been going every four weeks to get my hair trimmed and just had highlights put in a few days ago. I had proven myself during a couple visits from Child Services by not letting them know anything that was going on. I just told them that I was fine being home and plan to attend school again in September. For this, Leah had been letting me come downstairs for a couple hours a day, during which time Father hardly spoke to me. I think he asked where he put his damn coffee once, and where the hell Leah was.

If Frank pulled up, Father would yell from the shop and Leah would almost have a heart attack trying to get me up into the attic. I was allowed outside every other day for an hour as Leah thought it would be good for my skin. I had to lie on a blanket behind the house, in some tall grass, with yellow weed-like flowers. Leah, of course, had to be with me and she would play her word puzzles.

Today Ellen would be coming to pick us up. We were going to Kamloops to find a wedding dress that Leah liked on me. We sat at the kitchen table finishing up some breakfast when Ellen arrived.

"Okay, finally she is here. Let's go meet her outside or she'll be taking forever to leave here. Let's go." Leah pulled me by my wrist out the doors and through the boot room. She opened my door and quickly pushed me in. "Do up your belt and stay down. You never know when that Frank is going to just pop over," Leah blurted while looking around nervously.

"Oh calm yourself, let the girl have some enjoyment." Ellen snarled.

"She will be in wedded bliss in just over a week with a man I should have married when I was twenty," Leah replied. Ellen laughed out loud. "You were far too much of a moody slut when you were twenty! A man like Alec McGuire wouldn't come near you without a lawyer and a couple of body guards."

It was kind of comical seeing Ellen and Leah get along sometimes, but I had some deep worries. I didn't want to have sex with this older man. I mean, he was like twenty years older than Frank. I just wanted to get away from where I was and find a way I could get Luke back.

I wasn't even over Frank yet to think about being with anyone. Frank was my first, and I felt somehow bonded to that.

I could feel myself starting to get sick to my stomach. Would Alec make me do that or try to do that with me? I mean was he kidding when he said he wanted me as an adopted daughter? My last wedding was consensual and I guess this one is too, a bit. I just don't want to be married to Alec the way I was to Frank. I loved everything about my wedding and my wedding night with Frank, and I knew in my heart that I still loved Frank. I have no idea how I am going to tell Alec I don't want him on our wedding night.

Alec was an attractive man for his age. In fact he looked like he was ten or fifteen years younger. He was trim and toned, he had light brown eyes if I remembered correctly, and salt and pepper hair. Often he sported a well-trimmed beard and moustache, but once in a while he would be clean shaven. You could tell he wasn't covering any horrible features or birthmarks by wearing a beard. I think Alec was around the same height and build as Frank. He had the most alluring Scottish accent. I remember my sisters thinking he was handsome and talking about how they could just melt from his accent.

Here we were at Ellen's friend's bridal shop trying on about the twenty-fifth dress I didn't care about. "No, don't even bother putting her in that, it looks too fairy princess. She wants to look more grown up and something with a little sex appeal would make my purse open," Leah squawked at Ellen's friend.

"Leah, don't be so rude, she is a good friend of mine." Ellen pleaded to Leah. "I thought I was a good friend of yours," Leah replied sarcastically. I could see Ellen's friend look pretty uncomfortable as she went to the back room to retrieve another dress.

I was really getting tired of changing and unchanging for something I wasn't really shopping for. "That's the kind of dress I mean," Leah said as she stood up to touch the fabric. "It is long and shiny, form fitting, and not all puffed out like a Cinderella dress. Let's try this one on." Leah passed the dress to me.

As soon as I came out of the dressing room Leah said "That is the one, that's it! Will I be able to get it hemmed and altered in a few short day's?" Leah looked worried.

"I am sure Lily can do that Leah, and I will drive it out when we I get off work on Friday. Don't worry, it will work out," Ellen reassured Leah.

Getting Married in Vancouver

It was the morning before the wedding and Alec had bought everyone plane tickets. We were all running around and making sure we had everything. I picked up my backpack and headed towards the door.

"You're not bringing that old thing with you!" Leah demanded as she tried pulling it off my back.

"It's my backpack with all my favorite things in it. It's my stuff and I will never be coming back, so I need it now." I yelled. My father pushed Leah's hand off and scolded her; "It is her stuff. If you think it's junk then you won't have to look at it anymore. If Alec thinks its hideous, Alec can deal with it then." He had Leah's hand firmly until it looked like she relaxed.

"Fine! Did you contact the lawyers and bring that new birth certificate you ordered?" Leah sounded moody and uptight. You'd almost think she was getting married.

"Yes, I did. Were having a couple drinks on the plane and were going to enjoy ourselves. This is my daughter's wedding and we have a free hotel and round trip." Father bent down to tie his shoes. I felt numb all over.

Within hours we were in a small little church and Ellen's hairdresser was trying to fix my hair, and Leah was fidgeting with my dress. I felt like I was going to faint. I was hot all over, and then Leah was worried about how long the groom was waiting at the altar.

"Great, you look all flush. You had better keep it together. You had better be Alec's dream bride. Take some deep breaths and drink some of this cold water." Leah looked at me disappointed.

"Okay, let's do it now. Right now or I won't be able to," I said while dabbing my eyes with a Kleenex.

"Oh, okay your Father is waiting for you around the corner. Remember, walk with him," Leah reminded me.

I walked around the corner and Father took me by the arm and led me down the aisle. I never saw my father in a tuxedo before. I didn't believe he could clean up on the inside ever, as well as he cleaned up on the outside this day.

We made it to the front of the almost empty church were Ellen and some man where taking a few pictures. Alec looked very nice in his tuxedo and he was clean-shaven today. He looked into my eyes proudly and excitedly. I could feel my legs get weak as the minister started to speak. I couldn't make out a word of it. It sounded underwater. I remembered to breath and when I felt faint I just kept thinking about Luke. We were at the part where we had to repeat what the minister said, I really tried to psych myself up so I could do it right.

Now it was time to for the kiss. Alec immediately leaned toward me and his hand wrapped around me as he kissed me. His kiss was not too short but not uncomfortably long.

Chapter 7

Awkwardly I came out the washroom and stood in front of Alec. I was wearing the satin, short nightgown with spaghetti straps Leah picked it out. She told me I needed to wear it on my wedding night. Leah had picked everything out, from my wedding dress to my undergarments. I wasn't about to argue with her though. I was willing to do anything to get away from her and that house and find a way to get Luke back.

My head was slightly down and my arms were across my chest. I felt I had to cross my legs as this cream coloured and extremely short nightgown made me feel exposed.

Alec looked at me as if he was a bit puzzled, and then he took off his dinner jacket of a chair and covered me with it.

"There are some things we need to talk about Christina," Alec looked concerned as he sat me down on the end of the bed. He pulled a chair up close in front of me and continued in his Scottish accent. "I had no plans to ever marry again after the death of my first wife when I was twenty-eight. I have more than doubled those twenty-eight years, and now I have entered the sanction of marriage once again. Marriage is a very important covenant in which I do not intend to break. I did not see marriage s an option in which to remove you from your Father, as I know how young you are. Also I did not feel you would be comfortable. And I don't blame you, but this was the only way your father would release you to me.

Still, you need to know some important facts; you are my wife and I am your husband now, and in all ways you will be my wife except one: There will be no non-consensual intimacy; I have no plans to force anything upon you. However, you will be known as my wife to all who know me in any situation. I will not hide that fact. We will do many things together and eventually will grow to know each other very well. We will have only one bed in our bedroom and you will be by my side and I will be by yours. As time passes, and if we develop a romantic feel for each other, then we might at that time have those kinds of relations. I don't want you walking on eggshells or doing something you shouldn't be," Alec exhaled loud.

"Christina, I have no intention of divorcing you at anytime. I don't believe in divorce. I didn't prepare or have you sign any prenuptials for that very purpose," Alec paused for a moment and held one of my hands with both of his. "I give you all that I am. If at any point you choose to divorce me, I will understand. But know that I won't be doing the divorcing. You will be entitled to half of what was once just mine. Half of all I have inherited and of what I have worked my whole life for. If we stay married, I think we both understand that you will outlive me. In the event of my death all will go to you. There are some small things I would like to give if this happens. I do hope you would respect and carry out my wishes," Alec explained.

I was starting to feel dizzy at the thought of what was being said. I mean, it wasn't that long ago that I was told I could be killed and buried in the basement. It wasn't long ago that no one really loved me. No one would care or notice me missing. After all of Alec's explanations I still don't know why he would want me to be this person he keeps talking about.

A fondness

"Since I met your family long ago I have always carried you in my thoughts and my heart very deeply. I don't know if I can ever explain to you why. It is much too hard for me to talk about. Maybe one day Christina, one day you might see. For now let's work on getting to know each other," Alec smiled as he released my wrist.

I felt a large weight lift off my shoulders. I knew Alec seemed like a caring person, but I had never had any deep talks with him in the past. They were always light hearted and brief conversations with my father present.

The next day we spent in Vancouver shopping for clothes. It made me think of the clothes shopping expedition with Frank about two years ago. Alec had no regulations on what clothes I picked. He did say I should get some comfortable jeans. Most of the clothes I picked out were casual, but I also got a lot of classy stuff. I kind of grew to like a variety of different styles.

Alec had us stop at a specialty store for horse riding apparel. He wanted me to have proper riding gear so I could take lessons when we got home. We bought four pairs of riding pants; two were black, one pair was brown, and one pair white. We also got two pairs of riding boots and a riding helmet. Alec told me that horses were therapeutic, and soon I would have one special horse to call my very own—although he pointed out that all the horses would be mine as well. He just knew that I would bond with one very special horse.

Last, we stopped at a luggage shop and bought suitcases to carry all my new clothes in. I was actually looking forward to getting back. I had my heart set on coming up with a new plan to track down Luke and get him back with me as soon as I could. Something inside me told me he needed his mother, his true mother. There was no way I wouldn't take action on these feelings.

My New Home

We flew into Kamloops where Alec had his car parked. His car was none like any I had driven in before. It looked like it was old, like an antique, but in brand new condition. I had to ask him what kind of car it was, and how old it was? Alec told me that one of his hobbies was collecting all kinds of cars. "This, My Dear, is a 1959 Rolls-Royce. I have had this car since it was brand new. There is much we have yet to learn about each other," Alec smiled.

The outside of the car was silver with a black roof and it had a very long front end. Inside was full of white leather and real wood paneling. I noticed that even the carpet was white and it all seemed to be in pristine condition. "Alec, why does the car seem so new if you have had it since it was brand new?" I asked.

With a prideful smile Alec answered. "I have a collection of cars; approximately twenty-seven, and at one time I had thirty-six. I switch the cars around often and make sure I get them detailed on a regular basis.

I still have the same man take care of the interior and exterior of all my cars. He was just a young man from a very low-income family, so I thought he might need a job. After time, I grew to see and appreciate his love for cars and his loyalty to me for giving him work. I ended up putting him through an auto body trade course and he is on my payroll to this day. He has never worked for anyone else and he keeps quite busy looking over all my cars." Alec seemed please to talk about cars and happy I had an interest.

Twenty-seven cars, I thought—that is a lot. I wonder where he would keep twenty-seven cars. I decided not to ask as I am sure he will show me soon enough.

Alec lived much further north than my father's house, about four hours of driving had already past. It was a good thing that we started out in the morning from the airport. I was getting tired from all the driving.

It was around 4:30 PM when Alec announced we were almost home We were traveling a very narrow, recently paved road for what seemed like another three miles. I could only see trees on either side of the road. Finally, off to the right I could see a bit of a clearing.

We turned into it, and before us was a very high gate, and on either side were statues of bucking horses. To the left on a metal pillar was a box with buttons that had numbers. On the sides of the box there were what looked like speakers. Alec rolled down his window and punched in some numbers. As soon as he finished, the gate opened and we drove in.

I looked behind as we passed through to see if the gate would shut, and it did. We followed an extremely long driveway with more trees on each side of the drive. It seemed like it was a little under a mile until we came to a slight hill with a clearing. When we crested the hill I saw what looked like a beautiful hotel with immaculate landscaping.

The house, which was actually a mansion, had a huge paved cul-de-sac in front of it. Then the driveway went past the mansion quite a ways where I could see a huge warehouse building. The front of the mansion had a wide set of steps and a row of three thick pillars on each side that led to a huge set of double doors. On the right side of the doors was another box with numbered buttons where Alec punched in a code. When he finished, a lady with a Spanish accent flung open the doors and welcomed us. She said without any tones of judgment "This must be Mrs. McGuire?"

Soon, another, much older lady who also looked Spanish approached picking up one of my suitcases. "Christina, this is Lucia and her mother Manuela. They live here. They help with cooking and cleaning and I consider them part of the family. I don't know what I would do without them," Alec remarked. "Gracias, gracias," Lucia replied.

"This is my new wife, her name is Christina. Please, can you take the luggage up to my room? I would like to show her around," Alec seemed excited.

The Strange Spanish Lady

Manuela, who was about fifteen feet away, took a couple more steps towards me and put on a pair of glasses she had hanging out of a pocket on her shirt. "Shannon, this is not true. How does this be? Senor salvar mi Corazon ella espiritu ser antes de nosotros." Manuela was holding her hand over her mouth. I had no idea what she was saying but she looked pretty upset. Her eyes were watering and they were open widely. Lucia led her mother out of the room while pulling a suitcase and looking a little stunned at me.

Maybe they were judging me for my age. I think Manuela saw how young I looked when she put her glasses on and was getting mad at Alec. I looked at Alec who had is head down and was shaking it. "What happened? What did she just say?" I asked eagerly and concerned.

Alec looked up at me like he was trying hard to smile "Don't worry about her, she gets that way when something is touching to her. She's a little bit emotional right now. I have had her on my staff for thirty-eight years now and it's not very often I bring home a bride," Alec added. "Are you sure? I don't think she likes me." I felt rather worried.

"Let's not over think things now," Alec said. This is going to be a hard place to get used to, with Spanish and my Scottish accent.

I realized about twenty-five feet in front of us was the most beautiful grand marble stair case I have ever seen in my life. The floor in the entrance was all marble and led to the staircase that had wide, long stairs and large, marble pillars at the start of the staircase on both sides. You could walk six or eight people side by side up that staircase. The staircase had a bend, then a landing that had a crossing to both sides on the second floor. Then it continued it's spiral upwards.

First Alec explained that we were in the grand entrance. Here I noticed a lot of artwork, plants, and statues. From there you could go either right or left. Alec took me to the left.

"This is the main living room where I entertain guests. I don't often take others back to far off places in the house, although you can go anywhere and see anything you want," Alec smiled.

In the main living room the floors were a natural rock until about ten feet before the fireplace. There they turned into marble, which connected directly to the marble fireplace. The fireplace in its entirety was the size of a whole wall in most homes. About half way up the fireplace was what Alec explained to be his family crest, engraved in marble. He told me how sections of the fireplace were moved into the house when it was being built and how they fit it all together. I could hardly tell. To me it looked like one solid piece. It was very beautiful.

The second floor had an indoor pool, hot tub, and a steam room. The pool room itself was very sizable and had shelves with towels and lounging furniture. The walls were murals with ocean and tropical beach scenes. They matched the palm trees in the fancy planters that were throughout the poolroom. The entire floor was of stone tile. I was very excited about the pool. I couldn't imagine getting board in the winter.

Behind the mansion was a huge outdoor pool and barbeque area. I could see through a back window, a large area of lawn covering rolling mounds at the one end. I could see a tennis court at one end and the other, a small golf course. Beyond the golf course I could see a big stable, and far off to the left were some other small building structures. Looking straight between the golf course and tennis courts was a bridge over a stream that led to a gazebo and what looked like another small home.

Room after room, we drifted through the mansion and each room seemed to have a story. By the time we were done a couple hours had gone by. I was sure I could get lost easily trying to fine my way. The only area we didn't go down was the maid's quarters. Alec didn't want to disturb Manuela at this time. I did peek down the hallway that led to their quarters but didn't see much but other doorways. Alec told me that they had their own living and cooking area, but they mostly ate what they cooked for him. He wanted them to have their own comfort area.

Alec took me back to our room that was the size a whole floor of some homes. Our room was on the third and final floor, although I noticed down the hall and around the corner was a set of stairs. When I asked Alec where they went he said it was just an attic used for storage. Sometimes he had to get things from there for his lab projects.

"I'm going to show you where you can put your things, since Lucia and Manuela are having a little break. This dresser over here that matches mine will be yours, and the second walk in closet here is yours also. I'm sure in time we will fill it," Alec smiled. "I always sleep on the left side of the bed nearest the washroom, but would be willing to trade if you so wanted? You can unpack your things while I go talk to Manuela. It looks like it is going to be a late dinner tonight. If you want to freshen up you will find a load of towels in a cupboard in the washroom.

"Tomorrow we will take out a golf cart and I will show you all the property, including the horses. I want you to start riding lessons Monday morning. I hope that pleases you," Alec asked looking deep into my eyes almost trance-like, almost like Manuela had.

"I would be happy to, I have always loved horses." My reply seemed to make Alec snap back to reality. "Good, then we will begin on Monday!" Alec, startling voice almost seemed like he was trying to camouflage his trance-like state.

Life at the Mansion

I had been enjoying the last couple of months living with Alec in the mansion. I had a fairly scheduled life. This was something I never had before. Still I would wake up with Luke on my mind early every morning so I would go down to the second floor and have an hour or two swim, including using the steam room.

I found that the steam room was a good outlet to organize my thoughts. I felt like the four walls would hide my thoughts from everyone on the outside. The steam seemed to help me to have some feeling beneath the numbness I felt when my childhood haunted me.

Luke's first birthday had come and gone and I tried to envision what he might look like now and how he was doing. I sat in the steam room with my arms wrapped around my legs and rocked back and forth. I repeated to myself over and over 'November 8th, 1984, 7PM seven pounds and seven ounces. I felt that repeating this and memorizing how he looked when he was first born would make Luke sense me somewhere. I knew it likely wasn't true, but it made me feel a little better. I never stopped praying that one day we would be together again. I prayed for that every night and often during the day, when I found myself in a dark moment.

Martial Arts

I had walked into a room in the mansion one day where Alec was fencing with his trainer. I was ever so quiet while I watched their session. I think this was the first time I looked at Alec as being sensual. I did always find Alec attractive, in an older man sort of way. But watching him fence with such strength brought out a lot that I never saw in Alec before. For his age he did not look too much older than Frank. Still, it was a hard pill to swallow being that he was older than my father. After his session was done he came over to me wiping his face with a towel.

"I know you want to learn, don't you?" Alec asked while taking off his fencing clothes.

"Yes, I would love to. I used to take martial arts years ago and I really enjoyed it." I was very excited.

"I know," Alec replied. "You'd be excited to know Sven teaches a variety of martial arts also. So figure out what you want to learn and we'll get things rolling," Alec looked excited for me.

Days later I was fencing, kick-boxing, and learning Taekwondo. I was very passionate about it and the workouts would take some of the pain away from my heart: my heart that was broken for Luke. I also had my riding lessons and was going to take tennis lesson in the New Year.

There were a lot of distractions in my life at this point, but nothing stopped me from keeping Luke number one on my list. I had been searching Vandenhoff through information on the phone line. It was really hard to connect. I knew their first and last name, but with no Dutch phone book and little access to phone information for Holland, it was starting to look like Luke would be lost forever. I couldn't bare that thought.

More than a few times I head another line in the house pick up while I was on the phone. It would hang up just before I did. Alec had also walked in and might have heard a bit of information on two separate occasions. Alec had no idea I was pregnant before and maybe even somewhat married to someone else. I wasn't even sure if my marriage to Frank still stood.

Secret Phone Calls

One night lying in bed, Alec actually asked me what was holding me down. "You are not one-hundred percent here. I am sensing a distraction. I have looked at the phone bills, and I see many calls to Holland all under the last name Vandenhoff. Is there a young man, or a lost love in your life? If you are in love with someone else and you want a divorce, I understand. I just want some time to prepare my heart, Christina. I am not ready to lose at love again so soon," Alec voiced sounded very sad in his Scottish accent.

"No, it's not like that! But yes, I did love someone once. But I know it would not have worked, especially since I . . . I lost something important. I know he is still not meant for me. I wouldn't have known this, even months ago, but now it is very clear to me. I am not looking for someone that I am in love with, or could even have an intimate relationship with. It is someone I love though, but I can't explain this to you. I think I've lost this person forever, and it is all my fault. There will always be the biggest piece of my heart missing, a part I can never replace." I was now starting to sob as we lay side by side in bed with the fire crackling.

"Christina, I can help you. I can't let you be this heartbroken. If I have to make it mission in my life and you will stay by my side I will find this loved one for you; no matter where he or she is in this world. I have some really good connections that have found people in the strangest of places. When you are ready to talk to me and explain, I will help you find this loved one." Alec slipped his arm around me and pulled me towards him so that my head was on his chest and my arm rested across his stomach.

My tears streamed down my face onto his chest although I was trying my hardest to hold back. I had not had a cry about Luke like this, ever. It just seemed to come out for about an hour until I started to fall asleep from crying. As I slipped off, I heard Alec say these odd words: "I am not going to lose you again. I won't let it happen this time." I was too tired to even respond and the blackness closed in on me. This was the first time Alec and I had ever been this close to each other. It felt really good to be held and to be heard by someone who did not want to judge me.

Chapter 8

It seemed the days and the months passed so quickly and June was in full bloom already. I think it was because I kept myself so occupied. I was really getting to be an excellent rider and I could go for hours on my own. I loved to explore through the woods into different mountain trails. Riding made me feel free; Freer than I could ever feel in my life, I think.

Alec complained a lot when I was gone for long periods of time by myself. A few times he had found me in the woods. Once I had my horse tied and I was lying on a blanket by a stream. He was angry as I was ridding quite long and the sun would be going down soon. He was worried that it might have gotten dark before I got back to the stable. I was just enjoying the nature and the quiet, but somehow lost track of time.

Another time we almost went head to head on a trail. Alec did appreciate that I loved nature. He knew there was something on my mind since I arrived there. He did try to talk to me about it on several occasions, but I didn't know how to explain it to him. I couldn't put it into words, and if I did, I feared I would lose it and break down in front of him. He was a good man to me. He always assured me that when I was ready to tell him he would be ready to help me, in every way possible.

Alec

Alec was like my best friend now. We would fence together, play tennis, swim, go for walks, and go riding together, when I wasn't off on my own. We went to bed cuddling every night now, and Alec seemed to be completely happy with that. He never tried to touch me anywhere I didn't want, nor did he try to spark any romance. We would lay in bed talking about our day, and he would gently kiss me on the forehead once in a while until I drifted off to sleep. I never drifted off to sleep without a silent prayer for Luke in my head.

Lucia and Manuela were very kind to me. I guess the first day they met me must have been hard. Alec has never remarried after his first wife died, and Manuela knew his first wife. Alec said she was very fond of her. It was Alec's deceased wife that had hired Manuela and Alec has still kept her to this day, as a cook and maid

I would like to know how Manuela had her daughter Lucia over the time she worked for Alec. Lucia was thirty years old and there was no talk of her father. I could tell that whoever her Father, was he must have been Caucasian. Lucia did not look like she was fully Spanish. She was a pretty girl of about five-foot-even inches. Her eyes were a hazel green and her hair was medium to light brown. She was big boned like Manuel—not heavy by any means.

Since I had been living here, we had celebrated both Manuela's and Lucia's birthdays so I knew Manuela had to have had Lucia when she was thirty-three. If I did the math correctly Lucia would have been conceived a few years after Alec's wife's death. I wonder if it would be possible that Lucia was Alec's daughter.

I had spotted in the hall of the maid's quarters, several pictures of Alec leading Lucia as a young girl around on a horse. There were also a lot of pictures of Alec holding Lucia as a toddler. I had never seen any pictures of Lucia as a child with any other man. I didn't want to ask Alec at this point. I was curious, but how could I when I hadn't told him about Luke. I felt like we were kind of even in that way. I never even asked him how his wife died or any details about her. I think I felt it would open wounds that he didn't want picked at; the way I felt about my situation with Luke. Still, I knew it was kind of unfair, but my curiosity about Lucia was overwhelming. I needed to know if Alec was her father. If I look around maybe I might happen upon some information that would reveal the truth without having to talk to Alec.

Mrs. McGuire

I was in the stable brushing my horse after a good hard ride. Lucia came racing up to me. "Senora, come, you will be late for Alec's guest. We need to get you freshened up and dressed. Let us go, Senora." Lucia handed the brush to the grounds man who also worked in the stable. Lucia practically dragged me by my arm.

When we got to the house, a tub was already for me and Lucia pointed to me indicating to get in quick. Normally I would bath or shower in the Stable, and that was where I left my blue jeans and my t-shirt. It was nice as I could walk back to the house clean and ready for the rest of the day. Already I was in the tub and my ridding clothes were in a pile on the floor.

"Alec wanted you to be wearing a nice summer dress. You have no summer dresses in your closet," Lucia said with question in her voice.

"Yeah, I guess I never thought too much about summer dresses when I went shopping. That was almost a year ago. We haven't gone since, and as you know, there are no local clothing stores for miles," I said in a calmer voice than Lucia.

"Oh no, Madre come Madre." Lucia yelled while Manuela walked in the bathroom. They started talking in Spanish quite loudly over me. Manuela looked at me again, covering her mouth with her eyes bulging again. I was thinking. 'do I look irregular naked? Is there dirt on my face, maybe in some weird place? Why is she looking at me that way?' Now she looks a bit watery eyed. Maybe she thinks I'm going to have her fired.

Manuela, who was still speaking in Spanish to Lucia, covered part of her face with her hand again and was nodding to her. Lucia yelled one last thing in Spanish and Manuela hurried off.

"You must hurry, Senora, they just arrived and are heading down to the gazebo by the little house; we need to be there soon. My mother will meet us over there after we get you a dress, now hurry," Lucia begged.

"Well she has a long way to go if she is getting me a dress. There are no stores." I felt confused now, but I started to rinse the conditioner out of my hair. I washed up and Lucia was standing holding a towel for me. She wrapped it around me and we walked into the bedroom.

Across the bottom of the bed was a white summer dress with eyelets of purple and blue flowers under the breast that went all the way around. The dress was long, down to my toes. Lucia told me to try some sandals with the dress. The sandals fit perfect; they had white, leather straps and a bit of a heel that was corked. This gave just enough lift so that the dress didn't go over my toes anymore.

"This is very pretty Lucia, was this yours when you were younger?" I smiled looking in a mirror. By comparing our height and frames, Lucia probably wasn't my size since she was twelve years old.

"No," Lucia said, as she brushed through my hair.

"Oh, well then was it your mothers?" I guessed, as I looked in the mirror at how perfect it fit me.

"No it was not. We must hurry." Lucia rushed me. I ran over to my makeup area and dusted on a little power. Lucia took my hand, and down the grand staircase we went. We took off outside, down the path. Lucia was walking so fast I could barely keep up. She stopped for a moment near a flower bed before the tennis court and picked some purple-blue flowers and put them in my hair.

"Here," she said, arranging the flowers into my hair, "I am going to walk ahead so I can help my mother." Lucia took off at a very swift pace. I just took my time, as I didn't want to sprain an ankle. I wouldn't be able to do martial arts of any kind for a while if I did that. Passing the end of the tennis court, I turned right onto the path to the gazebo where I could see Alec and four other men sitting with him.

I started to walk up some stairs that led to higher stairs on the gazebo. I could tell that Alec noticed me coming. In fact, he seem like he froze and was squinting as if to see me properly. I got to the gazebo entrance and Alec rose to meet me. Taking my hand, his eyes fell heavy on me and they seemed to be a bit watery.

"This can't be possible. I mean I saw it, but this is more real," Alec said as he brought me to the other side where he was sitting. His stare was so affixed on me that he didn't seem to remember his guests. I loosened my hand and sat myself in the chair Alec had pulled out for me.

"Are you talking about the new blood pressure pills we have been working on, or is this some private conversation you are having with yourself?" A young man around the age of thirty-five asked.

"This, Jim, is my wife. I would like you all to meet my wife Christina. Christina, this is Jim, Donald, Raymond, and Chuck," Alec finished.

"Are we robbing the cradle here or can I take her to prom next year?" Donald laughed.

"Well, Donald not all of us have the privilege of hand picking the perfect wife from a magazine, and then have her flown to Canada with all the right measurements," Alec laughed, as did the whole table.

"I told you Buddy, you could have gotten yourself a nice wife out here, bald or not," laughed Chuck again.

"Finally, here comes Manuela with those drinks and some appetizers." Alec looked across the gazebo where Manuela was walking up another set of stairs followed by Lucia, each holding a large tray in their hands. Manuela handed out Tom Collins around the table carefully watching her tray. Lucia took some plates of appetizers off her tray and placed them on the table. It looked like some small pastries, and skewered shrimp and other meats. Manuela put the last drink on the table that was Alec's.

"Christina, what would you like?" Alec asked me.

"Can I get a margarita, strawberry?" I asked.

"Certainly!" Alec replied.

Manuela suddenly looked down at me like she had seen a ghost. She started to speak in Spanish again like she was upset. Then to my surprise, Alec started talking fluent Spanish to Manuela with his arm over her shoulder. This went on for a few moments and Manuela picked up her tray that she had dropped. She then left the gazebo slowly looking back at me once in a while.

I felt very confused and looked at Alec when Donald laughed saying "You can't blame her if she doesn't want to serve alcohol to a minor, Alec."

Alec gave Donald a glare. "This is my wife, no more jokes. I expect you to respect her as my wife. Now let's go over the business so we can finish and try to enjoy this evening," Alec's accent was attractive even when he was upset. It seemed a little sexy when he was defending my honor.

"You got it Chief," Donald said, taking a swallow of his Tom Collins. Lucia came up with my margarita and just then everyone seemed to start happily talking amongst themselves.

"I didn't know you even spoke Spanish, never mind so clearly," I said to Alec.

"You didn't? Well you might want to know I speak a few other languages too. It's part of my business. Although the biggest pharmaceutical company I own is in the United States. I have some smaller labs in a couple other countries. I often introduce medications to labs all over the world that we have created." Alec seemed to like that I was attentive as he looked deep into my eyes again. He brought my hand to his lips and kissed it gently.

"I love you!" Alec caught me off guard. He looked at me when he said it but looked down and to the right, away from me. His eyes watered up a little bit. My heart raced at what to say next. Do I love him? I think I do, but we never had sex and I am his wife. Maybe that means I don't love him. But I do . . . I think. I had to say something; there would be too much of a time lapse if another few seconds went by.

"Thank you," I blurted taking a sip of my margarita.

"I guess I'll be the one presenting these new medications to Europe,' Jim cut right in over everyone's talking (which I felt took the attention off my abrupt answer to Alec's statement).

"Well I don't know Jim, do you think you are ready for that?" Alec asked. Now it seemed like business was on the table. And business talk went into the wonderful dinner Manuela and Lucia prepared desert as well as a few after dinner drinks.

Finally it was time for all to go, and this time Alec's employees politely said goodbye to me as Mrs. McGuire, each shaking my hand. I knew they could see this made Alec very happy.

After everyone was gone Alec and I had another drink out on the gazebo and thanked Manuela and Lucia. They were wonderful hosts and the cooking was delicious. Alec told them they could come and get our glasses tomorrow, and that they could just go on to their quarters.

Manuela

Lights were weaved all through the top of the gazebo, which gave the night a romantic flare. I could smell the different flowers from the gardens around the property as the wind lightly dusted them.

"Alec, why was Manuela acting so strange around me again? I really don't think she likes me, and she does it in such a creepy way." I could tell Alec was feeling a little tipsy so I thought I could get some answers from him tonight. In fact this is the first time I ever saw Alec tipsy. Maybe he drank a little more tonight because he was stressed at how his employees were acting. I was pretty sure it was a combination of different stressors.

"She doesn't Christina; in fact, she thinks you are beautiful," Alec started as I interrupted him.

"Okay, I need to ask this as now it is making more sense to me. Please don't feel like you have to hide it from me if it is true Alec." I looked deep into Alec's eyes as he gulped and looked like he had been caught at something that wasn't good.

"Okay, I will be honest Christina. But did I tell you how incredibly beautiful you look tonight? You are the light in all this darkness; the light has come back into my heart. I want to keep you in my heart until my last breath here on this earth. Go ahead Christina, ask me and I will answer truthfully even if it might hurt me." Alec had both my hands and looked deep within my eyes. I could tell he was nervous for some reason, so I was sure the answer to my question would be yes. He looked very handsome in the lights of the gazebo as the moon danced above. Once in a while a cloud would blow over part of the moon, but all in all it was a full moon tonight.

"Alec, is Lucia your daughter? Did you have a relationship with Manuela after your first wife died? Please just tell me, then the way that Manuela sometimes acts around me will make more sense," I gave Alec's hand a squeeze as I waited for him to answer. He suddenly got a smile on his face.

"Manuela? Oh no no-no-no. Manuela met someone actually, just before my wife died. They dated for a few years. He was a carpenter I had hired to build a guesthouse, where I own a home in Palm Springs.

He was with us for a while building, as you can imagine that does take some time. When I returned back from the Caribbean where my wife died, Manuela continued to see him. Manuela was good friends with my late wife and I think he comforted her through some really hard times she was having with the death.

Eventually Manuela got pregnant and the man disappeared. So Manuela just continued to work for me until it was too difficult. I still kept her on the payroll and hired someone to clean until Manuela felt she was able enough to work. I eventually hired her a nanny until Lucia was old enough to go to school. I knew my late wife would have wanted me to help her and she had already been tossed out by a man. Manuela actually gave her daughter my late wife's name as a middle name, Alec explained

"We moved to Canada a few years after Lucia's birth, and when Lucia became a teenager she wanted a job. Manuela had already taught her how to cook and clean so I put her on the payroll with her mother. It is quiet a story for sure. Lucia is helping to save money for a home for her mother, for when Manuela is too old to work. It's not too far from here.

They are practically the only family I have aside from you now. In most respects I did raise Lucia, not like my own, but maybe like a niece. It almost felt like God had gifted her to Manuela and even to me, to soften the blow of my late wife's unexpected end," Alec finished.

"Wow, not the answer I was expecting. How did your late wife die?" I asked.

"Let's get into that another time. I am still surprised. Not upset, just surprised by your question. But about Manuela; just give her some time. She likes you, I know it. When I talked to her she even said she was surprised at how you have so many of my late wife's qualities. She's just not herself lately. You need not worry about this. You are my beautiful wife and I just want to enjoy this evening with you.

He stood up and took my hand, moving me aside from the table. He placed one had around my waist and pulled me close to him with the other. We danced beneath the gazebo lights to the faint sound of the radio that was playing below us near the barbeque. As we moved around the gazebo I could smell Alec's cologne. I cuddled into him, and every few moments a warm breeze would carry the scent of flowers from the gardens to us. As the song ended, Alec looked down at me and pressed his lips against mine gently. "Shall we walk back together now?" Alec had his arm out leading the way.

As I was laying in bed waiting for Alec I realized something. It has taken me so long to get used to being here. I have been so consumed by Luke that I had not asked until tonight about how Alec's late wife died. I wouldn't want to force it from him though, as I don't know when I would be able to tell him about Luke.

Alec crawled into bed, slipping his arm under me and his other arm over me. Then he pulled me towards him nice and tight. I laughed which made him laugh.

"Good-night Christina," Alec whispered in my ear.

"Good-night Alec," I answered then Alec said, "Good-night Mary Ellen, good-night Jason, good-night Ben, Jim-Bob, and Elizabeth. Oh Yeah, and good-night John Boy," laughed Alec.

"You drank too much tonight," I laughed, "but I like it when you are funny," I laughed a little again.

"I did drink too much; you really shocked me when you walked in that dress. The way it fit you so perfectly, right down to the sandals; it was astounding." He must know whose dress it is.

"Yeah, Manuela gave it to Lucia for me to wear. I'm sure it's Lucia's from when she was younger. I don't think they wanted me to think it was used. They really don't know how much I don't mind. I am the youngest daughter of three girls. That involves a lot of hand me downs. It's hard to imagine Lucia my size even when she was younger. She is quite big-boned and her hips are quite wide. I guess we all can change rather quickly once hormones hit us," I finished.

"Hmm," Alec thought I could tell that he had fallen asleep, as the room grew loud with silence.

I prayed for Luke to be returned to me soon and that he would be safe and in good health. Then I too felt myself fall into the mercy of my unconscious mind.

I saw my mother. She was wearing the dress at the funeral parlor; the one she wore to church on occasion. We were in Sunday school and she was telling the story of Daniel in the lion's den with all the little felt figurines on a board in front of the class. Her hair was straight and brown and her nails and lipstick were mauve. I felt a sense of pride as she told the story. Suddenly I lifted out of the room towards outer space. My mother didn't notice, she just kept teaching the class. I lifted up higher and higher. Then I pulled away from the class. They were so tiny and far away until they disappeared. Abruptly, I started to fall. The wind was at my face and I couldn't breathe. I just kept falling and falling and falling. I could see the earth and I was coming towards it fast. It was getting, bigger and now I could see roads and buildings. I shot through a roof without getting hurt and I started to slow down as I went through the first floor, then the second floor, then last floor. I hovered above for a second, looking at my father and Leah argue and my siblings. Then I just dropped onto my mother's casket. I felt the coldness again, the hardness of her body, the smell of formaldehyde and perm solution. I gasped and shot up into a sitting position. I awoke at 6AM and slipped out of Alec's arms, careful not to wake him.

Naked

I felt an ache in my heart for Luke. I think I felt guilty for having fun the night before when I still had no idea how to get Luke back. I had more money at my disposal, so much I didn't even know how much, but it didn't matter; it couldn't help me. Nor could it remove the pain I felt for Luke in my heart.

I quickly strode down the hall and then down to the second floor. I made a left on the second floor and fled down a very long hallway. About midway down I could see the side of the hall that was all windows and that lead to the pool. I had bathing suites hanging in a closet but I just tore my PJ's off and dove into the pool naked. I did forty-five minutes of laps and decided to take a quick dip in the hot tub before entering the steam room.

When I got into the steam room I poured some eucalyptus oil into the cup that went under the area where the steam jets come from. I lay across one of the wooden benches with a towel in a roll under my head. I cried aloud for quite a few moments, as I knew no one could hear me. Then I fell back to sleep for a while, breathing in the eucalyptus scent.

I awoke again to the steam jets. Then I could hear my name being called and doors of the towel cupboard opening. I realized I was naked and that it was Alec's voice I was hearing. The panic started to leave me and I thought to myself, 'do I really care if he sees me? He is my husband; it is sure to happen one day. Would it not?' I could hear his footsteps coming towards the steam room, and I got up and walked toward the door.

The door opened outward and Alec was standing there in his swim shorts. "I thought . . . I . . . might . . . join you for a swim," he said, with many pauses while his eyes locked onto me. I came close to him and I took one of his hands with both of my mine and placed it on my shoulder and then directed downward and over my breast. I got up on my tippy-toes, brought my mouth towards Alec's, and kissed his soft lips. Alec received my lips and we began kissing passionately. He pulled his hands from my breast and ran it up the back of my neck.

My hair was through the fingers of both of his hands. I pulled my mouth away and turned away. Alec resisted, holding each side of my head with his fingers still in my hair. He pushed himself closer to me, smelled the top of my head, and kissed my forehead several times. He pulled his arms out and my hair slipped out of his fingers as I left.

No Entry

I turned towards the showers, grabbing a few towels, and as I looked back I saw Alec enter the steam room. I had a really quick shower and pulled my hair back into one long braid while it was still wet. I dried off and wrapped myself with a fresh new towel and walked back down the long hallway making my way to the third floor, and back to my room.

Before I opened the door I could hear something down the farthest end of the hallway. It sounded like a door closing. It couldn't have been Alec. There is no way he could have gotten past me or even close to the bedroom at the same time as me.

With my towel wrapped tight around myself, I walked down the hall until I could see the staircase leading to the attic. Coming down the staircase was Manuela. She looked at me as she came down the last couple of stairs.

"Senora, you must never go up there, never," Manuela stated as she put a large key into a pocket on the chest of her apron.

"Why are you up there Manuela?" I asked, a little annoyed at this. I am supposed to be the woman of this house. It's supposed to be my house, and she is telling me that I am not allowed to enter certain rooms. I couldn't help but think she must not know who she is messing with.

Now she has made it so that I have no choice but to sneak up there if need be and take a look around. And this wasn't my fault, I just had a natural curiosity in me. True, it often led to trouble, but it stopped my mind from playing guessing games about the unknown for days and days. I can recall so many times when I was younger how my curiosity was so much stronger than my fear. I face down monsters in my closet and dark scary rooms that none of the other kids would dare go near. I'd put a teacher to the test to know if they seriously were going to react the way they said they were. All of this was in the name of curiosity.

Manuela cleared her throat; "Senor Alec asked me to bring down some storage items for him this morning," Manuela answered, sounding a bit nervous.

"What storage things?" I asked, trying to sound strict. I think Manuela needs to know that I am the woman of the house now. She has been like the woman of the house for some time in her own way, but I wouldn't let her walk all over me.

"I just do what I am told, Senorita. Please can I go back to work now? She asked.

"What is up there that you don't want me to see?" I demanded. Manuela's eyes paced back and forth like she was thinking of an excuse. "Up there?" she pointed up the stairs, "oh, tons of junk. I tell Senor Alec to get rid of it for years. It is very dangerous with that stuff all over. You could get hurt very easily. Don't go up there Senorita, you don't know how easy it is to trip and fall. Look, see my arm has big scratch because I fell back into something today." Manuela twisted her upper arm and there was quite a scratch on it about eight inches long.

"Manuela, you need to go tend to this right away. It could get infected," I said.

"I know, I don't like to go in that nasty room myself. I will go clean it up Senorita, Thank you."

I walked back to my bedroom thinking that it wasn't so interesting after all. Sounds like she was just afraid I might hurt myself.

Safire

I went to the left of the closet and found the one pair of riding pants I hadn't used yet; the white ones. I put them on with my black ridding boots and headed out to the stable. I took the scenic route I always chose to get to the stable. It was only one of two ways I could use to get there. I could go down the drive-way and walk for sometime on pavement passing the warehouse full of Alec's car collection and then turn off through a pasture, or I could use the scenic route. The scenic route took me down some garden paths with miniature waterfalls, birdbaths, and statues of animals (and through Alec's golf area) until I got to the hedges.

The hedges were a pathway that twisted and turned with hedges on each side. They were about six feet tall on either side and were very well groomed and square on top. I followed them for awhile. The only break in them was over a bridge that carried the same stream that was near the other end of the property. It led to the area of the property that went to the gazebo. At the end of the hedges was a field where you could see the big green and brown stable.

I was excited to ride Safire today; she was my favorite horse. She was old enough to know better and young enough to play. Safire was a classic Arabian horse with her arched neck and high tail carriage. She was a solid chestnut colour with a silky, black main and tail. Like most Arabians she was very alert, good natured, quick to learn, and always willing to please. This made her the perfect horse for me and she knew it to. Anytime she even sensed me in the stable she would become alert and you could tell she was raring to go.

Today I wanted a good ride. I went inside and saw the grounds man already grooming Safire.

"She is ready for you, Madam. You usually ride around this time so I thought I'd give you a head start." The grounds-man slipped around to put the horse brush back.

"Thank you, but how did you know I was going to ride Safire today," I asked.

"Well that I wasn't sure; of but I do see you riding her a lot. If you would like me to prepare a different horse I will get right on that," he said with a laugh that was about as strange as it was funny. Might even be creepy to some people?

"No thank you, Sir, you got it right today," I said, throwing on a saddle blanket.

"Russell," he blurted.

"What?" I asked.

"My name, Russell, that's what most people around here call me. I thought I'd just keep that name as my mother said not too much else suited me," Russell laughed that strange little laugh again.

As serious of a mood I was in, it was hard to keep myself from laughing or even smiling from that funny sound. I climbed up on a bench and placed the saddle on Safire.

"Russell, okay I will remember that. You know what Russell?" I questioned.

"No I don't think I do, Madam," He said bopping from one foot to the next.

"I think I am going to ride western today so can you hang my hat up over there?" I asked. "You bet I can." Russell hung the hat up on a hanger.

"Christina." I said getting onto Safire.

"Huh?" Russell looked puzzled and scratched his head as he did his little bopping thing.

"They call me Christina, and so can you?" I started to walk Safire out of the Stable. "Oh yeah, I know that! You bet I will, Madam." Something told me that Russell wasn't the sharpest pencil in the box, but he seemed nice and thoughtful all the same.

Bang

I started at slow trot until we picked up into a good canter and before I knew it I was galloping with Safire over rolling hills. I felt like I was flying as the wind brushed my cheeks. I could see some hills up ahead so I slowed Safire down. I could tell she didn't appreciate it. Safire loved to stay going once she got going. I decide to take a new area I hadn't ridden before. It actually didn't really have any trails or markings, but I wanted a challenge.

We jumped a half broken fence and started up a mountainside. I was thinking I'd just go to the top and see if there's any kind of view, then down the other side. Then I'd head back from where I came. I thought to myself that if there is any time left I might take the trail down to the stream in the woods later.

Going up was quite tricky for Safire as there were a lot of old, broken tree rounds and large rocks. I certainly didn't want her to break anything and decided if the terrain didn't get better soon we might have to turn back. I really had to pull back on Safire. She wanted to go full throttle, badly. It was like she could sense something wasn't right. We crested the mountaintop within forty minutes. I had to pull back on the reigns so much. I didn't want Safire to hurt herself. I decided into go in direction that was more northerly. This way I might see if we couldn't connect to some of the trails we were familiar with.

We were going down now. Safire seemed a bit more annoyed as I pulled the reins back again. I told her it was okay and rubbed her neck to see if I could calm her a bit. It was tedious but we made our way down the north side much quicker than I expected and I began to see why. The mountain levelled off and then went up for a bit longer and down again. I was pretty sure we were off of it now and would soon hit some familiar trails. The woods were thick here, but I could see up ahead that we would soon be hitting a clearing, and it would be much thinner.

We walked into the clearing where I began to look for trails or markings. Alec had shown me many different markings in these woods that connected to well-used trails. I was sure we would come to some soon. Just as I was, thinking that I noticed a trail and a marker. Yes, we could probably make it to the stream and then come back out before anyone would worry. We moved on towards the trail when I heard a growl from behind us. Safire made a loud distress sound. Suddenly it was in beside us. Safire flung around. Then I could see rushing out towards us was a coyote. Safire bucked at it and kept trotting around in a circle. I could feel myself starting to slip off.

I awoke and it was dusky out. Safire was standing beside me. She hadn't left me. She walked over to me as if she knew I was waking up and sniffed my face. I raised my hand to pet her and everything went fuzzy.

I woke up again and I could see it was dark. I could hear people calling me and I could see flashlights and hear horses off to my left. Safire made a loud noise a couple of times and I could hear someone saying, "do you hear that?" It got fuzzy again and it went completely black. I woke again to Alec, frantic. "Don't move her! Get that neck brace on her then let's slip that board in behind her."

Next thing I remember, I was in the hospital somewhere. I awoke to Alec by my side. "Christina can you hear me?" he asked, sounding really concerned.

I was so thirsty I felt like I hadn't had a drink in a month. "I'm thirsty." I answered.

Alec pushed a button on my bed and started calling for a nurse when it got fuzzy again. I woke up again and I could hear Alec. His head was on my chest and he sounded like he was crying, "Shannon, I lost you once and you gave me this wonderful gift. Please Shannon, don't take it away? I won't lose you again." Then he started to pray to God as it went fuzzy once again.

I woke up to Alec and a doctor beside me. "Christina can you hear me?" the doctor asked.

"Yes, I answered." Alec moved pass the doctor to the top of the bed holding my hand.

"You had a pretty bad bang to your head that caused some swelling on your brain. From what we can see it looks like it has all come down now. Is it ok if I just give you a good check over?" he asked.

"Yes," I replied. he checked me over, "good, everything looks like it has gone back to normal," he reassured.

"My name is Dr. Peterson." He shook my hand. "I think you are healed enough, but you have been in and out of consciousness for five days now. I am going to keep you through the night and just see how well you do, and if all goes well I think your husband can take you home tomorrow. Is that ok with you?" he asked politely.

"Yes, thank you Dr. Peterson," I replied. "Okay, now I will be here to check you in the morning." He slipped through the curtains and out of sight.

Allowing to Be Loved

I had been home for four days now, and Alec wouldn't let me get up for anything. I would argue with him that the doctor didn't give me any restrictions, and he just warned me to wear a helmet when I am riding.

"I should be riding right now," I complained.

"You will be soon enough, Christina, and you can walk around now. You don't have to listen to me, but I would like it if you stayed away from any martial arts and riding for just one more week. I know that seems like a long time to you, but you have no idea what I just went through when this happened." Alec took a cup of tea Manuela made and put it on the lamp table beside me.

"When mid-afternoon hit I knew you were gone for too long, and when I saw your helmet at the stable my heart almost failed me. I don't know why you left your helmet, but I am not going to go into that. I got a search team and people from miles away came looking for you. It took until 10:30 PM to find you when you set off in the morning." Alec placed his hand on his chest and lowered his head as he sat on his knees beside me while I lay on the couch. "Please, Christina, you can go in the pool and the steam room for now. Please? Alec begged.

"I promise, I won't do anything else for now, and I am sorry that I worried you and caused such a problem," I said, seeing his pain and realizing what a mess I had made. Alec leaned forward and kissed me on the lips.

Chapter 9

It had been over six years now that I had been with Alec. I was twenty four-years old. I had grown used to life in the country, living in the mansion, and used to Alec. Alec had been remarkable to me over the past years and has never really asked for much in return. Still over all this time we had not been intimate with each other, and there was never any pressure to do so. The closest we ever got was years ago when he found me naked in the steam room. He never brought that up to me or tried to see if he could push things in that direction. We had gone on vacations together to many tropical places, and we celebrated our anniversary each year as if it were the most important day.

Alec was still a hard person for me to figure out. I still didn't understand why he felt such affection for a poor abused young girl like me. I also didn't understand why a lonely widower would be living in such a huge mansion practically by himself. Soon it had gotten to the point where I didn't ponder these things so much and just thanked God that he was in my life.

I knew God had a plan for everything and whether it was met with trials or happiness his path for me was the one I needed to follow. Understanding that path would come later. I had grown a large amount of faith and respect for the Big Guy Upstairs and with faith there is always trust, and with both of these things grows the greatest . . . Love!

Alec spent a good deal of his time in his lab, which was past the gazebo and the guesthouse. Once I asked him why he had built his lab so far away from the house. He told me it gave him a sense of going to work and putting him in that work mode. Also, he said that the lab has a lot of chemicals and such and if it started on fire it would be less likely to burn down every building on the property. We were really far out from town and for a fire truck to get to us could take a lot longer than in most situations.

Over the years I had searched the phone system endlessly in an effort to find Luke. I was trying to find any families by the name of Vandenhoff and there were a lot. I didn't even have a city to go with in my search. I knew it was my only way to Luke, but I wasn't doing a good job of detective work. I needed some other means. I thought of asking Alec if we could take a trip to Holland, but I knew he would suspect what my intents were. I would then have to tell him the whole story about Luke, and not only did I not want to put myself through all of those emotion, but I wasn't sure how Alec would take it.

Alec was turning seventy soon and he seemed to be slowing down somewhat. He didn't go riding with me half as much, nor did he do much fencing anymore. Now he only fenced about once every two weeks with Sven.

I definitely used Sven service as much as I could. I fenced and did two different martial arts. It helped to have private lessons. Every time I would go up a belt, we would go into town were Sven taught. He would graduate five to ten people at a time so it would be a ceremony. Alec was always ecstatic, snapping pictures and clapping. It was a good feeling to me. I worked really hard at it and Alec would pay Sven double for a private lesson for me, as Sven would have to travel out. Sometimes I would do three—two hour private lessons per week.

Kick-boxing is what I mostly did on my own now that I had learned it. The gym we had on the second floor was huge and just a few doors down the hall from the pool. Often I would get up early or even go late at night when I couldn't sleep and kick-box for an hour or longer. I always end it with a short swim and a soak in the hot tub.

Manuela was basically retired now. Lucia and she were able to get a mortgage for the nice, little house that was about a mile down the main road from where we lived. Manuela still came by about twice a week to cook a meal or two and insisted that she come and help prepare each holiday meal with Lucia. Of course we had no objections and we knew it was a way for her to be around family. We were just as much family to her as Lucia was.

I was just coming in from a two, hour ride with Safire. I had gone by myself this afternoon, as I knew it would be too long of a ride for Alec. Alec would normally just ride down to the stream with me or do a few short trails. He never went longer than one hour now. We still walked a lot together and would spend a lot of time in the pool. I knew Alec tired easily now, although I never let on that I noticed.

Unexpected Guest

After handing Safire over to Russell I went over to the washroom in the stable and had a nice soak in the tub. I changed and then started walking back through the trail with the hedges and through the golf course and the gardens.

As I got a little closer to the house I noticed a red car and remembered Alec saying he was having a business meeting with someone. As I got closer to the cul-de-sac, the car became clearer to me and my body felt numb except for the pounding of my heart. That looks like Frank's Ferrari. Was it? Any of Alec's business partners could afford to own a Ferrari. Maybe I am just being paranoid. I couldn't recall anyone that Alec knew owning or driving a red Ferrari. I had never told Alec about Frank and I, so if he is doing business with Frank, Alec wouldn't know that this would be extremely uncomfortable for me.

I slipped around to the front door eyeing the Ferrari up as if something might give it away as being Frank's. I then slipped in through the front doors where I could clearly hear Alec talking to Frank in his Scottish accent and Frank talking to Alec in his Italian accent.

"Well this is why I would like to go over all my assets with you; I am going to have to update my will again. I had tried to get a hold of you a couple years ago. I was unable to so I had an old friend of mine write it up. Apparently you were having a stressful time, going through a divorce. I was told you had decided to go back to Italy to have a little downtime," Alec said with a bit of question in his voice.

I stood halfway near the front doors and the grand staircase where I could make an emergency dash if needed. I needed to listen and maybe get Lucia to bring Alec to me so I could tell him to please not use Frank. I could say he is a friend of my father's I didn't much like. I know Alec new Frank was a friend of my father's so I am sure he would listen.

"Yes it has been stressing, she was pregnant with my child. I am not divorced though; she left and I have never seen her since. It was my fault though. I have a terrible temper and was upset with my brother. We had a bad fight and I think it scared her. But enough of me. So you have a wife now? I would never have thought you would marry again after so long. I heard many stories about your late wife . . . This tells me your new wife must be very lovely?" Frank stated.

"Oh yes, she is most lovely, I have asked Lucia to get her so you can meet her. She was out ridding a few hours ago so she should be back any moment," Alec said, as I heard their voices and their footsteps shuffle from the great living area, in my direction.

"She must be in wonderful shape to be ridding for hours like that," Frank stated as they came my way. Half frozen from shock, I thought of the door and the staircase. Which way should I run?

"Oh, yes she is younger than I and she does a lot of physical activities fencing, kick boxing, swimming, tennis, and Taekwondo she is very lively," Alec said.

'Stairs.' I thought at this point they would see me running away through the windows if I went out the door. I started to dash to the staircase as I could hear Alec and Frank were almost approaching the entrance where I was.

"Senora, there you are. I have been looking for you. Alec needs you," Lucia said as I proceeded up the first stair. Lucia grabbed my arm and spun me around as I stepped down.

"They are right over here." She pulled me forward. My body stiffened and my mind seized up on me. I was fifteen feet away from Frank.

"Well there she is. This is my beautiful wife, Christina, the one I have been bragging about." Alec had his arm raised out ahead of himself pointing towards me. I was still frozen with shock everywhere. Frank looked shocked too, maybe he would just leave.

"This is your new wife?" Frank asked as he walked towards me.

"Yes, she is the owner of my heart," Alec announced, prideful as Frank walked up to Lucia and me.

"Mine too . . . That is very interesting Alec, because this is my wife also, although I haven't seen here in years," Frank said, getting even closer to me. Alec now had a look of question on his face.

"Christina where is our baby? Did you have a miscarriage? Did you give it away? Is my baby here? Did the government apprehend it?" Frank raised his voice and caught my arm as I turned to leave.

"No, you are not running away this time. Was it a boy or a girl? Why didn't you contact me?" Frank sounded desperate. "Why didn't you contact me? I have never given up on you. I think of you everyday, many times a day. I see you in people everywhere I go and I have to turn around, or pass them again to make sure it is not you," Frank cried, as I stood there numb. To my surprise Lucia pulled my arm from him and yanked me towards her.

"You have hid from me and you never gave me a chance. I have wanted to say I am sorry for so long and tell you how much I still love you. Please, you don't belong here, you belong with me. Can I please see my child? I have a right to see my child," Frank begged in tears.

"Christina, is any of this true?" Alec asked looking quite stunned.

"No it's not true. It never happened. None of this is true," I said and started up the stairs. Looking back I saw Lucia walk in front of Frank as he was going to come after me.

"I am going to have to ask you to leave for now, Frank. I am sorry you seem so hurt, but I need to sort some stuff out with my wife." I heard Alec say to Frank as I ran up the grand staircase.

I made it to my room and pulled the covers over me. I felt like I needed to hide or escape. I could feel the numbness subside just to let an ocean of pain reveal itself. I began to bawl like when I was a small child. I sat up now, pulled my knees to my chest, and wrapped my arms around them so I was in a half circle. I rocked myself back and forth trying to slow down my crying. Alec arrived in the bedroom within about fifteen minutes.

The Truth Shall Set You Free

"Christina, you need to be honest with me. Were you married to this man? I can't see you as having a baby. Christina, answer me now! My heart is breaking as we sit here. Either Frank is crazy or this is true. It is one of those two things," Alec clarified.

"No, I don't want to do this, it is not true!" I answered rocking back and forth.

"Look here for a moment Christina, look!" Alec raise his voice and I looked up with a tear-drenched face to see my wedding ring Frank had bought me. I was shocked already, and at this point seeing my wedding ring from Frank just made me feel sick to my stomach. "This morning Lucia found this. It was hanging out of a tear in the old backpack you came here with. This is the love you couldn't tell me about, isn't it? I just can't put together why you would be calling Holland for Frank. I have known Frank for many years and he is a good businessman, but I have never known him to go to Holland to do business.

I told you a long time ago that I would help you find that loved one you have been looking for. I just never wanted it to be someone that would take you away from me. But a promise is a promise, and I love you too much to keep you against your will." Alec put his arms around my whole body and pulled me up on his lap where he rocked me. I could feel he had tears as he put his cheek near my temple.

"You have to tell me, what happened, Christina? I won't judge you and I will always love you unconditionally. "Are you married to this man?" Alec begged to know. I found it in myself to calm down. The story was unfolding whether I wanted it to or not.

"Yes, I am married to Frank—in a way." I heard Alec gasp and a small moan came from his lips. "But I was only fifteen and it was illegal. It was under a different name. The name of a dead person! She just happened to have the same first name as me. He did it because I had to be past the age of nineteen and she was twenty-one. I don't want to be with Frank, and he is not the one I'm searching for.

We did have a baby and I left Frank's when I was about five or six months pregnant. Frank's brother was touching me in the kitchen and Frank walked in when I was trying to get away. He beat his brother terribly bad. I wasn't thinking right. I was scared so I got in the car and drove. I realized the only people I knew or where I could go was home.

When Leah and Father found out I was pregnant they were planning to give me an abortion, and they locked me in the attic. Leah had another idea and she decided that I should continue the pregnancy and she would sell the baby to Dirk and Adana Vandenhoff, as Adana was infertile. They got impatient and induced labour on me. Leah and her friend Ellen helped deliver my baby, Luke.

Dirk and Adana came to Canada and took Luke the very next day. I haemorrhaged so badly, and I was so weak I couldn't tell them anything. I just told her my baby's name was Luke, and I asked her to tell him about me one day. He would be eight years old right now and he doesn't even know I exist," I cried.

"Then Leah wanted to kill me and bury me in the basement, or drop me off in the woods in subzero temperatures, miles away from civilization where I would freeze to death and animals would eat my remains. But Leah concocted another plan to sell me to one of Father's rich customers and that is where she came up with the idea of you buying me.

"You see, I am really not anyone special; just old garbage that gets in the way. You think I am more than what I really am, but I am just someone who shouldn't have been born to begin with." I really began bawling now.

Alec held me closer, telling me that this was not close to true and that he couldn't believe that my father and Leah had gotten away with what they did.

"I have still had your father make me guns since we have been together—well at least a couple of times. I knew they were totally dysfunctional. I just didn't know how entirely dark they really are. They need to be found out."

"No!" I cried, "Not until I find Luke." I wouldn't want them to give Dirk and Adana any kind of warning. They would and it would help them look better if it seemed that it didn't happen. "I just want to get my Luke," I cried.

"Christina, you know I will help you. I love you so much and would be elated to help you raise Luke. But I don't want to over step here. Do you want to be with Frank? It doesn't sound like your father sold you to Frank so I am guessing you were a willing participant? Am I correct?" Alec asked looking down my face and into my eyes.

"Yes, I was a willing participant, but I was young and stupid. I jumped at the first man that was kind to me and happened to be interested in me in a romantic way. I did love Frank for a time. I know I did, but I don't anymore. At that time all anyone had to do was show me the smallest kindness and I would have been theirs.

I am not sure if you have the whole picture, but after my mother died I pretty much forgot what love and kindness was. Frank took me by surprise; he was more kind than I could imagine and a little forward about things. I don't think he did it on purpose. I don't think it occurred to him that I was vulnerable and quite young. So he did the decisions making for both of us. I don't think I could bare that forever. My love for him slowly faded, and even more so when I came to live with you.

You let me make decisions and you give me space. You helped to let myself come out. You never have pressured me sexually or took advantage of me in any way.

I know from Leah that you wanted to just adopt me but my father didn't want Child Services to see a red flag and take Derrick from him. I know you were pushed into taking me as a young bride. I also know that you wanted to wait until I was at least seventeen before you and I were to marry. At the same time you wanted to ensure my safety by giving Father and Leah a quarter of the payment—which I might add was a lot more than they expected in the first place." I got everything out as fast as I could. I could feel a great weight subside the more truth I told.

The Facts

"You were worth more than any money to me and I had thought you had been living on the streets. For what must have been the whole time you were with Frank and for your whole pregnancy. I didn't know what you might have had happen to you before I got you. They made it sound like you might have been into prostitution and drugs. All I knew was I needed to save you at any cost. I knew the country and the horses would help heal you. I just didn't know it was healing you from something entirely different . . . And I didn't know that you would be healing me." Alec rocked me.

"You thought I might have been a prostitute or a drug addict and it didn't bother you?" I put my head back looking up at Alec with question.

"I would have taken the chance to have your love. I'm glad you know that marriage wasn't my idea of getting you here, but I also want you to know that I love you in every way possible. I have only grown in love with you more and more over time. Now I am so in love with you. It tears me up to say that my love for you has out-grown my love for my first wife. My late wife will always have a special place in my heart, and I think for some reason she picked you for me. One day I will explain that, but right now. I want to talk about getting Luke back for you. Then we can share a son together. So let's talk about that," Alec requested as he turned me towards him so that we were facing each other. I nodded and waited for him to speak.

"First off, Frank has no legal binding marriage to you. In fact, he could be in some pretty deep water trying to explain that to a judge. I don't think he would want to do that. He had no parental consent and he used a dead person's birth certificate. His rights to see Luke on the other had are a tricky thing. If he did want to see his son so badly, he might take the criminal charges of the illegal marriage and still try to get partial custody, or some kind of visitation. I think the judge would look at the whole picture and see him as being more of a hurdle than a benefit to the child, or the relationship with you and Luke. Either way there would be heavy stipulations that would apply, or the courts would just not see it beneficial." Alec's face showed he was methodically thinking the circumstances out.

However, your father and Leah would be looking at some serious jail time. This could affect me as well. They wouldn't just give me permission to marry you, they wanted money. This looks like what I didn't want it to be, but what it is. I bought you for marriage, which translates to a judge that I bought you for sex," Alec explained while I interrupted.

"But we have never even had sex. I would tell them that and they would have to believe me. Can we just not tell them about the money part?"

Alec interrupted. "They would still say that Christina. Although I paid them on two different occasions they might trace that back to one of my accounts . . . hum . . . Wait, I took the money from the safe. This means it would be untraceable. Even if Leah or your father said I gave them money in a cash form, they would have no trace to it. It would look like a marriage with parental consent," Alec sighed with relief.

"I remember when they took Luke. Adana said to do a bank draft or transfer the funds. Would that trace the money to them?" I asked Alec.

"Yes, and now that you say Adana and Dirk. I know why that last name you kept looking up seemed so familiar. I just didn't put it together until you told me this today. I remember an Adana and Dirk from a couple hunting trips I was on that your father guided. One time Adana came and another time Dirk came by himself as he and Adana where having problems. He got really drunk and told a bunch of us around the fire about an illegal adoption that fell through. The young girl that was pregnant had a stillborn child.

Okay, this is really coming together. I just never associated them with their last name. I think I only heard their last name a few times. Now they could be in some terrible trouble too, with a country-to-country illegal adoption. Do you know the date, the time, and the weight that Luke was when he was born?" Alec asked while in deep thought.

"I never forgot it." I answered. "You are a poor Dear. We are going to try to rectify this if it takes my last dying breath, I promise you Christina. I didn't know things were this bad for you." Alec looked very sympathetic, almost like he could feel my pain.

"I trust you Alec, but how are we going to do this? When I can't even find the city they live in to obtain their phone number?" I asked

"Christina I have some really good connections. I have never thought a time would come that I would talk about or need to secure them again. I can see that now the time has come.

Caribbean Murder

When I was in the Caribbean, with my late wife on a holiday, she had gone for a quick stroll at dusk. She never came back, and after a few hours I went out looking in the direction she went. I couldn't find her and she didn't respond to my calls, so I got a hold of the authorities. They had a few officers come by and comb in and around the beach.

They found nothing until the next morning. A person driving down a road directly above the beach found my late wife's bloody and beaten body on the side of the road. She was near some tire tracks. There were a bunch of different items found around the body and it didn't look like the authorities wanted to investigate thoroughly. It was a busy time of the year and I don't think they wanted to scare away the tourists.

A few evenings later I called Manuela from my hotel room. She was practically best friends with my late wife," Alec swallowed hard. I could tell this was hard for him. I could tell he felt he needed to share his pain with me.

"I got on the phone with Manuela and I told her she had been killed, and it didn't look like I was going to come home with even a suspect, as the authorities didn't seem to take an active interest in investigating. Manuela was so broken and infuriated that she decided to tell me of a family secret. Manuela had a cousin that worked in Spain as a secret agent. He worked in a subcontracting kind of fashion. Manuela did warn me that he was dangerous, but effective. Actually his entire family disowned him. He was known to have quite a short fuse, which might be good for his business, but very much scared his relatives. He was the best at what he did apparently, and that was what mattered to me at that moment.

I flew him out the next day and set him up in my same hotel. The next morning he was down to work for me. He had linked so much information together by that evening that I was very impressed. I went to the authorities there again the next day with all the new evidence. They were acting strange and wouldn't even lift their heads to listen to me. They just blew me off. The agent (who I will not name) told me to go back with the body and lay my wife to rest. He assured me he would update me every night as he learned more.

I flew back to Palm Springs. That was where we were living at the time. We had my late wife's funeral within days. Every night came in reports from Manuela's cousin that connected three rich American boys. Manuela's cousin followed them closely, and as it turned out they had been staying in our same hotel.

I could recall them eyeing up my wife in the lobby one night and at the pool on several occasions. I phoned the authorities and brought all of this information and the things I could recall to their attention. We had a lot of evidence; the tire tracks matched the vehicle they were driving, and the agent found strands of her long, blond hair matted with blood inside their car. Sill, the authorities snapped back that I hadn't any evidence. It was driving me mad, all that we had was evidence I yelled at Manuela's cousin. In anger and I told Manuela's cousin that if they didn't do something soon I was going to come down there myself and kill all three of those college boys.

I got a call back about three days later. It was from Spain and it was Manuela's cousin. He told me that his job was done and gave me an estimate of how much I owed him. He told me he had killed the three boys in their father's speed boat one evening while they were drunk out on the water. He overheard them discuss going out for a ride at the hotel. He got out to their boat and hid inside. After they were far enough out, he came up from the cabin and punched one in the head and knocked him overboard. He said the boy's leg hooked some rope and he hung head first in the water and drowned. He then hid above board and waited.

The other two boys went down into the cabin to find what all the commotion was about. They came up from the boat's cabin with broken bottles in case they had to defend themselves. The agent pushed the one boy's elbow up so that his broken bottle cut the others throats and they both fell down the stairs, back into the cabin of the boat. The live boy was trying to get out from under the boy with the slashed throat. The agent grabbed the dead boys hand making it again grasp the broken bottle, and he pushed his hand with the bottle deep in the others one's abdomen. He would have been alive for a while. Once the boat was found, the incident was looked at like a drunken fight between the three of them had turned fatal.

It wasn't what I had expected. I did not expect Manuela's cousin to take what I said as a cue to murder them. I was merely talking out of frustration. After the three boys had died it came out that they were troublemakers and hung onto the skirt tails of their rich parents for protection when they were in trouble. Five other girls came forward saying they were gang raped by the threesome. It might be a bad thing to say, but I am not sorry they are not here on this earth right now. I think the world is a little better off without them," Alec inhaled deep.

"Wow, I am sorry you went through all that. I mean, if it wasn't for Manuela's weird cousin there is a good chance you might never have seen justice," I sighed.

Our Plan

I don't aspire to use him for finding a child; he is old and pretty much retired now. I have used one of his sons who is a lot more mild and level headed. Actually, he has two sons and both of them followed into the family business. The youngest one, Rafael, is way out of hand and does a lot of his work for the mob. The oldest one, Sebastian, is good, he does his homework (well crosses his T's and dots his I's). He's good at getting facts together, and he is good at spying and being inconspicuous. He gathers information and facts, and best of all he does not believe in killing anyone unless it is in self-defence. Anyone who hires him is well aware of this. Yet he still has as much business as his younger brother." Alec looked in a deep thinking process.

"Christina, he could find Luke without anyone even knowing Luke was being looked for. Then we could figure out the best way to get him back. One rule though, I don't want your hands on or involved just yet. I will relay information to the agent, and until we get moving on it, you can then get more involved." Alec tapped a pencil on his knee.

We will just have to deal with Frank as we go. I want you to be with me on this part with Frank, Christina." Alec looked at me close to get my attention.

"Of course I will," I answered. I was feeling such hope again. I was almost glad Frank came by, as hard as it was to be open. I was feeling relieved that Alec knew now. It brought with it a fresh feeling of hope.

"We might need to have a sit down meeting with Frank. Just to let him know where he is sitting as far as the law goes." We must not tell him about any money exchange between your father and I. He can't have anything that can be used against us. Don't be afraid to speak your feelings about how you felt and how you feel about Frank. You are better to be on good terms with him . . . but he needs to know that if he cares for his son he will let him go, as it will be much too confusing for the boy if Frank still harbours romantic feelings for you.

I hope that you feel comfortable with it, and that his feelings change after he sees us together. If you are good with this I will get a hold of Sebastian tonight and plan a meeting with him so we can get started.

We have a large web to untangle. Are you ready for this Christina? Do you want this?" Alec rose from the bed still holding one of my hands.

"Yes, I know I am." I stood up and wrapped both my arms around Alec and gave him an affectionate kiss. We looked into each other's eyes for a few moments when Alec said he was going to his Lab where he could concentrate on the work at hand.

I washed my face in the bathroom and cleaned up a bit. I went into the walk in closet to find something nice to wear for dinner. I had told Lucia to make something special and that this was a good day for us. I noticed a section in my closet that kept filling up with clothes, mostly dresses and some jackets and lots of shoes. They were all very beautiful, but I had no idea where they were coming from.

Stranger than that, they all fit so perfect; nothing needed to be tailored in any way. Maybe Manuela had gotten them made or maybe she sews. But the shoes, they would have to have been ordered because my feet were so small. These were all of exquisite quality some from Italy. I have to not forget to ask Alec if he knows where these clothes keep coming from. There are so many now.

I found the perfect mauve dress that came just above my knees, I also found the exact mauve coloured matching shoes. They were wooden except for the mauve leather straps that went back and forth from the open toe to where they tied up behind the heel.

I did my make-up and my hair up to the tens. I looked at the time and it was 5:30 PM so I decided Alec would be waiting for me in the kitchen by now. I clicked down the grand staircase in my beautiful perfect fitting shoes that must have come from heaven. They felt so good, as did the dress. I went through the kitchen and saw the food was prepared and decided everyone must be in the dining room waiting for me. I opened the door to the dining room to see Lucia setting the table

"Senora, oh you look so beautiful. I don't think I have seen you look that beautiful. Look at that hair, some of it up some, of it down. I love the way you did your make-up. Alec will be very please," Lucia laughed.

"I am hoping so. Where is Alec? He usually likes to eat by five," I asked curiously.

"Oh, Senora I see he is busy talking to someone in a big black car so I turned the oven down a touch so Senor's dinner won't be cold," Lucia said, while putting out a basket of dinner rolls.

"We'll I am going to go get him or it is going to be cold." I turned and walked out of the dining room through the kitchen and to the front door.

Time Trap

I could hear Alec's voice as I was opening the door. I stepped out of the heavy door and it slammed shut behind me. It got quiet for a moment so I looked at Alec and told him that dinner would be getting cold. Alec told me that I look very beautiful, and then he looked down at the person sitting in the black car. I couldn't believe it. It was Frank again.

"I am not leaving, Christina, until you come home with me!" Frank yelped.

"What?" I said. "Frank I am not going anywhere. This is my home. You need to go. Don't make this so hard, just go," I pleaded.

"Maybe this is the time we need to sit down and have that talk Christina," Alec said with his comforting, Scottish accent. I could feel my celebration mood start to fade.

"Frank, were going to go into the house and find a spot where we can sit down and talk for a few moments. Then we can all be clear on some things. I'm sure you want some questions answered. I think it's important for you to know that Christina is here on her own free will, and maybe this will help you." Alec said firmly to Frank.

Frank responded, "Let's go!" and he got out of his black sports car. We proceeded through the doors.

"What about the dinner? Lucia made a special dinner for us, and she worked very hard." I added.

"I'm sure she will understand, and we can warm it up just as easy and it will still be special." Alec led us through the main living room down a hall through an office. Then he lead us into a smaller room behind the office that had a couple couches and a projector board. Alec directed Frank where to sit and we sat on the couch directly across from him.

"Can I see my child, Christina? Franks started out.

"I wish I could see our child. He is not with me as much as I wish he were. "I answered.

Frank moved to the edge of the seat. "You mean that we had a son? Why didn't you call me? Why haven't you let me see him all these years? What is his name?" Frank fired out so many questions.

"Frank, when I left you I went back home. I didn't know what else to do. I was really scared. I thought you may have killed Carlos. Leah and my father were going to give me an abortion. Then they decided not to and that they would sell the baby to a rich couple they knew and make some money from him. They made me go into labour in the attic where I delivered Luke." I could see Frank's eyes fire red, and he was bouncing his knee up and down.

"There is no way. I went by your Father's all the time looking for you. I still do. I didn't see you. I didn't hear you," Frank raised his voice.

"I know you did. I heard you the next day. You made an excuse up that your sister was missing and you were very upset. I heard you through the attic vent." Frank leaned back a bit more in his seat as I told of this.

"I sensed you might be there. I even went up to the attic door. I was going to open it, but Leah stopped me." I interrupted Frank. "Leah asked you what you were doing. I know you came around quite a bit, Frank, and there were times my heart ached for you and I wanted you to come rescue me."

Frank interrupted me. "Raymond, that asshole! And Leah, that filthy whore! They were going to kill my baby, and they sold him and kept money for him. I will make their lives miserable. I will make sure he has no customers. Christina, why didn't you come get me after? How did you get away?" Frank asked as he was tapping his leg really hard, and his eyes were red with fury.

Alec and I never discussed this part and I wasn't prepared to answer it.

"I came by the house on a day that Raymond and Leah had gone shopping, and I saw Christina through the window. I was told that she had been a runaway for sometime so I went to the side door of the house to see if I could talk to her. As you know, the side door has a latch on the outside. I unlatched it and she opened the door. I told her what I suspected, which was that her father and Leah were abusing her. I told her she could come with me. I later went down and told Raymond all I knew, including the baby. I told him I wanted to keep Christina with me. He didn't want to at first, but then later said he didn't want anything else to do with her so he wanted to give parental permission for me to marry her," Alec explained.

"So she is with you because of that? Well she married me willingly, because she was in love. And Christina, I still love you and I know you love me too. I want you and our baby back, and I won't stop until I get it." Frank pounded his fist on his knee.

"Frank stop! Understand that was the past—you and me. I was young and didn't have any love around, and you were good to me. I had nothing to compare it with. I did love you and I really want Luke back, but I don't love you anymore. I love Alec; he is truly my husband and legally my husband. You and I were never legally married and we both know it. I am sorry Frank, but I only have an interest in getting Luke back. I need you to not bother me so I can do that."

Frank interrupted me again. "You are telling me you are happy with this, must be seventy year old man? You want me to believe that you don't love me anymore? Why would you name the baby Luke; the name we picked out? How were you able to name the baby? I thought you said he was adopted? Who adopted him? I will go get him back myself, right now. I have every right as his father. That is my only child!" Frank screamed with emotion. He was angry and sad—I could see it in his eyes, his face, and the veins in his neck that bulged when he screamed.

"Frank, I don't know who adopted him. I don't know if they named the baby Luke. It was my request. I like the name Luke, and at the time I was still in love with you. I had a dream about it after I gave birth, and I just always see him as Luke in my mind. I do love Alec and I don't care about the age difference; you and I have a big age difference also. You must be coming up to fifty. I know the baby was born on your birthday, November the 8th right?" I thought telling him might make him calm down.

"He was he was born on my birthday? Tell me, what did he look like, Christina? How much did he weigh?" Frank cried. "He looked a lot like you, and like me a lot too. He had your eyes, really long lashes, dark brown hair, the most perfect little features, and an iron grip. He was born at 7:00 PM and he weighed seven pounds and seven ounces. He was beautiful.

Frank, you need to come to terms that I was way underage with you, and if you even tried to interfere you could get in some trouble. If the authorities knew about the death certificate you used to get us married, and the fact that I was fifteen when I had Luke." I felt myself start to get irritated as I continued. "Frank, you don't want that on your plate right now. Just let me get my son on my own. If you love me you will do that for me," I begged Frank.

"I do love you Christina, and I don't know if this is all real (you and Alec here), but I will be waiting for you to come back to me, and I know you will. You have grown into a beautiful young woman, and in my heart we are still married. I don't care about a certificate. I will try to do my best in honouring your request but it will be hard. I can hardly look at you; my heart still hasn't quit pounding and I feel like I am dreaming all of this."

Frank swallowed hard as he continued in his Italian accent with his many had gestures. "I won't interfere with you finding our son; our son Luke. I do want to know him and I want him to know I am his father. He would be eight now; I don't care if he is eighteen when you find him, he is mine too. That is all I can promise at this time, but please search your heart Christina, and remember the love we once had, and that I still have for you."

Frank stared straight at me. His voice was beginning to sound rough. I had my arm around Alec's arm and was probably pulling it really tight, feeling like I had to cover myself with him. I just wanted to hide from Frank. It was too much at one time. Having to have this conversation with him just added to my stress.

"Well I'm proposing we leave this meeting here for tonight and in the future Frank, if you could call before coming? I will be having my other financial partner help me with my business and personal endeavours. We will keep you updated to any changes about Luke. I think Christina has had quite an eventful day. I'm sure we all have," Alec said, as Frank got up.

We followed him to the front doors. I could smell the old Frank I remembered; the smell of leather and his yummy cologne. He was as attractive as ever, and I could feel I still had that animal attraction to him, but I knew I never wanted to act on that again. Alec was more than the man I wanted and twice the man I deserved.

"Christina, remember what I have said to you. I am true to you forever and that is how long my love lasts," Frank said abruptly as Alec was about to say goodbye.

"Goodbye Frank," I said and then I let go of Alec's arm and walked a way down the hall. I waited for Alec as he saw Frank out and locked the door.

Chapter 10

Alec hired three new guards to be sure that Frank couldn't find a way onto the property. He had one of the guards placed at the front gate as he couldn't figure out how Frank got in the second time that day. He had two guards tend the front doors and occasionally look over the grounds.

Alec had his new financial advisor go over all of the assets and finances with me. Alec told me that I was at an age now where he wanted me to understand how to run our home and do the payroll for all the employees. He ran it all by me and told me that every couple weeks he was going to make me do all the transactions that had to do with keeping our home and property going.

Alec had Sebastian meet with him at his lab where he went over all that was known about Luke and the Vandenhoffs. Alec got Sebastian a hotel in the town closest to where Father and Leah lived. He was going to somehow befriend my father and then break into his shop to see if he could get a list of his customers and their addresses.

Sebastian had been working at it for months, but Frank was causing trouble for my father and Leah and they were losing customers. Sebastian reported that Father and Leah were looking at moving to the Yukon to restart their business with what customers remained. Sebastian also reported that the way Father and Leah were getting along it didn't look like Leah would be making that move with him. He had seen Leah fooling around with a local customer when she had told Father she was going to be doing something with Ellen.

Frank had shown up drunk at Father's shop one evening and threw a bolder through his window. Father had the window replaced, and soon after Frank came by and broke it again.

Sebastian, who tapped the phone lines, heard Father talking on the phone to his weird mother. He told her he was out of ideas as what to do and was afraid to call the police on Frank, as he would spill all that they had done. He was smart enough to mention that he didn't think Frank would want the police involved as he could be arrested on so many levels. I know Father and Leah never knew about Frank and I getting married, so he must have had a few things in mind Frank could be charged with.

When the Time is Right

I was in the bathtub soaking while Alec was washing my back, telling me of what Sebastian had planned for scooping information from Father.

"Your father and Leah are going to Vancouver this weekend to pick up your father's brother, Chris. I guess he is going to be staying with your father for a while. Apparently he needs somewhere to stay and a little work. Your father said he would feel safer with two men in the house at his time. Frank sure is making Leah and your father pay already. He really could make him lose his whole business. The bad news is that Sebastian heard your father call Dirk and warn him, but he was unable to trace any number." Alec rinsed the soap off my back.

"That is great, like we don't have enough to contest with! Frank just infuriates me right now. Doesn't he know the kind of things that could happen? He has never been the best at emotional thinking and prediction; being a financial advisor, he can tell you when you are going in the whole by the penny. That's when it comes to math. He just never sees the outcome of his emotional tirades!" I half yelled and abruptly rose from the tub. Alec snatched a towel off the tub side shelf for me.

"Well we expected that with Frank there would be some fall out. What's done is done, and there is nowhere on the face of this earth I won't look for Luke." Alec pulled me towards him and held me for a moment.

Bitter Success

It had been a year since we had hired Sebastian and progress had been made, but it had not been as fast as what I had liked but it was much more than I could do in seven years. Sebastian had found the address of Dirk and Adana Vandenhoff. Alec flew Sebastian to Amsterdam, which is North Holland. When Sebastian arrived he found the address my father had down for Dirk and Adana, but the house was abandoned. He traced down information on the house and found that they still owned the home. Sebastian found a mail forward address to a Dr. Everhart Vandenhoff. He went to the address of Dr. Everhart Vandenhoff and found that he was a married man with teenage children.

Sebastian told Alec that he followed the doctor around for a while and bugged his phones. He then went through files in his clinic, and in the files he found a Dirk, Adana, and a Luke Vandenhoff. This was the best news that we had heard. It seemed too coincidental that these couldn't be the same people. If they were, I was happy to know that Adana named my baby Luke like I had asked her to. I just knew he was Luke in my heart so it had to be true.

Six weeks later we received a package in the mail from Amsterdam. Inside the package were some copies of medical files. The first file indicated that Dr. Everhart Vandenhoff had examined an Adana Vandenhoff the morning of November 10th, 1984, and that she had given birth the evening before to a seven pound, seven ounce baby boy. It said Dirk Vandenhoff was the father. The file read that Mrs. Adana Vandenhoff did not know she was pregnant, and she had no prenatal care. Despite that fact the baby was healthy, other than some mild jaundice. He was treated for it at Sint Lucas Andreas Ziekenhuis. My heart was pounding out of my chest hearing all this information; my head was just spinning with happiness that Luke was healthy, but angry that Adana was taking credit for birthing my child. How could they be this devious ?

I remembered how they were when they had been at our shop. They were signing up for a guided hunting trip on a few different occasions. They would always be bragging about things they had done, that they had, and how incredible they were. If it weren't for my baby they wouldn't even be together, I thought.

The last page was a photocopy of Luke's little birth certificate. I read it thoroughly and my eyes pierced at the names on it that didn't belong and a date that read November 9th, 1984.

"This is all wrong," I cried. "How can this be changed now? They have legalized this. I haven't got a chance when they have a doctor saying he examined her and she had given birth the night before. They ruined Luke's whole beginning; it is all one big, fat lie. He wasn't even born on the 9th, he was born on the 8th. People are going to believe them . . . How will I prove myself to a child who is almost ten, or when he is a teenager?" I cried and yelled as I paced back and forth throwing things about. Alec grabbed me up around my arms, holding the papers in one hand and then he fell to the couch with me.

"Christina, you have got to calm yourself. If you can't deal with this Christina I won't update you with all the information. I will only tell you the good stuff. Is that how you want it? I don't think you do. You need to pull yourself together! I need you to be together with me on this. I know where your heart is and the birth certificate doesn't mean anything. They had to do something to get one. You can't register a child for school, travel, or get a family doctor if you don't have a birth certificate.

Remember, we will have a money trace and that will be able to see their travel activity. Why would they have been traveling during the time she was giving birth? It would raise quite a commotion I'm sure, a forty-year-old woman giving birth on a plane? Now try to keep your thoughts together. I know this is hard for you, but this was never about being easy. We have to work through the hard stuff to get to the good." Alec started to release me when he felt my muscles become less tense.

"Okay, I'm sorry. You're right though, this is hard, much harder than I had anticipated. I'm glad to hear news. I've just missed out on so much. I'm at the point Alec, where I don't want to take him and uproot him if he is truly happy, but I don't feel he is. I don't know what it is about this but I don't think he fits into their too perfect, little world. If I'm wrong I would be happy just to meet him and let him know that I'm here. He's almost ten, and I don't know how long it will take before I will be with him again," I sobbed.

"Just wait, there's one more piece of paper here. It looks like a letter from Sebastian. It's just saying that Doctor Everhart Vandenhoff is Dirk's younger brother. Sebastian believes that the any further medical record in his clinic for his brother's family had to have been destroyed. He says the clinic's computer had Dirk's business down as Vandenhoff Enterprises. It's basically a bunch of oversea sweatshops where he has the poorest people (including children) manufacture products for a few cents per day. Then he moves the products to richer countries like the USA and sells them at a huge markup. He has several of these warehouses and he makes millions. Sebastian is going to look into his business and search hospital records. Then he will report back to us.

The One for Me

I saw my mother; she was wearing the dress at the funeral parlour, the one she wore to church on occasion. We were in Sunday school and she was telling the story of Daniel in the lion's den with all the little felt figurines on a board in front of the class. Her hair was straight and brown, and her nails and lipstick were mauve. I felt a sense of pride as she told the story. Suddenly, I lifted out of the room towards outer space. My mother didn't notice, she just kept teaching the class. I lifted up higher and higher. Then I pulled away from the class. They were so tiny and far away until they disappeared. Abruptly, I started to fall. The wind was at my face and I couldn't breathe. I just kept falling and falling and falling. I could see the earth and I was coming towards it fast. It was getting bigger. Now I could see roads and buildings. I shot through a roof without getting hurt and I started to slow down as I went through the first floor, then the second floor, then the last floor. I hovered above for a second, looking at my Father and Leah argue, and my siblings. Then I just dropped on my mother's casket. I felt the coldness again, the hardness of her body, the smell of formaldehyde, and perm solution. I gasped and shot up.

I awoke one morning at 5:00 AM my heart pounding. I felt like I needed to get down to the pool and swim the nightmare away. I left Alec sleeping to sneak down to the pool. I figured if I had a two-hour Taekwondo class at 10 AM I would be ready and prepped after a good swim. I planned to have a nice, two hour ride on Safire after my class, it always made me feel more level-headed when there was more activity in my day.

As I snuck out of bed pulling my arm out from under Alec I paused and looked at him sleeping. A deep sense of love seemed to pass through me as I watched him lay there peacefully. I thought about how accustomed I was to Alec. I think I have almost grown so accustom to Alec's unconditional love that I almost take him for granted. I know I try to remind myself all the time of where I came from and how much Alec has done for me. I don't think I will ever know exactly why he felt warmness towards me in the first place. I can only thank God that he did.

I don't know if or where I would be today if it weren't for Alec. He was everything to me now. His voice rang in my head as if it had been around my whole life. I moved towards him and kissed him gently on his forehead. Then I moved ever so slowly from the bed trying not to rouse him.

I don't know how many laps I did in the pool before I hoped into the hot tub and then into the steam room. In the steam room I searched my mind to make contact to the part that numbed and dulled events. I found most of my pain, guilt and regrets there. Thinking deep as I breathed in the hot eucalyptus scented air, I made a decision. I was not going to beat myself over the head at having to have Luke right this moment. As hard as it was I fought with myself trying to rationalize that Luke was a ten-year-old boy, and that Dirk and Adana must have some kind of love for him. I thought about the lengths they went through to have him.

I also didn't want to stress Alec out with my hurt. I know how bad he wanted everything for me, everything that I felt I needed and more. Alec would do or pay whatever it took to make me happy. Being happy just had to be with the knowledge that Luke was okay. I got up and opened the steam room door and looked at the time. It was 7 AM I should shower and go down stairs for breakfast before my 10 AM Taekwondo class.

The Closet

I felt invigorated after my Taekwondo class with Sven. He told me that he had never trained anyone with such determination and perseverance in his whole career. With our motivational talk I ran to my room to get dressed for my ride. As I entered my room I felt a chill go down my spine. My walk-in-closet light was on and I know I hadn't gone in there this morning. I am also quite sure that Alec doesn't go in my closet. I crept across my bedroom until I was dead in front of my closet then I peeked my head in.

There were more shoes, and all the racks looked dishevelled. I walked in to take a closer look, and I had about a third more clothes than I did the last time I looked. Most of the new items were packaged in zipped up bags. I opened a bunch and found pant suites, shirts, and a collection of jackets. I read the tag on one that said it was lamb leather made in Italy. Where was this all coming from? I think it was time for me go to Alec and address the problem.

I got dressed into my ridding gear and walked out of my room to find Manuela. I knew she was coming today at some point. We were her family here, and she would come over every couple of weeks and tinker around cleaning stuff. Then she would stay for lunch, dinner, and visit with Lucia and us.

"Senora, you riding this morning without any lunch?" Manuela asked.

"I was going to grab a sandwich and eat it on the walk over. Lucia was just bringing Alec's lunch to his lab, so you and Lucia can enjoy lunch together. Manuela, did you put some items of clothing in my closet?" Manuela paused and looked like she was thinking. "Manuela, were you in my closet?" I asked.

"Si, si senora, I was just going through it to organize it." She looked worried as she replied. I could see she had that large key around her neck that led to the attic. I didn't feel like I wanted to waste anymore time that I could be ridding, so I figured I wouldn't push her at right this moment. It was harder to talk to Manuela than Lucia as Manuela was right from Spain, and Lucia learned English and Spanish at the same time she learned to talk.

"Well I don't know why new things keep appearing in my closet all the time. It is getting weird, especially that everything seems to fit me. Anyhow, I will talk about this to you later; I want to get riding while the day is still young." I eyed Manuela as I walked away from her down the hallway.

"Adios Senora, you have nice ride." Manuela waved as I left.

I walked out the front doors to see the guards seated at a wooden lawn table eating their lunch. They immediately stopped talking and greeted me, asking where I would be. I was beginning to get irritated by guards always following me. They can't be that great if they see that I'm dressed to go riding and they still don't know where I'm going.

"I'm going for a walk on the grounds while, I eat my lunch," I smiled, thinking to myself; 'what a waste of money.' They smiled while they continued to eat their lunch.

I walked my scenic route through the golf course, the gardens, and through the hedge-lined trail.

Before I knew it I was flying through some bare, rolling hills just before the trails on my Safire. I took the path that led to the stream and hopped off Safire for a while, spreading a blanket on the ground. I loved to lay and watch what God does in places we don't always dwell.

There were so many different birds. I always tried to memorize what they looked like so I could get the bird book out and look them up when I got home. Again for the fourth time, I saw a deer and doe together eating amongst the woods. They must live around this area. I thought they have to be the same ones. Squirrels and chipmunks were abundant around the stream. I imagine the trees and the plants are healthier closer to the water.

I realized I had lost track of time. I looked down at my watch that was clipped to my pants and saw that almost two hours had passed. I still had a half hour ride back to the stable. I gathered up my things including the camera I brought to take pictures and headed back.

After taking off all of Safire's tack and giving her a brush down I was pretty achy. I decided I would take a bath right here at the stable. I had a drawer with some clothes in it and I could come back dry and clean, ready to spend the rest of my evening with Alec. I couldn't wait to see him and tell him I saw the deer and the doe again.

I filled the bathtub full, adding some bath salts and lavender oil. I might have over done it today with all the activity. I was up pretty early doing laps. I think I had done more laps in the pool this morning than I ever had.

The tub was like the tub we had at my father's. It was the old fashioned type with clawed paws at the end of the legs. The thing I liked about it most was that it was very deep and you could really have a good soak. I unbraided my hair and slipped into the tub. I made sure to carefully to hang my hair back over the tub behind me so it wouldn't get wet. I always did my hair last in the tub, with the shower nozzle.

I realized I didn't lock the washroom door, but I felt secure as I knew Russell the grounds-man and stable keeper was away for a couple days. Soaking in the tub was definitely relieving my sore achy muscles, but I knew I had to keep it short as I was a little late and Alec might worry. 'A few more minutes', I thought to myself, inhaling the relaxing vapours deeply as I closed my eyes. I could hear the horse neighing and every once in a while one would kick or bang the wall of their stall.

Conflict in the Stable

I knew I had spent too much time in the tub when I heard a door to the barn open. I'm pretty sure Alec sent one of the guards out to check on me and send me back to the mansion. I yelled out, as I didn't want some guard walking in on me in the tub.

"I'm in here, but please don't come in—I'm just going to finish washing my hair, so you can tell Alec I will be back at the house in twenty or thirty minutes," I yelled, waiting for a response. I heard doors opening and shutting. I hope the guard doesn't come in here, can't he hear me

"I'm in the washroom bathing. I will be out in a bit, just tell Alec I'll be back at the house in twenty or thirty minutes," I yelled again, louder. I heard the door creak open and in slipped Frank.

"What in the hell are you doing in here Frank? Someone will be here any moment and they aren't going to be gentle if they see you here." I crossed my arms over my chest to try and cover up.

"That is a chance that I am more than willing to take. There is now way Alec can keep me away from this property with a few security guards. His property is huge, and he would have to have thousands of guards to watch every area into here. I came here to talk some sense into you, My Love."

Frank grabbed a towel and pulled my arm upward so I had no choice but to exit the bath, even if I didn't want him to see me undressed. He wrapped the towel around me and forced me into his arms. Again, I could smell the Frank I remembered from so long ago. He used the same cologne and that smell of leather. He pulled me tighter into himself. "Christina, you need to come back. I need you, and I have been waiting for you for years. We have a son together and we were going to have more children. Our life together was planned. I am sorry I was not with you all the years that Alec has been. If I would have known how to find you I would have been the one to comfort you. We both know the marriage had to be illegal, but our words are still binding."

Frank had a mesmerizing way of talking, and when he was holding me so close and looking deep into my eyes it was impossible not to have some of those old feelings sneak up on me. He was very handsome, strong, and direct. "We have a wonderful, long life together Christina. And you are mine forever!" Frank pulled my face towards his and we began kissing very passionately. I could feel his happiness, and I could feel myself getting lost in him.

We smashed up against the wall and I could feel this animal instinct coming out of me. I wasn't sure I could contain it. Frank was the only man I had ever been with in my life. His hands were all over me and it was hard for me to find the strength to stop. It had been such a long time since I had been intimate, and Frank was not only familiar but also hopelessly attractive.

"You see, you still love me. You and Alec are not right. He can't take what is mine; you know you belong to me." Frank pressed himself against me, pinning me against the wall.

That was all I needed to break the temporary spell he had over me. He could have just said Alec's name and it would be over.

"Stop, Frank, you're wrong! My heart belongs to Alec and his to me. I admit I am attracted to you and I have a love for you, but not the love you are looking for. I love you because I think you had good intentions for me to a degree, and you are the father of my child. I don't want to be with you Frank, that was the past." I squirmed loose from Frank's arms and shoved him hard away from me.

"What do you mean the past? You can't start something that is real and not finish it Christina. I am real and your life with me is real. Our home, my family, and our friend's that is real. What about Crystal? You just shut her out? She was the best friend you ever had, you told me. You can't just throw people away Christina. You can't throw me away," Frank yelled.

"Our life was put together with lies, Frank. I'm not saying there wasn't love, and I'm not throwing you away. Too much time has passes and life has turned the page, were not even in the same book anymore. You need to close this book and stop reading it over and over. The ending is always going to be the same, and I still won't be in it." I explained.

Frank lunged at me holding me so hard I could barely breathe. "I won't, and you need to deal with us. That is what needs to be done; you have to come with me now. Then you will see." Frank responded.

I squirmed free again and shoved him hard. He went toppling backward losing his balance and started to lunge towards me again.

Holding my towel with one hand I stepped forward and spun around air kicking Frank in the chest. Frank went flying backward into a shelf when Alec and two guards came busting in the door. The guards pulled Frank away from the shelf and pushed him face first against the wall. Alec practically leaped across the room and pulled me into him.

"Don't hurt him, he just needs some help," I yelled. The guards wrestled with Frank until they got some handcuffs on him.

"I want my wife and my son. You can't keep her here," Frank demanded.

"Take him to your car and drive him to where his vehicle is. Then follow him until he is far away," Alec instructed the guards. The guards left the stable with Frank babbling and yelling.

Alec let go of me and opened a drawer that had some of my clothes. He pulled a complete outfit.

"I am tripling the guards, and you won't be riding alone, or walking, or anything. That man is out of control, and I'm not taking any chances. Who knows what he would have done had we not got there when we did. I knew something was up when I asked Manuela what time you went for your ride. How long did he have you here? Did he do anything to you?" Alec shook out my jeans for me so I could get into them.

"Not long, and I really don't feel like talking about it." I pulled my t-shirt over my head and reached for a pair of runners.

"He didn't have his hands on you, did he? You would tell me if anything bad happened, wouldn't you? You're not dressed and you have red marks on your arms and chest. I think we should get a doctor to check you," Alec suggested.

"No, I'm fine. I'm just a little shaken up and hurt from some of the things he was saying. If you guys hadn't of walked in when you did I would have been out any second anyhow. I just want to get back to the house." I opened the washroom door and walked briskly ahead of Alec.

Over the next month I thought about some of the things that Frank said and came to the conclusion that he was just pinning guilt on me to get what he wanted. I did think about Crystal though, and I realized just how much I had been missing our friendship. There had been many a time when I had wanted to call her, but I knew I couldn't as it might alert Frank to where I was. Now it is different though; Frank knew everything and there was nothing I could do to change that.

Friends

I lay on a lounge chair by the outside pool when Alec pulled a lawn chair up beside me. "Christina, I have noticed since that day with Frank that you have been acting strange, and I can't say this hasn't been troubling me. Can you please tell me what is on your mind? I won't judge! You know I only want you to be happy again," Alec looked very concerned.

"I am happy, Alec. I am happy with you and happy with my life now. It's just some things Frank said that have been bothering me. Well, one thing in particular." I took a deep breath and went on. "I know I had a kind of life with Frank and I'm not telling you I miss it. I'm just trying to tell you I miss someone from that life and I wish she could still be part of my life." I sat up right and faced Alec now.

"Well who is she?" Alec asked with a smile on his face. "A friend of mine, I met her in Vancouver and we really hit it off. But after that I was locked up at Father's and then consumed by Luke. Also I didn't know if Frank would somehow find out I was in contact with her, so this was a road block. I know now it really wouldn't matter, he knows where I am. Alec, I really miss having a girl for a friend. You know, that someone I could talk to and do girl things with. Crystal was the best friend I ever had. Right from the beginning I felt like I had known her my whole life." I looked at Alec.

"Well I see the dilemma, but honestly I don't see that being a problem. Contact this Crystal friend of yours and plan a visit. I think it would be good for you to have a friend other than just me. I'm not so good at watching chick flicks, and nail polish, just doesn't do anything for me." Alec laughed.

"Really, I have a piece of paper I kept in my old back-pack with her home number. I wonder if it changed or if she moved," I gasped happily.

"Well I am pretty good at finding people," Alec joked. "I am just so pleased to see you looking happy again. So let's find this Crystal and plan a get together." Alec lit up.

Lying on my bed with my phone, I dialed the number Crystal had written on a piece of paper so many years ago. I had no way of knowing if she had changed numbers, moved, or if she would even remember me after the amount of years that had passed.

The phone started to ring . . .

"Hello?" I heard a voice I was still familiar with.

"Hi I'm calling to talk to Crystal." I said, just to be sure.

"This is Crystal." Crystal responded.

"Hi Crystal, I'm not sure if you will remember me. It has been more than a few years since we both spoke. I met you in the spa at the." Crystal interrupted me.

"Christina! Is this you?" Crystal sounded excited as she waited for an answer.

"Yes, it's me! I can't believe you even remember me." I got up off the bed and sat on the bench at the end.

"Remember you? I haven't been able to forget you. Frank told me you left him, and over the years I have called directory assistants and always waited eagerly to see if you would come back to the hotel with Frank. I mean, you were pregnant, I just thought you had a little bit of a misunderstanding that would eventually repair itself. Well, how is your baby? What is going on with you? You can't believe how much I missed you." Crystal was talking so fast and I could tell we both had so much catching up to do.

"Well that is a long story. I was hoping maybe you could take some time off work. I would fly you here so we could have a visit to catch up?" I asked.

"Taking time off work won't be a problem. I lost my job about six weeks ago. I broke up with Jim three months ago and have been renting my own place. I'm being evicted for not paying my rent in two months. I just don't know if I can come out there now when I need to look for work and find a way not to lose all my things. I don't think we could even get together here until I'm settled and have a job. I do want to see you really badly though. I just don't know how that is possible right now. I can't go to my parents. They are still upset that I was with an older man for so long and I moved in him without being married," Crystal sounded sad.

"What if I could get you a job and help you keep your things?" I asked Crystal.

"You could do that? Do you know someone who would hire me?" Crystal eagerly asked.

"I think I just might. Can I call you back in a bit? I just want to check into this." I could almost hear the gears in my brain grinding up an idea.

"Yeah, sure I will be waiting for your call. This is so exciting! It would be cool to live right near you." At that, Crystal and I ended our phone call.

I found Alec in his lab out past the gazebo. I opened the door and called for him up the stairs. Alec called back down to me; "Um, one minute Christina. I'm just getting off the phone." A few seconds later Alec came swiftly down the stairs seemingly very happy.

"I just talked to our man Sebastian and he is going to make his way down here in a couple of weeks. He has some new information on Luke that he wants to share with us in person," Alec seemed delighted.

"So I will be meeting him then?" I held the front door open for Alec as we proceeded outside.

"Yes, I think you are handling the situation well. So now should be a good time for you to be more involved." Alec put his arm around me as we continued to walk towards the mansion. "So what brings you out here? You never come out to my lab," Alec looked down at me in question as we walked.

"Well, I got a hold of my friend Crystal, and we were excited to hear from each other." I spun around in front of Alec looking at him and walking backwards. "But there is a problem as far as us getting together." I folded my hands together trying my best to look sad as I walked backwards.

"Well, tell me what the problem is and I'm sure we can find a way that we can work around it." Alec smiled.

"It's a hard one." I began and told Alec the whole story of how Crystal got fired, left her fiancée, and was without work for so long that she is losing her home. "Alec, can't we just hire Crystal to work here for us? You go into the next town three days a week for massages and I go at least twice. She can have a room in the maid quarters and we could use one of the unused rooms that overlook the outdoor pool for a spa room. I mean, it would take a bit of work, but it would save us the trips into town and I already know she is good. Alec, she is in a really bad situation right now and I think we can help her." I begged while Alec looked at me with a big smile on his face. "Well? You're not saying anything. Can we, please? Can we?" I put my hand on Alec's chest to stop him from walking.

"I just love to see you excited and happy about something. We can hire Crystal. Whatever it takes to make you happy, but I want you to figure out what supplies will be needed and how much she should be paid. It will be a good learning project for you. Prepare a plan and as soon as Crystal is ready I will get her plane tickets and have her things brought here." I jumped in the air and threw my arms around Alec's neck, almost knocking him backwards. "Yes, thank you! And I will do the best job. You will see," I assured Alec.

One week later I was pacing the house waiting for the security guard that Alec hired to get Crystal from the airport. I had gotten a list of things needed for the spa from Crystal. The majority of it was going to arrive in a large truck, but this morning some couriered boxes had arrived with products in them. I completely stripped a room in the maid's quarters and redecorated it for Crystal. It was decided to put most her furniture and larger items in storage. She defiantly wouldn't need them at the mansion. We had everything she could use already here.

I heard Lucia answer the door from the kitchen where I was getting myself some tea. I dropped what I was doing and dashed through the house towards the front door.

"Christina!" Crystal dropped a bag she was holding and we both leapt towards each other and hugged. We were overwhelmed to see each other after so many years. Crystal was just the same as I remembered her with short, blonde hair and striking pale blue eyes. I was so happy to hear that I was always somewhere in her mind through the years, as she was in mine.

I had taken Crystal to her new room where we caught up and unpacked her things together. After that I showed her the new spa that was all painted and had new artwork I had chosen myself. It was pretty empty at the time except for the boxes of products that had arrived, a desk and some shelves. Crystal was excited about the products.

We got a box-cutter to open up the boxes and look at them. Crystal said she never could imagine opening her own spa, even if it was little and she would never be able to purchase all the expensive products at one time. We started placing the products on the spa shelves while we thought of a name for Crystal's new spa. We eventually agreed on *Desert Bliss Day Spa*.

Later we met up with Alec for dinner and he and Crystal got along wonderfully. Crystal went over the whole story of how we met and later, how she lost her job and couldn't go to her parents for help. Alec was very understanding and made Crystal feel very welcome. He did say he would like to see her repair her relationship with her parents eventually. I could tell Alec was glowingly pleased with Crystal living in the mansion and that I would have that female friendship and be even happier.

Chapter 11

Four years have passed since Crystal has been living and employed at the mansion. She had started dating Colin, our only remaining security guard. We didn't need more than a guard or two since Frank had gone to jail about three and a half years earlier.

Frank had turned to the bottle to deal with his anger and his inability to stay away. Then one evening he was driving back to his hotel from a business dinner, highly intoxicated, and broadsided a carload full of young men that were bar hopping. He killed two men in their mid-twenties and injured three men in the back seat; one of which will be disabled for the rest of his life. The police informed the court that he was more than twice the legal limit and he was sentenced to eight years in prison. I felt bad about the whole thing and even blamed myself for a while, but I knew he had deeper issues. Being with Frank for his happiness and not mine wouldn't help him. He had some changing to do, I was just sad that it had to be under the circumstances it was.

He had been writing me from prison, but Alec sent the first few letters back 'return to sender'. Later he paid our mail carrier personally to return them before they reached the front door. Alec told me that I had enough things to deal with. He didn't think I needed to wade around feeling guilty for Frank. I knew he was right and I had to agree with him.

Father and Leah had separated over three years ago. Leah managed to get one of my father's married customers to leave his wife and they moved in together. Father moved back to Langley, British Columbia, a city on the BC coast that we once lived in when we were a lot younger.

Apparently he did the odd gunsmith jobs and worked mainly on a few different farms.

Colin, Crystal's new boyfriend is a great guy by all accounts, not surprising as Alec had selected him. He had blonde hair like Crystal, but his eyes were an adorable medium-brown color. Crystal and I would joke that they were puppy-dog brown. Crystal made it pretty clear to me how she loved his muscular build and his bright white smile. She got to know his physique really well as she did massages for everyone on the payroll. That was how Crystal got to know Colin. Colin was pretty happy that he was the only security guard that would be coming to her for massages now.

Colin and Crystal started dating within the first eight months that Crystal moved in. Colin said he knew he wanted to date Crystal the first time he set eyes on her, but it took him a while to get past his nervousness around her. Finally when Devon (another security guard) told Colin if he wasn't going to ask her out, that he would. That is when Colin found it in himself to get past his fear.

Crystal's New Love

I was glad Crystal found love again. Interestingly enough, Colin was actually a couple years younger than Crystal. Crystal and I joked about what her much older ex would think about her and Colin.

Colin had asked Crystal to marry him a couple Christmases ago, and they were taking a two week holiday to spend with Crystal's folks, preparing for the wedding. Alec had pushed Crystal to heal her relationship with her parents and it was amazing how much happier Crystal was to be connected with them again. Crystal's parents had been out to the mansion on many occasions, but more often lately, as they were planning to have the wedding on the grounds in the garden.

Colin had been staying in the guest house with the other guards, Alec promised once he and Crystal were married they could stay in the guest house as long as they were employed at the mansion.

My friendship with Crystal grew strong over the years, so much that she felt more like a sister than a friend. I got Crystal into taking some kick-boxing classes and riding lessons. It was nice to have a riding partner again; a ridding partner that could go for hours with me on the trails. Crystal preferred to ride Shadow—a black Arabian stallion. Safire and Shadow had been bred years before, a few times, producing some really good quality horses for us. I knew Alec was happy that Crystal learned to ride. It gave him more of a piece of mind that I wouldn't be out there on my own so much.

It was refreshing to have a girlfriend in the picture now, and we did virtually everything together. Alec and Colin knew that if they couldn't find both of us at the same time there was a great chance we were off doing stuff together. We liked so many of the same things so we were inseparable.

Alec had me taking some computer, business administration, and business management courses over the past four years. We knew that computers where going to be the wave of the future. We wanted to transition all of our business information into computer files and documents as soon as possible. Also, I found that taking the courses gave me a huge boost in self-esteem and made me feel like I had all of our information at my fingertips at any given time.

Finally Sebastian was coming with some breaking updates about Luke. He informed Alec that we were inches away from making a connection. Sebastian was supposed to meet with us four years ago but found a trail to Luke that he had abruptly follow, before it ran cold. Today he would be coming and was expected to arrive any minute. I had just finished cleaning up from a hard ride and was anxiously digging through my drawers for something to wear. Manuela was at the mansion helping Lucia prepare lunch for the important occasion, and was going to stay for a few days.

Alec came up to our room and encouraged me to hurry, as Sebastian would be here soon. He wanted to get the main part of the meeting in before lunch. I finished dressing and dusted on some last minute make-up before making my way to the staircase. As I approached the stairs I could hear Alec greeting Sebastian.

"Here she is," Alec announced as I took the last few steps down the grand staircase. "Sebastian, this is Christina." Alec introduced us.

As if in a dream, time froze for a moment. If I could ever see a real male angel I could only imagine he looked like Sebastian. His dark, brown hair and olive coloured skin struck a soft spot in me I never knew about. His eyes were beautiful, piercing brown in contrast with his thick, dark eyelashes. His nose was small and shapely and his lips slightly fuller on the bottom than the top. Everything about his face was perfectly symmetrical, and from what I could see his body was as well. He had the type of hairstyle that is clean cut but tapers out longer on top. He looked to be in his mid to late thirties.

Sebastian

Alec had his hands on one side of his jacket when Sebastian leaned forward to shake my hand, when his other hand was still in the arm of his Jacket. This all seemed to happen in a blur. I do remember his eyes as he said, "Mrs. McGuire, it is very good to finally meet you. I can see where Luke gets his looks from." I seemed to wake up a bit from the spell I was under.

"What? You have seen Luke? Do you have any proof?" I felt my arms cross in disbelief.

"Oh, yes I do." Sebastian held up a black leather brief case.

"Let's hurry down to the office so we can go over some facts," Alec said with his most loved Scottish accent, which was even more sobering for me.

I started to feel like I should hit myself for noticing this attractive, young man when I had my wonderful Alec. We shuffled quickly through the main living room down a hall and into the same office that we had talked to Frank in. This time we didn't go in the sitting room behind the office; this time we all took a seat at a long table.

"Sebastian, I know you have had four or five other jobs to work at other than ours, so if you have any pertinent information, I am delighted." Alec rubbed his hands together eagerly.

"He has four or five other jobs! How can you possibly keep track of Luke when you are mixed in with four or five other investigations?" I demanded.

"Christina, the man has a business to keep which he does well, and I can assure you he is on top of everything as it becomes available, or he makes it available." Alec snapped.

I didn't know why I felt mad at him and for nothing in particular. Maybe I was mad at him because I found myself so attracted to him, and maybe I unconsciously blame him for my hidden embarrassment.

"Sorry Sebastian, it has been a long time. I think Christina is just a little stressed right now," Alec apologized for me.

Sebastian continued to unload his brief-case making piles while he looked up at me sideways and smiled. I stood up and walked over to a window so I could distract myself from starring.

"Sebastian, how is it that you don't have a Spanish accent like Lucia or Manuela? You are from Spain, aren't you?" I asked with my back turned waiting for the table.

"I am from Spain and was born in Spain. I was raised in the US. My parents moved us there a little after my younger brother was born. I had an American nanny and American education. I don't normally tell too many people details about myself, but I am afraid Alec could tell you almost everything about me. He has been around before I was born. He's a very good friend of the family . . . That is why I put his case on the highest priority above all others. It has been my main case for years. I hope that comforts you for what it's worth Christina?

I think this is all ready if you would like to take a seat so we can go through everything." Sebastian was standing with his hand ushering me to sit as I turned around. I took my place glancing at all the piles on the table. Alec gave me a look of disapproval when I looked over at him.

"Here is some information I acquired while I broke into the Sint Lucas Andreas Ziekenhuis. That is the hospital that Luke went to for his jaundice, after he was brought to Dirk's family doctor. I confirmed and concluded years back that this doctor was Dirk's younger brother, which is very convenient for them. The files here indicate that Luke had been back to the hospital when he was four. He had a case of Whooping-Cough. I went back to the home and was able to brake in. Although the house looked empty from the outside, and would to a common burglar, I found these." Sebastian pushed six photo's of a beautiful baby boy across the table to me.

It Was Luke

My mouth dropped open as I looked on. One was a professional picture and the baby looked to be between six or eight months old. I knew it was Luke. I could definitely see myself and Frank. He had brown hair and light brown eyes with very long lashes. His eyes looked to be a mixture of mine and Frank's. He had my nose and a variation of both of our features.

There were five other pictures of Luke as a toddler. One in a highchair with some cake—his face was covered in chocolate. He looked like he was about two in this picture. I wondered if it was a picture of his second birthday. Another picture was of Luke standing on a couch between Dirk and Adana. It appeared to be Christmas time by all the decorations I could see in the background. I could tell that Adana adored him and he always seemed well dressed and healthy. Another picture of Luke in a baby swing next to a house; the house Sebastian identified as listed in my father's customer information book. The last two pictures were of Luke asleep on the living room floor, on two different angles, one being closer up than the other.

I could feel tears roll out of my eyes before I even realized just how emotional this actually was for me. Luke was so perfect, so sweet, and soft. I longed to hear his little voice and touch his soft baby skin. It hit me like a train as I realized time had passed me by in this situation. Luke would now be turning fourteen. I felt Alec sit down beside me, placing his arm around me.

"I'll give you a minute," Sebastian stated.

"No, keep going, I'll be fine. I need to know everything." I said unable to stop the huge dropping tears.

Sebastian handed me a tissue that was on the desk behind him.

"Christina, are you sure? We can take a break. I know this must be incredibly difficult. I can't even imagine how this is for you right now." Alec stated as Sebastian handed me about five more tissues.

"I am sure, we need to just proceed," I sniffled out, trying my very hardest to suck it up and not cry.

Sebastian looked at Alec for his permission to go on. Alec looked at Sebastian and nodded yes.

"Also, at the hospital I found a file that indicates the family moved to Spain. We know Adana is Spanish and has family in Spain. I then tracked a Dirk and Adana Vandenhoff to an address in Barcelona." Sebastian proceeded to put papers and papers of information in front of us.

"Of course, I immediately made my way to Barcelona and found the address. My problem there was that this house was so tight with fences, vicious guard dogs, guards, high tech security systems, alarms, and motion lasers. I am sure Luke would be a reason for high tech security, but Dirk has much uglier reasons. He is not a very well liked man because of his career choice. As I told you before, Vandenhoff Enterprises is an international group of overseas sweatshops. They gain an enormous income by taking advantage of the poor including small children. We all have at sometime bought something that was connected with Vandenhoff Enterprises. If any of us have ever shopped at a large department stores we have. Those are the types of stores he might make a good mark up while massively importing his goods to them." Sebastian paused and started to dig in a file folder.

"No one seems to completely connect that to Dirk, but there are people who do and these numbers are growing. Dirk has been stalked, threatened, and he has even had hits out on him over the years." Sebastian took a drink of his water.

"Here are some pictures of his oversea warehouses, and the property in Barcelona in which Luke lives. You can see in these photos just how high the security actually is. Luke goes to a very privileged school." Sebastian placed a picture of Luke's school on the table in front of us. "And this is how he gets to school every day." Sebastian placed two pictures in front of us; one with a distant picture of a limo. You could see a young teenage boy in the passenger seat and the other was a close up picture. It was through glass but again I could tell he was mine and Frank's.

"It hasn't always been this busy for Dirk. Ten or fifteen years ago he only had a couple of these sweatshops and they weren't as big. Now with the increase of supply and demand, his business exploded and has grown very large. He's not the only supplier of these types of exports and imports, but all of these business owners have had the same kind of threats.

I was able to break through the security for a while using a lot of high tech equipment in order to mess up their equipment. This and many years worth of physical training helped me break in. I hooked up a wire lead to a phone in the house.

I then found that Dirk is still in contact with your father. I found myself thinking I could have easily figured that out by rigging up your father's new place in Langley, but as I was in Spain I got their first contact call after a long while. I can tell you that from that call your Father and Dirk seem quite confident that no one important knows where he lives anymore. If no one can produce Luke, they feel pretty safe. Also Dirk is paying Raymond (your father) five thousand Canadian dollars per month, just to keep him updated as to what is going on in Canada." Sebastian stopped to take a sip of his water when Manuela knocked and opened the door.

"Senor, lunch is ready. Oh my Sebastian, I haven't seen you since you were fifteen!" Manuela threw her arms in the air and embraced Sebastian.

"Oh, I think I was seventeen or eighteen," Sebastian said looking at me through the corner of his eye while his face turned red.

I never thought he would be so well educated and professional. I was kind of feeling embarrassed at how I attacked him and later ended getting teary eyed.

"Well that concludes most of the information I have for you now. It is going to take a lot longer to decide how to make a plan to proceed from here—also to figure out what we want to do with this information and what new information we want to get." Sebastian finished and Alec suggested that tomorrow we have lunch and discuss the points that Sebastian just made. That will give him a chance to wind down and get reacquainted with his family.

"Thanks Alec, you know that you are like family to me and I would like to spend time with you and get to know your wife better as well." Manuela grabbed Sebastian's arm and they both started a conversation in Spanish.

I learned a lot about Sebastian and his family over lunch. Sebastian looked a little embarrassed, as Manuela was so open. Alec had known Sebastian since he was a small child so he was considered part of the family, and as he was related to Manuela and Lucia there were no family secrets. The fact that I am Alec's wife made no one think twice about me knowing anything about Sebastian.

An Informative Lunch

From the information that I got in the dining room at lunch, Sebastian's father had trained each of his boy's to be secret agents. Sebastian, who is close to his mother, chose not to work for the same type of people as his father and brother. Sebastian's mother used to be Manuela's best childhood friend. They had continued their friendship over the years in a very guarded way. Sebastian's father was away on a lot of cases. Sometimes Sebastian's mother would come and visit with her young boys at Alec's to see Manuela. That is how Alec got to know the boys when they were younger.

Sebastian branched away from the kind of work his father and younger brother Rafael chose to do. Apparently Rafael was more dangerous than even his father. He had a shorter fuse and would kill most of the time even if it weren't ordered. Sebastian had seen this kind of killing as a young man while out on a mission with his father and decided right then that he would make himself a rule—he did not want that to be part of his business.

Sebastian had a real love for spying and reconciling wrongs. He said he loved the technology part and all the physical training. But Sebastian's law was not to kill unless his life was being threatened or if he was present and had to protect the life of his client. Even then if he could find a way to defend without killing he would rather resort to that.

Over the years, Rafael was favored by his father and Sebastian by his mother. Rafael grew hatred towards Sebastian and the two of them avoided each other. In fact, they had not spoken since they were teenagers. Lucia can remember growing up with both Sebastian and Rafael around and, she knew them as her only relatives.

Lucia told a story of how Sebastian stood up for her when Rafael smashed in her dollhouse and tied her to the foot of her bed. Sebastian put Rafael in a headlock while he untied Lucia. Both Alec and Sebastian laughed as they talked about how long ago that was. They worked together putting the dollhouse back together. Sebastian suggested an addition, and when they gave it back to Lucia she had never smiled so big. Immediately they had to play with it.

I found out that Sebastian was thirty-nine years old; about three years younger than Lucia and ten years older than me. I thought he was more likely to be in his mid thirties, but could possibly be in his late thirties.

I bothered me that I was so interested in Sebastian and that I found him more attractive than I have ever found a man to be. I made a point of not letting it show and trying not to feel that way. My love was for Alec and that was where my loyalty would always lie.

"Well all, I hate to mix business with pleasure, but I have some of my employees and associates flying in for dinner. I think while the weather is still good we should take dinner/business out to the gazebo. They will all be in suits so it will be a dress up kind off dinner. Sebastian, if you need something we can go into the next town and buy you an outfit." Alec offered.

"I always come prepared, Alec. I think I can manage. Thank you though." Sebastian smiled at me.

"You might try one of those nice dresses in your closet, Christina. Last time we had a dinner/business meeting you looked striking," Alec bragged.

"Will I be having time for a ride this afternoon?" I placed my napkin on the table, looking at Alec. "I think it would be better if you stuck around this time. I really want you to listen and learn, and I don't want to have to be tracking you down and having you show up late." Alec was firm. I noticed Sebastian gazing at me and forcefully looking away when our eyes met.

"Well I am going to the pool, the inside pool, so I can do some laps at least." I began to rise from the table when Alec stood and pulled out my chair.

Lying in the steam room after a few hours of swimming and soaking in the hot tub, I tried to think of things at hand and push thoughts of Sebastian out of my mind. I thought about Crystal's wedding here on the grounds. How beautiful it would be. Then the two would live in the beautiful guesthouse past the gazebo. Crystal could just walk to the mansion spa for work, and her new husband would never be far away.

I thought about how with free room and board for both of them they, could save so much money. They wanted to get that cabin they were looking at about ten kilometres away. Now they could easily afford it. It also wouldn't be that far for them to come back to the mansion and work.

Maybe Crystal will have a baby and I would be Auntie Christina. I wonder if Sebastian ever thought about having kids. Maybe he does have kids. Maybe he is married. His mother was married to an agent and had children. Why was I thinking about this? Who cares about Sebastian and his life choices? I am just happy he has a warm lead on Luke. If his lead proves that Luke is completely happy, than I will leave him alone, but I still want to meet him.

Adana said she would tell Luke of his adoption, as far as I can remember. I just want to tell him that I am his real mother and I didn't abandon him. I would tell him I was young and my parents made me give him up. I just wanted him to know where and who he really comes from, and let him know that I would be open to a relationship with him when he is ready.

Our lunch had been late; at 1:30 PM and ended at almost three with our visiting and everyone's catching up. I opened the door the steam room to look at the time it was 5:45 PM. Oh no!` I am going to be late. Alec is going to be upset with me.

I grabbed a towel and wrapped my hair. I stripped down to nothing, putting my bathing suit in a laundry basket and wrapping myself with a towel. I pushed open the exit doors from the pool room. Down the hallway I ran until I got to the landing. Then I made a left turn to go up to the third floor on the marble, grand staircase. I kept dripping and getting water under foot making the marble quite slippery. I could see at the end of the hall that it looked like the bedroom door was already open. I am sure Alec was looking for me already. I quickly got in and started the shower. I don't remember having such a fast shower in my life.

I could hear some humming or singing, so in my mad rush I turned down the shower water trying to get the last of the conditioner out of my hair. I was sure that was humming or someone out there, but as soon as I turned the water off it abruptly stopped. I got out, wrapping my hair up in a towel and my body in another. I quickly dried myself off and took the towel out of my hair.

Someone in My Closet

As I finished the final touches of my make-up I noticed a light on in my walk-in-closet. I slipped on some panties and made my way to the closet door. I opened it and there again were five or six more outfits. I noticed a beautiful deep, red dress with some red shoes below it. I immediately thought Alec must have gotten me this. This must be what he wants me to wear.

I took the dress down and unzipped the translucent plastic case it was in. I noticed a tiny bag around the neck of the hanger with something in it. I slipped it off the hanger and unzipped the bag to find a box inside. Opening the box revealed a beautiful, deep red ruby necklace and earrings. The necklace had a ruby shaped like a teardrop free-falling out of its setting where it was only held at the top. The earrings were the same shape and setting, dangling downward. I put them on with the dress and the shoes. Again, everything fit me perfectly which inspired me to do my hair long with ringlets just on the bottom and then I pulled the strands of the sides up, leaving spaces where the hair hung down. I put the selected pieces up with a gold hairpin.

The dress was amazing. It had bare shoulders and something inside just seemed to push my breasts up like a built in push-up bra. Alec must have paid a lot for this dress. Just after the waist the dress was made with a flowing sheer, deep red material. I could see my legs through it and at the back of the dress slightly trained out. The material was so beautiful and light, it would flow behind me not touching the floor as I walked.

"Christian, everyone is at the gazebo waiting. Alec sent me here to get you, are you ready?" I could hear Lucia yelling through the door. I opened the door to find Lucia leaning in towards it. "I am ready," I laughed.

Lucia laughed. "Awe Senora, you look . . . more beautiful than I have ever seen! I love it! Alec is going to be speechless. You look so beautiful, but we do have to get going. Manuela has already served appetizers and seconds on the drinks.

We got to the gazebo and I noticed all the wives or dates of the employees were there for this business meeting. In fact, the only one who didn't have a date was Sebastian. His gaze fell upon me strongly as I approached. I couldn't help but notice how extremely striking he looked in his suit.

I held up the front of my dress and quickly came up the gazebo stairs where Alec was. Alec immediately rose to his feet and to my surprise Sebastian did the same. I looked back at my dress and I could see the deep, red train blowing weightlessly through the air behind me in the light summer breeze.

"Christina?" Alec looked at me with this almost indescribable expression. "You are the most beautiful woman I have ever seen," Alec said, walking around the gazebo room until he could reach me. "You must forgive me everyone. I was planning to give my wife heck for being late but she has this very stubborn way about her that just . . . it just stops me every time," Alec smiled. He took me around to where I was seated between him and Sebastian.

Sebastian was still standing as I approached, his eyes burned over me with unquenchable energy. It made me feel like I was alone with just him for a brief few seconds. It took all of my self-control to push my mind from Sebastian. Again I felt angry with myself. What is the matter with me? I know who I love and that person is Alec. That will never change. Alec is the only man for me. I repeated that in my mind.

Alec and I took our seats and Sebastian was still standing, now looking down at me. "Sebastian, please have a seat." Alec urged, as he looked deep into my face. Alec's eyes started to glaze over what was once teary. Alec then proceeded to reintroduce me to his employees and associates and their wives.

Manuela came up the gazebo to see if anyone wanted another beverage. Alec asked her if she could get me a strawberry margarita. Manuela waved down to Lucia and in Spanish she rambled to her, sounding quite upset. Alec then asked Sebastian if he could go and tend to his aunt and see if he couldn't bring her back.

"Alec, I am going to talk to Lucia for a moment. I think I left something back at the house and I want to see if she might have grabbed it. I started to get up. Alec pulled on my wrist, "Right now Christina? You just arrived," Alec started.

"I won't be long, don't worry." I proceeded down the gazebo stairs to where I could see Lucia putting some steaks on the barbeque.

"Lucia, I know you know something about the ridiculous way your mother treats me when I am dressed up for Alec. What is it and what is going on with her?" I demanded. Lucia kept putting meat on the barbeque with an irritated look on her face.

"I don't know, she just gets that way sometimes." Lucia rushed as she started to whip something in a small bowl.

"Not good enough Lucia I know exactly those times and they are always times like this. I know you understand and speak Spanish very well. I know you know why Sebastian went to consol her. So why did he?" I made my voice more demanding.

"Sebastian has no idea why she is upset. Why don't you go to her and find out, Christina. I will make sure Alec is fine. It's between you and my mother and it is not my business to say," Lucia sounded insistent.

I walked ferociously down the path that led to the mansion and twisted my ankle which made me pace it a bit better. Four-inch heels were not ideal for a brisk walk. What could make this woman go from loving me to hating me in a few short seconds? I have no idea, but what I do know is that I am going to find out once and for all. I don't care if I have to pull teeth to get an answer. This is not fair, and not fair to Alec. Every time I think I look pretty for him Manuela always throws it off with some made up emotional emergency.

I opened the double front doors and I could hear some talking. It sounded like it was coming from up the staircase. It was Manuela and Sebastian speaking in Spanish. "Great," I thought. I went into the main living room and walked across from the marble fireplace where there was a liquor cabinet. I took a crystal stopper off a bottle and poured about half a glass of whatever it was. I shot it back and felt my stomach burn.

I waited and tried to listen. Manuela was talking in and out of English and Spanish. Maybe if I could hear some of the English I could get some of the Spanish. She said something about a spirit coming down; a spirit that she knows. "This is just getting weird," I thought I went back to the liquor cabinet and popped off the crystal stopper and poured another half glass of whatever. Feeling my stomach burn again I took up speed and headed for the grand staircase. I noticed the voices disappeared farther up the stairs.

The Ghost in the Attic

I got to the landing not knowing which way Manuela and Sebastian were I decided the third floor. Maybe she was in my bedroom. I turned down the hall that led to my bedroom and was approaching the door when I noticed something. If I looked a little further down the hall I could see the staircase that stuck out from the hall. It was the small, windy staircase that led to the attic. I could see that at the top the door was ajar. I thought to myself that they were up there. If not, it would be nice to see what is there. I have been curious for a long time, but each time my curiosity has been plugged by something Manuela has said.

I own this place and I have lived here twelve years and still have not been up there. I grabbed the front of my long, red dress and started up the stairs. When I came through the door there was a short, narrow hall that led to another door. The door was unlocked, so I opened it to find myself in a large room. There was a side room containing bottles of wine on a rack and a bunch of shelves of liquor. There was also a small table and one chair in the room. It was as if someone came up there once in a while to have a drink. There were alcohol decanters with different coloured alcohol in them and tumblers about. I also noticed a small rack that had a variety of red wines.

Moving forward a bit I came to a big, room with racks of clothing in zippered bags and an area with shoe; many shoes all looking to be the same size . . . my size. I knew I had at least thirty pairs in my closet but there must have been about two-hundred pairs up here. To the right there were some neatly piled boxes, and to the left there was an opening past the clothing racks.

I decided to go that way. It was a bit dark but I got around. I could make out the shape of a lamp on a tabletop over in the corner. I slowly inched my way there, clicking on the light. At first glance when I looked around it just looked like a bunch of various sized photos of me. Then I thought to myself, "Why are these pictures all out like this? And why are they up here in an attic?" One large oil painting off to the side really got my attention. It was an oil painting of me and Alec, but Alec looked so young. I never remembered having an oil painting taken of us. I didn't recognize the background. It looked like we were on lawn chairs in a yard, but we don't have palm trees in our yard. Why does Alec look so young? He has to be about twenty-five in that picture. Maybe he got someone to paint a picture with us closer to age. This is terrible. I hope Alec doesn't have this make-believe world up here where we are closer in age.

Another picture caught my eye; it was a picture of me in my white sundress with eyelet of purple and blue flowers under the breast; the one I last wore when Alec had company over for a business meeting. The strange thing about this picture was that I was on a sail boat hanging onto a pole, and in the background I could see Alec coming up from down below the deck with a big smile. But this Alec was different; this was a photo and Alec was about twenty-three maybe twenty-five; younger than Sebastian.

I felt myself getting dizzy like I might faint. I got down to the floor really quick and put my head between my legs. I made myself breathe in and out slowly about ten times. I looked at the photo again and it was Alec at that young age, but the woman was me. My heart was pounding and my hands were getting sweaty. I looked around the room and there were many more pictures of me and Alec, all of them with Alec; around this young age or a little older, but no older than his later twenties.

Breathe, Christina, breath. I went back over to the large oil painting and held it up realizing I was wearing my mauve dress and matching shoes in this one. Tears streamed down my face as I sat on the attic floor holding this picture. What is going on? Is this some kind of weird joke. I heard a creak and I dropped the oil painting, getting to my feet in a very dizzy state. I looked around with my pounding heart and nothing was there. I went to sit down and realized the painting was upside down and there was some writing on the back in pen. I got back down on the ground close to the painting so I could read what it said. *Our Palm Springs home. Alec and Shannon McGuire, summer of 1947.*

Instantly my head started to spin. I pulled myself across the floor crawling as far away from the picture as I could. I can't believe this. This isn't true. I could see everything I believed and trusted to be my reality over the past years slipping from me. Manuela must have done this.

I got up, really dizzy, and tripped my way through to the room that had the chair and table with the wine racks. I sat down at the table feeling more than just a little confused. I still needed to know more though. I had to go back in before someone caught me up here.

I grabbed a bottle of merlot out of the rack and opened a drawer where I found a opener. I uncorked the wine and took the whole bottle back to the room where the pictures were of me . . . or of Shannon? I stood amongst the room of pictures all set out along the floor and on short tables. I guzzled down a good amount of wine, straight out of the bottle. "This can't be Alec's deceased wife. She can't be me, and she can't look like me, like this?" I thought out loud, confused.

I grabbed at some of the clothing racks. "These are her clothes; she can't just be my size like this. This is impossible." I went over to the other side where there were some neatly stacked boxes. I found a wooden box that had 'Shannon McGuire' carved into the side. I opened it. At the very top I found a ring box. Inside was what looked to be her wedding and engagement ring together. Next a folded piece of paper that was Shannon and Alec's certificate of marriage dated November 11, 1945. This was becoming too real.

I began grabbing for more information. Next I unfolded another paper it was Shannon's birth certificate saying she was born in 1928. Next there were some very old black and white photographs of a young girl who looked remarkably like me when I was little. She was playing with two young boys. I flipped the first photo over where it said 'Alec and Connor McGuire and Shannon Campbell, Summer of 1938 Scotland,'

"Who in the world was this Connor McGuire I thought. He was much younger than Alec, but who the heck was he? Alec looked to be in his late teens but the girl, who resembled me, and this Connor couldn't be older than ten. I put the box on a large sewing table in front of me and slugged some more wine, then banging the bottle down on the table beside the box.

I looked through more and more of these pictures, and as I passed through them I could see the three of them growing up. The thing was, it was Connor when he turned a teen that was kissing Shannon and holding her hand, not Alec.

Great, no more pictures. I was back to the pictures that were on top of the pile. I opened the box again spreading out a type of time chart down on this huge sewing table. I grabbed what looked like a folded newspaper article. I began to read it. A terrible accident occurred in

Inverness, Scotland, Monday April 27th, 1942. The Campbell family was heading home in the rain from an evening out when their car slide down a rocky bank. It rolled several times before crashing into a guardrail from the road below. The two adults believed to be the parents of the surviving girl were pronounced dead at the scene. The dead body of a young man who was found thrown from the vehicle several yards away. I then grabbed the next piece of paper, and in my hand was the obituary of Connor McGuire.

I felt tears run down my face. I felt panicked and almost like I was a ghost with all these pictures around me everywhere. I tried to get my thoughts together. Shannon was born in 1928 and Alec married her in 1945. That means she was seventeen when he married her. This is too much.

I grabbed the bottle of wine and backed away from the information. Alec wanted me to wait until I was seventeen when I married him. Was he trying to repeat something, something that was long over? Could God have repeated me in history? I knew these questions weren't even worth an answer, but I still didn't understand what was happening, what happened, and what was going to happen. I took another glug of the merlot hoping it would numb me out or I would wake me from a very bad dream. My eyes met up with all the pictures when I backed into Sebastian.

"Oh no, Senora, you can't be up here," Manuela started at me.

"Don't even begin Manuela, you knew this all along. Who are you guys anyway? What are you trying to do? I approached Manuela. "You put those clothes in my closet, didn't you? You knew they were hers and you did it anyway. You call me a ghost. It is not me that is the ghost it's her," I yelled almost falling over when Sebastian caught me.

"Easy now, I don't understand. The pictures of you, they are ghost pictures?" Sebastian smiled.

"Oh Mr. Secret Agent man doesn't even know? Well Manuela you sure can keep as secret, can't you?" I yelled at Manuela.

"Ok now let's go easy on my aunt. I am sure I can get the story and figure it out so we can calm down and be friends," Sebastian said. Manuela looked frightened and nervous all at the same time.

"Look, go look at the information on the table. These pictures aren't me Sebastian. These are all Shannon. This dress is Shannon's and these . . . these shoes are too." I started to take the shoes off still holding the bottle of wine and threw them towards the pictures.

"Okay, now were starting to sound a bit too drunk. Lets just go over to the table and see what we have here." Sebastian approached the table and picked up each piece of information going through it very quickly as he rubbed his chin.

"Christina, I can see how you would be upset. I wasn't even told about this. I mean, I never met Alec's wife. She died before I would have been able to remember her, I think. I mean I just can't get over the likeness. This has got to be so rare, it is almost impossible. But yet it is true, right in front of me here. I just can't explain it. Maybe Alec thought going through this with you would just freak you out?" Sebastian then started a loud conversation with Manuela in Spanish.

"That is it, I am out of here." I sat my bottle of wine down on a table and made my way out of the attic. As soon as I got to the hallway I started running in my bare feet.

When I got outside I ran on the pavement and I kept running and running until I reached the car warehouse. I could see it was open a crack and some man wearing jeans and a muscle shirt was under a car about six cars down. I tiptoed in and quietly checked doors for being unlocked. I found an old car in the back row that had a big back seat. I closed the door, but not enough that it would click shut. I didn't want to make a sound. I lay in the backseat with my head spinning. I knew this was the most I had ever drank in my life. I think that in combination of some ghostly information, was more than enough to upset and confuse me.

After about an hour the man in the warehouse must have decided to call it a night. He shut off the lights and locked the door of the warehouse. I fidgeted around until I found an interior light I switched on. It was so quiet in the warehouse. When he shut the door it grew even quieter. That gave my mind the solace it needed to get a few thoughts together. I found myself wondering if Alec really loved me, like the Christina me, or if he just saw Shannon the whole time. I had no idea how I could be born in a whole different time and end up with the same man who married someone with such a likeness to me, in what seemed like eons ago. I don't remember when but at some point I blacked out into a deep sleep in the back of that old car.

My Dead Doppelganger

I woke up to Sebastian of all people. He handed me a couple Tylenol and some soda water in a bottle. I took them quickly.

"How long were you starring at me for?" I asked.

"Oh, maybe twenty minutes. I wanted you to wake-up on your own." Sebastian opened the passenger's side of the door. "It is funny you picked this car to sleep in! If you looked deeper into the front cab you would see this is the car they used on their wedding day. Look at this here, right on the glove compartment box. It's a gold plaque with their names and wedding date, right here." Sebastian moved to the left so I could see. I pulled myself to a sitting position again.

"It's because I am a freak. I'm not even me. I'm an image of an image of a person who once was and doesn't exist anymore. It doesn't surprise me the only damn vehicle unlocked in here would be this one and I wouldn't know that. I think I have been living blindly for too many years now." I rubbed my head.

"How did you find me here anyhow?" I asked.

"You dropped this ruby earring on the ground, and this gold hair barrette was near the door of the warehouse." Sebastian reached and handed me the earring and barrette.

"Well how did you get in here without tripping the alarm? The guy sets it every night when he leaves. I couldn't even tell you it unless I looked it up." I stood up getting the hugest head rush.

"Be careful now. You're going to need awhile to feel better, girl. To answer your question about the alarm this is not the highest tech alarm system I have been through. Also, you are not a freak, Christina. I had a talk with Alec at the hospital last night and he is broken up about this. He doesn't want to feel like he has deceived you. He loves you for you and this wasn't what he planned either." Sebastian started.

"In the hospital, why is he in the hospital? Did he get hurt? Is he okay?" I panicked.

"He is Okay, Christina, and he should be back right now. He came back to the house a little after you left. When he learned what you found out, he had an angina attack. We thought it was a heart attack. When he got to the hospital they did tons of tests and found out his blood pressure is a little high and he has angina. It just means he'll have to be careful, and he'll have some new medications he is going to need to take. One he has to take every day for his blood pressure and the nitro-glycerine he only needs to take if he feels an angina attack coming on." Sebastian explained.

"What he needs you to know is that he loves you for who you are. He doesn't understand why life sent him such unusual circumstances twice. Shannon was Alec's brother Connor's girlfriend. When Shannon literally lost everyone she loved in that car accident she had to live with her father's alcoholic sister. Alec stayed in touch with her and they bonded from the tragedy. They both lost people they loved dearly.

Things got too much for Shannon, living with her alcoholic auntie, I might add that her auntie treated Shannon like a slave. Well Alec and Shannon had bonded and dreamed of marrying each other. When Shannon turned seventeen they did marry. We all know the story of Shannon's tragic death while she and Alec were on holiday. It wasn't until years and years later that he came upon you. You were just a young child and you took him back to the only family in his life.

Yes, you looked like someone he loved romantically, but remember the age you were when he first met you. That was the age Shannon was when he was quite happy with her being with his brother. I have seen love before, Christina, and I know he loves you," Sebastian said looking downward.

Chapter 12

I stayed out in the warehouse with Sebastian while Manuela and Lucia got Alec into bed. Sebastian had already gone back to the house once to make sure that Manuela told Alec where I was. He didn't want him to have any extra worry.

It wasn't long before Lucia arrived at the warehouse to inform me that Alec had been asking for me. I knew I loved Alec, but even after talking to Sebastian for such a long time it wasn't completely clear to me how Alec loved me, or for what reason he loved me. I wanted to believe what Sebastian was saying, but I still wasn't so sure.

I had never felt unsure about Alec ever until now. This was a really big thing for me to be unsure about. I wished last night didn't happen and that none of it was true. I thought this as my gaze met the wedding plaque on the car glove box.

Shannon

Lucia then climbed into the back seat of the car with me. "Christina, I want you to know that I did not know how similar you and Shannon look. I had never met Shannon before or seen the pictures in the attic. My mother told me that when Alec moved here from Palm Springs he put all of the pictures and Shannon's things in the attic.

My mother wanted me to tell you that she never meant to hurt you by slipping some of Shannon's things into your closet. She loved Shannon a great deal and she has grown to love you also. In fact, that is why she gave you Shannon's things. Alec told my mother it was time to start getting rid of all Shannon's clothes. Alec wanted to move on and he knew it was more than time to do so. My mother agreed, but she thought it would be a kind gesture to pass some of the clothing down to you.

She didn't know at first how emotional she would get actually seeing you in Shannon's clothes. She, as Alec, were stunned by how well they fit you. Alec and my mother had a few fights about giving you the clothing, but mother insisted. She didn't want Shannon's clothing going to just anyone. Alec was afraid how you might react if you knew. At one point they were even going to show you, but when Alec had Frank come to the house he learned about your relationship with him. He saw how upset you were so he wanted it to wait.

Unfortunately, things got in the way and time passed. You found out in the way that Alec didn't want you to find out. Alec loves you Christina. My mother and I have never seen him so happy again until you came here. He loves you for you. I saw the pictures in the attic last night and I admit I was stunned at how crazy the similarities are between you and Shannon. Believe me, Christina, Alec had no ill plans for you.

When you lived with your Father of course he had a curiosity and warmness towards you because of your resemblance to Shannon. I can tell you though that Alec never suspected he would be your husband one day. I have heard him talk to mother about it after you came, and he never dreamed it would be that way. He just couldn't let you slip away and have your future be so uncertain. Christina, please forgive Alec for not telling you sooner. It was a hard thing for him to explain.

Think about how he has forgiven you in the past. I know I was there remembering.

Mother and I are very afraid for his health; I have never seen him look so bad in my entire life. I will leave you here with Sebastian and if you can find it somewhere in yourself, Alec will be upstairs in your room. Please think about it clearly, Christina." Lucia hugged me and slid back across the car seat to go back to the mansion.

I looked at Sebastian and told him Lucia is right, and I know it. It's just so hard to see clearly right now with all this in my head." I ran my hands over my face and pushed my fingers through my hair.

"Just sit here for a while longer and go over everything in your head from beginning to end. I know that when I'm spying on people I come upon some really shocking and bizarre stuff. Most people wouldn't believe it if they saw it right in front of their own eyes. I try to put it in a type of order in my head and eventually it explains it's self. Then I realize how it got so out of hand. Then once I can wrap my head around it I can precede to what is really important. You have to keep your eye on what you know to be real in your heart and your mind." Sebastian placed his hand on my heart then lifted it, putting his hand to the side of my head.

I sunk back in the seat and thought to myself. I wasn't up front with Alec about a lot of things. He didn't even know I had a baby never mind that I had gone through a wedding with Frank. I kept things secret from Alec for a long time. I just didn't want to be judged or to dredge up anything that was hard for me to talk about. Alec has always been so patient with me about things even though he knew something was going on. He waited, and when he did end up finding out it wasn't because I wasn't being forthright. It was because it blew up right in my face and I had nowhere to go but to the truth.

"I am going to see Alec," I said as I moved my way out of the backseat. Sebastian looked kind of shocked.

"Are you sure you are ready so soon?" He stepped in front of me. "Yes, I'm sure. I was just in shock last night, and I still am right now, but I'm being selfish. It is not like Alec hasn't had to deal with his share of my lovely mistakes that I wasn't up-front about." I looked at Sebastian watery eyed.

Sebastian looked at me with his head tilted. "If you are sure, he then stepped out of my way.

Reconcile

I approached Alec's side of the bed, kneeling on the floor. His eyes suddenly opened as if he knew it was me.

"Christina, I am so sorry you had to find out about Shannon this way. You need to understand that she was my past and you are my future. I have grown to know you over the years. As much as you look alike and have a few things in common you are two totally different people. I love you Christina, for being the girl I met and married who turned into the woman I know and love right now. I never meant to cause you all this turmoil. I always wanted healing and good things for you. You must believe me." Alec's hand was in mine and I interrupted him.

"Alec, I know, I believe you." The look of distress seemed to peel off Alec's face at those words. "I was just a little stunned at first and I know you didn't want to hurt me by holding information or not explaining. I did the same thing to you about Luke and Frank. I think we were just afraid of what the other would think, and we didn't want to dig up pain from the past. I'm sorry Alec, for not being as forgiving as you were right away. I shouldn't have run from it. I should have waited for your company to leave and then gone over things in my head. I acted in haste." I placed my head down on the bed

Alec pushed himself up and I placed some pillows behind his back so he could sit up. I then kissed him and we embraced. "I won't be lying around here for much longer. We need to get back to normal again." Alec said.

"Oh, I think you will be here as long as you need to." I adjusted the pillows behind Alec's back.

"No, the doctor said I could do things as usual. I just need to take my blood pressure pills everyday and keep my nitro on me in case I have an episode. I will stay in bed here for the day to appease Manuela, but I'll go nuts if I'm here another day," Alec teased

Over the next few months Alec was as busy as ever. He seemed quite energetic but I could see something different in him. He wasn't quite the same. I could tell the age was getting to him and he didn't want to admit it, even to himself. It was as if he thought keeping himself busy would suspend the inevitable.

He was a great help with Crystal's wedding and took a lot of the worry off her shoulders. He surprised Crystal and Colin's parents by picking up the entire bill for the wedding as their wedding present. And of course he kept his promise letting Crystal and Colin live together in the guest house. It was wonderful to see Crystal and Colin so happy together.

Almost three years had passed now since Crystals wedding. A new hope rung through the mansion and its grounds; Crystal was expecting—something we needed around here, some new life. I was sure that might brighten Alec up even more so.

About Luke

Sebastian had been doing a lot of work for us in Spain. He had been in and out of Dirk's security system quite a bit. He found a way to override the system for at least an hour at a time without anyone acknowledging it. He did have some disturbing news for us about Luke though. Through his slipping in and out of Dirk's property it became clear to him that Dirk and Luke's relationship was strained. Dirk was very hard on Luke about his grades and about Luke taking over his business enterprise. Adana was constantly sticking up for Luke and getting Dirk off Luke's heels.

Luke had learned through gossip in school about what Dirk's company was all about. Luke didn't want any part of it. In fact, Luke was constantly volunteering for raising money for those less fortunate. He volunteered in school programs, after school programs and in his spare time he would use his allowance money to buy blankets and food for the local shelters and food banks.

On one occasion Dirk through a fit at Luke for selling an expensive stamp collection that Dirk had given Luke. It was very old and rare; it was handed down to Dirk from his grandfather and then to Luke. Luke gave the money from the stamp collection to an organization that helped dig wells in Africa to provide clean water to its people.

Luke was later awarded for organizing and raising the most money ever raised for a school program supporting the poor. Luke had a hard time though, especially from a select group of kids. Their parents hated Dirk and would tease Luke about how he would raise money for the poor only so his family would go back and collect it later. I was devastated to hear these things about Luke, but I tried to keep a level head about it. We all had hard times in school or at home. Growing up wasn't easy for anyone.

I knew Sebastian would be arriving back at the mansion in a few weeks, and with Alec we would come up with a plan; a plan that would decide what would be the next step in what was left to do about Luke. He would be over sixteen years old now and was scheduled to graduate at the end of this year. He was very intelligent and I was very proud, but also relived he wouldn't have to deal with the group of kids that would pick on him.

It was a hot July day and I was hurrying down the trail to the mansion. I had been out for a long ride and I knew dinner was ready and probably waiting for me. When I got to the dining room Alec was not there and Lucia came in with a jug of ice water.

"Where is Alec?" I asked Lucia.

"He had a headache this afternoon and went up stairs to lie down for a while. I haven't seen him since." Lucia wiped her hands on the sides of her apron."

I'll go upstairs and get him," I smiled and skipped off.

I entered the bedroom and I could hear Alec snoring loudly. I called Alec as I approached his side of the bed. He kind of mumbled something I couldn't understand. I sat down on the end of the bed and took his hand.

"Alec, are you coming down for dinner? Everything is ready and we're just waiting for you." I kissed his hand.

"No, my head just hurts too badly, Dear. Can you grab me some more of those Advil off my lamp table and hand me my water?" Alec asked with some light moans. "I reached over and opened the bottle of Advil and took a couple out. I put them in Alec's mouth and put the water to his lips for him to sip.

"Christina, can you grab me one of my sleeping pills. I just want to fall asleep for the night and hopefully this will be gone in the morning." He looked pale to me. I got his sleeping pills and gave him one.

"When I come to bed I will try not to disturb you. I love you and hope you will feel better soon." I kissed him again and slipped off the bed.

I was in the office where we usually met with Sebastian. I was going over the new information including documents and pictures of Luke. I had been in the office for several hours now, racking my brain about my Luke. I finally decided to call it a night. I filed all the pictures and documents in their designated areas and locked everything up including the office door.

I entered our room and slipped into my bed clothes. I quickly went into the washroom to clean my face and brush my teeth. I could hear Alec moan a little, as I got ready for bed. I thought to myself, "I will need to book a relaxation message and scalp message for Alec first thing in the morning." I quietly entered the bedroom from the washroom and slipped into the bed and under the covers. I could tell Alec realized I was there as he pulled me towards him and wrapped himself around me, moaning softly. I kissed him on his chest as I cuddled up closely to him.

"I love you, good-night," Alec whispered.

"I love you too. Hope you feel better by morning," I added, nuzzling up closer. I quickly felt myself start to fall asleep to the comfort of Alec's scent that I was so used to over the years.

No

I saw my mother. She was wearing the dress at the funeral parlour; the one she wore to church on occasion. We were in Sunday school and she was telling the story of Jesus' Death, with all the little felt figurines on the board. Her hair was straight and brown and her nails and lipstick were mauve. I felt a sense of pride as she told the story. Suddenly I lifted out of the room into outer space, but my mother didn't notice, she just kept teaching the class. I lifted up higher and higher and then I pulled away from the class to the side. Now they were so tiny and far away. Abruptly, I started to fall. The wind was at my face and I couldn't breathe. I just kept falling and falling and falling. I could see the Earth and I was coming towards it fast. It was getting bigger. Now I could see roads and buildings, I shot through the roof without getting hurt and I started to slow down as I went through the first floor, then the second floor, then the last floor.

I landed on my twin bed with the frilly, pink bedspread. My mother was shaking me telling me it was time to get up.

"Christina, wake up! Wake up Christina! Christina, you need to wake up now!" She shook me hard.

I felt myself gush into alertness. I realized I had been having the dream again. I tried to stop my heart from beating so fast, but something was actually moving underneath and, around me. I reached up to feel Alec's face. I slid my hand up Alec's neck. It felt all cold and clammy.

"Alec, wake up Alec!" I raised my voice. I could feel Alec's body give a last few jolts as his arm was underneath me. I pulled myself into a sitting position telling Alec to wake up over and over again. He did not answer and his body stopped its jolting around.

I slowly and carefully reached over Alec to the lamp on the table beside him. I could see the alarm clock said it was 2:45AM. I clicked the lamp on. What I saw was one of the most shocking things I have ever seen in my life. I looked over at Alec who was now on his back but tilted slightly towards me. His lips were blue and his eyes were wide open. His eyes had a white, foggy coating over the irises.

I heard a scream come out of me in the form of the word 'No!' I kept screaming it over and over again as inched my way off the other side of the bed. I ran out of the bedroom and through the house yelling 'NO!' I ran out one of the back doors past the outdoor pool and toward the guesthouse where Crystal and Colin lived. I pounded as hard as I could and I screamed for them to open the door.

The door finally opened with Colin standing there with a grave look of concern on his face.

"Christina, what is going on? Why are you so upset?" Colin stepped outside and the door opened again as Crystal came out.

"It's Alec "He's dead, He's dead, help please, help he is dead!" I screamed with my arms crossed pacing a small circle.

"Where is he?" Colin asked. "He's in the bed, I saw his eyes. They are dead and he is cold feeling." I pointed quickly at the mansion and continued my pacing.

"Crystal, bring Christina over to the mansion and make her some tea or something," Colin instructed as he ran off towards the mansion. Crystal and I followed behind him at a slower pace. I can't remember everything I muttered to Crystal on the way over. Crystal had tears in her eyes as she led me with one arm over my shoulder and the other arm was gripped around my forearm.

We entered the mansion through the front door and I could hear Lucia crying and screaming as Colin yelled to her to call 911. My legs felt weak and I fell to my knees in the entrance area. Crystal pulled me upward until I was on my feet again. She then led me toward the main living room with the marble fireplace. She sat me on the leather couch and lifted my feet up and onto it.

"Wait here Christina, I am just going to grab a blanket for you. I will only be a minute." Crystal ran her hands through my hair as she got up off the couch beside me to go fetch a blanket.

I Did All I Could Do

It seemed like hours had come and gone by the time the ambulance had arrived. Colin had not come down the stairs and would not let anyone come up. Lucia, Crystal, and I sat on the couch each taking our turn crying comforting on another. It was 6 AM when the paramedics came back down the stairs. We all ran around the corner just to see the gurney that carried Alec down the stairs. We saw that they had put a sheet over his face. He was gone. Colin came down the stairs with tears in his eyes

"I did everything," he sobbed. "I did all I could do. He just wasn't coming back." Colin wiped his tears on the sleeve of his shirt. "I'm so sorry Christina. We all loved him, Sorry!" Colin came down the final few stairs. "I'll give you some time to clean up, but we need to travel to the hospital in Kamloops. They need you to give some information and sign some things." Colin cleared his throat and left the mansion. The three of us girls huddled together crying loudly.

"You need to get ready Christina," Crystal cried.

"I can't, I don't want to. I just want him back here right now. Can we please get him back?" I found myself on my knees again and to my surprise Lucia and Crystal met me there weeping as well.

"Let's just go lay on the couches in the living room for a few moments." We went back to the living room and we all found a spot on one of the four couches. Slowly we feel asleep to our own weeping.

I awoke at 9 AM to Crystal. She must have gotten up and dressed since we feel asleep here.

"Christina, it's time. I'm going to take you upstairs and I'll stay with you until you get cleaned up and changed." Crystal gently pulled me up until I was sitting.

"No I'm not going up there," I said. "I'll clean up in one of the washrooms down here, and maybe you and Lucia can find me some clothes and bring them to me."

I looked up and started to cry again. "Okay, we'll get some for you, don't worry." Crystal helped me up the rest of the way.

I made myself walk to the back of the mansion where I found a guest room with a bathroom attached. I turned the water on in the bath and started to undress. I sat down in the tub feeling completely numb. I tried my hardest to recall what we had last said to each other, and I remembered before bed we had said I love you. I pulled my legs up to my chest trying in my head to imagine rewinding time, to that moment. I thought of how he would cuddled me when I climbed into bed. Was there some way I could have stopped this? I thought and began to cry out loud again.

Crystal came in the bathroom with some clothes that Lucia and she had picked from the attic. They told me they were a little nervous themselves to go into our bedroom. They seemed afraid that I would be mad about the clothes coming from the attic. I just told them that it was fine, as I numbly started to dry off.

At the Hospital

I arrived at the hospital with Crystal and Colin at one 1 PM. I still felt like I was dreaming. I was just floating through time. Nothing felt real to me. I didn't want this to be real. I felt like I was waiting a long time to get up from this nightmare.

Crystal and Colin had gone to the front of the admitting desk to let them know that I had arrived. The lady at the desk told us to have a seat for a moment while she brought me some forms to sign. She had informed me that a doctor would be out shortly to talk to me, and a police officer had to ask me a few questions as well. I had to get Crystal to read over the forms and tell me where to sign. I was shaking so hard and my eyes seemed to well up with an endless supply of tears—they continuously plunked down on the documents.

A police officer came into the waiting room and the admitting lady at the front desk pointed him toward the three of us. The police officer then went directly up to Crystal, addressing her as Mrs. McGuire. When Crystal corrected him he said he was sorry and that he was expecting someone older; you did look too young, but you seem to be the oldest female."

"Uh, this is Mrs. McGuire," Crystal corrected him as she rubbed my back.

"Oh?" The officer replied looking like he was half shaking his head. "I am truly sorry for your loss Mrs. McGuire. I won't take much of your time." The short heavy-set officer said, and proceeded to flip open a notebook. He asked me question such as whether or not I was the one that found Alec? Where were we at the time? Does he have any health issues, had we been arguing in the past while? Did we get along most of the time?

I was really having a hard time answering. I just leaned on my hands with my elbows on my knees letting the tears drop out onto my pants. Crystal interrupted him a few times asking him why he would you ask that, and is that really a necessary question? The officer replied that it was procedure when someone dies at home and the cause of death is not clear-cut. He then said something about the doctor being sure that it was an aneurism. I signed permission for an autopsy to verify the cause of death.

Crystal was quite snappy with the officer, "Can't you see she is in shock right now?" She insisted that the questions were ridiculous. The officer insisted that they were procedure under the circumstances. Crystal snapped at him to hurry up. The officer finished looking a bit nervous at Crystal. He even asked me if I would like to be questioned in private. I grabbed Crystal's hand and refused. The police officer left stating that he would possibly be in touch later if it was deemed necessary.

About twenty minutes later a bald, thin doctor came out to the front desk. The lady at the front desk directed him toward where Crystal, Colin, and I were sitting.

He approached us. "Which of you two ladies is Mrs. McGuire?" I cleared my throat looking at him through my blurry burning eyes. "I am Mrs. McGuire." The thought passed through my mind that there will never be a Mr. and Mrs. McGuire again, and then I felt a stabbing pain surge through my heart.

"Well can you please come with me then?" He took one hand off his clipboard and pointed towards a closed door aside the admission desk. I got up slowly, holding my stomach as I felt a wave of nausea come over me.

We entered the little booth room that had two padded, high back chairs and a small desk. "I am very sorry for your loss Mrs. McGuire. I'm sure you want some answers right now. I had time to view Mr. McGuire for injuries, and a cause of death. With what I found from the test that I took it looks like Mr. McGuire suffered from an aneurism. If that is the case upon further examination I would like you to know that he would have gone fast and not felt a thing."

I interrupted the doctor and told him how I could feel him jolting around in the bed and how his arm was under me. The doctor explained that it was because the brain was dying and was is called posturing. He assured me that it was much too late at that point, and that even if we lived across the street from the hospital it would be extremely rare for someone to survive. He made it clear that the autopsy would give a better means to determine what he suspected.

He then asked me if Alec had complained of a headache, pain in his head, visual disturbances, or fatigue. I started to tell him while I wept uncontrollably that he didn't come down for dinner and he told our maid he was going to lie down. When I came upstairs he was sleeping. I tried to wake him but his headache was still there and I gave him Advil and a sleeping pill as he requested, so he could sleep it off. I told him how he cuddled into me so closely when I came to bed and we said I love you to each other. I told him that was the last that happened until I awoke to the jerking motions in the wee hours of the morning.

The doctor assured me that that was common onset for an aneurism and even at that point it is often hard to diagnose and, most often fatal. He then asked about Alec's medical history and went on to medications he was taking.

"Can you just stay put for a moment? I have some of Mr. McGuire's belongings that you will need to sign for. Also, you are welcome to view your husband one last time before we take him for autopsy. If you would like to I will get a nurse to walk you to the room where we have him," he explained. Again I felt that stabbing pain surge through my heart as the image of his blue lips and his wide-open eyes with the foggy coating over the pupil and irises passed through my mind.

"No, I can't see him like that again," I cried. The doctor put his arm across my shoulders.

"That is Okay Mrs. McGuire. It's completely understandable. I think I will just write you a prescription that you can fill if you think you need it. It will help reduce any anxiety you may be feeling and also help you sleep at night. It will likely be hard for you over the next while. I'm going to go and get the clerk so you can sign for his belongings." The doctor wrote on his prescription pad and handed me the paper before he slipped out of the small room.

I waited ten minutes and felt myself starting to feel sleepy at the ticking of the rather large wall clock. It was much too small for a closet sized room. Finally a lady entered addressing me as she took a seat and placed a manila envelope on the table in front of me.

She was a very short with a round shape to her body and had a beefy, red face. The distinct smell of onion and sweat seemed to follow her into the small room; so much so that I wanted to request she leave the door open. However, my good sense told me that might sound rude and at the time I couldn't find another excuse to have it stay open. I did find the smell kept me awake, leaving me on the edge of my seat, fearing I might vomit as my nauseated stomach taunted me.

"Here we have a wedding band, a wallet that contained three one-hundred dollar bills a fifty and two twenties, and this gold necklace with a Celtic cross and inscription on the back. Does that look right to you Mrs. McGuire?" She cleared her very gruff voice inching a pen towards me. She eyed the pen in her hand as if she could move it from her hand to my fingers with the power of her two tiny bulging eyeballs. I nodded and reached for the pen. The clerk to my surprise pulled the pen back not moving her eyes from it.

"Mrs. McGuire, this requires an audible answer. It is only regulation and I don't intend to be in violation of this. Believe me it is not worth risking my job," She never lifted her eyes from the pen, but raised the side of her head as if she was listening for an answer before her eyes could release to me the black pen.

"Yes, that looks right," I answered.

"Awe, now we have reached the conditions right." She eyed the pen over to my hand as I reached for it. I signed quickly on every required line. It was getting to the point where I couldn't breathe in the little room much longer.

"Thank you. You can watch me put these items back in this bag for you, and then the good doctor would like to meet with you in the waiting room one last time. He needs to see you for just a quick moment." The round clerk smelling of onions and sweat got up and abruptly left the room. I quickly grabbed the door behind me while I was still sitting and inhaled the cool air-conditioned air as I got up to leave.

I realized I was pulling on my shirt and dusting off my pants as I walked back in the waiting room. It was as if some of the onion/sweat smell had clung onto me.

I didn't see Crystal and Colin in the waiting room so I took a seat in a corner away from any people and picked up a newspaper to distract myself. I went through the pages just kind of glancing through, until I got towards the back where something stood out to me. A box in the corner read; the flower for the month of July is *Forget me not*. I felt a sad but warm feeling come over me, as if Alec had one last thing to say to me. I started to rip the tiny square out of the newspaper careful so I could cut it out straight when I got home.

Crystal and Colin walked into the waiting room with paper coffee cups in their hands. "Finally, I would have grabbed you something but

I was starting to wonder if you where ever going to come out of there."
Crystal sat down beside Colin and next to me.

"Me too," I replied.

"So are we able to go now or?" Crystal didn't get to finish as the
clerk at the admitting desk interrupted her.

"Did Mrs. McGuire get that prescription from the doctor?" She
was standing and looking over the glass window in front of her, as if it
would obstruct her view of us.

"I have it," I answered.

"Oh, you can go then. For some reason the clerk that was in the
room with you thought you didn't get it yet." She looked down at her
papers. "So you are free to go as far as I can see." She sat back down at
her desk.

"Well let's fill that prescription and get you home," Crystal said as
we all got up.

Since He's Been Gone

Four days had gone since Alec passed. I used a guest bedroom downstairs to sleep in, and I insisted that no one was to go in or disrupt mine and Alec's bedroom. I had not been in it myself since that night. I found having a hard time sleeping after 2:45 AM even with the sleeping pills, so I would often sleep in or sleep during the day.

The coroner ruled Alec's cause of death as an aneurism, verifying the diagnosis of the doctor that first saw Alec in the hospital. I burned inside trying to convince myself that I couldn't have prevented Alec's outcome, had I noticed and identified the symptoms. I found myself constantly wrestling with that. I tried to pull to mind the words of the doctor when he stated that often aneurisms are misdiagnosed and overlooked.

I found myself obsessed with the medical books in our library. I kept looking up aneurism causes, symptoms, and treatments. I learned that the symptoms mimicked many other things and that often delay treatment. In the end it is often too late. I prayed that the burning of guilt that pulsated through my being would be snuffed out so I could focus on the duties that Alec would want done.

I was waiting for our lawyer and the executor to Alec's will to arrive. He had all the funeral plans that and I needed to get them. As hard as it was going to be for me I wanted Alec's funeral to be perfect. He was everything to me and I need to honour him one last time.

I heard the doorbell go and I put my cup of tea down on the lamp table by the couch. I was in the main living room. I arrived at the front doors to see that Colin had opened them from the outside and was calling me.

"Christina its Michael Davis, the lawyer you've been waiting for." Colin smiled.

"Come in Mr. Davis." I pushed the door open further for him.

"I won't need to come in today, Christina, as Alec's executor I have a few instructions to follow before we meet up in two days. Alec specifically asked me to give you this letter to read. Over the next few days I will get a hold of the funeral home to get them to prepare. Alec prearranged his funeral years ago before he died. He didn't want you to have to be left with any extra burdens at this time. After you have taken a few days to digest his letter we will go over things. It is not too complicated as Alec had prepared for this day wisely."

Mr. Davis then handed me a fancy, beige envelope. It had a wax seal on the back with our last name on it. I took it from him, feeling the shocked look on my face. I pressed the letter to my chest.

"No one knows what that letter says; it has been in my office for about four years now. You meant a lot to him Christina! That is one thing I do know," Mr. Davis said as he turned to leave.

The Letter

I walked past Lucia and let her know that I needed to be alone and not to let anyone interrupt me. I then walked through the main living room and towards the back of the mansion to where I was sleeping in a guest room. I pulled the blinds open and crawled onto the middle of the bed crossing my legs. I started to pick at the seal, but I could see I couldn't open it without breaking the seal. I thought for a moment that breaking the seal might actually solidify the fact that Alec is gone forever. I will then be reading a letter that Alec actually wrote me years ago for the purpose of a day he would not exist with me.

I quickly forced myself to be brave and not to think so weak. I looked through the window and up to the skies and prayed to God. I asked him to please see the pain that is within me right now, and to take it from me. I'm sure that from the talks I have had with Alec about You that he believes in you full heartedly. God, just please let him know that I love him so much. Let him know that I will never forget him, but give me the strength God, to live without him. I then popped open the seal on the envelope and pulled the letter out. I unfolded it and began to read.

My Dear Christina,   July 14, 1997

I know it has only been a few short days that I have been gone from you, but I think we both knew that if nature was going to have its way I would be the first to depart. I have made all the arrangements for my funeral, as I don't want you to be burdened at this time. You have had a lot of pain in your young life. This makes one of my deepest regrets that I won't be there to support you through the rest of your life as it unfolds.

I want you to know that my love for you is the strongest love I have ever known. That love is for the Christina I married in 1985 and the Christina I have seen you transform into over the years. You are as beautiful on the inside as you are on the outside.

I continued to find that you lifted the darkness in my life and brought me joy. I have hurt seeing you hurt and rejoiced seeing you happy. I hope that through the years I have returned as much happiness and love to you as you have to me.

It pains me now to think of you hurting or suffering in any way, and I want you to have peace in knowing that I have gone to meet my Maker. Remember the talks we had about your mother being in better place now? I need you to know the same of me. Imagine me in the heavenly realms always looking over you with your mother. We are in the hands of God now.

There are places you will find me when you need to. At the stream where you go to think when you go on a ride. I will be there in all the nature that surrounds you. I will be part of that ray of sunshine that warms your back in the spring when winter hasn't quite retreated. I will also be in that cool breeze when the sun beams down on you too hot. When you go for walks I will still be walking right beside you smelling the flowers as you walk about the grounds. Keep yourself strong and know that my love for you is stronger than even death.

Today as I write this I will take in every moment I have with you and burn it into my head and my heart as if there will be no more moments ahead. I will cherish what I have with you always. Thank you for being the inspiration that kept my life moving. Making it beautiful and exciting, You have meant more to me than you could ever fathom.

My hopes for you are that you will have a peaceful life and to focus on the things that really matter. Don't ever despair if a storm blows your way. I know how strong you really are. Continue to have faith in your abilities and use what I have left you wisely. I have no request for you to carry on my career path. That was my calling. But promise to invest in your own.

If Luke is not with you by the time you read this letter, I pray that will connect, however this unveils. I continue to pray that one day you will find true love and step into it unjaded. I hope that as you soar through your life there will be evidence that in some way I gave you a little help, and a presence of me will remain in your heart never to be forgotten.
Remember I will see you again.

Love never dies and I will always love you

Alec S. McGuire

I held the letter to my chest with tears streaming down my face. I then lay down on the bed hugging the letter. I remember thinking the letter was almost a last conversation I had with Alec, but he didn't let me speak. If he would I would tell him that he can't leave and he needs to come home to me right now. I can't be missing him like this and if this is the way he wants it, I will never get over him. It's just not right.

Alec, please will you come home to me? I want to go for a ride to the stream with you. I want to go for a walk with you and hold your hand. I need to swim with you and soak in the hot tub while we have our deep talks. I remember that you taught me God is bigger than science and is the creator of all we have that. I want you to come with me when I go up a belt in Taekwondo. I want to see the pride beaming on your face.

A couple days later I met with Mr. Davis who read out Alec's last will and testimony. As Alec had said, he had left everything to me, but had paid off Manuela's home and left her and Lucia each a gift of two hundred-thousand-dollars. This was important to me too as Manuela had sent money to her mother and sister to help them out over the years and didn't really get to save for herself until she was in her forties. Also, Alec left three of his antique cars to go his mechanic and auto-body friend. He added a clause that he would remain employed at the mansion to keep his collection (which had grown during our life together) in the utmost condition unless or until I wanted to sell them.

Alec's generosity warmed my heart. It was as if he was still here showing how thoughtful and caring he was. These were the people that Alec had carried through since they were young. As far as any other employees or future employees, they would all be to my discretion.

Alec had hired Mr. Davis to change all the accounts and his pharmaceutical companies into my name. He knew it would be a very hard and stressful time for me. It was just another gesture of love from Alec even after he was gone.

He also provided me with a list of buyers for the companies if I chose to sell. Alec had attached some suggested selling prices that spread over a ten-year period and got higher. I thought that the accounts and the annual income generated from the companies were huge. Seeing how much they could sell for including his shares in parts of companies just showed how much money I didn't know we had. Also I realized how Alec and I had much money tied up in these companies, and that to liquidate it all would take care of me and my grandchildren's grandchildren for the rest of their lives and probably much longer. I didn't want to make any decisions about that anytime soon. I knew Alec had brought it up to me over the years; it was like he wanted to make sure I didn't feel guilty selling it.

I also found that Alec hadn't sold the property in Palm Springs in which he lived with Shannon. He had about five other properties. Only three of them I knew of as we had vacationed at them at different times. I was a bit shocked about this, but I knew that Alec had a lot going on with work and our relationship. He was trying to teach me how to run the property, and the payroll. His will indicated that he hired a man named Angus McCloud: an old school friend of his. He was to run things in the companies the same way he had been; until of course I make a decision on what I might do about them.

The Funeral

The funeral was the very next day. It was set up so I just had to get dressed and go. It was very heartfelt, and there were hundreds of people who attended and many who made speeches about Alec and how he had helped them over the years. I learned how outstanding of a person Alec was throughout his whole life. Many were there from all over. Some had known Alec as early as his late twenties.

I was glad to see it was closed casket and I appreciated that Alec had took my feelings into consideration. Alec knew what happened at my mother's open casket wake. I had told him that I never wanted to go to an open casket wake or funeral again.

At the end of the service, Crystal, Colin, Manuela, Lucia, and I were followed in a limo by the rest of the attendants to Alec's gravesite. When we arrived we were greeted by the playing of at least ten bagpipers dressed in kilts. The beautiful casket was stationed above the open grave on some sort of apparatus. To the side was the stone that would later be placed above his grave. It had a huge marble polished angel. When I looked closely at the angel it had my face on it. The angel was large and the wings where half spread were the ends dipped downward. The angel had a slight tilt in her head and her arms rested on the top of the stone that read.

{*Alec Shaymus McGuire—March 14th 1922-July 27th 2001. Safe in the arms of Jesus.* The next lines read: *Husband of Christina Dianne McGuire. His love for her will carry on into eternity.*}

I would go over his letter at least twice a day to obtain much needed strength, but the dense, empty feeling was overwhelming. I was using the anxiety drugs the doctor prescribed me on a daily basis. It helped to take the edge off, and I could feel that deep inside, if I didn't not take them, functioning would be near to impossible.

Today I decided to take a walk and test out what I considered a promise in Alec's last letter. It was a very still and quiet day. The sun was out and I could hear a bird, but there was not a sign of wind in the air anywhere. This made the day even better. I wouldn't have the wind to contest with and I could concentrate on reading the letter when I reached the gazebo.

I had cleaned up well that day and put the long, white sundress on—the one that Manuela put in my closet that had once belong to Shannon. I decided that I would keep the things that belonged to Shannon and think of them as a kind gesture from Manuela and a part of Alec's distant past. To me the clothes were familiar to Alec over the years before I was born, and I now looked at them as being an honor to wear.

This particular dress was one of the first ones I wore of Shannon's. I remembered the evening I wore it so clearly. I remember when everyone left and Alec and I danced in the gazebo. There was the smell of Alec and the smell of the flowers that were carried over to us through the late summer night breeze.

The Dance

Wearing the white summer dress with eyelet of purple and blue flowers under the breast, I started to walk toward the gazebo. The sun caught my body like tiny little kisses making the temperature just right. I stopped at the purple and blue coloured flowers and picked a few, placing them in my hair behind my ear just like Lucia had done for me that night. I climbed the gazebo stairs. When I reached the top I walked around the hexagon-pieced section. I looked out at the views from all angles until I found myself standing right were Alec and I danced that first time in the gazebo.

I came up close to the rail where I could feel the sunlight, and hear the chirping of some nearby birds. I closed my eyes trying to relive that dance one more time. Alec's voice became clear in my mind as if he were right with me. I could hear him sing a few words as we moved around the gazebo to the rhythm of a love song. I felt my cheek brush his chest and then rest on it. His heart, I could hear it. It was beating again strong and fast as we tightly embraced in our dance together. The music carried us away as he pressed his lips ever so gently on mine and a warm breeze filled my nose. I opened my eyes as the breeze took me from my wonderful daydream. Again I could feel another breeze carrying this wonderful sent.

A thought suddenly hit me. As long as I keep the same flowers in the garden I would always smell them the way I always had with Alec. I realized Alec was here; he was all over our home and our grounds. I think the letter was an indirect way for Alec to indicate to me that he wanted me to never move from the mansion and its grounds. I think he just didn't want to make that decision for me.

I walked down the stairs of the gazebo and found a soft place on the ground to sit. I knew in my heart that this was where I always wanted to be. I felt tears run down my face as I felt the warm caresses of the sun embrace me there on the grass. I was holding the letter in my hand but I couldn't find it in me to read it. It would take away the dance I just remembered and the warm feeling in my heart. To read it now would just reiterate Alec's physical death. I sobbed as I laid the stuffed envelop in front of me on the grass. A flower filled breeze wafted around me at that moment and I found myself lying on my stomach with my cheek rested on the envelope.

I cried out, "Alec, I don't ever want to leave here. All of our memories are here and all I love is here. I know what you were trying to tell me Alec, and I wouldn't leave anyhow. Thank you for not letting me be alone today." I continue to sob. I felt a hand on my back.

"Why would Alec want you to leave here Christina? Are you okay? Why are you crying?" A familiar voice from behind me came. I pushed myself to my knees to see Sebastian there. To my surprise I found myself hugging him and sobbing even louder.

"Alec, he is gone. He died. Didn't Manuela or Lucia tell you?" I said as I hung onto him tight. He placed his arms around me and began rubbing my back.

He replied with his mouth to my ear. "No, I never heard this. I was just heading to the lab to meet Alec. I just talked to him over two weeks ago. Didn't he tell you I was meeting him in a couple of weeks? Manuela and Lucia have no way of getting a hold of me when I'm away in Spain, and I didn't go into the house. When I parked my motorcycle, the guard, Colin told me to go that way. I thought he was meaning Alec was waiting in his lab for me. He does that a lot so I never thought anything of it. Don't cry Christina, tell me how this happened? Did he have an accident or . . . Please tell me what happened?" Sebastian begged.

"He had an aneurism when we were sleeping about two weeks ago—I guess just after you talked to him last. I can remember now he told me you were coming," I sobbed. It felt good to be in someone's arms again and to be held. Sebastian pulled me closer as I cried.

"I was bringing news about Luke and then I was going to quit my profession. Not until after everything is said and done with Luke, but that will be it after. I was coming to tell Alec about Luke. Alec said he had a proposition for me for work instead. I can't believe this; it feels like I just spoke to him. I am so sorry Christina. I'm not going to bring up Luke until you are more settled. I'm going to stay with you here until I'm sure you're doing better. That is if it is okay with you." Sebastian added. "Yes I want you to stay. I'm afraid in the house alone and you can have another one of the guest bedrooms." I pulled away a bit."But why are you quitting your job? And what was Alec's work proposition for you?" I managed to sob out the questions.

"I won't get into that right now, as it is a long story. Alec was going to pay me to be a guard here. He knew Frank will be coming around soon and he said he would pay me what he pays five guards if I would agree to it. I had just agreed to it two weeks ago. Alec said he was going to be writing the agreement up in his office that afternoon. Did he not tell you about it?

Anyhow, don't worry about that. I'm just here for you. I know Alec wanted me to be here before he died, and I am sure he would want it even more now that he's gone. Let's go make our way back to the mansion. You can show me a room and I'll bring in my bags from the bike. I have something I need to talk to Manuela and Lucia about." Sebastian helped me up with his arms still around me. He walked me back to the house holding me close and tight.

Colin met us at the doors and opened them.

"Welcome back stranger," Colin smiled.

"Thanks, it feels good to be here, however I'm sorry about the circumstances that have commenced in my absence," Sebastian said as we walked into the house and closed the doors.

"Sebastian, I have an idea. Let's go into the office and see if we can find the agreement," I said as I wiped tears from my cheeks.

"Are you sure you want to do that right now Christina? We could just get me settled in a room and take a look later." Sebastian stopped and looked at my face.

"No, we are going by the office anyhow. I just want to look now." I sniffled and started to walk through the main living room and down the back hall as Sebastian followed.

New Employee

In the office I found a pile of documents on the desk and I shuffled through them. I looked through file drawers for almost twenty minutes and Sebastian kept trying to prompt me to look later. "Not yet there are a few more places," I said feeling an ache in my heart as I looked at papers with Alec's handwriting.

I finally opened a drawer on the right side of the desk where I saw a file that said 'employment agreement' with Sebastian's name. "Here, I found it, finally!" I pulled the file and sat at the desk while Sebastian sat at the table. I sat down and opened the file. I could see the agreement, but was distracted by some hand-written notes. They read.

> July 26, 2001
> Reasons to have Sebastian on staff as a guard:
> - Sebastian is reliable and never gets distracted
> - No way Frank could get past him
> - Truly has a good heart
> - Sebastian does the job of at least 15-20 guards
> - Sebastian is like family and it would allow him to be around Manuela and Lucia as well
> - He gives 100% and strategizes until he is correct
> - He would be good suitor for Christina when I am gone
> - He would still be doing an extension of what he loves
> - Very organized
> - Trustworthy

"What have you got there? Read it to me!" Sebastian exclaimed.

"Yeah, just one second," I shuffled the notes deep down under documents in the drawer and pulled up the file on the desktop.

The agreement in short read that Sebastian would stay on the property with free room and board and that he would be paid the sum of $60,000 per month for his duties as a guard. It said he would be guarding the property and the grounds. It then stated that his main duty would to be to watch over Christina McGuire. It went on to state other areas of important duties for Sebastian."

I knew the finances and I knew Alec was actually paying Sebastian like he was paying five security guards. I do the payroll and Colin and the others were paid *$12,000* per month.

"So would you have agreed to that agreement Sebastian?" I asked as I turned on the computer.

"I have enough money now from my work over the years. I would do it for Alec for free and I will if you'll have me Christina. I don't plan on going back to what I used to do. My last job is Luke and I'll take that to the finish for you, but I'm done after that," Sebastian stated firmly.

I found a document in the computer under Sebastian's employment agreement. I went into it and wrote today's date and changed Alec's name to mine. I then put it into print.

"What happened to make you so adamant to get out of your kind of work? It must have been something really bad?" I asked as I walked over to the printer.

"Yeah, Christina, I just can't get into that. Before I got here I thought I was dealing with one loss already, and then I hear about Alec. I'm ashamed to even let you know right now. I need to grasp it still myself and then I'll tell you. I just hope it doesn't change your opinion of me. What is that you got there?" Sebastian asked as I put the agreement before him on the table.

"So what do you think my opinion is of you anyhow? I asked.

Sebastian shut his eyes and sat back in his chair. "I'm not sure Christina. I just hope it doesn't get worse once you know. I'm pretty upset with myself right now." Sebastian sat up and cleared his voice then looked at the agreement.

"Read it and please sign." I handed Sebastian a pen.

Sebastian read it over quickly. "I told you Christina I would do this for free." He looked up at me kind of shocked. "Let's not complicate it; this is how Alec wanted it. It is his exact words. I want things to run the way he would have done it." I wiped a small tear.

Sebastian shook his head and signed the agreement. "You are on the payroll and you'll get paid for the full month of August as I dated it August 1st instead of the 10th.

I need you to take the guest room right beside me. I'm not sleeping well at night; sometimes I don't sleep for days. I think it will make me feel more secure." I found this hard to admit to Sebastian.

"Of course, I will be honoured to do this for you and for Alec," Sebastian nodded. I filed the agreement and started out of the office.

"I'm not worried about whatever it is you did Sebastian. You told Alec and it didn't bother him, and I trust whatever Alec trusts." I took Sebastian further down the hall and led him to the room next to mine.

Chapter 13

It had been two years now since Alec died. A new magic was in the air now that Crystal had her baby boy. She named him Shawn and he was just the cutest and was now a year and a half old. He had light blonde hair. I was sure he got that from his parents. His eyes were turning an almost honey-brown color and he was very smart for his age. He called me Auntie Christy and would light up every time he saw me.

Crystal was an amazing mother and she just doted on Shawn. She bought him the cutes clothing and made sure he ate really well. Colin was Shawn's best friend as well as his Daddy. He would hang off of him when he finished work like he was an indoor playground. It warmed my heart to see the family that had evolved since Crystal moved to the mansion. I was glad to be a part of it. I considered Crystal to be a sister to me. I knew I had my own two sisters, but I never seemed to find the right time to open that painful part of my past. I knew one day I would have to. For now I would love the family I had around me in the present.

I decided that I would sell the pharmaceutical companies, and I was working with Mr. Davis and Angus McCloud to find a potential buyer. It wasn't that there was a lack of buyers I just wanted to find one that had the right intentions for the company. Angus could figure that apart out and Mr. Davis could make everything legal.

I had overheard Sebastian talking to Manuela and Lucia about what he did that was so wrong. He was on a case where his brother Rafael was hired, but the opposing end. He didn't know it at first. Then one night he was on a tall office rooftop trying to get a wire going when

Rafael jumped him from behind. Although they recognized each other and came to realize they were working on separate sides, Rafael tried to take Sebastian out.

Rafael shot Sebastian in the arm and wouldn't back off. They ended up in a long, drawn out fight. Rafael had run out of bullets and pulled out a knife. He stabbed Sebastian in the side somehow during the battle. Rafael jumped on Sebastian and had a knife to his throat. Sebastian threw Rafael off the rooftop trying to get the knife from his throat. Sebastian said that from that moment on there were going to be no more jobs for him. He wanted to have a real life.

Sebastian was the greatest for the first half year that he worked at the mansion. He was there to comfort me 24/7. I was so traumatized and it was so hard to sleep at night. I had a door way put in between mine and Sebastian's bedrooms. It didn't have an actual door put on it but it was at the end of our beds. I had it put in just so that I knew he was there, but so we couldn't see each other sleeping.

Many times in the night when I was afraid he came into my room to comfort me and would fall asleep on a lazy boy chair. A few times when I had a nightmare I made him crawl into the bed beside me and wrap around me. I couldn't remember by the next day what those dreams where; I just knew they made me so afraid I was almost inconsolable.

This last year I had Sebastian put up a curtain rod with a dark curtain on it so we could both slowly get our privacy. Sebastian insisted to go everywhere I went to the point that it was getting annoying. He insisted it was what Alec had talked about.

His worrying got even worse when Frank showed up on the property. I couldn't believe how fast Sebastian figured that out. He jumped out of bed one night and when I asked him where he was going he yelled that he was going to get Frank off the property. He told me under no circumstances was I to leave the house. I waited for some time and then I did get to a window near the front of the house. I saw him talking to Frank and it didn't look like a pleasant conversation. I couldn't help but try to get the best look at Frank that I could. I mean it had been years and being that he was the father to my son I kind of wanted to see how he was aging.

He looked terrible; his face was all drawn and he looked like he lost his youthful lustre. He looked thin, and from what I could tell he didn't have near the muscle mass he used to. I saw Frank hesitantly walk back down the driveway and Sebastian push him faster from behind as he escorted him away.

Later when Sebastian came back in the house I asked him how in the heck he knew Frank was around. Sebastian said he heard a Ferrari engine about a mile or so away, which means he must have heard him just before the gate at the end of our driveway.

I was happy that Sebastian was around for that and I knew he would always be good in an emergency.

Scott

In the past six months I had been on a few dates—if you could even call them dates. One was with a businessman that was a partner of Angus McCloud's. He had been helping Angus with some of the business accounting, so I had been meeting him regularly for appointments. His name was Scott. He was a suit and tie sort, but very attractive. He had light brown hair with darker brown eyes, and was very tall with broad shoulders.

Getting to know Scott had kind of evolved from being to so many meetings together lately. This was since I was contemplating selling the business. Scott, as an accountant, didn't think it was in my best interest. He thought he and Angus together could run the business as employees to me and that would be very successful. Angus didn't seem to care one way or another. He was doing it for Alec. He had known Alec since elementary school.

Sometime during those meetings I noticed Scott's fondness for me and I think he might have been able to tell I had given him a second look or two. It started out that he asked me out for coffee. For some reason Sebastian was none too happy about it. He said I didn't know him from Adam and he could be after my company money. When that didn't work he tried to guilt me out about how Alec would feel about the situation.

I remember one evening I had a meeting with Angus and Scott in the office. Towards the end I offered them a drink. The meeting seemed to go well and I thought why not wind it down nicely with a drink. When we left, we proceeded down the hallway of the office and was there was Sebastian. He was leaning against the wall just when Scott asked me to have dinner with him the following Friday. I was about to say yes but Sebastian interrupted and told him I had other obligations on Friday. Surprised, I asked, "I do?" and looked at Sebastian.

"Yes, yes you do we have to go over it tomorrow." He concluded, putting his hand on my back and gesturing for me to move them to the door faster.

"Well, what about Saturday night? I know this really nice Greek restaurant in Kamloops I could take you to." Scott looked at me for an answer.

I started to answer. "Well I'm sure we can make that work."

Sebastian interrupted me. "Well I think you had better see how our Friday goes before you commit to Saturday. It could mean we might have to use Saturday to work that little problem out," Sebastian said as we reached the front doors.

"Oh, okay then we have a meeting on Wednesday and when I get all the numbers together maybe we can put something on paper then," Scott smiled.

"Guess we'll have to cross that bridge when we come to it? I wish you two gentlemen the loveliest of evenings. Goodbye now," Sebastian snapped as practically pushed Scott out the door and then shut it.

"What are you doing Sebastian? That was rude. How could you be so rude to my guest? You know that is not part of your job description." I stood with my hands on my hips.

"How could you like that pompous-ass momma's boy? I mean, how old is twenty-four? He is probably younger than you?" Sebastian waved his hands with a look of discuss.

"He is thirty-six, thanks for the compliment. That is three years older than me. And if I'm so old looking maybe he likes my look. Unlike yourself! It's not like a date at this point. It's just a get together anyhow!" I could feel my blood start to flow.

"I didn't mean it that way. He's just not right for you and it's too soon. You don't get out enough to know what you want. You can't just grab the first thing your age that comes along." Sebastian seemed a little calmer, but I wasn't.

"Well then maybe I need to get out then. And you need to practice not being rude. I am going on the date with Scott and you better not follow me. I'm sure he has no intent to assassinate me or something." I crossed my arms and could feel my anger start to rise.

"Okay, so now it is a date. I don't think you are being true to me Christina. You are not telling me what your intentions are with this guy really are. What do you think Alec would think of this?" Sebastian started to get mad again.

"Sebastian, how could you say that to me? You have no idea. Alec wanted me to find true love one day. Be careful what you say. Maybe you should think about what Alec would think of you?" I cried.

"Oh, I know a lot more than you think and I know about what Alec wanted for you if he was ever going to die. This Scott is not true love for you." Sebastian urged.

"I don't know what you are saying exactly Sebastian, but I'm thirty-three years old. I'm not going to be young forever! You are taking me to Spain in six months to see Luke for the first time. It will be just after his nineteenth birthday. Have you ever thought that maybe I lost Luke's whole childhood and maybe I would like to meet someone and start a family while I still can? It doesn't mean I'm replacing Luke; I have never thought that way. I have a biological clock like any other woman and I would like to have a little family." I paused to calm down

"I'd like to bring some life back to this mansion. I would like to have what Crystal and Colin have. Do you think it doesn't bother me to see how happy they are and how they are already planning their second child? I love them to pieces, I do. I'd just like to have a little of what they have. I probably would feel guilty for saying this if Alec didn't leave the letter and tell me he wanted that for me. Can't you understand that?" I was angry and talking very fast, but I had tears.

Sebastian paced back and forth. "I do want that exact thing for you, Christina. You have no idea how much I want that. You know Alec wanted me here for a reason so please just try to trust my judgment . . . Maybe you need to go on a few dates yourself." He stopped pacing and placed his hand on the side of his chin looking down.

"Just do what you need to, but don't expect that I will be happy, or that I won't give you my opinion. I'm retiring for the night. Good luck with the boy/man," Sebastian added as he started to head towards his room.

"You could also try to work on not being rude to Scott when he comes over." I added, placing my hands back on my hips.

"Yeah, I'll get right on that cause he is such a nice guy and is deserving of my respect," Sebastian mumbled down the hallway.

After this Sebastian seemed a bit more distant, but he was still protective as ever. Somehow my meetings with Scott had turned into dates and were getting a bit more regular. I had to get Sebastian to promise not to bring it up during in our day-to-day life, as it was killing me.

Spain to Luke

The time had arrived and we were going to Spain to see if we could get through to Luke. I had my suitcase packed and so did Sebastian. I almost couldn't believe it was finally happening. Sebastian was following me around the house making sure I had my passport, my wallet, and my sleep medication.

I took the pills the doctor gave me for the flight about a half an hour before we boarded the plane. I was never good with flying and had to take the relaxation pills while flying with Alec as well. Sebastian was concerned if they were going to work for me now as I was so used to taking sedatives. I took a little extra as I did think Sebastian had a valid point.

Sebastian found our seats and we got settled. I grabbed on to Sebastian as the plane started its take off. Sebastian looked happy and smiled. I think he liked it when I looked to him for comfort. I have to admit he had been there for me through some of the hardest times.

As tired as I was, when the plane started to make a bunch of noises my heart pounded and I put my arm through Sebastian's and put my head closely on his shoulder.

"It's okay Honey, as soon as we get off the ground it will be smooth and you won't even know it. You will be sleeping." He then kissed my forehead, which reminded me of Alec. I thought that was a really nice feeling, but I never heard him call me Honey before. I felt myself falling asleep.

Panic on the Plane

It didn't seem like too much time had passed by when I suddenly awoke. My eyes just blinked open, and to my surprise Sebastian had his face really close to mine and it seemed like he was staring at me.

"Hi. You were a bit agitated in your sleep. I was wondering if you were waking up or not." Sebastian rubbed my arm as I started a big stretch. I looked out the window beside Sebastian and saw sky and an itty bitty piece of land, and ocean below. I started to feel like I couldn't breathe.

"Okay, just calm down; you're hyperventilating. You woke up too soon. We still have another four hours." Sebastian said, looking at me concerned.

"What?' I asked, as I made loud breathing noises—it felt like I couldn't get enough air if I tried.

"Where are the pills the doctor gave you? You just need to take a few more and in a half hour you will be sleeping again." Sebastian smiled and continued to rub me on the back now.

"They are in my suitcase. I normally only had to take a couple before. Why the hell are we still in the air?"

Sebastian looked like he was thinking for a minute when he called a flight attendant over and told me to act as normal as possible. I could hardly act normal as I couldn't breathe, but I did my best. I grabbed the magazine off Sebastian's lap and started to pretend I was reading it.

"Can you get me a handful or so of those mini alcohol bottles mixed, diet soda, and a couple glasses of wine for me and my new fiancé? I just proposed to her so we have reason to celebrate."

The flight attendant looked smitten and attracted to Sebastian until he said the fiancé thing. She then looked down at me with my red face as I was holding my breath trying not to hyperventilate.

"Congratulations to you Miss," she said. It took all I had to look up, as I was shocked at Sebastian and in the middle of a panic attack. I just slightly looked up at her and nodded rather fast. Words would not come from my mouth until she left.

"Sebastian, how could you say that?" I gasped halfway hyperventilating. Sebastian laughed and replied, "How else do you think I'm going to quickly get lots of alcohol to you when we are thousands of feet in the air?" His smile faded as he started to see me hyperventilate more. He started to rub my back and tell me to calm down and take deep breaths. He said he was sorry about saying the thousands of feet thing, but the lady was coming back with our loot.

"Are you sure you wanted to tell her you just asked me to marry, she was checking you out and she's pretty cute." I gasped.

"Yeah I'm sure. Now calm yourself here she comes." Sebastian opened the trays in front of us while the flight attendant placed the drinks on the trays.

"Congratulations again, that is a lovely way to ask. We don't have that happen too often thousands of feet in the air." She smiled as I let out a loud gasp. "Oh are you okay?" she asked.

"Oh yeah she is fine, she is still just a little in shock." Sebastian looked at me as I nodded yes. The flight attendant smiled as she walked away. Sebastian opened one of the six mini bottles and dumped it straight into a glass by its self.

"Here, just shoot that back. Sebastian placed the glass on my tray. I did what he asked. He then poured the other half and told me to do the same.

I had finished three of the bottles and then started to sip on my glass of wine. Within about fifteen minutes from the time the flight attendant left us the pilot came on the overhead speaker.

"I'd like to say congratulations to the couple in seats seventy-four and seventy-five who just got engaged on my flight. I have to admit I have heard of this happening, but this is the first time it's happened on my watch. The champagne you will be receiving in a few short moments is on me. Again, I'd like to congratulate the happy couple in seats seventy-four and seventy-five. The entire plane of people started to clap as I sunk in my seat.

Sebastian started laughing, "You better sit up. Here comes the attendant again."

The attendant came down the aisle again with a tray containing a small bucket with a mini champagne bottle in it. She smiled and handed us two plastic champagne glasses.

"Congratulations again, Oh let me see that ring?" She smiled removing three empty miniature bottles. I held up my hand and showed her the ring that Alec had gotten me. I still hadn't taken it off.

"That is so beautiful. You are one lucky lady!" she said as she turned to look at Sebastian with a big smile. Then she left with her tray, stopping to grab other passenger's dirty dishes and wrappers.

I could feel myself starting to relax now. In fact I felt quite tipsy as I took my last sip of wine. Sebastian opened the bottle of champagne with a little chuckle as he poured it into the two champagne glasses.

"Oh, no more for me thank. I'm feeling it already." I put my hand out to stop him from pouring. "I'll drink it, but you can have a sip or two to pretend you are having some. We don't want to seem ungrateful. Look, the attendant is looking back here right now to see if we are enjoying our complimentary champagne. The bottle only holds two small glasses. You can pretend and I'll drink it." Sebastian smiled and sipped his champagne.

"The attendant is looking back here because she thinks you're a hot and that is the only reason she's looking back this way. I can't believe you can't tell when someone likes you. Especially when they make it as blatantly obvious as she is. She could probably use one of those napkins she has piled there on the tray to wipe her drool up," I laughed.

Sebastian looked down at me inquisitively. "If she did think I was, however you say it 'hot', she is too. She looks much too . . ." I interrupted. "Much to what . . . Like a model? Her teeth are too white; her hair is too shinny for you? I can't see how you could find any fault with her?" I smiled up at Sebastian.

"Well I think she looks plastic, and she's way too tall for my liking. I'm more partial to women who are at least a couple inches shorter than me when they wear heels.

You are one to talk Christina; you couldn't tell if a guy, well at least if a good guy liked you. He could write it to you in a letter and you would think he was just being kind." Sebastian said, sipping his champagne. "Oh, you just know that I am right and that just kills you." My laugh faded as I looked just past Sebastian and out the plane window.

"Christina. It's Okay you're doing fine. Look, you can see part of France and to the side is the North Atlantic Ocean. We are going to make a slight turn and then we will be above Spain. Soon we will be off this plane and you will feel much better."

I realized I was draped across Sebastian with my head rested on his far shoulder looking out the window. Sebastian had his fingers through my hair rubbing the back of my head. I picked up a small bottle of the strong alcohol off his tray and I drank it back quickly as I started to get a falling feeling.

"You're going to be okay, just breathe. You are doing better already.

"How is everything? Can I get you something else?" The same flight attendant approached us again. I laughed and Sebastian told her we were quite fine.

"Oh, I see someone looks like they are doing very fine here. I will let you two relax now, we should be landing in about forty-five minutes." She smiled again looking back over her shoulder as she walked away. I'm not sure how she managed to not trip looking backwards while she was balancing a tray in heels.

Drunk talking

"I can't believe how good you're doing, granted you have a stomach full of alcohol. But you're awake and you even looked out the window." Sebastian looked at me like he was proud.

"Well I have this nice handsome body guard to watch over me and help pull me through things," I responded, as placed my head back on Sebastian shoulder. "So you do appreciate me? He laughed. "But the question is how much do you appreciate me? A list, I want a list right now please." Sebastian started.

"Well you help me with everything from opening doors to keeping weirdo's off my property and finding my son. I know you have gone beyond the call of duty since Alec died. You slept in my room and even with me when I was very scared. You always give me pep talks and try to make me feel better." I felt myself starting to get sleepy.

"You got amazing abs," I said rubbing my hand roughly across his stomach as he lifted his hand away. Then you got a rock-solid crop of chest muscles." I rubbed my head hard against his chest and pulled my arm across to his other shoulder. "And you have these broad shoulders and stone biceps! I don't think I have seen a more beautiful man in my life," blurted slowly as I felt myself fading into sleep again.

I awoke to the plane shaking and bouncing around.

"Sebastian, what's going on?" I half yelled.

"It's okay, we're just landing. It's always a bit bumpy." The plane started to slow down and before we knew it we were in a line up slowly making our way off the plane.

I could feel myself losing my balance even though everything was still.

"We are going to our hotel right away and you are going to have a little nap." Sebastian stated.

"It's day time. I wanted to look around and maybe see if we can see Luke today," I said excitedly.

"It's only morning hear right now. You can have a sleep and then we will have some brunch. Then we can consider going out." Sebastian grabbed my hand as we exited the plane.

"Why does it always have to go the way you want it?" I snapped. "Well I guess that's because I have a rock-hard chest and well, look at my amazing abs. Perhaps it's more to do with my stone biceps?" Sebastian laughed as he put my arm under his, leading me down a ramp and into the airport.

"I thought I was dreaming that part. I was trying to cheer you up, when I said that." I tried to search myself for things to say, but nothing came to me that would smoothly explain what I had said.

"As I remember it, I was pretty happy already. You were the one who needed encouragement," Sebastian smugly remarked as we reached the luggage conveyer.

Checking in at the hotel I could feel my intoxication.

"Yes, we have reservations under Christina McGuire for room 1209," Sebastian prompted the desk clerk.

"No, no way am I staying in a hotel room that is higher than the fifth floor. I'm not going to do that again. Alec respected that and you should too." I insisted rather loudly.

"Please give us a moment?" Sebastian said to the desk clerk."What is the big deal with a floor that is higher than the fifth floor? Look, I you need to just lay down and calm down."

I interrupted, "I am not going." I crossed my arms being extremely stubborn. "Every time I went to Vancouver with Frank he always made us take the seventeenth floor and if you haven't noticed today, I do not do well with heights. Unless you want me to be completely drunk for the whole time we are here. I need a lower level. Please tell me you're not another Frank?" I huffed.

"Okay, first, don't compare me to Frank, and second, just give me a second." Sebastian looked at the lady at the front desk and they began to have a conversation in Spanish. I rolled my eyes causing myself to stumble a bit. Sebastian grabbed both sides of me to support me as he continued his conversation with the desk lady. Of course I had no idea what they were saying. I just knew it ended with Sebastian being handed keys to a room on the fifth floor. Sebastian asked the lady in English if she would get our things brought up to our new room.

Sebastian helped me lay on one of the beds. He pulled the covers over me and instructed me to remove my clothes under the blanket so I would be more comfortable, as our luggage hadn't been delivered to our room yet. I did as he said and he gathered my clothing and laid it over a chair.

"Sebastian I'm sorry I suggested you would be anything like Frank, and I'm sorry about all the things that I said to you on the plane. I don't want to ruin our working relationship. I know Alec wanted you to take care of me for a reason. Please forgive my foolishness. I'm so sorry Sebastian." I apologized, feeling suddenly really tired. "There is nothing to forgive Christina. Alec wanted me to be your personal guard for many reasons. As you know Alec was a smart man and he saw the obvious in me, and he called me on it. He saw strait through me and knew my true feelings for you. We had a really good talk. Trust me Christina! Alec wanted me to be around for a long time even after he would pass on. Of course he didn't know he would be passing so soon," I heard Sebastian's voice start to fade as I started to fall asleep in the very cozy hotel bed.

Real Dream

I saw my mother. She was wearing the dress at the funeral parlour, the one she wore to church on occasion. We were in Sunday school and she was telling the story of Jacob and how much he loved Rachael and how he worked hard to have Rachael's hand in marriage. My mother put little felt figurines on a board telling the story. Her hair was straight and brown and her nails and lipstick were mauve. I felt a sense of pride as she told the story. Suddenly I lifted out of the room into outer space, but my mother didn't notice. She just kept teaching the class. I lifted up higher and higher and then I pulled away from the class to the side. Now they were so tiny and far away. Abruptly, I started to fall. The wind was at my face and I couldn't breathe. I just kept falling and falling and falling. I could see the earth and I was coming towards it fast it was getting bigger. Now I could see roads and buildings. I shot through the roof without getting hurt, and I started to slow down as I went through the first floor, then the second floor, then the last floor. I landed on my mother's lap in a childhood home we had lived in.

She looked younger and more beautiful than ever; I was about ten years old. She kissed me tenderly on the forehead when I felt someone behind her rubbing my head. I turned around to see Alec. He looked younger like he did in the pictures strewn about the attic with his first wife Shannon. He also looked healthy and spry.

My mother handed me to him and he took me on his lap. He told me that he would never stop loving me and that I needed to be smart about things. He told me that I only have one life and I need to do good by it. Then he smiled as he brushed his hands across my cheek and told me to never forget his notes.

He picked me up and started walking with me in his arms. We were outside on the lawn at the mansion. I saw myself. I was on the grass near the gazebo. I was wearing the white summer dress with eyelet of purple and blue flowers and weeping on the grass with my cheek on Alec's letter. I could hear what I was saying. "Alec, I don't ever want to leave here. All of our memories are here and all I love is here. I know what you were trying to tell me Alec, and I wouldn't leave anyhow.

Thank you for not letting me be alone today." I continue to sob to myself. I felt a hand on my back.

"Why would Alec want you to leave here Christina? Are you okay? Why are you crying?" A familiar voice from behind me came. I pushed myself to my knees to see Sebastian there. I saw myself throw my arms around him.

Alec placed me on the grass beside my older self that was now frozen in an embrace with Sebastian. "Christina, you know how much I love you and I only want good things for you?" He looked at me for an answer so I nodded at him. "This is where you need to be and I must leave you here until one day we can see each other again." Alec knelt down and hugged me and then kissed my forehead one last time.

Then this young Alec walked away from me through the green grass. I stood and watched him with a longing heart. A few clouds started to depart from the sky and a sunbeam glinted as it shone on Alec, making him look like he disappeared into the surroundings. I then turned around looking at me and Sebastian in a frozen embrace. I noticed that everything on the side where my adult self stood was frozen and when I looked the other way where Alec had left everything was moving. I started to panic, my heart was thumping and I couldn't breathe.

I awoke with a loud scream in our hotel room. I was air hungry as I hyperventilated.

"Christina?" I saw Sebastian jump from his bed over to mine. He wrapped himself around me and I pulled on each of his arms individually to make them tighter around me.

"Baby it's Okay; you just had another one of those bad dreams. I'm here, I'm not going to leave you. Just breathe. Take deep breaths. You need to take some nice deep breaths." Sebastian was holding me so tight he was talking really close into my ear.

"Please don't leave. I'm scared, and you know Alec wouldn't want you to" I added.

"You know what? I wouldn't want to leave either." Sebastian kissed my forehead and rocked me in his arms. "I tried to go back over the parts of my dream before I forgot all of it. I especially wanted to go over the parts with Alec in it. It seemed so real and I hadn't seen him for such a long time. What was he trying tell me? Some of it was starting to get foggy already. I mostly remembered him bringing me to the mansion and I remembered him saying something about not to forget his notes. Notes! I saw some notes of his. What were those last notes?

Of course, I thought; the notes in the file drawer on top of Sebastian's employment agreement. I could see them in my mind. I couldn't remember them. They all seemed fuzzy but one seemed to stand out. I tried hard to put my mind into focus. I tried as hard as I could to zone in on what the notes said until I could see a faint picture of them in my head. There was a line on the note that stood out in my mind. It was almost too blurry to make out.

July 26, 2001

Reasons to have Sebastian on staff as a guard:
- Sebastian is reliable and never gets distracted
- No way Frank could get past him
- Truly has a good heart
- Sebastian does the job of at least 15-20 guards
- Sebastian is like family and it would allow him to be around Manuela and Lucia as well
- He gives 100% and strategizes until he corrects
- He would be good suitor for Christina when I am gone
- He would still be doing an extension of what he loves
- Very organized
- Trustworthy

Sebastian wouldn't know about these notes, so he wouldn't even know what Alec was thinking. Or did he? I thought I recalled him saying something about that he and Alec talked. I wonder what they had talked about. I couldn't wrestle with it anymore. My eyes were heavy and Sebastian's rocking me made me fall back to sleep. I remember before I fell asleep how safe I felt with Sebastian and how strong he felt draped around me.

Sebastian's Heart

Sebastian and I finally woke up together at 2 PM. He released his hold on me and I realized I had flipped over in my sleep and was cuddled into him the same way I used to cuddle into Alec. We were facing each other. I never really saw Sebastian this close face to face even the times when he had to sleep with me at the mansion. We used to always break apart during the night.

We lay there for what seemed a long while just looking into each other's eyes. It was hard for me not to want kiss him, but I still wasn't sure what to make of him and the dream I had. The dream felt fuzzy and faded. I knew I would have to really think deeply it over and over to remember it, as it was when I dreamed it.

"You are so beautiful Christina. Why don't you be mine? You say you want to have a family and to find true love. Maybe you are looking right at it? I know that's what I see when I look at you. I knew that the day I walked in the front door and Alec introduced us. I know that doesn't sound good, but when I read your profile, and the conditions under which you were married didn't seem legitimate. I felt a kind of connection; it seemed like you felt it as well.

"Later it was clear that Alec truly loved you as his wife and I backed off. I don't want to force anything that you don't feel. Please take your time and make sure it is or it isn't what you think. I'll try not to pressure you, and for me that will be hard. I have never felt this way for anyone in my life ever.

"I don't know what I feel right now. I had some odd dreams and Alec was in them. It feels like it really happened although, I know it was a dream. The strangest thing is that I can't quite remember the dreams. I guess I just need to go back over it many times in my head and hope it comes to me. It's confusing I know you were in the dream too, but I don't remember why.

I do admit that when I first met you I did feel a connection. I felt guilty for looking at you that way, maybe even mad. I loved Alec so much and I still love Alec. I don't know if I will find a more loving and trustworthy man in my life. I almost don't expect there is anyone else in this world that is even near to Alec in his traits. I just hope that whoever is my true love of my future will have some of Alec's qualities. I guess it is too important for me, not to just make a spur of the moment decision.

I hope we can just not complicate the time that we are here about where we stand with each other. Just give me some time to think about my feelings and explore what might be my future." I was looking at the expression change on Sebastian's face, which started to look less pleasant as I paused.

"That will be extremely hard for me, especially if you feel you still need to see Scott. But when that falls through, if it proves to you that I am that man that you are looking for, I will give it my best effort." Sebastian placed his hand on the side of my cheek and kissed my forehead.

"We do need to get moving here it's 2:20 PM and Adana will be hitting the ladies gym at 6 PM. We should clean up; get something to eat so we are ready to go." Sebastian pushed the blankets off of us revealing that I was only wearing my bra and panties. I quickly pulled the sheet back over me. "Oh, sorry I forgot. My bad!" Sebastian covered his eyes with his hand while he smiled.

Confronting Adana

It was 5:46 PM and we were sitting outside the ladies gym where we were planning to intercept Adana before she went in.

"Just stick to the plan. I will follow right behind you if anything goes wrong. Let's just check your wire before you go," Sebastian said while he adjusted it under my shirt. "Okay, that's her right there. Get going, she'll grab her bag out of the back seat and go in." Sebastian reached around me, and opened my door, and gave me a little push out.

I walked swiftly up to the white Mercedes as I saw Adana open her door and step up on the sidewalk and towards her back seat.

"Adana?" I called out to her. She looked over the hood of her car towards me as I scurried onto the sidewalk until she was directly in front of me.

"Do I know you?" she asked. "Yes, as a matter of fact you do know me, although it has been a long time . . . if you think nineteen years is a long time." I placed my hand on the back door of her car and rested it there so she couldn't get her gym bag. She looked a little nervous. It was kind of like she was recalling something. Perhaps it was some deep, dark thing in her distant past.

"Well I certainly don't recall you. I mean, you don't look familiar." She put her hand on her hip. She was defiantly the tall woman I remembered, and her sleek, dark red, tight gym suite and jacket enhanced her height.

"Funny, you still look the same as you did nineteen years ago, but I guess that could be due to the facelift you had three years ago. I'm sure you can remember that. You know, maybe I'm not recalling you right. Last time I saw you I could barely open my eyes because I was losing so much blood." I raised my voice ever so slightly at her. When I finished, her eyes popped, she rubbed her hand over her neck, and she took a step back.

"I um . . . I really don't recall what you're talking about. I don't remember such an incident. I think you might have me mixed up with someone else?" Adana's eyes widened as she started to nervously pull the pendant on her necklace back and forth.

"I don't think that could be possible. I could never forget the woman who walked away with my newborn baby . . . Luke!" I made sure to spit out Luke's name extra loud.

"You can't prove that. I have papers, medical records, and I have a birth certificate for him naming Dirk and me as his parents!" Adana came back at me quickly as her eyes bulged.

"Yeah, I know exactly what you have because I have copies. But I have one other thing that connects me to Luke as his real mother. I have his DNA and you're never going to have that, Adana," I retorted confidently.

"You had better just leave. I know no one will look twice, they will just laugh at you if you even claimed this. No one would waste their time and money to prove such an unlikely situation." She looked as if she was trying hard to convince herself.

"Adana, I have money; lots of it. And I have time and have already put together a case that proves you faked your documents. I have been working on this for years, and if you don't let me see Luke I will make sure you go to prison for a very long time," I fired back at her.

"A doctor saw me and he witnessed on paper that I had just given birth." Adana looked like she was running out of things to say.

"Yeah I know, and it's so convenient that the doctor that looked at you was Dr. Everhart Vandenhoff, if I recall correctly! I'm sure I could go refer back to my documentation. I'm pretty sure I do have it right though. Don't, I Adana? And isn't it true that he is your husband, Dirk's brother. Hmm . . . man, he could be in some pretty deep trouble for that once the DNA results roll in. I can't even imagine how he would explain that one. Although, he and you have all been pretty crafty in the past . . . but you just aren't that good.

I think that if you want to avoid being prosecuted and a lengthy jail sentence I would get into the black car about three cars behind us. Then we can weigh the pros and cons." I suggested looking at the red mark forming on Adana's neck from her nervously pulling her pendant.

"Okay, I'll agree to go talk with you, but I don't think it's a good time to see Luke right now. He's taking some college courses right now that need his undivided attention. He has to have it to take over his . . . Dirks business when Dirk retires." Adana's face looked red as I led her to the rental car Sebastian was sitting in. Sebastian got out of the car and opened the roadside back door for Adana and I to get in. We slid in and I shut the door behind us.

"So you and Dirk are planning to hand Dirk's business down to Luke?" I asked. Before she could answer I began to speak again. "Did it ever occur to you that Luke is not interested in Dirk's business and the fact that Luke despises Dirk's business? It's against everything that Luke believes in and you know that Adana." I looked at her confused face.

"Yes, I know that. Remember, I have mothered Luke since he was born. What I don't know is how you know this?" Adana looked inquisitively at me for an answer.

"Let me introduce my agent to you. This is Sebastian." I stretched my arm out towards the driver's seat where Sebastian was turned around and leaning forward with an outstretched hand. Adana looked hesitant and shook it. "This is the man who has been messing up your security systems for about the past eight to ten years." Adana interrupted me.

"Yes, we have had some intermittent problems with the electrical system. Are you telling me that this man has been spying on my family?" Adana looked at me as if she had been violated.

"Well just hold on there a minute. It is a legitimate business and you took something that didn't belong to you. Don't be looking at me like I'm some kind of monster, Adana. What you did was so illegal and just . . . wrong, and I've seen it's not the first time you have tried to do it either. I have paper and money trails on all of your activities, and you know what? They can't be destroyed. You wouldn't even be able to guess where I hid them," I laid that out to her. Sebastian stepped in. "Now what about this making Luke go to college to learn how to take over his father's business. I know you understand perfectly clear that Luke hates what his Father does. You yourself have even argued with Dirk about how he has been hard on Luke about learning the family business. What are you thinking?" Sebastian surprised me at how upset he sounded for Luke.

"I know . . . It's true I have tried to talk to Dirk about it and he just won't let up. He makes me feel guilty by reminding me that he got the baby that I wanted, and he should have the son he wanted to take over his business to carry on his legacy." Adana looked ashamed as she looked down, still playing with her pendant.

"I know you truly do love Luke, Adana. I've read and discussed the reports over the years. What I don't understand is that if you love him so much why didn't you tell him he was adopted like you told me you would?" I asked, feeling myself getting a little heated.

"I was going to but on the plane coming back Dirk and I came up with a plan about how to obtain a birth certificate, and we knew we needed one if Luke was going to have a normal life. That destroyed my plan to tell him when he was old enough. I didn't want him to find out that he was adopted and then correct and explain how he was born at home. Dirk wouldn't have it, he just wouldn't." Adana took a few deep breaths.

"I didn't know if there were hereditary disorders in your family and I didn't want him to go back into his medical records even after I'm gone. Please don't make me tell him he isn't mine, Christina," Adana cried as she looked at me with pleading eyes.

"Adana, I remember feeling like I was begging you to tell Luke I was his real mother, and you walked away with him and took him out of my life for what I thought was forever. I think it's time that you tell Luke the truth as soon as possible so you don't damage your relationship with him any further. If you don't tell him, I won't leave here until I tell him.

Adana, I don't want to damage your relationship with Luke, but this needs to be done. Also you need to stop Dirk from forcing Luke to do something that would make him miserable for the rest of his life. You have three days; no longer. And don't try to pull anything. We have your house completely wired and you will never figure out where and how." I warned Adana.

"Let's do it right now then. I don't want to do it around Dirk and I know exactly where Luke is right now. If you're going to destroy me in front of my son . . . you might as well get it over with!" Adana turned around in her seat and did up her seat belt.

"He's studying in the college library," she said, signalling for Sebastian to drive forward. I couldn't believe this was actually going to be happening. Adana crossed her arms and instructed Sebastian where to go until we pulled up to a castle sized college where we pulled over to the opposite side of the road. We got out and followed Adana across the street and into the building. We walked down several hallways until we came to an elevator.

Finally My Luke

Adana looked miserable, so I didn't want to look happy or take my guard down in any way. The elevator opened and we followed Adana out and took a sharp, right turn.

"The library is over here." Adana walked swiftly, but we kept up to pace with her.

"Hello Mrs. Vandenhoff. Luke is in the hallway." A group of girls giggled as they walked by. "I'm sure you know just where he is, you flock of vultures." Adana replied to them rudely.

"Hey, go easy on them. They're just young girls," Sebastian snapped.

Adana looked back while she continued her swift pace. "If you had to deal with all the girls that try to swoon in on my son you'd be saying the same thing. But you should know that right? With all your high-tech, yet invisible spying you do." Adana looked back again with a snarl.

"Yeah, I have seen; it's called hormones, and you should trust your son's choices. It might surprise you how much smarter he is than you are in this area," Sebastian retorted.

Adana turned the corner into the library when some girls indicated to her where Luke was studying. She then waved for us to walk up beside her. I could see some rows of long tables with high, back padded chairs. The library was enormous with what looked like thirty foot ceilings, high bookshelves, and large stain glass windows portraying characters from famous books.

Towards the end of the section of library I could see Luke. I knew it was him. My heart was pounding hard now. I felt Sebastian squeeze my hand. I don't know if he did it to signal to me that the boy before us was Luke, or to calm me down.

"Luke, My Darling, I'm here! Adana flung her arms up and Luke quickly got out of his seat and embraced Adana. "You are such a good boy, studying as hard as you do." Adana winked.

"Thanks Mom, but I think you know what I would rather be doing. I think you forgot to introduce me to your friends." Luke looked at us with the most beautiful smile. Hearing his voice was like music to my ears. I found myself pinching myself to figure out if this was real.

"Yes, please have a seat." Adana gestured us to sit, and she pulled a chair out for herself. "First of all, Luke, I will tell you that this here is Christina and this man here is Sebastian. Christina and Sebastian, this is my son Luke . . . for what it's worth to you." Adana put her elbows on the table and leaned her head on her fists.

"Mom, why are you being rude?" Luke said as he slowly pushed his mother's elbows off the table as he looked around at all of us confused.

"Luke, there is no good way to explain this to you. We need to talk. I've been keeping something from you, and I know I need to come strait with you." Adana looked down.

"Mom, do you think maybe you can find a better time than now? Maybe when we don't have these people here?" Luke said, looking very uncomfortable. I couldn't believe she didn't have the decency to look Luke in the eye.

"It involves them, Luke. Please don't hate me. Believe me when I tell you this; I love you and I have devoted my life to you. I really don't want to lose you. I did this with the best intentions, so please keep that in mind as you listen to what I'm about to say," Adana gasped.

Luke sat up and moved to the end of his seat, grabbing Adana's wrist as his eyes scanned over the three of us.

"Okay Mom, please tell me . . . . . I'm listening." Luke looked genuinely concerned.

"Luke, you're not my biological son; you were adopted," Adana cried and covered her mouth with her hand careful not to move the arm that Luke held. "I did a bad thing, Luke. It was an illegal adoption. Your biological mother was very young, and I didn't learn until much later that she always wanted you . . . It was her father that wanted to sell you. They were embarrassed about their daughter having a baby at such a young age, and they needed some money to keep their business going." Adana cried some more as Luke pushed her arm away from him.

"You bought me? What the hell, Mom? How old was the girl?" Luke asked looking like he was going to throw up.

"She was only fifteen years old. She had the same complexion as your father, and the boy that impregnated her had the same complexion as me—that's why you never questioned it." Adana cried.

"Mom, I didn't question it because I didn't know. That doesn't mean I didn't feel different. I'm nothing like Father . . . or Dirk. I would absolutely expect this from him, but you . . . why wouldn't you tell me?"

"Wait . . . oh my God . . . are you going to tell me these are my parents? Luke sat back with a disgusted look on his face as his eyes went between Sebastian and I. He crossed his arms. "Go on Mother, tell me some more. I want it all to come out right now." Luke then looked over to Adana for an answer.

"Not exactly . . . I mean the girl . . . Christina here is your biological mother; the man is her agent, he found you for her," Adana explained.

Luke interrupted, "She had to pay someone to find me? So you weren't going to tell me on your own after all?" Luke looked at me in a gentler fashion now as he questioned Adana.

"Luke, your father wouldn't let me. We had documentation from your uncle stating that I gave birth to you at home. I thought about it over the years, but your father was against it. In fact, he doesn't even know I'm telling you right now. You're father is going to kill me when he finds out!" Adana placed her hands over her eyes and started to cry.

"Don't call him my father anymore. I can't believe you. You only hurt for yourself and what happened to you. What about this woman over here who has been searching for her son . . . me . . . ever since I was taken from her. I just can't even bare to look at you right now. I won't be going home tonight. I have my own money now, and I'm going to find a hotel until I can find a place for myself. And I won't be studying here to learn Dirk's inhumane business because I refuse to take it over, ever.

"You know, I used to think I would do it for you and then change it slowly. I was going to pay those poor people a wage they could actually live off of. But now I feel relieved because I don't feel guilty about ditching it." Luke got up slamming his books shut, and Adana started to get up after him. Luke placed his hand on her chest and told her not to follow him before he took off out of the library.

"Adana, you need to give him a little time. He needs it; you kind of dumped that on him a bit rough," Sebastian said.

"I'm going to try to talk to him." I got up and dashed out of the library. I could see Luke walking down the hall. I ran and caught up to him. "Luke, please. I've been dreaming and looking for you my whole life. If you could just give me a few moments of your time . . . I won't interfere with your life anymore if you don't want me to." I pulled on his arm and he hesitantly turned around to face me. I saw the tears running down his face dripping from his long, black lashes. He hung his head down and started to cry.

"It's too much . . . just way too much . . . I'm . . . so sorry you had to go through this. It must have been terrible for you. Don't think I don't want to see you, I do I'm . . . just overwhelmed," Luke sobbed.

He was so tall next to me; I estimated that he was about six feet tall compared to my own five foot stature. I could see what Adana meant by girls swooning over him. He was adorable, and I guess young girls would find him completely attractive. I really admired his sense of others and how he worried about what effect things might have had or were having on me.

"You know, you're really helping me out at this time in my life. You saved me from going against every moral and value I have in myself," Luke sobbed. I pulled him towards me and put my arms around him. He started to bawl on my shoulder. He was so heartbroken and it felt so wonderful that I could comfort him during a bad time in his life. I only dreamed I would be able to be there for him at a time like this.

"It's okay Luke. It's going to take some time Sweetheart, but you need to know that Adana does love you, and she just badly wanted a baby to love. She does love you Luke. I love you too; I always have and always will. You will get through this, and I will always be here for you if ever you need me. Well, I'll be in Canada, but I can come here and I hope you will come and see me when the shock of this wears." I was crying a bit too.

"I'm sorry. I shouldn't be such a baby. But it will take me a long time to trust my mother . . . Adana, my adopted mother again. The whole scenario to me is just so wrong. I'm sorry about what happened to you. I don't even know what to call you," Luke cried a little louder.

"You can call me whatever you like. I can be your second Mom, or just Christina, whatever you want, Luke. I think you need to talk to

Adana though. I think I'll leave tomorrow and let the two of you work through the initial shock of this.

I want you to call me anytime you need me, so I'll give you my phone number and my mailing address. When you're ready you can call me or write me . . . And I hope one day you will come visit me. You can stay as long as you like; I mean that." I tried to stress to Luke to contact me, and I really felt I needed to not be there to complicate his relationship repair with Adana.

"Let me get you a pen. I really want to get to know you . . . I really want to know my real mother." Luke sobbed, let go of me, and wiped his eyes. He stepped away from me and turned towards a payphone that was stationed in the hallway. He tore a piece of paper from the back.

"The pen is attached to the book, so you'll need to come here to write it down. I would prefer that you write it so I can have something of you with me." Luke laid his arm up against the top of the payphone and sobbed a bit more, rubbing his face on his sleeve. His head was turned away from me and he gestured the pen towards me.

"Luke, I want you to have this until we meet again—then you can give it back to me. I pulled off my most beloved wedding ring that I hadn't removed since Alec's death—not even to bathe—and I put it in his hand and closed it. I pulled his closed hand up to me and I kissed it. Luke, who was still sobbing handed me the torn paper and then the pen. I put the paper against the wall and wrote all of my information on it. I wrote below it: *I love you Luke*.

Chapter 14

We had been back at the mansion for about three weeks. I was missing Luke and longing to see him again—or at least have him call. I was so happy with the way Luke had turned out. I could only sum it that Luke had a naturally good heart.

Dirk had absolutely no integrity, was careless of others, and had a greedy wife. Being raised by this particular set of people, held little hope that Luke wouldn't turn out to be like one of them. I could tell from the way that Luke talked to Adana in the library that he was empathetic and very moral, even when he was the one that was hurting.

In the hallway of the college where I got to speak alone with Luke I could see that he was selfless again. He seemed to care more about my feelings than he did about what was happening to him.

I replayed my short, first introduction to my son over and over. I thought about how Adana broke the news to Luke. To Sebastian and I, it seemed she was more concerned about how informing Luke was going to affect her, not Luke. I jumped every time the phone rang, and often clipped the phone to my pants hoping that if Luke called I would be the first voice he heard on the line. I didn't want him to hang up if he heard an unfamiliar voice and think that he had the wrong number . . . Maybe he might even think that I gave him a wrong number. I really wanted him to come and stay with me soon.

I had only been on a few dates with Scott. They were quite awkward as I could sense Sebastian's frustrations. He would be waiting for me outside the mansion when Scott and I pulled up, and he would rant at Scott if he were more than ten minutes late getting me back. I felt quite embarrassed as if Sebastian were treating me like I was a teenager late for my curfew. I tried to balance my frustration out by remembering that Alec wanted Sebastian to be here. Also, I kept in mind that this was difficult for Sebastian as well.

Sebastian and I had a long talk when we arrived home where I explained to him that I just needed to give Scott a chance and just see if maybe he was the match for me. I just didn't want to lose an opportunity with someone who was meant to be in my life, and I didn't want to ruin my relationship with Sebastian due to some animal attraction we had for each other. I basically didn't want to stoke the fire that Sebastian and I already felt for each other just to have it burn out and then be left with nothing.

It was early in the evening on a Friday, and I was dressed up to have dinner with Scott at some fancy restaurant. Although I had many dresses to choose from that were still in the attic, I chose to wear the long, deep dark red one. It was strapless and was made of a sheer type of material at the upper thigh area so that my legs showed through. At the back, it had a slight V-shaped, short train. I wore the ruby tear-shaped earrings and necklace. I also wore the matching deep red shoes and found a matching red shawl. Years before, I had Manuela take some of the clothes that were Shannon's back up to the attic as my walk in closet was getting crowded.

Crystal did my hair and make-up; she did such a good job. I swear she made me look better than the hairdresser and make-up artist had done it at the Vancouver hotel. Crystal knew how important this night was to me. I was so glad to have a friend that was so close to me and really understood me. I really thought this was the night that I would know whether or not Scott was the guy for me. He seemed almost too perfect, and I needed to know in fact that he was all he seemed or if he was guarded.

I heard Lucia call out to let me know that Scott was just let in the gates and would be there soon. I told Crystal again how I had a feeling that this would be the night I would really question Scott and dig deeper to see who he really was and what his intentions were. Crystal picked my shawl up and followed me down the stairs, beaming at the job she had done on my hair and make-up. At the bottom of the stairs stood Sebastian, and I could tell by the reaction on his face that he liked my choice of dress and the way Crystal had done my make-up.

"Wow . . . you look amazing, stunning . . . I mean . . . so beautiful. I'm telling you the truth when I say I have never seen someone so beautiful in my life . . . But . . . you really shouldn't wear that tonight with Scott. Christina, that is not fair!" Sebastian crossed his arms like he was blocking me from coming down the last stairs.

Frustration

"I'm going to let you guys alone to work this one out." Crystal walked around me and passed Sebastian.

"I've stood here and watched you go on dates and out for coffee with this guy and I'm telling you I don't get a good vibe from him. You say that we will explore us to see if we're meant to be, but have you gone on a date with me? Have you dressed up like this for me? The last time I saw you wearing that dress I swore it felt like my heart was going to fail and here you are wearing it again and you look even more stunning . . . But you're wearing it on a date with someone I don't believe to be genuine.

"No way should you leave this house with him wearing that; he is not trustworthy. You know I have a feel about things like this Christina, and when have you known me to be wrong?" Sebastian pushed his hands up across his face, through his hair, and held them there as he paced in front of me.

"Sebastian, I'm thirty-three years old. I can make some decisions on my own. And I'm sorry, but if you didn't notice you have never even suggested we go on a date. This is an important night Sebastian. I'm going to drill Scott and get down past his surface layer. I plan to make a decision tonight if I will continue seeing him. You might like to know that I already have my doubts to a degree, as he doesn't seem to open up and tell me much about himself.

"Sebastian, trust me. I know what I'm doing. Can you give me a little credit? I promise that if he doesn't open up tonight that we can start going on some dates. I'm sorry, we just never planned how to deal with us, and it's hard since you're my employee as well." I felt flustered with frustration and confused too. I always preferred to deal with one thing at a time so that I could feel I had one thing out of the way and could start on the next as it arose. It seemed it was unavoidable, and I was going to have to do two things at once.

"Can't you wear a wire in your dress then? Let me follow at a far distance? I promise I won't cut in on you or go anywhere near the two of you. Can I just listen in so I know what is going on? I can't stand this anymore. Christina, it's driving me so crazy," Sebastian let out as he paced continually in front of me.

"Hey Sebastian, is it okay for Scott to come in? He's standing right here." Colin opened the front doors.

"No, not yet; give us a few moments," Sebastian yelled to Colin and Colin shut the doors.

"No you can't come. That's so ridiculous. Why do you have Colin guarding the door? I'm going Sebastian, and you're just going to have to trust me. I started to rush towards the doors when I felt something wrap around my arms and pull me back.

"It's cold outside—you need to wear a jacket." Sebastian grabbed me by the sides of my arms with a jacket he started to wrap around me. "Just be careful. I hope you find out whatever it is you think you need to know. I'll wait up for you." Sebastian opened the front doors where Colin was talking with Scott. "Don't be late with her, Scott!" Sebastian warned.

The Dodger

The restaurant was very elegant and the food was incredible.

"So Scott, what do you see in your future?" I looked at Scott very seriously.

"Hmm . . . I see a very beautiful woman in a sexy, red dress and a sexy pair of high heels on," Scott laughed.

"I mean in your distant future, Scott. What do you hope for?" I looked again at Scott and for some reason he was looking a little bit uncomfortable. "What do you want in your future?"

"That is exactly what I want." Scott reached across the table grabbing both of my hands and looked at me.

"Well you have to have something in that head of yours that is attached to your heart; something that is your own?" I begged the question of him.

"I don't know. I just know that right now I have what I want, and I know that I don't want to lose that. I also know that what I want has some strange body guard that would love to see me lose you." Scott looked at me for consolation.

"Let's not bring up Sebastian when I'm on a date with you, Scott." I pulled my hand out of his and Scott pulled them back and smiled with his response.

"Let's not do that then. Let's just do whatever we feel we want when we are with each other."

For about half an hour I asked Scott questions that he dodged over and over. I finally got him to take me home nearly an hour early.

We arrived back at the mansion and parked near the front entrance. I could tell by the whole drive back that Scott was nervous and it bothered me that he couldn't just ask or answer a simple question.

"Christina, I'm sorry that it's been such an awkward evening. I really wanted this evening to be special, and I didn't want to ruin it by saying the wrong thing or acting like I was nervous. In an effort to avoid that I just made it happen instead. Please forgive me and let me have this last hour with you. We can stretch out in the backseat where it's more comfortable, and I promise I'll answer every question you throw at me, and you won't be past your curfew," Scott laughed.

I thought to myself that I should give the guy a second chance. I guess some people are just a bit more nervous than others. "Okay, but you have to promise to answer how you would answer yourself, not try to answer what you think I would answer. Do you promise?" I asked with a smile.

"I absolutely promise," Scott retorted. We got out and opened the back doors and sat beside each other in the backseat.

"Okay, what plans do you have for your future? Think about where you would like to live, employment, children, marriage, would you like to live in a house or a condo? Stuff like that." I shifted my body so I was facing him.

"I would love to be married, have a few kids, and live in a nice home . . . Hmm . . . being self employed would be a bonus. I would like to show my children the world when they are at least ten; take them out of school and home school them for a year, and just travel with them from country to country. Teach ourselves about culture as a family." Scott looked like he was honestly getting into this now. We talked for half an hour and I was feeling like I was getting a good picture of Scott, and the picture was looking like a bright one. The windows were fogged so it seemed to give us that extra sense of privacy.

"I do have to say, Christina, that you look so ravishing tonight and that I almost felt like I was going to start stuttering." Scott moved closer to me and slowly pulled his face to mine and we kissed.

"This is what I have really been waiting for. I just didn't know if you were open to it," Scott said as he slipped his hand up my dress and between my thighs.

"What . . . no Scott, I'm not open to this." I tried to push myself up.

"Come on Christina, do you expect me to believe you didn't think sitting in the backseat of a car wouldn't lead to making out or making love? I gave you what you were looking for. You need to give me a little back now," Scott laughed, pushing me back and grabbing my breasts.

"Get off me, Scott! Right now! I'm warning you." I brought my elbow up and over and smashed him in the neck with it. He started coughing when I saw the door on his side of the car open. It was Sebastian. He grabbed Scott by the back of his collar, ripping him out of the car. Sebastian punched Scott in the stomach and in the face a couple of times. Then he left him on the ground moaning long enough to reach through the backseat and grab me.

"Get out, now Christina!" Sebastian pulled me out by the arm as I pushed myself along, digging my high heels into the carpet until I could step out.

"You are a useless son of a bitch! I knew you were bad news from the start." Sebastian punched Scott in the head again just as he was starting to get up. Then he pulled him up by the collar until he could get a grip on his ear. He opened the driver side door and led him in by his ear and then gave him a good thrust into his car and slammed the door shut.

I was standing by the door, frozen as I watched Sebastian. He slammed his fists on Scott's car trunk and kicked out his headlight. I heard the car turn over and Scott backed the car up and turned it around, squealing out of the cul-de-sac and down the driveway. Sebastian stood for a moment and watched Scott as he rounded the corner.

I noticed he was only wearing jeans and a t-shirt while it had just started to lightly snow. It looked like he had his arms crossed in front of him. Seeming like he was satisfied that Scott was gone, he turned around with his arms crossed. The motion detector lights turned on as Sebastian started to walk towards me.

"Are you convinced now Christina? How was that for a special, romantic night? Damn it, why didn't you just listen to me. You know I have to know things about people. It's been my job since I was old enough to work. I have to learn how to read people. I don't know Christina; you really make me sad sometimes. Can you please just go inside so I can be by myself? Is it okay for me to have the peace of mind to know that nothing else is going to happen tonight?" Sebastian opened the door.

I didn't say anything. I just went into the mansion exactly like Sebastian had asked. I saw him lock the doors and then he walked by me, towards his bedroom with his head down.

A Little Shaken Up

I stood in the entranceway thinking to myself about how this all happened. How could Scott behave that way? Why didn't I see that coming? Why didn't I sense that he was a creep? I felt so ashamed to Sebastian. I didn't know if he was going to even want to work here now. I was pretty positive that if he did love me he didn't anymore. I felt some tears roll from my eyes as I walked to my bedroom. I reached my room feeling a little numbed and shocked at what had happened. I never thought for even a moment that Scott was like that. I can't understand how Sebastian could sense that about Scott. I felt a few more tears come down my face as I tried to unzip my dress. When the zipper got snagged on some of the inside material, I couldn't reach back to see to get it out.

There was no way that I was going to bother Sebastian to help me with this. I decided the dress—although beautiful—carried a bad track record when I wore it. Not to mention it would always remind me of Scott slipping his hand up my thigh and the whole incident. I decided I would just try to rip it off, so I took a hairpin off my dresser and started a small hole in the sheer material near the legs. Once I made a hole in the fabric I pulled on it and tore it until the material at the crotch got thicker and I couldn't tear it anymore. I grabbed a pair of scissors out of the drawer in my nightstand and started to cut it up the center. I kept cutting until the dress fell off of me into a heap on the floor. I sobbed to myself as I walked over to my dresser and placed the earrings on it.

"Christina, please don't cry." Sebastian had walked into my room through the curtain-covered doorway. I lifted my hand from the dresser were I placed my earrings and froze. I realized my body was hardly covered and Sebastian was at the front of the foot of my bed. I turned towards Sebastian; he was still in front of my bed. Sebastian's eyes were wide open and he seemed frozen as well. Finally, he dashed towards the bed and grabbed a throw that was lying on the end of it.

"Oh man, I'm so sorry. I heard you crying and moving around in here for a while. I thought you would be in bed clothes by now." Sebastian wrapped the throw around me and led me to the end of the bed where he sat down beside me.

Enlightened

"I was harsh Christina, and I admit it. I've been dying inside slowly watching you date this creep. I heard his car motor from at least a mile away and I knew you were back early. I guess I kind of hoped it was because you figured out he's a fake . . . And maybe I wanted you to want me to be there for you. It really hurt to see you get into the backseat of his car. I know you, and I know you wouldn't have the intentions for the backseat that Scott had. In my anger and hurt I tried not to interfere, but the windows started to fog and I don't trust Scott so I had to go outside and spy. I just wanted to protect you . . . When I heard what that creep said to you I knew he was doing something to you, and then it was clear that that son of a bitch was forcing himself on you . . ." Sebastian shook his head a little and then stretched his hands out in front of himself.

"Christina, can't you see that I'm the one you're looking for? I love you and I want to take care of you—not just as an employee. The day before Alec died, the day that I had the long talk with him on the phone and I told him that after Luke I was quitting my profession . . . That was the day that Alec told me he wasn't going to be around forever.

I don't know if he knew something or he had a feeling, but not only did he propose the employment contract, he talked to me about taking his place one day. He actually wanted me to be with you. I almost didn't know what to say. I can't say it didn't feel strange, but at the same time it ignited the feelings I had for you the day I first met you by the front doors. You know, the same doors I have been seeing you off on dates through. Alec asked me what my thoughts were about it, and I believe that was the first time I had ever stuttered in my life. I told him . . . that I was very attracted to you, and I didn't quite know what to say. He told me . . . I don't know if Alec would want me to tell you . . . but it's only something you and he would know and I hope it can help you believe me when I say it. So I'm just going to say it; Alec told me that you never had been intimate . . . and that he thought it wasn't healthy for you to not be in a relationship where you would want to share that." Sebastian looked over at me.

I was absolutely floored; there is no way Sebastian would know that. Alec and I never really even talked about that. There was no way he could have gotten it from a wire or overheard us. My mind flashed around as emotions flooded it.

Then my mind flashed to the dream I had in the hotel, and I remembered the young Alec who picked up my child self and took me to a place in time; that place and time that he chose was the day I saw Sebastian after Alec died. I could just make out the words that came out of Alec's mouth:

"*Christina, you know how much I love you and I only want good things for you.*" He looked at me for an answer so I nodded at him. "*This is where you need to be, and I must leave you here until one day when we can see each other again.*" He left me in front of Sebastian and I, embracing.

"I believe you Sebastian. I know you're telling the truth, and I know you wouldn't lie to me." I got up and wrapped the throw around me so that it would stay on better. "I was upset the day we went to the office to see if we could find the employment agreement Alec wrote up."

I walked out of my room and told Sebastian to follow me. I headed a few doors down to the office. I opened the drawer that originally held the agreement that Alec made up for Sebastian. I dug around under a bunch of papers and other files until I found Alec's handwritten notes. I pulled out the paper and handed it to Sebastian.

July 26, 2001

Reasons to have Sebastian on staff as a guard:

- Sebastian is reliable and never gets distracted
- No way Frank could get past him
- Truly has a good heart
- Sebastian does the job of at least 15-20 guards
- Sebastian is like family and it would allow him to be around Manuela and Lucia as well
- He gives 100% and strategizes until he corrects
- He would be a good suitor for Christina when I am gone
- He would still be doing an extension of what he loves
- Very organized
- Trustworthy

Sebastian looked over it. "These are the things that Alec was telling me on the phone that day. He must have been taking these notes right when he was talking to me," Sebastian smiled. I took the notes and placed them back in the drawer, and Sebastian followed me back to my room.

I sat back down on the end of my bed. "I just feel so strange. The dream I had at the hotel was about you and Alec. Alec led me to you in the dream! As soon as I awoke I remembered that note but I couldn't quite recall the dream. Later I had forgotten all about the note, and before I knew it I was immersed in what was going on with Luke."

Sebastian interrupted me. "Christina, you don't know how happy I am to know that you believe me realize that Alec thought highly of me . . . But what I really want to know is how you feel about me. Were you ever as attracted to me like I am to you?"

"Sebastian, you have no idea how attracted I am to you." I flopped back on my bed with a big smile. "I was so guilty about the feelings I felt when I saw you. I felt like I had to be mad at you or make myself hate you, or maybe even find fault in you so that I wouldn't look at you with lust."

Sebastian flopped back on the bed beside me with a huge smile on his face.

"Then when I tried to do that I only saw how intelligent you intelligent and caring you were and it made it even harder. You're hard person to hate, you know that?" I laughed.

"You're a hard person not to love." Sebastian turned to face me, pulled me tight up against him, and kissed me soft and sensually. I could feel my heart flip around in my chest. He rolled up on top of me and we kissed again.

"Please be careful with me; it's been about twenty years," I laughed, as did Sebastian.

"I'll be careful with you. I'm your bodyguard after all."

Sebastian pulled the blanket off of me and reached his hand over his head, pulling his shirt off. My heart leaped at the sight of his shirtless torso. He was gentle with me. There is nothing I would have changed about that night with Sebastian—or the next night, or the next, or the next. I wouldn't have changed the month later when we got married in the Bahamas.

It had been a few months after the wedding. I was heading upstairs to meet Sebastian for a swim when I heard a phone ring in the hallway of the second floor. I picked it up and answered.

"Mom it's me, Luke!" the voiced announced on the other end of the telephone.

"Luke! Is this really you? I was wondering if you would even call me." I was feeling surprised and more than pleased that he called me Mom.

"Can I come up there to visit you?" Luke asked.

"I would love that so much! When you book your plane ticket, make it to Kamloops, British Columbia and I will come and pick you up myself to drive you back here." I was feeling so happy.

"Is it okay if I come in one week, or is that too soon?" Luke asked.

"It's never too soon, Luke. I meant it when I said anytime," I told him.

"Thank you Mom. I love you but I'm going to have to go now," Luke said as I felt my eyes water up with happy tears.

"I love you too Luke." I waited for him to hang up first and then I ran towards the pool to tell Sebastian the good news.

I got to the door and I could already see Sebastian through the windows sitting by the edge of the pool with his feet in it. I pulled open the door as Sebastian got out of the pool to greet me. Suddenly I started to feel myself go down. I heard Sebastian yell something and I saw a streak of Sebastian's leg coming towards me when all of a sudden it got black. As suddenly as I went down, sound came to my ears. I could hear Sebastian yelling over my head, and suddenly I could feel pressure on my head. I looked up and saw that Sebastian was pressing down on my head.

"Christina, can you hear me?" Sebastian asked with a terrified look on his face which was starting to scare me.

"Yes, I can hear you," I answered as I started to sit up with his hand on my head.

"Okay let's just stand up slowly and then we'll walk over here together." I walked with Sebastian's hand on my head over to the towel shelves. "You just fainted. I caught you, but your head hit the rail." Sebastian said and I could see he was soaking up what looked like a lot of blood on a white towel. "It looks like we're going to need to take you to get some stitches and hopefully find out why you fainted like that." Sebastian walked with me slowly out of the poolroom and downstairs.

We passed a bunch of construction workers on the way down. They were working on our new bedroom on the third floor. We had it built beside my old room that I shared with Alec. Some of the construction workers commented on my cut as we passed them on the stairs.

"Yes, we're going to get it looked at right now," Sebastian said as he led me down the stairs.

On the ride to the doctor's I told Sebastian about Luke's call and that he was flying down next week. I looked over at Sebastian with my tipped up head and I could see he was happy.

"See, everything is coming together. We'll be like a happy family of three while he is here," Sebastian glowed with happiness.

At the Walk-In Clinic

We pulled into the parking lot at a walk-in-clinic.

"Perfect, the waiting room looks empty." Sebastian hopped out of the car and came around to my side to let me out. He led me to the door and found me a seat.

"My wife has a cut on her forehead that I think might need some stitches. Here's her medical card," he added, handing it to the desk clerk.

"You guys are in luck. You can just follow me and the doctor will be with you in a few short moments." She gestured for us to go into the room. We went in and Sebastian picked me up and put me on the examination table.

"You don't know how good that felt to say my wife to the clerk." He then leaned in towards me and kissed me on the lips just as the doctor walked in.

"Looks like someone got a pretty hard bump on the head. How did this happen?" He walked up to me and placed his hand on my head as Sebastian slipped off to the side.

"I don't know, I was running down the hall and when I opened the door to the pool room I felt myself start to black out. Next thing I knew, my head was on my husband's knees and he was trying to stop the bleeding."

The doctor took the band-aid off while I was talking. "Well it's still oozing blood. Lucky for you it's right up in your hairline. This is going to need some stitches, probably about eight. I have to say, I'm worried about the cause of your fall more than I am the injury. There are many things that can cause fainting so I'm going to take a few simple tests and maybe that will tell us something. But first I'll set you up with some brand new stitches. Is that okay with you?" The doctor asked.

"Sure," I said, shrugging my shoulders. After he stitched my cut up he checked my reflexes, took my blood pressure, looked in my ears and my eyes, got me to take a quick eye test, and topped it off with a urine test.

"The nurse will be back with the results to that urine test any moment now," the doctor assured us as he was writing in his file. "So tell me, how long have the two of you been married?" The doctor continued to write in the file he was holding.

Sebastian answered, "Just over two months—the best two months of my life," Sebastian added when the nurse came in and handed the doctor a piece of paper.

"Well I guess it has been the best two months of your life. You're going to need to make room for one more to your happy little family though. All the rest of the tests look normal to me, except the urine test which shows you are going to be parents pretty soon. Can you recall the date of your last menstrual cycle?" The doctor looked up aiming his pen on his paper as if he was waiting for me to come up with an immediate answer.

I looked over at Sebastian for an answer, mostly because I was astonished that this was the outcome of the test—I never would have thought. Sebastian put his hand over his mouth and walked over to me placing his other hand on my knee.

"When was it, Babe?" Sebastian asked

"I've been so busy, but now that I think of it I would say that I'm probably two weeks late. I imagine with the wedding and the rebuilding that I just lost track." I pushed down on the padded examination table in almost disbelief. They must have gotten my test mixed up, or maybe the test made a mistake. This would be just too good to be true.

"Well it sounds to me like you are about six weeks pregnant. I want to give you a quick internal exam to see if we can get a better idea of how far along you are. Here is a gown you can slip into. Your husband can stay for the test if you would like. I'll be back in a few moments to see if you're ready." The doctor smiled at Sebastian as he went out the door closing it behind him.

Sebastian looked quite pleased. "I am the happiest man on this planet right now!" Sebastian busted out. I laughed at his peculiar behaviour as I was undressing and slipping into the gown the doctor left me.

"I didn't know anything. It's been so long since I was pregnant; I think I forgot what the initial symptoms are. Sebastian, I'm so happy, I just can't imagine that this could be happening right now. I mean, think about where we were five months ago. Sebastian, what are you thinking?" I looked at Sebastian seriously as I lay down on the exam table. I tried to push my past memories of Leah and Ellen doing this same sort of examination on me in the attic bedroom of my father's home.

The doctor knocked asking if I was prepared yet.

"Yeah, she's ready . . . and I'm ecstatic, Christina. I love you and I promise I'm going to be the best father," Sebastian stated as the doctor came in placing my feet on the stirrups. Sebastian stayed up near my head through the whole examination.

"You're wrong about the dates dear; your uterus is at least ten.

"Was your last period a heavy one?" the doctor questioned.

"No, actually when I think back, it was extremely light and short. I've had a lot of stress and changes over the last few years so they haven't been quite regular." I pushed myself up on my elbows looking at the doctor for answers.

"Well I can say you are ten . . . maybe twelve weeks pregnant. That means you are entering or going to be entering your second trimester very soon.

Here's the name of some prenatal vitamins I'd like you to pick up at the drug store, and at the front desk the clerk will give you a book that will explain the stages of pregnancy so you'll know what to expect.

Congratulations to you both on the Marriage and the pregnancy!" The doctor smiled as he handed me a piece of paper and left. Sebastian pulled me up from the exam table into his embrace.

It had been about three months since we found I was pregnant and that Luke was coming for a visit. In fact, Luke was still with us and had decided that he would stay for a while. I was just delighted to have him and didn't want him to go.

Luke tried to understand Adana and Dirk's explanations and reasons for doing what they did. He had worked hard for months to rationalize the whole situation, but it just made the fact that he felt different and didn't fit with the Vandenhoffs was more clear. Adana would call our house occasionally to talk to Luke, but he definitely didn't have the same relationship with Adana that he used to have.

Luke seemed to be bonding really well with Sebastian. They would toss a football on the grass, play tennis, or lift weights together. Luke said he wished Sebastian was his real father, but he still really wanted to meet Frank despite that I told him he was unstable. I knew I had to respect the way Luke felt, and Sebastian promised he would track Frank down for Luke.

Luke was thrilled that he was going to have a sibling. Sebastian and Luke would feel the baby kicking in my stomach and watch the baby move under my skin anticipating his or her arrival. Luke had decided that he wasn't going back to Spain anytime soon. He was excited to be with us and eager for the baby's birth.

Our bedroom had been finished for some time now. It was next door to my old room and every bit as big. The arrangement of the room had a much different layout than my other room, which made me feel like I had a new start to life.

It was early November and I could feel the contractions starting. They were a couple weeks earlier than my predicted due date.

Sebastian was out looking for information as to where Frank had disappeared. It was almost like he went off the grid and Sebastian really wanted to find him for Luke. He knew how important it was for Luke to meet his biological father, and he wanted to make it happen. I tried calling Luke several times on his cell phone but it would go immediately to his voice mail. I decided I would have a warm bath to ease the pain.

I didn't want to miss Sebastian en route to the hospital; there were too many areas where there is no cell service. I was soaking in the tub when I heard Sebastian yelling for me as he ran into the bathroom out of breath.

"I got your message. I was so worried; I've been out of cell phone range for about half an hour." He caught his breath.

I interrupted Sebastian. "We need to go. I feel really bad pressure. Please help me out of this tub." I tried pushing myself up when this enormous pain shot through my belly followed by some extreme downward pressure.

"Let me help you!" Sebastian put his arms up under my arms and proceeded to lift me.

"No! Stop! It hurts, it really hurts! Wait a minute until this contraction stops." I just remembered to do the breathing. I made myself slow my breaths and then start to take them less shallow.

"Christina, is this right for you to be in this much pain so quickly?" Sebastian started pushing a speed dial number on his cell phone while he reached for a couple towels.

"I don't know, it was a lot slower with Luke. It's getting much worse," I cried out in pain.

"Luke, you need to come up here! Your mother is in labor and I'm going to need some help lifting her out of the bath. I don't want to chance her slipping. We're in the bathroom in our bedroom. Okay! Come quickly then." Sebastian hung up the phone and put a towel over the front of me, right in the water.

I screamed in pain as it felt like this baby was trying to rip his or her way out of me. "Lets try and time these. Sebastian looked at his watch, placing his hand on my belly. It didn't seem like very long when the next contraction started.

"That's about four minutes apart, Christina. I don't think we can drive you to the hospital without you giving birth in the car. Luke, finally, I need you to grab her under her knees when I bring her up. Then we need to carry her onto the bed." Sebastian looked at Luke ever so seriously. Luke nodded his head and told Sebastian that he understood.

"Okay, I'm going to start now." Sebastian came in behind me and started to lift. I screamed in pain, so Sebastian quickly grabbed a quilt off the bed with one hand as he leaned into one corner of my body to support it. He spread the quilt out on the bedroom floor as best he could. I wouldn't let them lift me any higher due to the pain.

"Stop it! Don't, I need to push! It's coming right now! I'm serious. Ahhh, it hurts, it hurts!" I cried out. Luke paced a few times as Sebastian tended to me.

"Luke, go get the phone in our bedroom and call 911. When it rings hold it to my ear." Sebastian instructed.

I started to feel this overwhelming urge to push so I went with it.

"Okay, I can see it coming and it has lots of hair. Keep pushing, push . . . push . . . push. Sebastian pulled a towel over me as Luke entered the bedroom with the phone in his hands. "Grab me a pile of those towels in the bathroom and get Lucia to come up here, now!" Sebastian took the phone and Luke ran to get Lucia.

Sebastian got on the phone with the emergency responder. "I need someone to come here now. Please, my wife is giving birth in our tub. Can you hold on for just a minute?" Sebastian pushed the speakerphone and literally threw the phone on some towels on the floor. He told the 911 attendant that he put her on speaker but the reception wasn't good.

"Here it comes again! It hurts; I can't stand this, it hurts too much! I have to pus!." I pushed my legs against Sebastian.

"Push . . . push . . . I see the head . . . Oh my God!" Sebastian panicked.

"Sir, now try to get her to not push with this next contraction until one shoulder slips out," the voice instructed over the phone.

"Christina, did you hear that? You can't push with the next contraction." Sebastian sat up a bit more and pushed my legs out more.

"Tell her to take short, shallow breaths with this contraction." The phone sounded a bit crackly.

"Okay, did you hear her? Don't push . . . You need to pant, short little breaths. Yeah, like that . . . Keep panting . . . Keep panting. Good Job! I see the shoulder." Sebastian was moving onto his knees and putting light pressure on the baby's head. Again I had to push.

"Okay push . . . push . . . push . . . push. Oh my God, it's out. I have the baby." Sebastian brought the baby up to his chest and looked down at its face when Luke and Lucia rounded the corner.

"Oh no, Senora. Is she okay Sebastian?" Lucia had her hands covering her mouth and Luke's face dropped.

"Go get that baby suction bulb on the changing table, quick," Sebastian instructed. Lucia and Luke both ran out. Luke came back in seconds, handing it to Sebastian. Sebastian immediately started to suction the baby's nose and throat with his shoulder supporting its head. Finally the baby started to cry a tiny little 'whaaa'. The lady on the phone was going in and out with all the noise.

Sebastian was a natural; it was like he knew what to do once the baby was out. He picked the baby up and looked at it in the air as it had a little cry.

"It's a girl; it's my baby girl." He kissed my forehead. "Lucia, can you get me a towel for my little girl?" He poured some fresh water into the tub. I spread the towel over me and straitened while pushing myself up to look at the baby. Luke and Lucia went up near Sebastian to look at the baby. Sebastian was holding the baby close to his chest wrapped in a towel trying to keep her warm.

Luke was so affectionate to the baby, and he looked so happy. He kept saying that he couldn't believe he actually had a baby sister and that their birthdays were three days apart.

Sebastian noticed the phone had been kicked over and it was off the hook. He was going to dial back 911 to make sure they had the address and were on the way. He carefully handed our baby girl to Lucia. He then sat down beside me and continuously brushed his hands through my hair as he waited for the call to connect. He quickly explained to the emergency call center what had transpired and they told him help was already en route.

At the hospital the baby and I were checked over. They found that both of us were in excellent condition considering an unplanned home birth, and nurses and doctors congratulated Sebastian for doing an exceptional job. I couldn't believe how well he did. He was calm and seemed to know what to do in each step of the delivery.

We soon learned in the hospital that I was not producing any milk. I was disappointed that I could not feed my baby in a more natural way, but it did give Sebastian a more active role in caring for our baby. Sebastian was great with the baby; he was more than happy to change the baby's diapers, feed her, and tend to her colic.

Luke and Lucia arrived at the hospital later in the evening with flowers and gifts for the baby and I. Luke held his baby sister like she was the most fragile treasure in the world. She was beautiful; she had light brown hair and the most beautiful brown, Spanish eyes. Her lips were full; a mixture of Sebastian and mine. She would look attentively as we spoke, like she seemed to recognize our voices.

We named her Tianna; a name that Sebastian found in a baby book. He just loved it because it meant 'Princess', and Tianna was defiantly Daddy's little princess. Sebastian would joke saying he used to just have a queen and now he has a princess too.

The Lost and Found

It has been just over a year now since Tianna's birth, and Sebastian finally managed to track down Frank. He had been in Thailand for a few years trying to move forward from his past. Unfortunately alcohol had taken him over. He lost his business and a good part of his investments and savings due to his addiction. He finally came back to Canada as his health was finally starting to catch up with him.

Sebastian found him shortly after he re-enter the country and was admitted to the hospital the very same day. After a battery of tests were run on him it was clear that his cirrhosis was at a terminal state. There was no way to repair or treat it other than a transplant, and the doctors said he had to be healthy enough to even be a candidate for transplant surgery. At this point, Frank's other organs were shutting down and his liver was not doing its job. His kidneys were hardly functioning and he had edema throughout his body causing his lungs to fill with fluid. They had put tubes in through his ribs so they could drain lots of water from his body every day.

Luke and I left Sebastian and Tianna in the waiting room of the Vancouver General Hospital as we slipped into an elevator. As we arrived on the floor that housed the Intensive Care Unit, I looked at Luke and I could see he was nervous. I felt a deep sadness that Luke wanted to get to know his father on some level, and it looked unlikely that he would get that chance at this point.

We carried on through the hallway until we got to the double glass doors that read 'ICU'. There was a panel next to the door instructing us to ring a bell to gain entrance. Luke rang the bell and a voiced asked us who we were there to see and what our names were. We had called in before we came to get permission and it was standard practice that they looked in their log to see who was scheduled for visitation. Soon the doors slid open to the sides and a nurse led us down a hallway of curtained rooms until we were instructed to wait in front of one. It was Frank's room that was directly in front of a nurse's station.

I could hear the sound of machines beeping and ringing and respirators pumping. People were moaning and there was some faint crying in the background. The nurse pulled back the curtains and got Frank's attention.

"Mr. Shamanskii, your son and his mother are here. Do you still feel up for a visit?" The nurse adjusted Frank's oxygen tubes in his nose.

"Yes, I do. Please let us alone. Frank's voice sounded really scratchy and rough. He had tubes and gadgets attached to him everywhere. He looked extremely gaunt and more ill than I had ever seen anyone, yet I could see a glimmer of that twinkle in his eyes that had not yet left him.

"Frank, this is our son, Luke. He's living with Sebastian and I right now. I tried for some time to find you so you could meet him sooner." I led Luke into the chair closest to Frank and I sat in the one next to Luke's.

"My son, finally you are with me. I have waited so long for this moment. I thank you Christina, for bringing him to me." Frank tried to lift his head off his pillow and dropped it back down as if he had no strength. Luke inched his chair closer to Frank's side. Frank turned his head and looked over at Luke.

"You look like me when I was your age, but I see a lot of your beautiful mother in you as well." Frank tried to look downward past Luke at me to compare. "I am going to get better now, and you and I are going to go fishing and hunting and play some sports. Do you like that kind of stuff, My Son?" Frank's eyes got teary and I could see that Luke was trying not to get teary himself.

"I do. And I would love to spend that time with you too." Luke placed his hand on Frank's shoulder. Frank put his head back.

"I have something to live for again." His eyes closed with exhaustion and a nurse opened the curtains.

"Are we a little tired Mr. Shamanskii? Maybe we shouldn't be having company right now." The nurse squeezed past us and started taking Frank's blood pressure. Frank seemed to be taking a short rest. "Well that's a much better pressure than a few hours ago." The nurse released the cuff.

"Please give me a few more seconds with them?" Frank looked over at Luke again.

"Okay, a couple more, but I'm going to wait right at the end of your bed. You really need to get your rest." The nurse smiled at Frank and moved to the end of the bed writing in her clipboard.

"When can you come again? I promise I will be able to spend more time with you." Frank looked at Luke and then at me.

"Next week, same day, we will fly again so we won't be late due to traffic." I picked my purse off the ground preparing to go. I didn't know how much longer I could be in the room without crying. I have always seen Frank as a tough, strong man and seeing him reduced to this bed ridden state was getting to me.

"Luke, I love you and I am always your dad. I will see you for a longer visit in a week. I promise." Frank place his other hand on Luke's and looked at him determined. I stood up and walked across to the nurse's station where I got a handful of tissues to catch the tears that were leaking from my eyes. The nurse ushered Luke out and we booked our next visit with the nurse behind the desk before we left.

Many months had passed and Luke visited Frank weekly. For the first two months it was always in the ICU, but Frank gradually started to improve. He was then moved to a different floor in the hospital and then he was able to leave to an apartment he rented where he had a home nurse visit him several days per week. He still had to come back to the hospital every three weeks for a blood transfusion. A few times he had to have the tubes placed back in his ribs to remove fluid from his lungs. He was now an eligible candidate for a liver transplant and was on the waiting list.

The Picnic

About a year later in the spring, we enjoyed a family celebration picnic with Luke on a Vancouver Beach. Luke had been accepted by a Vancouver college to attend medical school. It was his dream to become a general practitioner and then travel to third world counties to help the poor. He planned to stay with his father in his apartment as it was close to the college. We would miss each other when he was gone, but he we would visit each other as much as possible.

As we walked along the beach I was holding Sebastian's hand watching Luke carry his little sister across the sand. He was beautiful, and so was she. A breeze blew through Tianna's hair as Luke bent down with her to place her bare feet in the ocean. He pulled her up and spun around holding Tianna in the air above his head. She laughed and squeaked out Luke's name over and over.

Sebastian led us to a bench near a bunch of foliage. As we approached it I saw many bunches of beautiful, little blue tinged flowers. We sat down and Luke placed Tianna on Sebastian's lap. I stood up to say goodbye to Luke as I saw Frank slowly walking up to the beach to pick up Luke.

I watched Luke and Frank as they left the beach disappearing around a corner of bushes. I felt a deep peace around me that I had never quite felt before. It felt as if my mother and Alec were looking down from heaven smiling. In the background, sounds of the waves rolling in and out from the shore comforted me. I could hear Sebastian talking to Tianna and as he held a handful of the blue tinged flowers in front of her.

"Look at this flower, it is blue. Can you say 'blue', Tianna? I saw Sebastian looking down at Tianna with anticipation.

"Boo!" Tianna said three times.

"Good girl! You are so smart. Now, you know what kind of flower this is? I bet you don't? It is called a Forget Me Not. It is for Mommy." Sebastian smiled and handed the flowers to me.

CPSIA information can be obtained at www.ICGtesting.com
Printed in the USA
LVOW081202241012

304133LV00002B/25/P